Robert Ludlum

THE OSTERMAN WEEKEND

THE MATLOCK PAPER

WH SMITH

EXCLUSIVE
· BOOKS ·

The Osterman Weekend first published in
Great Britain in 1972 by Rupert Hart-Davis Ltd
Copyright © Robert Ludlum 1972

The Matlock Paper first published in Great Britain
in 1973 by Hart-Davis, MacGibbon Ltd
Copyright © Robert Ludlum 1973

This edition first produced exclusively
for WH Smith in 1990 by Grafton Books
A Division of Harper Collins, Publishers.

ISBN 0 286 12599 4

Printed and bound in Great Britain by
The Bath Press, Avon

THE OSTERMAN WEEKEND
THE MATLOCK PAPER

CONTENTS

THE OSTERMAN WEEKEND

PART ONE

Sunday Afternoon

1

Saddle Valley, New Jersey, is a Village.

At least real estate developers, hearing alarm signals from a decaying upper middle-class Manhattan, found a Village when they invaded its wooden acres in the late 1930s.

The white, shield-shaped sign on Valley Road reads

SADDLE VALLEY

VILLAGE INCORPORATED 1862

Welcome

The 'Welcome' is in smaller lettering than any of the words preceding it, for Saddle Valley does not really welcome outsiders, those Sunday afternoon drivers who like to watch the Villagers at play. Two Saddle Valley police cars patrol the roads on Sunday afternoon.

It might also be noted that the sign on Valley Road does not read

SADDLE VALLEY, NEW JERSEY

or even

SADDLE VALLEY, N.J.

merely

SADDLE VALLEY

The Village does not acknowledge a higher authority; it is its own master. Isolated, secure, inviolate.

On a recent July Sunday afternoon, one of the two Saddle Valley patrol cars seemed to be extraordinarily thorough. The white car with blue lines roamed the roads just a bit faster than usual. It went from one end of the

Village to the other – cruising into the residential areas – in front of, behind and to the sides of the spacious, tastefully landscaped one-acre lots.

This particular patrol car on this particular Sunday afternoon was noticed by several residents of Saddle Valley.

It was meant to be.

It was part of the plan.

John Tanner, in old tennis shorts and yesterday's shirt, sneakers and no socks, was clearing out his two-car garage with half an ear cocked to the sounds coming from his pool. His twelve-year-old son, Raymond, had friends over, and periodically Tanner walked far enough out on the driveway so he could see past the backyard patio to the pool and make sure the children were all right. Actually, he only walked out when the level of shouting was reduced to conversation – or periods of silence.

Tanner's wife, Alice, with irritating regularity, came into the garage through the laundry-room entrance to tell her husband what to throw out next. John hated getting rid of things, and the resulting accumulation of junk exasperated her. This time she motioned toward a broken lawn spreader which had lain for weeks at the back of the garage.

John noticed her gesture. 'I could mount it on a piece of wrought iron and sell it to the Museum of Modern Art,' he said. 'Remnants of past inequities. Pre-gardener period.'

Alice Tanner laughed. Her husband noted once again, as he had for so many years, that it was a nice laugh.

'I'll haul it to the curb. They pick up Mondays.' Alice reached for the relic.

'That's okay. I'll do it.'

'No, you won't. You'll change your mind halfway down.'

Her husband lifted the spreader over a Briggs and Stratton rotary lawn mower while Alice sidled past the small Triumph she proudly referred to as her 'status symbol'. As she started pushing the spreader down the driveway, the right wheel fell off. Both of them laughed.

'That'd clinch the deal with the museum. It's irresistible.'

Alice looked up and stopped laughing. Forty yards away, in front of their house on Orchard Drive, the white patrol car was slowly cruising.

'The gestapo's screening the peasants this afternoon,' she said.

'What?' Tanner picked up the wheel and threw it into the well of the spreader.

'Saddle Valley's finest is on the job. That's the second or third time they've gone down Orchard.'

Tanner glanced at the passing patrol car. The driver, Officer Jenkins, returned his stare. There was no wave, no gesture of greeting. No acknowledgement. Yet they were acquaintances, if not friends.

'Maybe the dog barked too much last night.'

'The baby-sitter didn't say anything.'

'A dollar fifty an hour is hush money.'

'You'd better get this down, darling.' Alice's thoughts turned from the police car. 'Without a wheel it becomes father's job. I'll check the kids.'

Tanner, pulling the spreader behind him, went down the driveway to the curb, his eyes drawn to a bright light about sixty yards away. Orchard Drive, going west, bore to the left around a cluster of trees. Several hundred feet beyond the midpoint of the bend were Tanner's nearest neighbors, the Scanlans.

The light was the reflection of sun off the patrol car. It was parked by the side of the road.

The two policemen were turned around in their seats, staring out the rear window, staring, he was sure, at *him*. For a second or two, he remained motionless. Then he started to walk toward the car. The two officers turned, started the engine and sped off.

Tanner looked after it, puzzled, then walked slowly back toward his house.

The Saddle Valley police car raced out toward Peachtree Lane; there it slowed and resumed cruising speed.

Richard Tremayne sat in his air-conditioned living room watching the Mets blow a six-run lead. The curtains of the large bay windows were open.

Suddenly Tremayne rose from his chair and went to the window. The patrol car was there again. Only now it was hardly moving.

'Hey, Ginny!' he called to his wife. 'Come here a minute.'

Virginia Tremayne walked gracefully down the three steps into the living room. 'What is it? Now you didn't call me to tell me your Mets or Jets hit something?'

'When John and Alice were over last night . . . were he and I . . . all right? I mean, we weren't too loud or anything, were we?'

'You were both plastered. But pleasant. Why?'

'I know we were drunk. It was a lousy week. But we didn't do anything outlandish?'

'Of course not. Attorneys and newsmen are models of decorum. Why do you ask?'

'Goddamn police car's gone by the house for the fifth time.'

'Oh.' Virginia felt a knot in the pit of her stomach. 'Are you sure?'

'You can't miss *that* car in the sunlight.'

'No, I guess you can't . . . You said it was a rotten week. Would that awful man be trying to . . .'

'Oh, Jesus, no! I told you to forget that. He's a loudmouth. He took the case too personally.' Tremayne continued looking out the window. The police car was leaving.

'He did threaten you, though. You said he did. He said he had connections . . .'

Tremayne turned slowly and faced his wife. 'We all have connections, don't we? Some as far away as Switzerland?'

'Dick, please. That's absurd.'

'Of course it is. Car's gone now . . . probably nothing. They're due for another raise in October. Probably checking out houses to buy. The bastards! They make more than I did five years out of law school.'

'I think you're a little edgy with a bad head. That's what I think.'

'I think you're probably right.'

Virginia watched her husband. He kept staring out the window. 'The maid wants Wednesday off. We'll eat out, all right?'

'Sure.' He did not turn round.

His wife started up into the hall. She looked back at her husband; he was now looking at her. Beads of perspiration had formed on his forehead. And the room was cool.

The Saddle Valley patrol car headed east toward Route Five, the main link with Manhattan twenty-six miles away. It stopped on a road overlooking Exit 10A. The patrolman to the right of the driver took a pair of binoculars from the glove compartment and began scanning the cars coming off the exit ramp. The binoculars had Zeiss-Ikon lenses.

After several minutes he tapped the sleeve of the driver, Jenkins, who looked over through the open window. He motioned the other man to give him the binoculars, and put them to his eyes, tracking the automobile specified by his fellow officer. He spoke one word: 'Confirmed.'

Jenkins started the car and headed south. He picked up the radio-phone. 'Two car calling in. Heading south on Register Road. Tailing green Ford sedan. New York plates. Filled with niggers or PR's.'

The crackling reply came over the speaker. 'Read you, two car. Chase 'em the hell out.'

'Will do. No sweat. Out.'

The patrol car then turned left and sped down the long incline into Route Five. Once on the highway, Jenkins pressed the accelerator to the floor and the car plunged forward on the smooth surface. In sixty seconds the speedometer read ninety-two.

Four minutes later the patrol car slowed down rounding a long curve. A few hundred yards beyond the curve stood two aluminum-framed telephone booths, glass and metal reflecting the harsh glare of the July sun.

The police car came to a stop and Jenkins' companion climbed out.

'Got a dime?'

'Oh, Christ, McDermott!' Jenkins laughed. 'Fifteen years in the field and you don't carry the change to make contact.'

'Don't be a smartass. I've got nickels, but one of them's an Indian head.'

'Here.' Jenkins took a coin from his pocket and handed it to McDermott. 'An ABM could be stuck and you wouldn't use a Roosevelt dime to alert operations.'

'Don't know that I would.' McDermott walked to the phone booth, pushed in the squeaky, shiny door, and dialed '0'. The booth was stifling, the still air so close that he kept the door open with his foot.

'I'll head down to the U-turn,' yelled Jenkins from the car window. 'Pick you up on the other side.'

'Okay . . . Operator. A collect call to New Hampshire. Area Code three-one-two. Six-five-four-oh-one. The name is Mr Leather.'

There was no mistaking the words. McDermott had placed a call to the state of New Hampshire and the telephone operator put it through. However, what the operator could not know was that this particular number did not cause a telephone to ring in the state of New Hampshire. For somewhere, in some underground complex housing thousands upon thousands of trunk lines, a tiny relay was activated and a small magnetized bar fell across a quarter-inch space and made another connection. This connection caused – not a bell – but a low humming sound to emanate from a telephone two hundred and sixty-three miles *south* of Saddle Valley, New Jersey.

The telephone was in a second-floor office in a red brick building fifty yards inside a twelve-foot-high electrified fence. The building was one of perhaps ten, all connected with one another to form a single complex. Outside the fence the woods were thick with summer foliage. The location was McLean, Virginia. The complex was the Central Intelligence Agency. Isolated, secure, inviolate.

The man sitting behind the desk in the second-floor office crushed out his cigarette in relief. He'd been waiting anxiously for the call. He noted with satisfaction that the small wheels of the recording device automatically started revolving. He picked up the telephone.

'Andrews speaking. Yes, operator, I accept the charges.'

'Leather reporting,' came the words rerouted from the state of New Hampshire.

'You're cleared. Tape going, Leather.'

'Confirming the presence of all suspects. The Cardones just arrived from Kennedy Airport.'

'We knew he landed . . .'

'Then why the hell did we have to race down here?'

'That's a rotten highway, Route Five. He could have an accident.'

'On Sunday afternoon?'

'Or any other time. You want the statistics on accidents for that route?'

'Go back to your Goddamn computers . . .'

Andrews shrugged. Men in the field were always irritated over one thing or another. 'As I read you, all three suspects are present. Correct?'

'Correct. Tanners, Tremaynes and the Cardones. All accounted for. All waiting. The first two are primed. We'll get to Cardone in a few minutes.'

'Anything else?'

'Not for now.'

'How's the wife?'

'Jenkins is lucky. He's a bachelor. Lillian keeps looking at those houses and wants one.'

'Not on our salary, McDermott.'

'That's what I tell her. She wants me to defect.'

For the briefest of seconds Andrews reacted painfully to McDermott's joke. 'The pay's worse, I'm told.'

'Couldn't be . . . There's Jenkins. Be in touch.'

Joseph Cardone drove his Cadillac into the circular drive and parked in front of the stone steps leading to the huge oak door. He turned off the engine and stretched, bending his elbows beneath the roof. He sighed and woke his boys of six and seven. A third child, a girl of ten, was reading a comic book.

Sitting beside Cardone was his wife, Betty. She looked out the window at the house. 'It's good to get away, but it's better to get home.'

Cardone laughed and put his large hand on his wife's shoulder. 'You must mean that.'

'I do.'

'You must. You say it every time we come home. The exact words.'

'It's a nice home.'

Cardone opened the door. 'Hey, Princess . . . get your brothers out and help your mother with the smaller bags.' Cardone reached in and withdrew the keys from the ignition. He started toward the trunk. 'Where's Louise?'

'She probably won't be here till Tuesday. We're three days early, remember? I gave her off till then.'

Cardone winced. The thought of his wife's cooking was not pleasant. 'We eat out.'

'We'll have to today. It takes too long to defrost things.' Betty Cardone walked up the stone steps, taking the front-door key out of her purse.

Joe dismissed his wife's remark. He liked food and he did not like his wife's preparation of it. Rich debutantes from Chestnut Hill couldn't begin to cook like good South Side Italian mamas from Philadelphia.

One hour later he had the central air-conditioning going full blast throughout the large house, and the stuffy air, unchanged for nearly two weeks, was becoming bearable again. He was aware of such things. He'd been an exceptionally successful athlete – his route to success, both social and financial. He stepped out on the front porch and looked at the lawn with the huge willow tree centered in the grass within the circular drive. The gardeners had kept it all up nicely. They should. Their prices were ridiculous. Not that price ever concerned him any more.

Suddenly there it was again. The patrol car. This was the third time he'd seen it since leaving the highway.

'Hey, you! Hold it!'

The two officers in the car looked briefly at one another, about to race away. But Cardone had run to the curb.

'Hey!'

The patrol car stopped.

'Yes, Mr Cardone?'

'What's with the police routine? Any trouble around here?'

'No, Mr Cardone. It's vacation time. We're just checking against our schedules when residents return. You were due this afternoon, so we just wanted to make sure it was you. Take your house off the check list.'

Joe watched the policeman carefully. He knew the officer was lying, and the policeman knew he knew.

'You earn your money.'

'Do our best, Mr Cardone.'

'I'll bet you do.'

'Good day, sir.' The patrol car sped off.

Joe looked after it. He hadn't intended to go to the office until mid-week, but that had to be changed now. He'd go into New York in the morning.

On Sunday afternoons, between the hours of five and six, Tanner closeted himself in his study, a walnut-paneled room with three television sets, and watched three different interview shows simultaneously.

Alice knew her husband had to watch. As Director of News for Standard Mutual, it was part of his job to be aware of the competition. But Alice thought there was something sinister about a man sitting alone in a half-lit room watching three television sets at the same time, and she constantly chided him for it.

Today, Tanner reminded his wife that he'd have to miss next Sunday – Bernie and Leila would be there, and nothing ever disturbed an Osterman weekend. So he sat in the darkened room, knowing all too well what he was going to see.

Every Director of News for every network had his favorite program, the one to which he gave extra attention. For Tanner it was the Woodward show. A half hour on Sunday afternoon during which the best news analyst in the business interviewed a single subject, usually a controversial figure currently in the headlines.

Today Charles Woodward was interviewing a substitute, Undersecretary Ralph Ashton from the State Department. The Secretary himself was suddenly unavailable, so Ashton had been recruited.

It was a gargantuan mistake by the Department. Ashton was a witless, prosaic former businessman whose main asset was his ability to raise money. That he was even considered to represent the Administration was a major error on someone's part. Unless there were other motives.

Woodward would crucify him.

As Tanner listened to Ashton's evasive, hollow replies, he realized that a great many people in Washington were soon going to be telephoning each other. Woodward's polite inflections couldn't hide his growing antagonism toward the Undersecretary. The reportorial instinct was being frustrated; soon Woodward's tones would turn to ice and Ashton would be slaughtered. Politely, to be sure, but slaughtered nevertheless.

It was the sort of thing Tanner felt embarrassed watching.

He turned up the volume of the second set. In ponderous, nasal tones a moderator was describing the backgrounds and positions of the panel of experts who were about to question the UN delegate from Ghana. The black diplomat looked for all the world as if he were being driven to the guillotine in front of a collection of male Madame Defarges. Very white, well-paid Madame Defarges.

No competition there.

The third network was better, but not good enough. No competition there either.

Tanner decided he had had enough. He was too far ahead to worry, and he'd see Woodward's tape in the morning. It was only five-twenty, and the sun was still on the pool. He heard his daughter's shouts as she returned from the country club, and the reluctant departure of Raymond's friends from the backyard. His family was together. The three of them were probably sitting outside waiting till he finished watching and started the fire for the steaks.

He'd surprise them.

He turned off the sets, put the pad and pencil on his desk. It was time for a drink.

Tanner opened the door of his study and walked into the living room. Through the rear windows, he saw Alice and the children playing follow-the-leader off the pool diving board. They were laughing, at peace.

Alice deserved it. Christ! She deserved it!

He watched his wife. She jumped – toes pointed – into the water, bobbing up quickly to make sure that eight-year-old Janet would be all right when she followed her.

Remarkable! After all the years he was more in love with his wife than ever.

He remembered the patrol car, then dismissed the thought. The policemen were simply finding a secluded spot in which to rest, or listen to the ball game undisturbed. He'd heard that policemen did that sort of thing in New York. Then why not in Saddle Valley? Saddle Valley was a lot safer than New York.

Saddle Valley was probably the safest place in the world. At least it seemed that way to John Tanner on this particular Sunday afternoon.

Richard Tremayne turned off his one television set within ten seconds after John Tanner had shut off his three. The Mets had won it after all.

His headache had left him and with it his irritability. Ginny had been right, he thought. He was simply edgy. No reason to take it out on the family. His stomach felt stronger now. A little food would fix him up again. Maybe he'd call Johnny and Ali and take Ginny over for a swim in the Tanners' pool.

Ginny kept asking why they didn't have one of their own. Heaven knew they had an income several times that of the Tanners. Everybody could see that. But Tremayne knew why.

A pool would be that one symbol too much. Too much at age forty-four. It was enough that they had moved into Saddle Valley when he was only thirty-eight. A seventy-four-thousand-dollar house at thirty-eight years of age. With a fifty-thousand-dollar down payment. A pool could wait until his forty-fifth birthday. It would make sense then.

Of course what people – clients – didn't think about was that he had graduated from Yale Law in the top five percent of his class, had clerked for Learned Hand, had spent three years at the bottom of his present firm's ladder before any real money came his way. When it came, however, it came rapidly.

Tremayne walked out to the patio. Ginny and their thirteen-year-old daughter Peg were cutting roses near a white arbor. His entire backyard, nearly half an acre, was cultivated and manicured. There were flowers everywhere. The garden was Ginny's pastime, hobby, avocation – next to sex, her passion. Nothing really replaced sex, thought her husband with an unconscious chuckle.

'Here! Let me give you a hand,' shouted Tremayne as he walked toward his wife and daughter.

'You're feeling better,' said Virginia, smiling.

'Look at these, daddy! Aren't they beautiful?' His daughter held up a bunch of red and yellow roses.

'They're lovely, sweetheart.'

'Dick, did I tell you? Bernie and Leila are flying east next week. They'll be here Friday.'

'Johnny told me . . . An Osterman weekend. I'll have to get in shape.'

'I thought you were practicing last night.'

Tremayne laughed. He never apologized for getting drunk, it happened too seldom, and he was never really difficult. Besides, last night he had deserved it. It *had* been a rotten week.

The three of them walked back to the patio. Virginia slipped her hand under her husband's arm. Peggy, growing so tall, her father thought, smiled brightly. The patio phone rang.

'I'll get it!' Peg dashed ahead.

'Why not?' shouted her father in mock exasperation. 'It's never for us!'

'We've simply got to get her her own telephone.' Virginia Tremayne pinched her husband's arm playfully.

'You're both driving me on welfare.'

'It's for you, mother. It's Mrs Cardone.' Peggy suddenly covered the receiver with her hand. '*Please* don't talk too long, mother. Carol Brown said she'd call me when she got home. You know, I told you. The Choate boy.'

Virginia Tremayne smiled knowingly, exchanging a conspiratorial look with her daughter. 'Carol won't elope without telling you, darling. She may need more than her week's allowance.'

'Oh, mother!'

Richard watched them with amusement. It was comfortable and comforting at the same time. His wife was doing a good job with their child. No one could argue with that. He knew there were those who criticized Ginny, said she dressed a little . . . flamboyantly. He'd heard that word and knew it meant something else. But the kids. The kids all flocked around Ginny. That was important these days. Perhaps his wife knew something most other women didn't know.

Things . . . 'things' were working out, thought Tremayne. Even the ultimate security, if Bernie Osterman was to be believed.

It was a good life.

He'd get on the phone with Joe if Ginny and Betty ever finished with their conversation. Then he'd call John and Ali. After Johnny's television shows were over. Perhaps the six of them could go over to the Club for the Sunday buffet.

Suddenly the memory of the patrol car flashed across his mind. He dismissed it. He had been nervous, edgy, hung over. Let's face it, he thought. It *was* Sunday afternoon and the town council *had* insisted that the police thoroughly check out the residential areas on Sunday afternoons.

Funny, he mused. He didn't think the Cardones were due back so early. Joe must have been called by his office to get in on Monday. The market was crazy these days. Especially commodities, Joe's speciality.

Betty nodded yes to Joe's question from the telephone. It solved the dinner problem. The buffet wasn't bad, even if the Club had never learned the secret of a good antipasto. Joe kept telling the manager that you had to use Genoa salami, not Hebrew National, but the chef had a deal with a Jewish supplier, so what could a mere member do? Even Joe, probably the richest of them all. On the other hand he was Italian – not Catholic, but nevertheless Italian – and it had only been a decade since the Saddle Valley Country Club first let Italians join. One of these days they'd let Jews in – that'd be the time for some kind of celebration.

It was this silent intolerance – never spelled out – that caused the Cardones, the Tanners and the Tremaynes to make it a special point to have Bernie and Leila Osterman very much in evidence at the Club whenever they came east. One thing could be said for the six of them. They weren't bigots.

It was strange, thought Cardone as he hung up the phone and started toward the small gym on the side of his house, strange that the Tanners had brought them all together. It had been John and Ali Tanner who had known the Ostermans in Los Angeles when Tanner was just starting out. Now Joe wondered whether John and Ali really understood the bond between Bernie Osterman and him and Dick Tremayne. It was a bond one didn't discuss with outsiders.

Eventually it would spell out the kind of independence every man sought, every worried citizen might pray for; there were dangers, risks, but it was right for him and Betty. Right for the Tremaynes and the Ostermans. They had discussed it among themselves, analyzed it, thought it through carefully, and collectively reached the decision.

It might have been right for the Tanners. But Joe, Dick and Bernie agreed that the first signal had to come from John himself. That was paramount. Enough hints had been dropped and Tanner had not responded.

Joe closed the heavy, matted door of his personal gymnasium, turned on the steam dials and stripped. He put on a pair of sweatpants and took his sweatshirt off the stainless-steel rack. He smiled as he noticed the embroidered initials on the flannel. Only a girl from Chestnut Hill would have a monogram sewn on a sweatshirt.

J. A. C.

Joseph Ambruzzio Cardone.

Giuseppe Ambruzzio Cardione. Second of eight children from the union of Angela and Umberto Cardione, once of Sicily and later South Philadelphia. Eventually, citizens. American flags alongside countless, cosmeticized pictures of the Virgin Mary holding a cherubic Christ-child with blue eyes and red lips.

Giuseppe Ambruzzio Cardione grew into a large, immensely strong young man who was just about the best athlete South Philadelphia High had ever seen. He was president of his senior class and twice elected to the All-City Student Council.

Of the many college scholarships offered he chose the most prestigious, Princeton, also the nearest to Philadelphia. As a Princeton halfback he accomplished the seemingly impossible for his alma mater. He was chosen All-American, the first Princeton football player in years to be so honored.

Several grateful alumni brought him to Wall Street. He'd shortened his name to Cardone, the last vowel pronounced very slightly. It had a kind of majesty, he thought. Like Cardozo. But no one was fooled; soon he didn't care. The market was expanding, exploding to the point where *everyone* was buying securities. At first he was merely a good customers' man. An Italian boy who had made good, a fellow who could talk to the emerging new-rich with money to spend; talk in ways the new-rich, still nervous about investments, could understand.

And it had to happen.

The Italians are sensitive people. They're more comfortable doing business with their own kind. A number of the construction boys – the Costellanos, the Latronas, the Battellas – who had made fortunes in industrial developments, gravitated to Cardone. Two syllables only. 'Joey Cardone,' they called him. And Joey found them tax shelters, Joey found them capital gains, Joey found them security.

The money poured in. The gross of the brokerage house nearly doubled, thanks to Joey's friends. Worthington and Bennett, members, NY Stock Exchange, became Worthington, Bennett and Cardone. From that point it was a short leap to Bennett-Cardone, Ltd.

Cardone was grateful to his *compares*. But the reason for his gratitude was also the reason why he shuddered just a bit when a patrol car appeared too frequently around his house. For a few of his *compares*, perhaps more than a few, were on the fringes – perhaps more than the fringes – of the underworld.

He finished with the weights and climbed on his rowing machine. The perspiration was pouring out and he felt better now. The menace of the patrol car began to diminish. After all, ninety-nine percent of the Saddle Valley families returned from vacations on Sunday. Who ever heard of people coming back from a vacation on a Wednesday? Even if the day were listed as such at the police station, a conscientious desk sergeant might well consider it an error and change it to Sunday. No one returned on Wednesday. Wednesday was a business day.

And who would ever take seriously the idea that Joseph Cardone had anything to do with the Cosa Nostra? He was the living proof of the work ethic. The American Success Story. A Princeton All-American.

Joe removed his sweatshirt and walked into the steam room, now dense with vapor. He sat on the bench and breathed deeply. The steam was purifying. After nearly two weeks of French-Canadian cooking, his body needed purifying.

He laughed aloud in his steam room. It was good to be home, his wife was right about that. And Tremayne told him the Ostermans would be flying in Friday morning. It'd be good to see Bernie and Leila again. It had been nearly four months. But they'd kept in touch.

Two hundred and fifty miles south of Saddle Valley, New Jersey, is that section of the nation's capital known as Georgetown. In Georgetown the pace of life changes every day at 5:30 P.M. Before, the pace is gradual, aristocratic, even delicate. After, there is a quickening – not sudden, but with a growing momentum. The residents, for the most part men and women of power and wealth and commitment to both, are dedicated to the propagation of their influence.

After five-thirty, the games begin.

After five-thirty in Georgetown, it is time for stratagems.

Who is where? . . . Why are they there?

Except on Sunday afternoon, when the power-brokers survey their creations of the previous week, and take the time to restore their strength for the next six days of strategy.

Let there be light and there *was* light. Let there be rest and there *is* rest.

Except, again, not for all.

For instance, not for Alexander Danforth, aide to the President of the United States. An aide without portfolio and without specified activities.

Danforth was the liaison between the all-securities communications room in the underground levels of the White House and the Central Intelligence Agency in McLean, Virginia. He was the compleat power-broker because he was never in evidence, yet his decisions were among the most important in Washington. Regardless of administrations, his quiet voice was heeded by all. It had been for years.

On this particular Sunday afternoon, Danforth sat with the Central Intelligence Agency's Deputy Administrator, George Grover, beneath the bougainvillea tree on Danforth's small backyard patio, watching television. The two men had reached the same conclusion John Tanner had reached two hundred and fifty miles north: Charles Woodward was going to make news tomorrow morning.

'State's going to use up a month's supply of toilet tissue,' Danforth said.

'They should. Whoever let Ashton go on? He's not only stupid, he *looks* stupid. Stupid and slippery. John Tanner's responsible for this program, isn't he?'

'He is.'

'Smart son of a bitch. It'd be nice to be certain he's on our side,' Grover said.

'Fassett's assured us.' The two men exchanged looks. 'Well, you've seen the file. Don't you agree?'

'Yes. Yes, I do. Fassett's right.'

'He generally is.'

There were two telephones on the ceramic table in front of Danforth. One was black with an outdoor plug-in jack on the ground. The other was red and a red cable extended from inside the house. The red phone hummed – it did not ring. Danforth picked it up.

'Yes . . . Yes, Andrews. Good . . . Fine. Ring Fassett on Redder and tell him to come over. Has Los Angeles confirmed the Ostermans? No change? . . . Excellent. We're on schedule.'

Bernard Osterman, CCNY, Class of '46, pulled the page out of his typewriter and glanced at it. Adding it to the bottom of a thin sheaf of papers, he stood up. He walked around his kidney-shaped pool and handed the manuscript to his wife, Leila, who sat naked in her lounge chair.

Osterman was naked too.

'You know, an undressed woman's not particularly attractive in sunlight.'

'You think you're a portrait in beige? . . . Give.' She took the pages and reached for her large, tinted glasses. 'Is this the finish?'

Bernie nodded. 'When are the kids getting home?'

'They'll call from the beach before they start back. I told Marie to make sure they phone. I wouldn't want Merwyn to find out about naked girls in sunlight at his age. There's enough aversion to that in this town.'

'You've got a point. Read.' Bernie dove into the pool. He swam back and forth rapidly for three minutes . . . until he was out of breath. He was a good swimmer. In the Army they made him a swimming instructor at Fort Dix. 'Speed-Jew' they had called him at the Army pool. But never to his face. He was a thin man, but tough. If CCNY had had a football team instead of a joke, he would have been its captain. An end. Joe Cardone told Bernie he could have used him at Princeton.

Bernie had laughed when Joe told him that. In spite of the surface democratization of the Army experience – and it was surface – it had never occurred to Bernard Osterman, of the Tremont Avenue Ostermans, Bronx, New York, to vault time-honored barriers and enter the Ivy League. He might have been able to, he was bright and there was the GI Bill, but it simply never entered his thinking.

It wouldn't have been comfortable then – in 1946. It would be now; things had changed.

Osterman climbed up the ladder. It was good that he and Leila were going to the east coast, back to Saddle Valley for a few days. It was somehow akin to taking a brief, concentrated course in pleasant living whenever they returned. Everyone always said the east was hectic, pressurized – far more so than Los Angeles; but that wasn't so. It only seemed that way because the area of action was more confined.

Los Angeles, *his* Los Angeles, which meant Burbank, Hollywood, Beverly Hills, was where the real insanity was practiced. Men and women racing crazily up and down the aisles of a palm-lined drug store. Everything on sale, everything labeled, everyone competing in their psychedelic shirts and orange slacks.

There were times when Bernie just wanted to see someone dressed in a Brooks Brothers suit and a button-down broadcloth. It didn't really mean anything, not actually; he didn't give much of a damn what costumes the tribes of Los Angeles wore. Perhaps it was just the continual, overbearing assault on the eyes.

Or perhaps he was entering one of his downswings again. He was wearying of it all.

Which was unfair. The palm-lined drug store had treated him very well.

'How is it?' he asked his wife.

'Pretty good. You may even have a problem.'

'What?' Bernie grabbed a towel from a stack on the table. 'What problem?'

'You could be stripping too many layers away. Too much pain, maybe.' Leila flipped over a page as her husband smiled. 'Be quiet a minute and let me finish. Perhaps you'll snap out of it.'

Bernie Osterman sat down in a webbed chair and let the warm California sun wash over his body. There was still a smile on his lips; he knew what his wife meant and it was comforting to him. The years of formula writing hadn't destroyed his ability to strip away the layers – when he wanted to.

And there were times when there was nothing more important to him than to want to. To prove to himself that he could still do it. The way he used to back in the days when they lived in New York.

They were good days. Provocative, exciting, filled with commitment and purpose. Only there was never anything else really – just commitment, just purpose. A few flattering reviews written by other intense young writers.

He'd been called *penetrating* then; *perceptive, incisive.* Once, even, *extraordinary.*

It hadn't been enough. And so he and Leila came to the palm-lined drug store and willingly, happily trained their talents for the exploding world of the television residual.

Someday, though. Someday, thought Bernard Osterman, it would happen again. The luxury of sitting down with all the time in the world to really do it. Make a big mistake if he had to. It was important to be able to think like that.

'Bernie?'

'Yes?'

Leila draped a towel over her front and pushed the latch on the lounge chair so the back raised itself. 'It's beautiful, sweetie. I mean really very beautiful, and I think you know it's not going to work.'

'It does work!'

'They won't sit still for it.'

'Fuck 'em!'

'We're being paid thirty thousand for a one-hour drama, Bernie. Not a two-hour exorcism ending in a funeral home.'

'It's not an exorcism. It happens to be a sad story based on very real conditions, and the conditions don't change. You want to drive down to the barrio and take a look?'

'They won't buy it. They'll want rewrites.'

'I won't make them!'

'And they'll hold the balance. There's fifteen thousand coming to us.'

'Son of a bitch!'

'You know I'm right.'

'Talk! All Goddamned talk! This season we'll have *meaning*! *Controversy*! . . . Talk!'

'They look at the figures. A rave in *The Times* doesn't sell deodorant in Kansas.'

'Fuck 'em.'

'Relax. Take another swim. It's a big pool.' Leila Osterman looked at her husband. He knew what that look meant and couldn't help smiling. A little sadly.

'OK, fix it then.'

Leila reached for the pencil and yellow pad on the table next to her chair. Bernie stood up and approached the edge of the pool.

'You think Tanner might want to join us? You think maybe I can approach him?'

His wife put down her pencil and looked up at her husband.

'I don't know. Johnny's different from us . . .'

'Different from Joe and Betty? Dick and Ginny? I don't see he's so different.'

'I wouldn't jump at him. He's still a newshawk. Vulture they used to call him, remember? The vulture of San Diego. He's got a spine. I wouldn't want to bend it. It might snap back.'

'He thinks like we do. He thinks like Joe and Dick. Like us.'

'I repeat. Don't jump. Call it the well-advertised woman's intuition, but don't jump . . . We could get hurt.'

Osterman dove into the pool and swam thirty-six feet under water to the far end. Leila was only half right, he thought. Tanner was an uncompromising newsman but he was also a sensible and sensitive human being. Tanner wasn't a fool, he saw what was happening – everywhere. It was inevitable.

It all came down to individual survival.

It reduced itself to being able to do what one wanted to do. To write an 'exorcism' if he was capable of it. Without worrying about deodorants in the state of Kansas.

Bernie surfaced and held on to the side of the pool, breathing deeply. He pushed himself off and slowly breast-stroked back toward his wife.

'Did I box you into a corner?'

'You never could.' Leila spoke while writing on the yellow pad. 'There was a time in my life when I thought thirty thousand dollars was all the money in the world. Brooklyn's house of Weintraub was not Chase Manhattan's biggest client.' She tore off a page and secured it under a Pepsi-Cola bottle.

'I never had that problem,' said Bernie, treading water. 'The Ostermans are really a silent branch of the Rothschilds.'

'I know. Your racing colors are puce and pumpkin orange.'

'Hey!' Bernie suddenly grasped the ledge and looked excitedly at his wife. 'Did I tell you? The trainer called this morning from Palm Springs. That two-year-old we bought did three furlongs in forty-one seconds!'

Leila Osterman dropped the pad on her lap and laughed. 'You know, we're really too much! And you want to play Dostoyevski!'

'I see what you mean . . . Well, someday.'

'Sure. In the meantime keep an eye on Kansas and the other on those cockamamie horses of yours.'

Osterman chuckled and plunged toward the opposite side of the pool. He thought once more about the Tanners. John and Ali Tanner. He'd cleared their names with Switzerland. Zurich was enthusiastic.

Bernard Osterman had made up his mind. Somehow he'd convince his wife.

He was going to talk seriously to John Tanner next weekend.

★ ★ ★

Danforth walked through the narrow front hallway of his Georgetown house and opened the door. Laurence Fassett, of the Central Intelligence Agency, smiled and extended his hand.

'Good afternoon, Mr Danforth. Andrews called me from McLean. We've only met once before – I'm sure you don't remember. It's an honor, sir.'

Danforth looked at this extraordinary man and returned the smile. The CIA dossier said Fassett was forty-seven, but to Danforth he seemed much younger. The broad shoulders, the muscular neck, the unwrinkled face beneath the short-cropped blond hair: this all reminded Danforth of his own approaching seventieth birthday.

'Of course I remember. Come in, please.'

As Fassett stepped into the hallway, his gaze fell on several Degas watercolors on the wall. He took a step closer. 'These are beautiful.'

'Yes, they are. Are you an expert, Mr Fassett?'

'Oh, no. Just an enthusiastic amateur . . . My wife was an artist. We used to spend a lot of time in the Louvre.'

Danforth knew he shouldn't dwell on Fassett's wife. She had been German – with ties in East Berlin. She had been killed in East Berlin.

'Yes, yes, of course. Come this way, please. Grover's out back. We were watching the Woodward program on the patio.'

The two men walked out onto the flagstone and brick backyard. George Grover rose from his chair.

'Hello, Larry. Things are beginning to move.'

'Looks that way. It can't be too quick for me.'

'Nor for any of us, I shouldn't think,' said Danforth. 'Drink?'

'No, thank you, sir. If you don't mind, I'd rather make this as quick as possible.'

The three men sat down around the ceramic table. 'Then let's pick up from where we are right now,' Danforth said. 'What is the immediate plan?'

Fassett looked bewildered. 'I thought it had all been cleared through you.'

'Oh, I've read the reports. I just want the information first-hand from the man in charge.'

'All right, sir. Phase one is complete. The Tanners, the Tremaynes and the Cardones are all in Saddle Valley. No immediate vacations planned, they'll be there throughout the coming week. This information is confirmed from all our sources. There are thirteen agents in the town and the three families will be under constant surveillance . . . Intercepts have been placed on all telephones. Untraceable.

'Los Angeles has established the Ostermans' flight on Friday to be Number 509, arriving Kennedy at 4:50 Eastern Daylight Time. Their usual procedure is to take a taxi directly out to the suburbs. The cab will be followed, of course . . .'

'If, by then, they're adhering to normal patterns,' interrupted Grover.

'If they're not, they won't be on that plane . . . Tomorrow we bring Tanner down to Washington.'

'He has no inkling at the moment, does he?' asked Danforth.

'None at all – other than the patrol car, which we'll use if he balks tomorrow morning.'

'How do you think he'll take it?' Grover leaned forward on his seat.

'I think it'll blow his mind.'

'He may refuse to cooperate,' Danforth said.

'That's not likely. If I do my job, he won't have a choice.'

Danforth looked at the intense, muscular man who spoke so confidently. 'You're anxious that we succeed, aren't you? You're very committed.'

'I have reason to be.' Fassett returned the old man's stare. When he continued it was in a matter-of-fact tone. 'They killed my wife. They ran her down on the Kurfürstendamm at two o'clock in the morning – while I was being "detained". She was trying to find me. Did you know that?'

'I've read the file. You have my deepest sympathy . . .'

'I don't want your sympathy. Those orders came from Moscow. I want them. I want Omega.'

PART TWO

Monday
Tuesday
Wednesday
Thursday

2

Monday – 10:15 A.M.

Tanner left the elevator and walked down the thickly carpeted corridor toward his office. He'd spent twenty-five minutes in the screening room watching the Woodward tape. It confirmed what the newspapers had reported: Charles Woodward had exposed Undersecretary Ashton as a political hack.

There had to be a lot of embarrassed men in Washington, he thought.

'Quite a show, wasn't it?' his secretary said.

'Out-of-sight, as my son would put it. I don't think we can expect many dinner invitations to the White House. Any calls?'

'From all over town. Mainly congratulations; I left the names on your desk.'

'That's comforting. I may need them. Anything else?'

'Yes, sir. The FCC called twice. A man called Fassett.'

'Who?'

'Mr Laurence Fassett.'

'We've always dealt with Cranston down there.'

'That's what I thought, but he said it was urgent.'

'Maybe the State Department's trying to get us arrested before sundown.'

'I doubt it. They'd at least wait a day or two; it'd look less political.'

'You'd better get him back. To the FCC everything's urgent.' Tanner crossed into his office, sat down at his desk, and read through the messages. He smiled; even his competition had been impressed.

The telephone intercom buzzed. 'Mr Fassett's on one, sir.'

'Thanks.' Tanner pushed the appropriate button. 'Mr Fassett? Sorry I was out of the office when you called.'

'It's my place to apologize,' said the polite voice at the other end of the line. 'It's just that I have a difficult schedule today, and you're a priority.'

'What's the problem?'

'Routine but urgent is the best way I can describe it. The papers you filed with us in May for Standard's news division were incomplete.'

'What?' John remembered something FCC's Cranston had said to him a few weeks ago. He also recalled that Cranston had said it was unimportant. 'What's missing?'

'Two signatures of yours for one thing. On pages seventeen and eighteen. And the breakdown of projected public service features for the six-month period commencing in January.'

John Tanner did remember now. It had been Cranston's fault. Pages seventeen and eighteen had been missing from the folder sent from Washington for Tanner's signature – a point which the network's legal department had made to Tanner's office – and the service feature blanks were to be left open for another month, pending network decisions. Cranston, again, had agreed.

'If you'll check, you'll find your Mr Cranston omitted the pages you refer to and the specific service features were postponed. He agreed to that.'

There was a momentary pause from Washington. When Fassett spoke his voice held a touch less politeness than it had previously.

'In all deference to Cranston, he had no authority to make such a decision. Surely you have the information now.' It was a statement.

'Yes, as a matter of fact, we do. I'll send it out Special Delivery.'

'I'm afraid that's not good enough. We'll have to ask you to get down here this afternoon.'

'Now, wait a minute. That's kind of short notice, isn't it?'

'I don't make the rules. I just carry them out. As of two months ago Standard Mutual Network is operating in violation of the FCC code. We can't allow ourselves to be put in that position. Regardless of who's responsible, that is a fact. You're in violation. Let's get it cleared up today.'

'All right. But I warn you, if this action is in any way a harassment emanating from the State Department, I'll bring down the network attorneys and label it for what it is.'

'I not only don't like your insinuation, but I don't know what you're talking about.'

'I think you do. The Woodward Show yesterday afternoon.'

Fassett laughed. 'Oh, I heard about that. The *Post* did quite a story on it . . . And I think you can put your mind at ease. I tried to reach you twice last Friday.'

'You did?'

'Yes.'

'Wait a minute.' Tanner pushed the *hold* button and then the *local*. 'Norma? Did this Fassett try to get me Friday?'

There was a short silence while Tanner's secretary checked Friday's call sheet. 'Could be. There were two calls from Washington, an Operator thirty-six in DC for you to reach if you returned by four. You were in the studio till five-thirty.'

'Didn't you ask who was calling?'

'Of course I did. The only answer I got was that it could wait until Monday.'

'Thanks.' Tanner got back on the line with Fassett. 'Did you leave an operator's number?'

'Operator three-six, Washington. Till 4:00 P.M.'

'You didn't give your name or identify the agency . . .'

'It was Friday. I wanted to get out early. Would you have felt better if I'd left an urgent call you couldn't return?'

'Okay, okay. And this can't wait for the mails?'

'I'm sorry, Mr Tanner. I mean I'm really *very* sorry, but I have my instructions. Standard Mutual's not a small local station. The filing should have been completed weeks ago . . . Also,' here Fassett laughed again, 'the way you keep stepping on exposed toes, I wouldn't want to be you if some wheels in the State Department found out your whole damn news department was in violation . . . And that's no threat. It couldn't be. We're both at fault.'

John Tanner smiled at the telephone. Fassett was right. The filing *was* overdue. And there was no sense risking bureaucratic reprisals. He sighed. 'I'll catch the one o'clock shuttle and be at the FCC by three or a little after. Where's your office?'

'I'll be with Cranston. We'll have the papers, and don't forget the schedules. They're only projections, we won't hold you to them.'

'Right. See you then.' Tanner pushed another button and dialed his home number.

'Hi, darling.'

'I've got to hop down to Washington this afternoon.'

'Any problems?'

'No. "Routine but urgent" was the description. Some FCC business. I'll catch a shuttle back to Newark by seven. I just wanted you to know that I'd be late.'

'Okay, darling. Do you want me to pick you up?'

'No, I'll get a cab.'

'Sure?'

'Very. It'll make me feel good to think Standard's paying the twenty bucks.'

'You're worth it. By the way, I read the reviews on the Woodward Show. You're a regular triumph.'

'That's what I wrote across my jacket. Tanner the Triumph.'

'I wish you would,' said Alice quietly.

Even in jest she could never let it go. They had no real money problems, but Alice Tanner forever thought her husband was underpaid. It was the only serious argument between them. He could never explain that to seek more from a corporation like Standard Mutual meant just that much more obligation to the faceless giant.

'See you tonight, Ali.'

'Bye. I love you.'

As if in silent deference to his wife's complaint, Tanner commandeered one of the news cars to take him to La-Guardia Airport in an hour. No one argued. Tanner was, indeed, a triumph this morning.

During the next forty-five minutes, Tanner tied together a number of administrative loose ends. The last order of business was a call to Standard Mutual's legal department.

'Mr Harrison, please . . . Hello, Andy? John Tanner. I'm in a hurry, Andy; I've got to catch a plane. I just want to find out something. Do we have anything pending with the FCC I don't know about? Any problems? I know about the public service features but Cranston said we could hold on those . . . Sure, I'll wait.' Tanner fingered the telephone cord, his thoughts still on Fassett. 'Yes, Andy, I'm here . . . Pages seventeen and eighteen. The signatures . . . I see. Okay. Thanks. No, no problems here. Thanks again.'

Tanner replaced the phone and got out of his chair slowly. Harrison had added fuel to his vague suspicions. It all seemed just a bit too contrived. The FCC filing had been complete except for the final two pages on the fourth and fifth copies of the document. They were merely duplicates, important to no one, easily Xeroxed. Yet those pages had been missing from the file. Harrison had just commented:

'I remember, John. I sent you a memo about it. It looked to me as though they had been deliberately left out. Can't imagine why . . .'

Neither could Tanner.

3

To Tanner's amazement, the FCC sent a limousine to meet his plane.

Cranston's offices were on the sixth floor of the FCC Building; at one time or another every major network news director had been summoned there. Cranston was a career man – respected by the networks as well as the changing administrations – and because of this Tanner found himself resenting the unknown Laurence Fassett, who could say with indignation, '. . . Cranston had no authority to make such a decision.'

He'd never heard of Laurence Fassett.

Tanner pushed open the door to Cranston's waiting room. It was empty. The secretary's desk was bare – no pads, no pencils, no papers of any kind. What light there was came from Cranston's office door. It was open and he could hear the quiet whirr of an air conditioner. The window shades in the office were down, probably to keep out the summer sunlight. And then, against the office wall, he saw the shadow of a figure walking toward the door.

'Good afternoon,' said the man as he came into view. He was shorter than Tanner by several inches, probably five ten or eleven, but very broad in the shoulders. His blond hair was cut short, his eyes set far apart beneath bushy light-brown eyebrows. He was, perhaps, Tanner's age, but without question a more physical man. Even his stance had a potential spring to it, thought Tanner.

'Mr Fassett?'

'That's right. Won't you come in?' Fassett, instead of retreating into Cranston's office, crossed in front of Tanner to the door and locked it. 'We'd rather not have any interruptions.'

'Why not?' asked Tanner, startled.

Laurence Fassett looked about the room. 'Yes. Yes. I see what you mean. Good point. Come in, please.' Fassett walked in front of Tanner into Cranston's office. The shades of the two windows overlooking the street were pulled all the way down; Cranston's desk was as bare as his secretary's, except for two ashtrays and one other item. In the center of the cleared surface was a small Wollensak tape recorder with two cords – one in front of Cranston's chair, the other by the chair in front of Cranston's desk.

'Is that a tape recorder?' asked the news director, following Fassett into the office.

'Yes, it is. Won't you sit down, please?'

John Tanner remained standing. When he spoke it was with quiet anger. 'No, I will *not* sit down. I don't like any of this. Your methods are very unclear, or maybe *too* clear. If you intend putting anything I say down on tape, you know perfectly well I won't allow it without the presence of a network attorney.'

Fassett stood behind Cranston's desk. 'This is not FCC business. When I explain, you'll understand my . . . methods.'

'You'd better explain quickly, because I'm about to leave. I was called by the FCC to deliver the public service hours projected by Standard Mutual – which I have in my briefcase – and to sign two copies of our filing which *your* office omitted sending. You made it clear that you would be with Cranston when I arrived. Instead, I find an office which obviously is not in use . . . I'd say you'd better have a good explanation or you'll be hearing from our attorneys within an hour. And if this is any kind of reprisal against Standard Mutual's news division, I'll blast you from coast to coast.'

'I'm sorry . . . These things are never easy.'

'They shouldn't be!'

'Now hold it. Cranston's on vacation. We used his name because you've dealt with him before.'

'You're telling me you intentionally lied?'

'Yes. The key, Mr Tanner, is in the phrase you employed just now . . . "I was called by the FCC," I believe you said. May I present my credentials?' Laurence Fassett reached into his breast pocket and withdrew a small plastic case. He held it across the desk.

Tanner opened it.

The top card identified Laurence C. Fassett as an employee of the Central Intelligence Agency.

The other card was Fassett's priority permit to enter the McLean complex at any hour of day or night.

'What's this all about? Why am I here?' Tanner handed back Fassett's identification.

'That's the reason for the tape recorder. Let me show you. Before I explain our business I have to ask you a number of questions. There are two switches which can shut off the machine. One here by me, the other there by you. If at any time I ask you a question you do not care to answer, all you have to do is push the OFF switch and the machine stops. On the other hand – and, again, for your protection – if I feel you are including private information which is no concern of ours, *I* shall stop the machine.' Fassett started up the recorder with his switch and then reached across the desk for the cord in front of Tanner's chair and stopped it. 'See? Quite simple. I've been through hundreds of these interviews. You've got nothing to worry about.'

'This sounds like a pretrial examination without benefit of counsel or mandate of subpoena! What's the point? If you think you're going to intimidate me, you're crazy!'

'The *point* is one of completely positive identification . . . And you're absolutely right. If it was our intention to intimidate anyone, we picked about as vulnerable a subject as J. Edgar Hoover. And even *he* doesn't have control of a network news program.'

Tanner looked at the CIA man standing politely behind Cranston's desk. Fassett had a point. The CIA wouldn't allow itself to use so blatant a tactic on someone in his position.

'What do you mean, "completely positive identification"? You know who I am.'

'It should give you some idea of the magnitude of the information I'm empowered to deliver. Just extraordinary precaution in line with the importance of the data . . . Did you know that in the Second World War an actor – a corporal in the British army, to be exact – impersonated Field Marshal Montgomery at high-level conferences in Africa and even some of Montgomery's Sandhurst classmates didn't catch on?'

The news director picked up the cord and pushed the ON and OFF switches. The machine started and stopped. John Tanner's curiosity – mingled with fear – was growing. He sat down. 'Go ahead. Just remember, I'll shut off the tape and leave any time I want to.'

'I understand. That's your privilege – up to a point.'

'What do you mean by that? No qualifications, please.'

'Trust me. You'll understand.' Fassett's reassuring look served its purpose.

'Go ahead,' said Tanner. The CIA man picked up a manila folder and opened it. He then started the machine.

'Your full name is John Raymond Tanner?'

'Incorrect. My legal name is John Tanner. The Raymond was a baptismal name and is not registered on my birth certificate.'

Fassett smiled from across the desk. 'Very good.'

'Thank you.'

'You currently reside at 22 Orchard Drive, Saddle Valley, New Jersey?'

'I do.'

'You were born on May 21, 1924, in Springfield, Illinois, to Lucas and Margaret Tanner?'

'Yes.'

'Your family moved to San Mateo, California, when you were seven years old?'

'Yes.'

'For what purpose?'

'My father's firm transferred him to Northern California. He was a personnel executive for a department-store chain. The Bryant Stores.'

'Comfortable circumstances?'

'Reasonably so.'

'You were educated in the San Mateo public school system?'

'No. I went through the second year of San Mateo High and transferred to a private school for the final two years of secondary school. Winston Preparatory.'

'Upon graduation you enrolled at Stanford University?'

'Yes.'

'Were you a member of any fraternities or clubs?'

'Yes. Alpha Kappa fraternity. The Trylon News Society, several others I can't recall . . . Photography club, I think, but I didn't stay. I worked on the campus magazine, but quit.'

'Any reason?'

Tanner looked at the CIA man. 'Yes. I strenuously objected to the Nisei situation. The prison camps. The magazine supported them. My objection still stands.'

Fassett smiled again. 'Your education was interrupted?'

'Most educations were. I enlisted in the Army at the end of my sophomore year.'

'Where were you trained?'

'Fort Benning, Georgia. Infantry.'

'Third Army? Fourteenth Division?'

'Yes.'

'You saw service in the European theater of operations?'

'Yes.'

'Your highest rank was First Lieutenant?'

'Yes.'

'OCS training at Fort Benning?'

'No. I received a Field Commission in France.'

'I see you also received several decorations.'

'They were unit citations, battalion commendations. Not individual.'

'You were hospitalized for a period of three weeks in St Lô. Was this a result of wounds?'

Tanner looked momentarily embarrassed. 'You know perfectly well it wasn't. There's no Purple Heart on my Army record,' he said quietly.

'Would you explain?'

'I fell out of a jeep on the road to St Lô. Dislocated hip.'

Both men smiled.

'You were discharged in July of 1945 and returned to Stanford the following September?'

'I did . . . To anticipate you, Mr Fassett, I switched from an English major to the journalism school. I graduated in 1947 with a Bachelor of Arts degree.'

Laurence Fassett's eyes remained on the folder in front of him. 'You were married in your junior year to one Alice McCall?'

Tanner reached for his switch and shut off the machine. 'This may be where I walk out.'

'Relax, Mr Tanner. Just identification . . . We don't subscribe to the theory that the sins of the parents are visited upon their daughters. A simple yes or no will suffice.'

Tanner started the machine again. 'That is correct.'

At this point, Laurence Fassett picked the cord off the desk and pushed the OFF switch. Tanner watched the reels stop, and then looked at the CIA man.

'My next two questions concern the circumstances leading up to your marriage. I presume you do not care to answer them.'

'You presume correctly.'

'Believe me, they aren't important.'

'If you told me they were, I'd leave right now.' Ali had been through enough. Tanner would not allow his wife's personal tragedy to be brought up again, by anyone.

Fassett started the machine again. 'Two children were born to you and Alice Mc . . . Tanner. A boy, Raymond, now age thirteen, and a girl, Janet, now eight.'

'My son is twelve.'

'His birthday is day after tomorrow. To go back a bit, your first employment after graduation was with *The Sacramento Daily News*.'

'Reporter. Rewrite man, office boy, movie critic and a space salesman when time permitted.'

'You stayed with the Sacramento paper for three and a half years and then obtained a position with *The Los Angeles Times*?'

'No. I was in Sacramento for . . . *two* and a half years – I had an interim job with the *San Francisco Chronicle* for about a year before I got the job at *The Times*.'

'On *The Los Angeles Times* you were quite successful as an investigative reporter . . .'

'I was fortunate. I assume you're referring to my work on the San Diego waterfront operations.'

'I am. You were nominated for a Pulitzer, I believe.'

'I didn't get it.'

'And then elevated to an editorial position with *The Times?*'

'An assistant editor. Nothing spectacular.'

'You remained with *The Times* for a period of five years . . .'

'Nearer six, I think.'

'Until January of 1958 when you joined Standard Mutual in Los Angeles?'

'Correct.'

'You remained on the Los Angeles staff until March of 1963 when you were transferred to New York City. Since that time you have received several promotions?'

'I came east as a network editor for the seven o'clock news program. I expanded into documentaries and specials until I reached my present position.'

'Which is?'

'Director of News for Standard Mutual.'

Laurence Fassett closed the folder and shut off the tape recorder. He leaned back and smiled at John Tanner. 'That wasn't so painful, was it?'

'You mean that's it?'

'No, not . . . *it,* but the completion of the identity section. You passed. You gave me just enough slightly wrong answers to pass the test.'

'What?'

'These things,' Fassett slapped the folder, 'are designed by the Interrogations Division. Fellows with high foreheads bring in other fellows with beards and they put the stuff through computers. You couldn't possibly answer everything correctly. If you did it would mean you had studied too hard . . . For instance, you were with *The Sacramento Daily News* for three years almost to the day. Not two and a half or three and a half. Your family moved to San Mateo when you were eight years, two months, not seven years old.'

'I'll be Goddamned . . .'

'Frankly, even if you had answered everything correctly, we might have passed you. But it's nice to know you're normal. In your case, we had to have it all on tape . . . Now, I'm afraid, comes the tough part.'

'Tough compared to what?' asked the news editor.

'Just rough . . . I have to start the machine now.' He did so and picked up a single sheet of paper. 'John Tanner, I must inform you that what I am about to discuss with you comes under the heading of classified information of the highest priority. In no way is this information a reflection on you or your family and to that I do so swear. The revealing of this information to anyone would be against the interests of the United States Government in the severest sense. So much so that those in the government service aware of this information can be prosecuted under the National Security Act, Title eighteen, Section seven-nine-three, should they violate the demands of secrecy . . . Is everything I've said so far completely clear?'

'It is . . . However, I am neither bound nor am I indictable.'

'I realize that. It is my intention to take you in three stages toward the essential, classified information. At the end of stages one and two you may ask to be excused from this interview and we can only rely on your intelligence and loyalty to your government to keep silent about what has been said. However, if you agree to the third stage, in which identities are revealed to you, you accept the same responsibility as those in government service and can be prosecuted under the National Security Act should you violate the aforementioned demands of secrecy. Is that clear, Mr Tanner?'

Tanner shifted in his seat before speaking. He looked at the revolving wheels of the tape recorder and then up at Fassett. 'It's clear, but I'll be damned if I agree to it. You don't have any right calling me down here under false pretenses and then setting up conditions that make me indictable.'

'I didn't ask if you agreed. Only if you understood clearly what I said.'

'And if that's a threat, you can go to hell.'

'All I'm doing is spelling out conditions. Is that a threat? Is it any more than you do every day with contracts? You can walk out any time you like until you give me your consent to reveal names. Is that so illogical?'

Tanner reasoned that it wasn't, really. And his curiosity now had to be satisfied.

'You said earlier that whatever this thing is, it has nothing to do with my family? Nothing to do with my wife? . . . Or me?'

'I swore to it on this tape.' Fassett realized that Tanner had added the 'or me' as an afterthought. He was protecting his wife.

'Go ahead.'

Fassett rose from the chair and walked toward the window shades. 'By the way, you don't have to stay sitting down. They're high-impedance microphones. Miniaturized, of course.'

'I'll sit.'

'Suit yourself. A number of years ago we heard rumors of a Soviet NKVD operation which could have widespread damaging effects on the American economy should it ever amount to anything. We tried to trace it down, tried to learn something about it. We couldn't. It remained rumor. It was a better-kept secret than the Russian space program.

'Then in 1966 an East German intelligence officer defected. He gave us our first concrete knowledge of the operation. He informed us that East German Intelligence maintained contact with agents in the West – or a cell – known only as *Omega*. I'll give you the geographical code name in a minute

. . . or maybe I won't. It's in step two. That's up to you. Omega would regularly forward sealed files to East German Intelligence. Two armed couriers would fly them to Moscow under the strictest secrecy.

'The function of Omega is as old as espionage itself, and extremely effective in these days of large corporations and huge conglomerates . . . Omega is a doomsday book.'

'A what?'

'Doomsday book. Lists containing hundreds, perhaps by now thousands, of individuals marked for the plague. In this case not bubonic, but blackmail. The men and women on these lists are people in decision-making positions in scores of giant companies in key fields. Many have enormous economic power. Purchasing as well as refusal-to-purchase power. Forty or fifty, acting in concert, could create economic chaos.'

'I don't understand. Why would they? Why should they?'

'I told you. Blackmail. Each of these people is vulnerable, exploitable for any of a thousand reasons. Sex, extracurricular or deviate; legal misrepresentation; business malpractice; price-fixing; stock manipulation; tax evasion. The book touches a great many people. Men and women whose reputations, businesses, professions, even their families could be destroyed. Unless they comply.'

'It's also a pretty low view of the business world, and I'm not at all sure it's an accurate one. Not to the extent you describe it. Not to the point of economic chaos.'

'Oh? The Crawford Foundation made an in-depth study of industry leadership in the United States from 1925 to 1945. The results are still classified a quarter of a century later. The study determined that during this period thirty-two percent of the corporate financial power in this country was obtained by questionable, if not illegal, means. *Thirty-two percent!*'

'I don't believe that. If it's true it should be made public.'

'Impossible. There'd be legal massacre. Courts and money are not an immaculate combination . . . Today it's the conglomerates. Pick up the newspaper any day. Turn to the financial pages and read about the manipulators. Look at the charges and countercharges. It's a mother lode for Omega. A directory of candidates. None of those boys lives in a deep freeze. Not one of them. An unsecured loan is granted, a stock margin is expanded – temporarily – girls are provided to a good customer. Omega digs just a little with the right people and a lot of slime gets in the bucket. It's not very hard to do. You just have to be accurate. Enough so to frighten.'

Tanner looked away from the blond man who spoke with such precision. With such relaxed confidence. 'I don't like to think you're right.'

Suddenly, Fassett crossed back to the table and turned off the tape recorder. The wheels stopped. 'Why not? It's not just the information uncovered – that could be relatively harmless – but the way it's applied. Take *you*, for instance. Suppose, just suppose, a story based on occurrences around twenty some-odd years ago outside Los Angeles were printed in the Saddle Valley paper. Your children are in school there, your wife happy in the community . . . How long do you think you'd stay there?'

Tanner lurched out of his chair and faced the shorter man across the desk. His rage was such that his hands trembled. He spoke with deep feeling, barely audible.

'That's filthy!'

'That's Omega, Mr Tanner. Relax, I was only making a point.' Fassett turned the recorder back on and continued as Tanner returned warily to his chair. 'Omega exists. Which brings me to the last part of . . . stage one.'

'What's that?'

Laurence Fassett sat down behind the desk. He crushed out his cigarette, while Tanner reached into his pocket and withdrew a pack. 'We know now that there's a time table for Omega. A date for the chaos to begin . . . I'm not telling you anything you don't know when I admit that my agency is often involved in exchange of personnel with the Soviets.'

'Nothing I don't know.'

'One of ours for two or three of theirs is the normal ratio . . .'

'I know that, too.'

'Twelve months ago on the border of Albania such an exchange took place. Forty-five days of haggling. I was there, which is why I'm here now. During the exchange our team was approached by several members of the Soviet Foreign Service. The best way I can describe them to you is to call them moderates. The same as our moderates.'

'I understand what our moderates oppose. What do the Soviet moderates oppose?'

'Same thing. Instead of a Pentagon – and an elusive military-industrial complex – it's the hard-liners in the Presidium. The militarists.'

'I see.'

'We were informed that the Soviet militarists have issued a target date for the final phase of Operation Omega. On that date the plan will be implemented. Untold hundreds of powerful executives in the American business community will be reached and threatened with personal destruction if they do not follow the orders given them. A major financial crisis could be the result. An economic disaster is not impossible . . . It's the truth.

'That is the end of stage one.'

Tanner got out of his chair, drawing on his cigarette. He paced up and down in front of the desk. 'And with that information I have the option to get out of here?'

'You do.'

'You're too much. Honest to Christ, you're too much! . . . The tape's running. Go on.'

'Very well. Stage two. We knew that Omega was made up of the very same type of individual it will attack. It had to be, otherwise the contacts could never have been made, the vulnerabilities never established. In essence, we basically knew what to look for. Men who could infiltrate large companies, men who worked either in or for them, who could associate with their subjects . . . As I mentioned previously, Omega is a code name for a cell or a group of agents. There is also a geographical code name; a clearing house for the forwarding of information. Having passed through this source, the authenticity is presumably established because of its operational secrecy. The geographical code name for Omega is difficult to give an accurate translation of, but the nearest is "Chasm of . . . Leather" or "Goat Skin".'

'"Chasm of Leather"?' Tanner put out his cigarette.

'Yes. Remember we learned this over three years ago. After eighteen months of concentrated research we pinpointed the "Chasm of Leather" as one of eleven locations throughout the country . . .'

'One of them being Saddle Valley, New Jersey?'

'Let's not get ahead of ourselves.'

'Am I right?'

'We placed agents within these communities,' continued the CIA man, disregarding Tanner's question. 'We ran checks on thousands of citizens – a very expensive exercise – and the more we researched, the more evidence we turned up that the Village of Saddle Valley was the "Chasm of Leather". It was a thorough job. Watermarks on stationery, analysis of dust particles the East German officer brought out in the sealed folders he gave us when he defected, a thousand different items checked and rechecked . . . But mainly, the information about certain residents unearthed in the research.'

'I think you'd better get to the point.'

'That will be *your* decision. I've just about concluded stage two.' Tanner remained silent, so Fassett continued. 'You are in a position to give us incalculable assistance. In one of the most sensitive operations in current US–Soviet relations, you can do what no one else can do. It might even appeal to you, for as you must have gathered from what I've said, the moderates on both sides are at this moment working together.'

'Please clarify that.'

'Only fanatics subscribe to this type of insurgency. It's far too dangerous for both countries. There's a power struggle in the Soviet Presidium. The moderates must prevail for all our sakes. One way to accomplish this is to expose even part of Omega and kill the target date.'

'How can I do anything?'

'You know Omega, Mr Tanner. You know Omega very well.'

Tanner caught his breath. For a moment he believed his heart had stopped. He felt the blood rush to his head. He felt, for an instant, somewhat sick.

'I find that an *incredible* statement.'

'I would, too, if I were you. Nevertheless, it's true.'

'And I gather this is the end of stage two? . . . You bastard. You son of a bitch!' Tanner spoke hardly above a whisper.

'Call me anything you like. Hit me if you want to. I won't hit back . . . I told you, I've been through this before.'

Tanner got out of the chair and pressed his fingers against his forehead. He turned away from Fassett, then whipped around. 'Suppose you're wrong?' he whispered. 'Suppose you Goddamn idiots have made another *mistake!*'

'We haven't . . . We don't claim to have flushed Omega out completely. However, we *have* narrowed it down. You're in a unique position.'

Tanner walked to the window and started to pull up the shade.

'Don't *touch* that! Hold it *down!*' Fassett leaped from his chair and grabbed Tanner's wrist with one hand and the string of the shade with his other. Tanner looked into the agent's eyes.

'And if I walk out of here now, I live with what you've told me? Never knowing who's in my house, who I'm talking to in the street? Living with the knowledge that you think someone might fire a rifle into this room if I lift up the shade?'

'Don't over-dramatize. These are merely precautions.'

Tanner walked back to his side of the desk but did not sit down. 'Goddamn you,' he said softly. 'You know I can't leave . . .'

'Do you accept the conditions?'

'I do.'

'I must ask you to sign this affidavit.' He took out a page from the manila folder and placed it in front of Tanner. It was a concise statement on the nature and penalties of the National Security Act. It referred to Omega in unspecific terms – Exhibit A, defined as the tape recording. Tanner scribbled his name and remained standing, staring at Fassett.

'I shall now ask you the following questions.' Fassett picked up the folder and flipped to the back pages. 'Are you familiar with the individuals I now specify? Richard Tremayne and his wife, Virginia . . . Please reply.'

Astounded, Tanner spoke softly. 'I am.'

'Joseph Cardone, born Giuseppe Ambruzzio Cardione, and his wife, Elizabeth?'

'I am.'

'Bernard Osterman and his wife, Leila?'

'Yes.'

'Louder, please, Mr Tanner.'

'I said, yes.'

'I now inform you that one, two, or all three of the couples specified are essential to the Omega operation.'

'You're out of your mind! You're insane!'

'We're not . . . I spoke of our exchange on the Albanian border. It was made known to us then that Omega, Chasm of Leather, operated out of a Manhattan suburb – and that confirmed our analysis. That Omega was comprised of couples – men and women fanatically devoted to the militaristic policies of the Soviet expansionists. These couples were well paid for their services. The couples specified – the Tremaynes, the Cardones, and the Ostermans – currently possess coded bank accounts in Zurich, Switzerland, with amounts far exceeding any incomes ever reported.'

'You can't mean what you're saying!'

'Even allowing for coincidence, and we have thoroughly researched each party involved, it is our opinion that you are being used as a very successful cover for Omega. You're a newsman above reproach.

'We don't claim that all three couples are involved. It's conceivable that one or possibly two of the couples are being used as decoys, as you are. But it's doubtful. The evidence – the Swiss accounts, the professions, the unusual circumstances of your association – point to a cell.'

'Then how did you disqualify me?' asked Tanner numbly.

'Your life from the day you were born has been microscopically inspected by professionals. If we're wrong about you, we have no business doing what we're doing.'

Tanner, exhausted, sat down with difficulty in the chair. 'What do you want me to do?'

'If our information is correct, the Ostermans are flying east on Friday and will stay with you and your family over the weekend. Is that right?'

'It *was*.'

'Don't change it. Don't alter the situation.'

'That's impossible now . . .'

'It's the only way you can help us. *All* of us.'

'Why?'

'We believe we can trap Omega during this coming weekend. *If* we have your cooperation. Without it, we can't.'

'How?'

'There are four days remaining before the Ostermans arrive. During this period our subjects – the Ostermans, the Tremaynes, and the Cardones – will be harassed. Each couple will receive untraceable telephone calls, cablegrams routed through Zurich, chance meetings with strangers in restaurants, in cocktail lounges, on the street. The point of all this is to deliver a common message. That John Tanner is *not* what he appears to be. You are something else. Perhaps a double agent, or a Politbureau informer, or even a bona fide member of my own organization. The information they receive will be confusing, designed to throw them off balance.'

'And make my family a set of targets. I won't permit it! They'd kill us!'

'That's the one thing they won't do.'

'Why not? If anything you say is true – and I'm by no means convinced that it is. I *know* these people. I can't believe it!'

'In that event, there's no risk at all.'

'Why not?'

'If they – any one or all couples – are not involved with Omega, they'll do the normal thing. They'll report the incidents to the police or the FBI. We'll take over then. If one or two couples make such reports and the other or others do not, we'll know who Omega is.'

'And . . . supposing you *are* right. What then? What are your built-in guarantees?'

'Several factors. All fool-proof. I told you the "information" about you will be false. Whoever Omega is will use his resources and check out what he learns with the Kremlin itself. Our confederates there are prepared. They will intercept. The information Omega gets back from Moscow will be the truth. The truth until this afternoon, that is. You are simply John Tanner, news director, and no part of any conspiracy. What will be added is the trap. Moscow will inform whoever runs a check on you to be suspicious of the *other* couples. *They* may be defectors. We divide. We bring about a confrontation and walk in.'

'That's awfully glib. It sounds too easy.'

'If any attempt was made on your life or the lives of your family, the entire Omega operation would be in jeopardy. They're not willing to take that risk. They've worked too hard. I told you, they're fanatics. The target date for Omega is less than one month away.'

'That's not good enough.'

'There's something else. A minimum of two armed agents will be assigned to each member of your family. Twenty-four-hour surveillance. They'll never be more than fifty yards away. At any time.'

'Now I know you're insane. You don't know Saddle Valley. Strangers lurking around are spotted quickly and chased out! We'd be sitting ducks.'

Fassett smiled. 'At this moment we have thirteen men in Saddle Valley. Thirteen. They're daily residents of your community.'

'Sweet Jesus!' Tanner spoke softly. 'Nineteen-eighty-four is creeping up on us, isn't it?'

'The times we live in often call for it.'

'I don't have a choice, do I? I don't have a choice at all.' He pointed to the tape recorder and the affidavit lying beside it. 'I'm hung now, aren't I?'

'I think you're over-dramatizing again.'

'No, I'm not. I'm not dramatizing anything . . . I have to do exactly what you want me to do, don't I? I *have* to go through with it . . . The only alternative I have is to disappear . . . and be hunted. Hunted by you and – if you're right – by this Omega.'

Fassett returned Tanner's look without a trace of deceit. Tanner had spoken the truth and both men knew it.

'It's only six days. Six days out of a lifetime.'

4

Monday – 8:05 P.M.

The flight from Dulles Airport to Newark seemed unreal. He wasn't tired. He was terrified. His mind kept darting from one image to another, each visual picture pushing the previous one out into the distance. There were the sharp staring eyes of Laurence Fassett above the tape recorder's turning reels. The drone of Fassett's voice asking those interminable questions; then the voice growing louder and louder.

'Omega!'

And the faces of Bernie and Leila Osterman, Dick and Ginny Tremayne, Joe and Betty Cardone.

None of it made sense! He'd get to Newark and suddenly the nightmare would be over and he'd remember giving Laurence Fassett the public service features and signing the absent pages of the FCC filing.

Only he knew he wouldn't.

The hour's ride from Newark to Saddle Valley was made in silence, the taxi driver taking his cue from his fare in the back seat who kept lighting cigarettes and who hadn't answered him when he'd asked how the flight had been.

SADDLE VALLEY

VILLAGE INCORPORATED 1862

Welcome

Tanner stared at the sign as it caught the cab's headlights. As it receded he could only think of the words 'Chasm of Leather'.

Unreal.

Ten minutes later the taxi pulled up to his house. He got out and absently handed the driver the fare agreed upon.

'Thanks, Mr Tanner,' said the driver, leaning over the seat to take the money through the window.

'What? What did you say?' demanded John Tanner.

'I said "Thanks, Mr Tanner".'

Tanner leaned down and gripped the door handle, pulling the door open with all his strength.

'How did you know my name? You tell me how you knew my *name!*'

The taxi driver could see beads of perspiration rolling down his passenger's face, the crazy look in the man's eyes. A weirdo, thought the driver. He carefully moved his left hand toward the floor beneath his feet. He always kept a thin lead pipe there.

'Look, Mac,' he said, his fingers around the pipe. 'You don't want nobody to use your name, take the sign off your lawn.'

Tanner stepped back and looked over his shoulder. On the lawn was the wrought-iron lantern, a weatherproof hurricane lamp hanging from a crossbar by a chain. Above the lamp, reflected in the light, were the words:

THE TANNERS
22 ORCHARD DRIVE

He'd looked at that lamp and those words a thousand times. *The Tanners. 22 Orchard Drive.* At that moment they, too, seemed unreal. As if he had never seen them before.

'I'm sorry, fella. I'm a little on edge. I don't like flying.' He closed the door as the driver began rolling up the window. The driver spoke curtly.

'Take the train then, Mister. Or walk, for Christ's sake!'

The taxi roared off, and Tanner turned and looked at his house. The door opened. The dog bounded out to meet him. His wife stood in the hall light, and he could see her smile.

5

The white French telephone, with its muted Hollywood bell, had rung at least five times. Leila thought sleepily that it was foolish to have it on Bernie's side of the bed. It never woke him, only her.

She nudged her husband's ribs with her elbow. 'Darling . . . Bernie. Bernie! It's the phone.'

'What?' Osterman opened his eyes, confused. 'The phone? Oh, the Goddamn phone. Who can hear it?'

He reached over in the darkness and found the thin cradle with his fingers.

'Yes? . . . Yes, this is Bernard Osterman . . . Long distance?' He covered the phone with his hand and pushed himself up against the headboard. He turned toward his wife. 'What time is it?'

Leila snapped on her bedside lamp and looked at the table clock. 'Three-thirty. My God!'

'Probably some bastard on that Hawaiian series. It's not even midnight there yet.' Bernie was listening at the phone. 'Yes, operator, I'm waiting . . . It's very long distance, honey. If it *is* Hawaii, they can put that producer on the typewriter; we've had it. We never should have touched it . . . Yes, operator? Please hurry, will you?'

'You said you wanted to see those islands without a uniform on, remember?'

'I apologize . . . Yes, operator, this *is* Bernard Osterman, damn it! Yes? Yes? Thank you, operator . . . Hello? I can hardly hear you. Hello? . . . Yes, that's better. Who's this? . . . What? What did you say? . . . Who *is* this? What's your name? I don't understand you. Yes, I *heard* you, but I don't understand . . . Hello? . . . Hello! Wait a minute! I said *wait* a minute!' Osterman shot up and flung his legs over the side of the bed. The blankets came after him and fell on the floor at his feet. He began punching the center bar on the white French telephone. 'Operator! Operator! The Goddamn line's dead!'

'Who was it? Why are you shouting? What did they say?'

'He . . . the son of a bitch grunted like a bull. He said, he said we were to watch out for the . . . *Tan One.* That's what he said. He made sure I heard the words. *The Tan One.* What the hell is that?'

'The *what?*'

'The Tan One! That's all he kept repeating!'

'It doesn't make sense . . . Was it Hawaii? Did the operator say where the call came from?'

Osterman stared at his wife in the dim light of the bedroom. 'Yes. I heard that clearly. It was overseas . . . It was Lisbon. Lisbon, Portugal.'

'We don't know anyone in Portugal!'

'Lisbon, Lisbon, Lisbon . . .' Osterman kept repeating the name quietly to himself. 'Lisbon. Neutral. Lisbon was neutral.'

'What do you mean?'

'*Tan One . . .*'

'Tan . . . tan. Tanner. Could it be John Tanner? John Tanner!'

'Neutral!'

'It's John Tanner,' said Leila quietly.

'Johnny? . . . What did he mean, "Watch out"?' Why should we watch out? Why place a call at three-thirty in the morning?'

Leila sat up and reached for a cigarette. 'Johnny's got enemies. The San Diego waterfront still hurts because of him.'

'San Diego, sure! But Lisbon?'

'*Daily Variety* said last week that we're going to New York,' continued Leila, inhaling smoke deeply. 'That we'd probably stay with our ex-neighbors, the Tanners.'

'So?'

'Perhaps we're too well advertised.' She looked at her husband.

'Maybe I'll call Johnny.' Osterman reached for the phone.

Leila grabbed his wrist. 'Are you out of your *mind?*'

Osterman lay back down.

Joe opened his eyes and glanced at his watch: six-twenty-two. Time to get up, have a short workout in his gym and perhaps walk over to the Club for an hour's practice on the golf range.

He was an early riser, Betty the opposite. She would sleep till noon whenever she had the chance. They had two double beds, one for each of them, because Joe knew the debilitating effects of two separate body temperatures under the same set of covers. The benefits of a person's sleep were diminished by nearly fifty percent when he shared a bed all night with somebody else. And since the purpose of the marriage bed was exclusively sexual, there was no point in losing the benefits of sleep.

A pair of double beds was just fine.

He finished ten minutes on the exercycle and five with seven-and-a-half-pound handbells. He looked through the thick glass window of the steam bath and saw that the room was ready.

A panel light above the gym's wall clock flashed on. It was the front doorbell. Joe had the device installed in case he was home alone and working out.

The clock read six-fifty-one, much too early for anyone in Saddle Valley to be ringing front doorbells. He put the small weights on the floor and walked to his house intercom.

'Yes? Who is it?'

'Telegram, Mr Cardione.'

'Who?'

'Cardione, it says.'

'The name is Cardone.'

'Isn't this Eleven Apple Place?'

'I'll be right there.'

He flicked off the intercom and grabbed a towel from the rack, draping it around him as he walked rapidly out of the gym. He didn't like what he had just heard. He reached the front door and opened it. A small man in uniform stood there chewing gum.

'Why didn't you telephone? It's pretty early, isn't it?'

'Instructions were to deliver. I had to drive out here, Mr Cardone. Almost fifteen miles. We keep twenty-four-hour service.'

Cardone signed for the envelope. 'Why fifteen miles? Western Union's got a branch in Ridge Park.'

'Not Western Union, Mister. This is a cablegram . . . from Europe.'

Cardone grabbed the envelope out of the uniformed man's hand. 'Wait a minute.' He didn't want to appear excited, so he walked normally into the living room where he remembered seeing Betty's purse on the piano. He took out two one-dollar bills and returned to the door. 'Here you are. Sorry about the trip.' He closed the door and ripped open the cablegram.

L'UOMO BRUNO PALIDO NON E AMICO DEL ITALIANO. GUARDA BENE VICINI DI QUESTA MANIERA. PROTECIATE PER LA FINA DELLA SETTIMANA.

DA VINCI

Cardone walked into the kitchen, found a pencil on the telephone shelf and sat down at the table. He wrote out the translation on the back of a magazine.

The light-brown man is no friend of the Italian. Be cautious of such neighbors. Protect yourself against the end of the week. Da Vinci.

What did it mean? What 'light-brown . . . neighbors'? There were no blacks in Saddle Valley. The message didn't make sense.

Suddenly Joe Cardone froze. The light-brown neighbor could only mean John Tanner. The end of the week – Friday – the Ostermans were arriving.

Someone in Europe was telling him to protect himself against John Tanner and the upcoming Osterman weekend.

He snatched up the cablegram and looked at the dateline.

Zurich.

Oh, Jesus Christ! Zurich!

Someone in Zurich – someone who called himself Da Vinci, someone who knew his real name, who knew John Tanner, who knew about the Ostermans – was warning him!

Joe Cardone stared out the window at his backyard lawn. Da Vinci, Da Vinci!

Leonardo.

Artist, soldier, architect of war – all things to all men.

Mafia! Oh, Christ! Which of them?

The Costellanos? The Battellas? The Latronas, maybe.

Which of them had turned on him? And *why*? He was their *friend*!

His hands shook as he spread the cablegram on the kitchen table. He read it once more. Each sentence conjured up progressively more dangerous meanings.

Tanner!

John Tanner had found out something! But *what*?

And why did the message come from Zurich?

What would any of them have to do with Zurich?

Or the Ostermans?

What had Tanner discovered? What was he going to do? . . . One of the Battella men called Tanner something once; what was it?

'*Volturno!*'

Vulture.

'. . . no friend of the Italian . . . Be cautious . . . Protect yourself . . .'

How? From *what*? Tanner wouldn't confide in him. Why should he?

He, Joe Cardone, wasn't syndicate; he wasn't *famiglia*. What could *he* know?

But 'Da Vinci's' message had come from Switzerland.

And that left one remaining possibility, a frightening one. The Cosa Nostra had learned about Zurich! They'd use it against him unless he was able to control the 'light-brown man', the Italian's enemy. Unless he could stop whatever it was John Tanner was about to do, he'd be destroyed.

Zurich! The Ostermans!

He had done what he thought was right! What he had to do to *survive*. Osterman had pointed that out in a way that left no doubts. But it was in other hands now. Not his. He couldn't be touched any more.

Joe Cardone walked out of the kitchen and returned to his miniature gymnasium. Without putting on gloves he started pounding the bag. Faster and faster, harder and harder.

There was a screeching in his brain.

'Zurich! Zurich! Zurich!'

Virginia Tremayne heard her husband get out of bed at six-fifteen, and knew immediately that something was wrong. Her husband rarely stirred that early.

She waited several minutes. When he didn't return, she rose, put on her bathrobe, and went downstairs. He was in the living room standing by the bay window, smoking a cigarette and reading something on a piece of paper.

'What *are* you doing?'

'Look at this,' he answered quietly.

'At what?' She took the paper from his hand.

> Take extreme caution with your editorial friend. His friendship does not extend beyond his zeal. He is not what he appears to be. We may have to report his visitors from California.
>
> Blackstone

'What is this? When did you get it?'

'I heard noises outside the window about twenty minutes ago. Just enough to wake me up. Then there was the gunning of a car engine. It kept racing up and down . . . I thought you heard it, too. You pulled the covers up.'

'I think I did. I didn't pay any attention . . .'

'I came down and opened the door. This envelope was on the doormat.'

'What does it mean?'

'I'm not sure yet.'

'Who's Blackstone?'

'The commentaries. Basis of the legal system . . .' Richard Tremayne flung himself down in an armchair and brought his hand up to his forehead. With the other he rolled his cigarette delicately along the rim of an ashtray. 'Please . . . Let me think.'

Virginia Tremayne looked again at the paper with the cryptic message. '"Editorial friend." Does that mean? . . .'

'Tanner's onto something and whoever delivered this is in panic. Now they're trying to make me panic, too.'

'Why?'

'I don't know. Maybe they think I can help them. And if I don't, they're threatening me. All of us.'

'The Ostermans.'

'Exactly. They're threatening us with Zurich.'

'Oh, my God! They know! Someone's found out!'

'It looks that way.'

'Do you think Bernie got frightened? Talked about it?'

Tremayne's eye twitched. 'He'd be insane if he did. He'd be crucified on both sides of the Atlantic . . . No, that's not it.'

'What is it, then?'

'Whoever wrote this is someone I've either worked with in the past or refused to handle. Maybe it's one of the current cases. Maybe one of the files on my desk right now. And Tanner got wind of it and is making noises. They expect me to stop him. If I don't, I'm finished. Before I can afford it . . . Before Zurich goes to work for us.'

'They couldn't *touch* you!' said Tremayne's wife with fierce, artificial defiance.

'Come on, darling. Let's not kid each *other*. In polite circles I'm a merger analyst. In the boardrooms I'm a corporate raider. To paraphrase Judge Hand, the merger market is currently insane with false purchase. False. That means fake. Buying with paper. Pieces of fiction.'

'Are you in trouble?'

'Not really – I could always say I was given wrong information. The courts like me.'

'They respect you! You've worked harder than any man I know. You're the best damned lawyer there is!'

'I'd like to think so.'

'You *are!*'

Richard Tremayne stood at the large bay window looking out at the lawn of his seventy-four-thousand-dollar ranch house. 'Isn't it funny. You're probably right. I'm one of the best there is in a system I despise . . . A system Tanner would rip apart piece by piece on one of his programs if he knew what really made it go. That's what the little message is all about.'

'I think you're wrong, I think it's someone you've beaten who wants to get even. Who's trying to frighten you.'

'Then he's succeeded. What this . . Blackstone is telling me isn't anything I don't know. What I *am* and what I *do* makes me Tanner's natural enemy. At least, he'd think so . . . If only he knew the truth.'

He looked at her and forced a smile. 'They know the truth in Zurich.'

6

Osterman wandered aimlessly around the studio lot, trying to get his mind off the pre-dawn phone call. He was obsessed by it.

Neither he nor Leila had slept again. They'd kept trying to narrow down the possibilities and when those were exhausted they explored the more important question of why.

Why had *he* been called? What was behind it? Was Tanner onto another one of his exposés?

If he was, it had nothing to do with him. Nothing to do with Bernie Osterman.

Tanner never talked in specifics about his work. Only in generalities. He had a low pressure point when it came to what he considered injustice, and since the two men often disagreed on what constituted fair game in the marketplace, they avoided specifics.

Bernie thought of Tanner as a crusader who had never traveled on foot. He'd never gone through the experience of watching a father come home and announce he had no job the next day. Or a mother staying up half the night sewing wonders into a worn-out garment for a child going to school in the morning. Tanner could afford his indignation, and he had done fine work. But there were some things he would never understand. It was why Bernie had never discussed Zurich with him.

'Hey, Bernie! Wait a minute!' Ed Pomfret, a middle-aged rotund, insecure producer, caught up with him on the sidewalk.

'Hello, Eddie. How's everything?'

'Great! I tried reaching you at your office. The girl said you were out.'

'Nothing to do.'

'I got the word, guess you did, too. It'll be good working with you.'

'Oh? . . . No, I didn't get the word. What are we working on?'

'What's this? Jokes?' Pomfret was slightly defensive. As if he was aware that Osterman thought he was a second-rater.

'No jokes. I'm wrapping up here this week. What are you talking about? Who gave you the word?'

'That new man from Continuity phoned me this morning. I'm handling half of the segments on *The Interceptor* series. He said you were doing four running shots. I like the idea.'

'What idea?'

'The story outline. Three men working on a big, quiet deal in Switzerland. Right away it grabbed me.'

Osterman stopped walking and looked down at Pomfret.

'Who put you up to this?'

'Put me up to what?'

'There's no four shots. No outlines. No deal. Now tell me what you're trying to say.'

'You've got to be joking. Would I kid powerhouses like you and Leila? I was tickled to death. Continuity told me to phone you, ask for the outlines!'

'Who called you?'

'What's his name . . . That new exec Continuity brought from New York.'

'Who?'

'He told me his name . . . Tanner. That's it. Tanner. Jim Tanner, John Tanner . . .'

'John Tanner doesn't work here! Now, who told you to tell me this?' He grabbed Pomfret's arm. 'Tell me, you son of a bitch!'

'Take your hands off me! You're crazy!'

Osterman recognized his mistake: Pomfret was no more than a messenger boy. He let go of the producer's arm. 'I'm sorry, Eddie. I apologize . . . I've got a lot on my mind. Forgive me, please. I'm a pig.'

'Sure, sure. You're uptight, that's all. You're very uptight, man.'

'You say this fellow – Tanner – called you this morning?'

'About two hours ago. To tell you the truth, I didn't know him.'

'Listen. This is some kind of a practical joke. You know what I mean? I'm not doing the series, believe me . . . Just forget it, okay?'

'A joke?'

'Take my word for it, okay? . . . Tell you what; they're talking to Leila and me about a project here. I'll insist on you as the money-man, how about it?'

'Hey, thanks!'

'Don't mention it. Just keep this little joke between the two of us, right?'

Osterman didn't bother to wait for Pomfret's grateful reply. He hurried away down the studio street, toward his car. He had to get home to Leila.

A huge man in a chauffeur's uniform was sitting in the front seat of his car! He got out as Bernie approached and held the back door open for him.

'Mr Osterman?'

'Who are you? What are you doing in . . .'

'I have a message for you.'

'But I don't want to hear it! I want to know why you're sitting in my car!'

'Be very careful of your friend, John Tanner. Be careful what you say to him.'

'What in God's name are you talking about?'

The chauffeur shrugged. 'I'm just delivering a message, Mr Osterman. And now would you like me to drive you home?'

'Of course not! I don't know you! I don't understand . . .'

The back door closed gently. 'As you wish, sir. I was simply trying to be friendly.' With a smart salute, he turned away.

Bernie stood alone, immobile, staring after him.

7

Tuesday – 10:00 A.M.

'Are any of the Mediterranean accounts in trouble?' Joe Cardone asked.

His partner, Sam Bennett, turned in his chair to make sure the office door was shut. 'Mediterranean' was their code word for those clients both partners knew were lucrative but dangerous investors. 'Not that I know of,' he said. 'Why? Did you hear something?'

'Nothing direct . . . Perhaps nothing at all.'

'That's why you came back early, though?'

'No, not really.' Cardone understood that even for Bennett not all explanations could be given. Sam was no part of Zurich. So Joe hesitated. 'Well, partly. I spent some time at the Montreal Exchange.'

'What did you hear?'

'That there's a new drive from the Attorney General's office; that the SEC is handing over everything they have. Every possible Mafia connection with a hundred thousand or more is being watched.'

'That's nothing new. Where've you been?'

'In Montreal. That's where I've been. I don't like it when I hear things like that eight hundred miles from the office. And I'm Goddamned reluctant to pick up a telephone and ask my partner if any of our clients are currently before a grand jury . . . I mean, telephone conversations aren't guaranteed to be private any more.'

'Good Lord!' Bennett laughed. 'Your imagination's working overtime, isn't it?'

'I hope so.'

'You know damned well I'd have gotten in touch with you if anything like that came up. Or even looked like it *might* come up. You didn't cut a vacation short on those grounds. What's the rest?'

Cardone avoided his partner's eyes as he sat down at his desk. 'Okay. I won't lie. Something else did bring me in . . . I don't think it has anything to do with us. With *you* or the company. If I find out otherwise, I'll come to you, all right?'

Bennett got out of the chair and accepted his partner's non-explanation. Over the years he'd learned not to question Joe too closely. For in spite of his partner's gregariousness, Cardone was a private man. He brought large amounts of capital into the firm and never asked for more than a proper business share. That was good enough for Bennett.

Sam walked to the door, laughing softly. 'When are you going to stop running from the phantom of South Philadelphia?'

Cardone returned his partner's smile. 'When it stops chasing me into the Bankers' Club with a hot lasagna.'

Bennett closed the door behind him, and Joe returned to the ten-day accumulation of mail and messages. There was nothing. Nothing that could be related to a Mediterranean problem. Nothing that even hinted at a Mafia conflict. Yet something had happened during those ten days; something that concerned Tanner.

He picked up his telephone and pushed the button for his secretary. 'Is this everything? There weren't any other messages?'

'None you have to return. I told everyone you wouldn't be back until the end of the week. Some said they'd call then, the others will phone you Monday.'

'Keep it like that. Any calls, I'll be back Monday.'

He replaced the phone and unlocked the second drawer of his desk, in which he kept an index file of three-by-five cards. The Mediterranean clients.

He put the small metal box in front of him and started fingering through the cards. Perhaps a name would trigger a memory, a forgotten fact which might have relevance.

His private telephone rang. Only Betty called him on that line; no one else had the number. Joe loved his wife, but she had a positive genius for irritating him with trivial matters when he wished no interruptions.

'Yes, dear?'

Silence.

'What is it honey? I'm jammed up.'

Still his wife didn't answer.

Cardone was suddenly afraid. No one but Betty had that number!

'Betty? Answer me!'

The voice, when it came, was slow, deep and precise.

'John Tanner flew to Washington yesterday. Mr Da Vinci is very concerned. Perhaps your friends in California betrayed you. They've been in contact with Tanner.'

Joe Cardone heard the click of the disconnected telephone.

Jesus! Oh, Jesus! Oh, Christ! It was the Ostermans! They'd turned!

But *why*? It didn't make sense! What possible connection could there be between Zurich and anything *remotely* Mafia? They were light-years apart!

Or were they? Or was one using the other?

Cardone tried to steady himself but it was impossible. He found himself crushing the small metal box.

What could he do? Who could he talk to?

Tanner himself? Oh, God, of course not!

The Ostermans? Bernie Osterman? Christ, no! Not *now*.

Tremayne. Dick Tremayne.

8

Tuesday – 10:10 A.M.

Too shaken to sit in a commuter's seat on the Saddle Valley express, Tremayne decided to drive into New York.

As he sped east on Route Five toward the George Washington Bridge, he noticed a light blue Cadillac in his rear view mirror. When he pulled to the left, racing ahead of the other cars, the Cadillac did the same. When he returned to the right, squeezing into the slower flow, so did the Cadillac – always several automobiles behind him.

At the bridge he neared the tollbooth and saw that the Cadillac, in a faster adjacent lane, came parallel. He tried to see who the driver was.

It was a woman. She turned her face away; he could only see the back of her head. Yet she looked vaguely familiar.

The Cadillac sped off before he could reflect further. Traffic blocked any chance he had to follow. He was certain the Cadillac had followed him, but just as surely, the driver did not want to be recognized.

Why? Who was she?

Was this woman 'Blackstone'?

He found it impossible to accomplish anything in his office. He canceled the few appointments he had made, and, instead, reexamined the files of recent corporate mergers he had favorably gotten through the courts. One folder in particular interested him: *The Cameron Woolens*. Three factories in a small Massachusetts town owned for generations by the Cameron family. Raided from the inside by the oldest son. Blackmail had forced him to sell his share of the company to a New York clothing chain who claimed to want the Cameron label.

They got the label, and closed the factories; the town went bankrupt. Tremayne had represented the clothing chain in the Boston courts. The Cameron family had a daughter. An unmarried woman in her early thirties. Headstrong, angry.

The driver of the Cadillac was a woman. About the right age.

Yet to select one was to dismiss so many other possibilities. The merger builders knew whom to call when legal matters got sticky. Tremayne! He was the expert. A forty-four-year-old magician wielding the new legal machinery, sweeping aside old legal concepts in the exploding economy of the conglomerates.

Was it the Cameron daughter in the light blue Cadillac?

How could he know? There were so many. The Camerons. The Smythes of Atlanta. The Boyntons of Chicago. The Fergusons of Rochester. The corporate raiders preyed upon old families, the moneyed families. The old moneyed families pampered themselves, they were targets. Who among them might be Blackstone?

Tremayne got out of his chair and walked aimlessly around his office. He couldn't stand the confinement any longer; he had to go out.

He wondered what Tanner would say if he called him and suggested a casual lunch. How would Tanner react? Would he accept casually? Would he put him off? Would it be possible – if Tanner accepted – to learn anything related to Blackstone's warning?

Tremayne picked up the phone and dialed. His eyelid twitched, almost painfully.

Tanner was tied up in a meeting. Tremayne was relieved; it had been a foolish thing to do. He left no message and hurried out of his office.

On Fifth Avenue, a Checker cab pulled up directly in front of him, blocking his path at the corner crossing.

'Hey, mister!' The driver put his head out the window.

Tremayne wondered whom he was calling – so did several other pedestrians. They all looked at one another.

'You, mister! Your name Tremayne?'

'Me? Yes . . .'

'I got a message for you.'

'For me? How did you? . . .'

'I gotta hurry, the light's gonna change and I got twenty bucks for this.

I'm to tell you to walk east on Fifty-fourth Street. Just keep walking and a Mr Blackstone will contact you.'

Tremayne put his hand on the driver's shoulder. '*Who* told you? Who gave you . . .'

'What do I know? Some wack sits in my cab since nine-thirty this morning with the meter on. He's got a pair of binoculars and smokes thin cigars.'

The 'Don't Walk' sign began to blink.

'What did he say! . . . Here!' Tremayne reached into his pocket and withdrew some bills. He gave the driver a ten. 'Here. Now, *tell* me, please!'

'Just what I said, mister. He got out a few seconds ago, gave me twenty bucks to tell you to walk east on Fifty-fourth. That's all.'

'That's *not* all!' Tremayne grabbed the driver's shirt.

'Thanks for the ten.' The driver pushed Tremayne's hand away, honked his horn to disperse the jaywalkers in front of him, and drove off.

Tremayne controlled his panic. He stepped back onto the curb and retreated under the awning of the storefront behind him, looking at the men walking north, trying to find a man with a pair of binoculars or a thin cigar.

Finding nobody, he began to edge his way from store entrance to store entrance, toward Fifty-fourth Street. He walked slowly, staring at the passersby. Several collided against him going in the same direction but walking much faster. Several others, heading south, noticed the strange behavior of the blond man in his expensively cut clothes, and smiled.

On the Fifty-fourth Street corner, Tremayne stopped. In spite of the slight breeze and his lightweight suit, he was perspiring. He knew he had to head east. There was no question about it.

One thing was clear. Blackstone was not the driver of the light blue Cadillac. Blackstone was a man with binoculars and thin cigars.

Then who was the woman? He'd seen her before. He knew it!

He started east on Fifty-fourth, walking on the right side; no one signaled him, no one even looked at him. Then across Park Avenue to the center island.

No one.

Lexington Avenue. Past the huge construction sites. No one.

Third Avenue. Second, First.

No one.

Tremayne entered the last block. A dead-end street terminating at the East River, flanked on both sides by the canopies of apartment house entrances. A few men with briefcases and women carrying department store boxes came and went from both buildings. At the end of the street was a light tan Mercedes-Benz sedan parked crossways, as if in the middle of a turn. And near it stood a man in an elegant white suit and Panama hat. He was quite a bit shorter than Tremayne. Even thirty yards away, Tremayne could see he was deeply tanned. He wore thick, wide sunglasses and was looking directly at Tremayne as Tremayne approached him.

'Mr . . . Blackstone?'

'Mr Tremayne. I'm sorry you had to walk such a distance. We had to be sure, you see, that you were alone.'

'Why wouldn't I be?' Tremayne was trying to place the accent. It was cultivated, but not the sort associated with the northeastern states.

'A man who's in trouble often, mistakenly, looks for company.'

'What kind of trouble am I in?'

'You *did* get my note?'

'Of course. What did it mean?'

'Exactly what it said. Your friend Tanner is very dangerous to you. And to us. We simply want to emphasize the point as good businessmen should with one another.'

'What business interests are you concerned with, Mr Blackstone? I assume Blackstone isn't your name so I could hardly connect you with anything familiar.'

The man in the white suit and hat and dark glasses took several steps toward the Mercedes.

'We told you. His friends from California . . .'

'The Ostermans?'

'Yes.'

'My firm has had no dealings with the Ostermans. None whatever.'

'But you have, haven't you?' Blackstone walked in front of the hood and stood on the other side of the Mercedes.

'You can't be serious!'

'Believe me when I say that I am.' The man reached for the door handle, but he did not open the door. He was waiting.

'Just a minute! Who *are* you?'

'Blackstone will do.'

'No! . . . What you said! You couldn't . . .'

'But we do. That's the point. And since you now know that we do, it should offer some proof of our considerable influence.'

'What are you driving at?' Tremayne pressed his hands against the Mercedes' hood and leaned toward Blackstone.

'It's crossed our minds that you may have cooperated with your friend Tanner. That's really why we wanted to see you. It would be most inadvisable. We wouldn't hesitate to make public your contribution to the Osterman interests.'

'You're crazy! Why would I cooperate with Tanner? On what? I don't know what you're talking about.'

Blackstone removed his dark glasses. His eyes were blue and penetrating, and Tremayne could see freckles about his nose and cheekbones. 'If that's true then you have nothing to worry about.'

'Of course it's true! There's no earthly reason why I should work with Tanner on anything!'

'That's logical.' Blackstone opened the door of the Mercedes. 'Just keep it that way.'

'For God's sake, you can't just *leave*! I see Tanner every day. At the Club. On the train. What the hell am I supposed to think, what am I supposed to say?'

'You mean what are you supposed to look for? If I were you, I'd act as if nothing had happened. As if we'd never met . . . He may drop hints – if you're telling the truth – he may probe. Then you'll know.'

Tremayne stood up, fighting to remain calm. 'For all our sakes, I think you'd better tell me whom you represent. It would be best, it really would.'

'Oh, no, counselor.' A short laugh accompanied Blackstone's reply. 'You see, we've noticed that you've acquired a disturbing habit over the past several years. Nothing serious, not at this time, but to be considered.'

'What habit is that?'

'Periodically you drink too much.'

'That's ridiculous!'

'I said it wasn't serious. You do brilliant work. Nevertheless, at such times you haven't your normal control. No, it would be a mistake to burden you, especially in your current state of anxiety.'

'Don't go. Please! . . .'

'We'll be in touch. Perhaps you'll have learned something that will help us. At any rate, we always watch your . . . merger work with great interest.'

Tremayne flinched. 'What about the Ostermans? You've got to *tell* me.'

'If you've got a brain in your legal head, you won't say a thing to the Ostermans! Or hint at anything! If Osterman is cooperating with Tanner, you'll find out. If he's not, don't give him any ideas about *you*.' Blackstone climbed into the driver's seat of the Mercedes and started the motor. He said, just before he drove off, 'Keep your head, Mr Tremayne. We'll be in touch.'

Tremayne tried to marshal his thoughts; he could feel his eyelid twitch. Thank Christ he hadn't reached Tanner! Not being prepared, he might have said something – something asinine, dangerous.

Had Osterman been such a gargantuan fool – or coward – to blurt out the truth about Zurich to John Tanner? Without consulting them?

If that were the case, Zurich would have to be alerted. Zurich would take care of Osterman. They'd crucify him!

He had to find Cardone. They had to decide what to do. He ran to a corner telephone.

Betty told him Joe had gone in to the office. Cardone's secretary told him Joe was still on vacation.

Joe was playing games. The twitch above Tremayne's left eye nearly blinded him.

9

Tuesday – 7:00 A.M.

Unable to sleep, Tanner walked into his study, his eyes drawn to the gray glass of the three television sets. There was something dead about them, empty. He lit a cigarette and sat down on the couch. He thought about Fassett's instructions: remain calm, oblivious, and say nothing to Ali. Fassett had repeated the last command several times.

The only real danger would come if Ali said the wrong thing to the wrong person. There *was* danger in that. Danger to Ali. But Tanner had never withheld anything from his wife. He wasn't sure he could do it. The fact that they were always open with each other was the strongest bond in their strong marriage. Even when they fought, there was never the weapon of unspoken accusations. Alice McCall had had enough of that as a child.

Omega, however, would change their lives, for the next six days, at any rate. He had to accept that because Fassett said it was best for Ali.

The sun was up now. The day was beginning and the Cardones, the Tremaynes and the Ostermans would soon be under fire. Tanner wondered what they'd do, how they'd react. He hoped that all three couples would contact the authorities and prove Fassett wrong. Sanity would return.

But it was possible that the madness had just begun. Whichever the case, he would stay home. If Fassett was right, he'd be there with Ali and the children. Fassett had no control over that decision.

He would let Ali think it was the flu. He'd be in touch with his office by phone, but he would stay with his family.

His telephone rang regularly; questions from the office. Ali and the children complained that the constant ringing of the telephone was enough to drive them crazy, so the three of them retreated to the pool. Except for a few clouds around noon, the day was hot – perfect for swimming. The white patrol car passed the house a number of times. On Sunday Tanner had been concerned over it. Now he was grateful. Fassett was keeping his word.

The telephone rang again. 'Yes, Charlie.' He didn't bother to say hello.
'Mr Tanner?'
'Oh, sorry. Yes, this is John Tanner.'
'Fassett calling . . .'
'Wait a minute!' Tanner looked out his study window to make sure Ali and the children were still at the pool. They were.
'What is it, Fassett? Have you people started?'
'Can you talk?'
'Yes . . . Have you found out anything? Has any of them called the police?'
'Negative. If that happens we'll contact you immediately. That's not why I'm calling you . . . You've done something extremely foolish. I can't emphasize how careless.'
'What are you talking about?'
'You didn't go in to your office this morning . . .'
'I certainly did *not*!'
'. . . But there must be no break from your normal routine. No altering of your usual schedule. That's terribly important. For your own protection, you *must* follow our instructions.'
'That's asking too much!'
'Listen to me. Your wife and children are at this moment in the swimming pool behind your house. Your son, Raymond, did not go to his tennis lesson . . .'
'I told him not to. I told him to do some work on the lawn.'
'Your wife had groceries delivered, which is not customary.'
'I explained that I might need her to take notes for me. She's done that before . . .'
'The main point is you're not doing what you usually do. It's vital that you keep to your day-to-day routine. I can't stress it enough. You cannot, you *must* not call attention to yourself.'
'I'm watching out for my family. I think that's understandable.'
'So are we. Far more effectively than you can. None of them have been out of our sight for a single minute. I'll amend that. Neither have you. You walked out into your driveway twice: at nine-thirty-two and eleven-twenty. Your daughter had a friend over for lunch, one Joan Loomis, aged eight. We're extremely thorough and extremely careful.'
The news director reached for a cigarette and lit it with the desk lighter. 'Guess you are.'
'There's nothing for you to worry about. There's no danger to you or your family.'
'Probably not. I think you're all crazy. None of them have anything to do with this Omega.'

'That's possible. But if we're right, they won't take any action without checking further. They won't panic, too much is at stake. And when they do check further they'll immediately suspect each other. For heaven's sake, don't give them any reason not to. Go about your business as if nothing happened. It's vital. No one could harm your family. They couldn't get near enough.'

'All right. You're convincing. But I went out to the driveway three times this morning, not twice.'

'No, you didn't. The third time you remained in the garage doorway. You didn't physically walk out onto the driveway. And it wasn't morning, it was twelve-fourteen.' Fassett laughed. 'Feeling better now?'

'I'd be an awful liar if I didn't admit it.'

'You're not a liar. Not generally at any rate. Your file makes that very clear.' Fassett laughed again. Even Tanner smiled.

'You're really too much, you know that. I'll go into the office tomorrow.'

'When it's all over, you and your wife will have to get together with me and mine for an evening. I think they'd like each other. Drinks will be on me. Dewars White Label with a tall soda for you and Scotch on the rocks with a pinch of water for your wife.'

'Good God! If you start describing our sex life . . .'

'Let me check the index . . .'

'Go to hell,' Tanner laughed, relieved. 'We'll take you up on that evening.'

'You should. We'd get along.'

'Name the date, we'll be there.'

'I'll make a point of it on Monday. Be in touch. You have the emergency number for after hours. Don't hesitate to call.'

'I won't. I'll be in the office tomorrow.'

'Fine. And do me a favor. Don't plan any more programs on us. My employers didn't like the last one.'

Tanner remembered. The program Fassett referred to had been a Woodward Show. The writers had come up with the phrase *Caught in the Act* for the letters CIA. It was a year ago, almost to the week. 'It wasn't bad.'

'It wasn't good. I saw that one. I wanted to laugh my head off but I couldn't. I was with the Director, in *his* living room. *Caught in the Act!* Jesus!' Fassett laughed again, putting Tanner more at ease than the news director thought possible.

'Thanks, Fassett.'

Tanner put down the telephone and crushed out his cigarette. Fassett was a thorough professional, he thought. And Fassett was right. No one could get near Ali and the kids. For all he knew, the CIA had snipers strapped to the trees. What was left for him to do was precisely what Fassett said: nothing. Just go about business as usual. No break from routine, no deviation from the norm. He felt he could play the role now. The protection was everything Fassett said it would be.

However, one thought bothered him, and the more he considered it, the more it disturbed him.

It was nearly four o'clock in the afternoon. The Tremaynes, the Cardones and the Ostermans had all been contacted by now. The harassment had begun. Yet none had seen fit to call the police. Or even to call *him*.

Was it really possible that six people who had been his friends for years were not what they seemed to be?

10

Tuesday – 9:40 A.M. *California Time*

The Karmann Ghia swung off Wilshire Boulevard onto Beverly Drive. Osterman knew he was exceeding the Los Angeles speed limit; it seemed completely unimportant. He couldn't think about anything except the warning he had just received. He had to get home to Leila. They had to talk seriously now. They had to decide what to do.

Why had they been singled out?

Who was warning them? And about what?

Leila was probably right. Tanner was their friend, as good a friend as they'd ever known. But he was also a man who valued reserve in friendship. There were areas one never touched. There was always the slight quality of distance, a thin glass wall that came between Tanner and any other human being. Except, of course, Ali.

And Tanner now possessed information that touched them somehow, meant something to him and Leila. And Zurich was part of it. But, Christ! *How?*

Osterman reached the foot of the Mulholland hill and drove rapidly to the top, past the huge, early-pastiche mansions that were peopled by those near, or once near, the top of the Hollywood spectrum. A few of the houses were going to seed, decaying relics of past extravagance. The speed limit in the Mulholland section was thirty. Osterman's speedometer read fifty-one. He pressed down on the accelerator. He had decided what to do. He would pick up Leila and head for Malibu. The two of them would find a phone booth on the highway and call Tremayne and Cardone.

The mournful wail of the siren, growing louder, jarred him. It was a sound effect in this town of devices. It wasn't real, nothing here was real. It couldn't be for him.

But, of course, it was.

'Officer, I'm a resident here. Osterman. Bernard Osterman. 260 Caliente. Surely you know my house.' It was a statement made positively. Caliente was impressive acreage.

'Sorry, Mr Osterman. Your license and registration, please.'

'Now, look. I had a call at the studio that my wife wasn't feeling well. I think it's understandable I'm in a hurry.'

'Not at the expense of pedestrians. Your license and registration.'

Osterman gave them to him and stared straight ahead, controlling his anger. The police officer wrote lethargically on the long rectangular traffic summons and when he finished, he stapled Bernie's license to it.

At the sound of the snap, Osterman looked up. 'Do you have to mutilate the license?'

The policeman sighed wearily, holding onto the summons. 'You could have lost it for thirty days, mister. I lessened the speed; send in ten bucks like a parking ticket.' He handed the summons to Bernie. 'I hope your wife feels better.'

The officer returned to the police car. He spoke once more through the open window. 'Don't forget to put your license back in your wallet.'

The police car sped off.

Osterman threw down the summons and turned his ignition key. The Karmann Ghia started down the Mulholland slope. Half in disgust, Bernie looked at the summons on the seat next to him.

Then he looked again.

There was something wrong with it. The shape was right, the unreadable print was crowded in the inadequate space as usual, but the paper rang false. It seemed too shiny, too blurred even for a summons from the Motor Vehicle Department of the City of Los Angeles.

Osterman stopped. He picked up the summons and looked at it closely. The violations had been marked carelessly, inaccurately, by the police officer. They hadn't really been marked at all.

And then Osterman realized that the face of the card was only a thin photostat attached to a thicker sheet of paper.

He turned it over and saw that there was a message written in red pencil, partially covered by his stapled license. He ripped the license off and read:

Word received that Tanner's neighbors may have cooperated with him. This is a potentially dangerous situation made worse because our information is incomplete. Use extreme caution and find out what you

can. It is vital we know – you know – extent of their involvement.
Repeat. Use extreme caution.

Zurich

Osterman stared at the red letters and his fear produced a sudden ache at
his temples.
The Tremaynes and the Cardones too!

11

Tuesday – 4:50 P.M.

Dick Tremayne wasn't on the four-fifty local to Saddle Valley. Cardone,
sitting inside his Cadillac, swore out loud. He had tried to reach Tremayne
at his office but was told that the lawyer had gone out for an early lunch.
There was no point in having Tremayne call him back. Joe had decided to
return to Saddle Valley and meet all the trains from three-thirty on.

Cardone left the station, turned left at the intersection of Saddle Road,
and headed west toward the open country. He had thirty-five minutes until
the next train was due. Perhaps the drive would help relax him. He couldn't
just wait at the station. If anyone was watching him it would look suspicious.

Tremayne would have some answers. Dick was a damned good lawyer,
and he'd know the legal alternatives, if there were any.

On the outskirts of Saddle Valley Joe reached a stretch of road bordered
by fields. A Silver Cloud Rolls-Royce passed him on his left, and Cardone
noted that the huge automobile was traveling extremely fast, much too fast
for the narrow country road. He kept driving for several miles, vaguely
aware that he was traveling through open country now. He would probably
have to turn around in some farmer's driveway. But ahead of him was a long
winding curve which, he remembered, had wide shoulders. He'd turn
around there. It was time to head back to the station.

He reached the curve and slowed down, prepared to swing hard to his
right onto the wide shoulder.

He couldn't.

The Silver Cloud was parked off the road under the trees, blocking him.

Annoyed, Cardone gunned the engine and proceeded several hundred
yards ahead where, since there were no other cars in sight, he made the
cramped turn.

Back at the station, Cardone looked at his watch. Five-nineteen, almost five-twenty. He could see the entire length of the platform. He'd spot Tremayne if he got off. He hoped the lawyer would be on the five-twenty-five. The waiting was intolerable.

A car pulled up behind his Cadillac, and Cardone looked up.

It was the Silver Cloud. Cardone began to sweat.

A massive man, well over six feet tall, got out of the car and walked slowly toward Cardone's open window. He was dressed in a chauffeur's uniform.

'Mr Cardione?'

'The name's Cardone.' The man's hands, which gripped the base of Joe's window, were immense. Much larger and thicker than his own.

'Okay. Whatever you like . . .'

'You passed me a little while ago, didn't you? On Saddle Road.'

'Yes, sir, I did. I haven't been far from you all day.'

Cardone involuntarily swallowed and shifted his weight. 'I find that a remarkable statement. Needless to say, very disturbing.'

'I'm sorry . . .'

'I'm not interested in apologies, I want to know why. Why are you following me? I don't know you. I don't like being followed.'

'No one does. I'm only doing what I'm told to do.'

'What is it? What do you want?'

The chauffeur moved his hands, just slightly, as if to call attention to their size and great strength. 'I've been instructed to bring you a message, and then I'll leave. I've a long drive. My employer lives in Maryland.'

'What message? Who from?'

'Mr Da Vinci, sir.'

'Da Vinci?'

'Yes sir. I believe he got in touch with you this morning.'

'I don't know your Mr Da Vinci . . . What message?'

'That you should not confide in Mr Tremayne.'

'What are you talking about?'

'Only what Mr Da Vinci told me, Mr Cardione.'

Cardone stared into the huge man's eyes. There was intelligence behind the blank façade. 'Why did you wait until now? You've been following me all day. You could have stopped me hours ago.'

'I wasn't instructed to. There's a radio-phone in the car. I was told to make contact just a few minutes ago.'

'*Who* told you?'

'Mr Da Vinci, sir . . .'

'That's not his name! Now, who is he?' Cardone fought his anger. He took a deep breath before speaking. 'You tell me who Da Vinci is.'

'There's more to the message,' said the chauffeur, disregarding Cardone's question. 'Mr Da Vinci says you should know that Tremayne may have talked to Mr Tanner. No one's sure yet, but that's what it looks like.'

'He *what*? Talked to him about *what*?'

'I don't know, sir. It's not my job to know. I'm hired to drive a car and deliver messages.'

'Your message isn't *clear*! I don't understand it! What good is a message if it isn't clear!' Cardone strained to keep in control.

'Perhaps the last part will help you, sir. Mr Da Vinci feels it would be a good idea if you tried to find out the extent of Mr Tremayne's involvement with Tanner. But you must be careful. Very, very careful. As you must be careful with your friends from California. That's important.'

The chauffeur backed away from the Cadillac and slapped two fingers against his cap's visor.

'Wait a minute!' Cardone reached for the door handle, but the huge man in uniform swiftly clamped his hands on the window ledge and held the door shut.

'No, Mr Cardione. You stay inside there. You shouldn't call attention to yourself. The train's coming in.'

'No, please! *Please* . . . I want to talk to Da Vinci! We've got to talk! Where can I reach him?'

'No way, sir.' The chauffeur held the door effortlessly.

'You prick!' Cardone pulled the handle and shoved his whole weight against the door. It gave just a bit and then slammed shut again under the chauffeur's hands. 'I'll break you in half!'

The train pulled to a stop in front of the platform. Several men got off and the shriek of two whistle blasts pierced the air.

The chauffeur spoke calmly. 'He's not on the train, Mr Cardione. He *drove* into town this morning. We know that, too.'

The train slowly started up and rolled down the tracks. Joe stared at the immense human being holding the car door shut. His anger was nearly beyond control but he was realistic enough to know it would do him no good. The chauffeur stepped back, gave Cardone a second informal salute and walked rapidly toward the Rolls-Royce. Cardone pushed the car door open and stepped out onto the hot pavement.

'Hello there, Joe!' The caller was Amos Needham, of the second contingent of Saddle Valley commuters. A vice-president of Manufacturers Hanover Trust and the chairman of the special events committee for the Saddle Valley Country Club. 'You market boys have it easy. When it gets rough you stay home and wait for the calm to set in, eh?'

'Sure, sure, Amos.' Cardone kept his eye on the chauffeur of the Rolls, who had climbed into the driver's seat and started the engine.

'I tell you,' continued Amos, 'I don't know where you young fellas are taking us! . . . Did you see the quotes for DuPont? Everybody else takes a bath and it zooms up! Told my trust committee to consult the Ouija board. To hell with you upstart brokers.' Needham chuckled and then suddenly waved his small arm, flagging down a Lincoln Continental approaching the depot. 'There's Ralph. Can I give you a lift, Joe? . . . But, of course not. You just stepped out of your car.'

The Lincoln pulled up to the platform, and Amos Needham's chauffeur started to get out.

'No need, Ralph. I can manipulate a door handle. By the way, Joe . . . that Rolls you're looking at reminds me of a friend of mine. Couldn't be, though. He lived in Maryland.'

Cardone snapped his head around and looked at the innocuous banker. 'Maryland? *Who* in Maryland?'

Amos Needham held the car door open and returned Cardone's stare with unconcerned good humor. 'Oh, I don't think you'd know him. He's been dead for years . . . Funny name. Used to kid him a lot . . . His name was Caesar.'

Amos Needham stepped into his Lincoln and closed the door. At the top of Station Parkway the Rolls-Royce turned right and roared off toward the main arteries leading to Manhattan. Cardone stood on the tarred surface of the Saddle Valley railroad station and he was afraid.

Tremayne!

Tremayne was with Tanner!

Osterman was with Tanner!

Da Vinci . . . Caesar!

The architects of war!

And he, Giuseppe Ambruzzio Cardione, was alone!

Oh, Christ! Christ! Son of God! Blessed Mary! Blessed Mary, Mother of Christ! Wash my hands with his blood! The blood of the lamb! Jesus! Jesus! Forgive me my sins! . . . Mary and Jesus! Christ Incarnate! God all holy! What have I done?

12

Tuesday – 5:00 P.M.

Tremayne walked aimlessly for hours; up and down the familiar streets of the East Side. Yet if anyone had stopped him and asked him where he was, he could not have answered.

He was consumed. Frightened. Blackstone had said everything and clarified nothing.

And Cardone had lied. To somebody. His wife or his office, it didn't matter. What mattered was that Cardone couldn't be reached. Tremayne knew that the panic wouldn't stop until he and Cardone figured out between them what Osterman had done.

Had Osterman betrayed them?

Was that really it? Was it *possible*?

He crossed Vanderbilt Avenue, realizing he had walked to the Biltmore Hotel without thinking about a destination.

It was understandable, he thought. The Biltmore brought back memories of the carefree times.

He walked through the lobby almost expecting to see some forgotten friend from his teens – and suddenly he was staring at a man he hadn't seen in over twenty-five years. He knew the face, changed terribly with the years – bloated, it seemed to Tremayne, lined – but he couldn't remember the name. The man went back to prep-school days.

Awkwardly the two men approached each other.

'Dick . . . Dick Tremayne! It *is* Dick Tremayne, isn't it?'

'Yes. And you're . . . Jim?'

'Jack! Jack Townsend! How are you, Dick?' The men shook hands, Townsend far more enthusiastic. 'It must be twenty-five, thirty years! You look great! How the hell do you keep the weight down? Gave up myself.'

'You look fine. Really, you look swell. I didn't know you were in New York.'

'I'm not. Based in Toledo. Just in for a couple of days . . . I swear to God, I had a crazy thought coming in on the plane. I canceled the Hilton and thought I'd grab a room here just to see if any of the old crowd ever came in. Insane, huh? . . . And look what I run into!'

'That's funny. Really funny. I was thinking the same sort of thing a few seconds ago.'

'Let's get a drink.'

Townsend kept spouting opinions that were formed in the traditions of corporate thought. He was being very boring.

Tremayne kept thinking about Cardone. As he drank his third drink he looked around for the bar telephone booth he remembered from his youth. It was hidden near the kitchen entrance, and only Biltmore habitués-in-good-standing knew of its existence.

It wasn't there any more. And Jack Townsend kept talking, talking, remembering the unmemorable out loud.

There were two Negroes in leather jackets, beads around their necks, standing several feet away from them.

They wouldn't have been there in other days.

The pleasant days.

Tremayne drank his fourth drink in one assault; Townsend *wouldn't* stop talking.

He *had* to call Joe! The panic was starting again. Maybe Joe would, in a single sentence, unravel the puzzle of Osterman.

'What's the matter with you, Dick? You look all upset.'

'S'help me God, this is the first time I've been in here in years.' Tremayne slurred his words and he knew it. 'Have to make a phone call. Excuse me.'

Townsend put his arm on Tremayne's arm. He spoke quietly.

'Are you going to call Cardone?'

'What?'

'I asked if you were going to call Cardone.'

'Who are you? . . . Who the hell are you?'

'A friend of Blackstone. Don't call Cardone. Don't do that under any circumstances. You put a nail in your own casket if you do. Can you understand that?'

'I don't understand *anything*! Who *are* you? Who's Blackstone?' Tremayne tried to whisper, but his voice carried throughout the room.

'Let's put it this way. Cardone may be dangerous. We don't trust him. We're not sure of him. Any more than we are of the Ostermans.'

'What are you saying?'

'They may have gotten together. You may be flying solo now. Play it cool and see what you can find out. We'll be in touch . . . but Mr Blackstone told you that already, didn't he?'

Then Townsend did a strange thing. He removed a bill from his wallet and placed it in front of Richard Tremayne. He said only two words as he turned and walked through the glass doors.

'Take it.'

It was a one-hundred-dollar bill.

What had it bought?

It didn't buy anything, thought Tremayne. It was merely a symbol.

A price. Any price.

When Fassett walked into the hotel room, two men were already bent over a card table, studying various papers and maps. One was Grover. The other man was named Cole. Fassett removed his Panama hat and sunglasses, putting them on the bureau top.

'Everything okay?' asked Grover.

'On schedule. If Tremayne doesn't get too drunk at the Biltmore.'

'If he does,' said Cole, his attention on a New Jersey road map, 'a friendly, bribable cop will correct the situation. He'll get home.'

'Have you got men on both sides of the bridge?'

'And the tunnels. He sometimes takes the Lincoln Tunnel and drives up the Parkway. All in radio contact.' Cole was making marks on a piece of tracing paper placed over the map.

The telephone rang. Grover crossed to the bedside table to pick it up.

'Grover here . . . Oh? Yes, we'll double check but I'm sure we would've heard if he had . . . Don't worry about it. All right. Keep in touch.' Grover replaced the receiver and stood by the telephone.

'What's the matter?' Fassett removed his white Palm Beach jacket and began rolling up his sleeves.

'That was Los Angeles logistics. Between the time Osterman left the studio and was picked up on Mulholland, they lost him for about twenty minutes. They're concerned that he may have reached Cardone or Tremayne.'

Cole looked up from the table. 'Around one o'clock our time – ten in California?'

'Yes.'

'Negative. Cardone was in his car and Tremayne on the streets. Neither could be reached . . .'

'I see what they mean, though,' interrupted Fassett. 'Tremayne didn't waste any time this noon trying to get to Cardone.'

'We calculated that, Larry,' said Cole. 'We would have intercepted both of them if a meeting had been scheduled.'

'Yes, I know. Risky though.'

Cole laughed as he picked up the tracing paper. 'You plan – we'll control. Here's every back road link to "Leather".'

'We've got them.'

'George forgot to bring up a copy, and the others are with the men. A command post should always have a map of the field.'

'*Mea culpa.* I was in briefing until two this morning and had to get the shuttle at six-thirty. I also forgot my razor and toothbrush and God knows what else.'

The telephone rang once again and Grover reached down for it.

'. . . I see . . . wait a minute.' He held the phone away from his ear and looked over at Laurence Fassett. 'Our second chauffeur had a run-in with Cardone . . .'

'Oh, Christ! Nothing rough, I hope.'

'No, no. The hot-tempered All-American tried to get out of the car and start a fight. Nothing happened.'

'Tell him to head back to Washington. Get out of the area.'

'Go back to DC, Jim . . . Sure, you might as well. Okay. See you at camp.' Grover replaced the receiver and walked back to the card table.

'What's Jim going to do "just as well"?' asked Fassett.

'Drop off the Rolls in Maryland. He thinks Cardone got the license number.'

'Good. And the Caesar family?'

'Primed beautifully,' interrupted Cole. 'They can't wait to hear from Giuseppe Ambruzzio Cardione. Like father, unlike son.'

'What's that mean?' Grover held his lighter under his cigarette.

'Old man Caesar made a dozen fortunes out of the rackets. His oldest son is with the Attorney General's office and an absolute fanatic about the Mafia.'

'Washing away family sins?'

'Something like that.'

Fassett walked over to the window and looked down at the long expanse of Central Park South. When he spoke he did so quietly, but the satisfaction in his voice made his companions smile.

'It's all there now. Each one is jolted. They're all confused and frightened. None of them know what to do or whom to talk to. Now we sit and watch. We'll give them a rest for twenty-four hours. A blackout . . . And Omega has no choice. Omega has to make its move.'

13

Wednesday – 10:15 A.M.

It was ten-fifteen before Tanner reached his office. He had found it nearly impossible to leave home, but he knew Fassett was right. He sat down and glanced perfunctorily at his mail and messages. Everyone wanted a conference. No one wanted to make a single decision without his say-so.

Corporate musical chairs. The network sub-brass band.

He picked up the phone and dialed New Jersey.

'Hello Ali?'

'Hi, hon. Did you forget something?'

'No . . . No. Just felt lonely. What are you doing?'

Inside 22 Orchard Place, Saddle Valley, New Jersey, Alice Tanner smiled and felt warm. 'What am I doing? . . . Well, as per the great Khan's orders, I'm overseeing your son's cleaning out the basement. And as the great Khan also instructed, his daughter is spending a hot July morning on her remedial reading. How else could she get into Berkeley by the time she's twelve?'

Tanner caught the complaint. When she was a young girl, his wife's summers were lonely and terrifying. Ali wanted them to be perfect for Janet.

'Well, don't overdo it. Have some kids over.'

'I might at that. But Nancy Loomis phoned and asked if Janet could go there for lunch . . .'

'Ali . . .' Tanner switched the phone to his left hand. 'I'd rather cool it with the Loomises for a few days . . .'

'What do you mean?'

John remembered Jim Loomis from the daily eight-twenty express. 'Jim's trying to boilerplate some market stuff. He's got a lot of fellows on the train to go along with him. If I can avoid him till next week I'm off the hook.'

'What does Joe say?'

'He doesn't know about it. Loomis doesn't want Joe to know. Rival houses, I guess.'

'I don't see that Janet's going to lunch has anything . . .'

'Just saves embarrassment. We don't have the kind of money he's looking for.'

'Amen to that!'

'And . . . do me a favor. Stay near the phone today.'

Alice Tanner's eyes shifted to the telephone in her hand. 'Why?'

'I can't go into it, but I may have an important call . . . What we're always talking about . . .'

Alice Tanner immediately, unconsciously lowered her voice as she smiled. 'Someone's offered you something!'

'Could be. They're going to call at home to set up a lunch.'

'Oh, John. That's exciting!'

'It . . . could be interesting.' He suddenly found it painful to talk to her. 'Speak to you later.'

'Sounds marvelous, darling. I'll turn up the bell. It'll be heard in New York.'

'I'll call you later.'

'Tell me the details then.'

Tanner placed the receiver slowly in its cradle. The lies had begun . . . but his family would stay home.

He knew he had to turn his mind to Standard Mutual problems. Fassett had warned him. There could be no break in his normal pattern, and normalcy for any network news director was a condition close to hypertension. Tanner's mark at Standard was his control of potential difficulties. If there was ever a time in his professional life to avoid chaos, it was now.

He picked up his telephone. 'Norma. I'll read out the list of those I'll see this morning, and you call them. Tell everyone I want the meetings quick and don't let anyone run over fifteen minutes unless I say otherwise. It would help if all problems and proposals were reduced to written half-pages. Pass the word. I've got a lot to catch up on.'

He wasn't free again until 12:30. Then he closed his office door and called his wife.

There was no answer.

He let the phone ring for nearly two minutes, until the spaces between the rings seemed to grow longer and longer.

No answer. No answer at the telephone – the telephone whose bell was turned up so loud it would be heard in New York.

It was twelve-thirty-five. Ali would figure no one would call between noon and one-thirty. And she probably needed something from the supermarket. Or she might have decided to take the children over to the Club for hamburgers. Or she couldn't refuse Nancy Loomis and had taken Janet over for lunch. Or she had gone to the library – Ali was an inveterate poolside reader during the summer.

Tanner tried to picture Ali doing all these things. That she was doing one, or some, or all, had to be the case.

He dialed again, and again there was no answer. He called the Club.

'I'm sorry, Mr Tanner. We've paged outside. Mrs Tanner isn't here.'

The Loomises. Of course, she went to the Loomises.

'Golly, John, Alice said Janet had a bad tummy. Maybe she took her to the doctor.'

By eight minutes after one, John Tanner had dialed his home twice more. The last time he had let the phone ring for nearly five minutes. Picturing Ali coming through the door breathlessly, always allowing that one last ring, expecting her to answer.

But it did not happen.

He told himself over and over again that he was acting foolishly. He himself had seen the patrol car following them when Ali drove him to the station. Fassett had convinced him yesterday that his watchdogs were thorough.

Fassett.

He picked up the phone and dialed the emergency number Fassett had given him. It was a Manhattan exchange.

'Grover . . .'

Who? thought Tanner.

'Hello? Hello? . . . George Grover speaking.'

'My name is John Tanner. I'm trying to find Laurence Fassett.'

'Oh, hello, Mr Tanner. Is something the matter? Fassett's out. Can I help you?'

'Are you an associate of Fassett's?'

'I am, sir.'

'I can't reach my wife. I've tried calling a number of times. She doesn't answer.'

'She may have stepped out. I wouldn't worry. She's under surveillance.'

'Are you positive?'

'Of course.'

'I asked her to stay by the phone. She thought I was expecting an important call . . .'

'I'll contact our men and call you right back. It'll set your mind at ease.'

Tanner hung up feeling slightly embarrassed. Yet five minutes went by and the expected ring did not come. He dialed Fassett's number but it was busy. He quickly replaced the phone wondering if his impetuous dialing caused Grover to find his line busy. Was Grover trying to reach him? He had to be. He'd try again right away.

Yet the phone did not ring.

Tanner picked it up and slowly, carefully dialed, making sure every digit was correct.

'Grover.'

'This is Tanner. I thought you were going to call right back!'

'I'm sorry, Mr Tanner. We've been having a little difficulty. Nothing to be concerned about.'

'What do you mean, difficulty?'

'Making contact with our men in the field. It's not unusual. We can't expect them to be next to a radio-phone every second. We'll reach them shortly and call you back.'

'That's not good enough!' John Tanner slammed the telephone down and got out of his chair. Yesterday afternoon Fassett had detailed every move made by all of them – even to the precise actions at the moment of his phone call. And now this Grover couldn't reach any of the men supposedly watching his family. What had Fassett said?

'We have thirteen agents in Saddle Valley . . .'

And Grover couldn't reach any of them.

Thirteen men and none could be contacted!

He crossed to the office door. 'Something's come up, Norma. Listen for my phone, please. If it's a man named Grover, tell him I've left for home.'

SADDLE VALLEY
VILLAGE INCORPORATED 1862
Welcome

'Where to now, Mister?'

'Go straight. I'll show you.'

The cab reached Orchard Drive, two blocks from his home; Tanner's pulse was hammering. He kept picturing the station wagon in the driveway. As soon as they made one more turn he'd be able to see it – if it was there. And if it was, everything would be all right. Oh, Christ! Let everything be all right!

The station wagon was not in the driveway.

Tanner looked at his watch.

Two-forty-five. A quarter to three! And Ali wasn't there!

'On the left. The wood-shingled house.'

'Nice place, mister. A real nice place.'

'Hurry!'

The cab pulled up to the flagstone path. Tanner paid and pulled open the door. He didn't wait for the driver's thanks.

'Ali! Ali!' Tanner raced through the laundry room to check the garage. Nothing. The small Triumph stood there.

Quiet.

Yet there was something. An odor. A faint, sickening odor that Tanner couldn't place.

'Ali! Ali!' He ran back to the kitchen and saw his pool through the window. Oh, God! He stared at the surface of the water and hurried to the patio door. The lock was stuck and so he slammed against it, breaking the latch, and ran out.

Thank God! There was nothing in the water!

His small Welsh terrier dog stirred from its sleep. The animal was attached to a wire run and immediately started barking in its sharp, hysterical yap.

He sped back into the house, to the cellar door.

'Ray! Janet! Ali!'

Quiet. Except for the incessant barking of the dog outside.

He left the cellar door open and ran to the staircase.

Upstairs!

He leapt up the stairs; the doors to the children's rooms and the guest room were open. The door to his and Ali's room was shut.

And then he heard it. The soft playing of a radio. Ali's clock radio with the automatic timer which shut the radio off at any given time up to an hour. He and Ali always used that timer when they played the radio. Never the ON button. It was a habit. And Ali had been gone over two and a half hours. Someone else had turned on the radio.

He opened the door.

No one.

He was about to turn and search the rest of the house when he saw it. A note written in red pencil next to the clock radio.

He crossed to the bedside table.

Your wife and children went for an unexpected drive. You'll find them by an old railroad depot on Lassiter Road.

In his panic, Tanner remembered the abandoned depot. It sat deep in the woods on a rarely used back road.

What had he done? What in Christ's name had he done? He'd killed them! If that was so, he'd kill Fassett! Kill Grover! Kill all those who should have been watching!

He raced out of the bedroom, down the staircase, into the garage. The door was open and he jumped into the seat of the Triumph and started the engine.

Tanner swung the small sports car to the right out of the driveway and sped around the long Orchard Drive curve, trying to remember the quickest way to Lassiter Road. He reached a pond he recognized as Lassiter Lake, used by the Saddle Valley residents for ice skating in winter. Lassiter Road was on the other side and seemed to disappear into a stretch of undisciplined woods.

He kept the accelerator flat against the Triumph's floor. He started talking to himself, then screaming at himself.

Ali! Ali! Janet! Ray!

The road was winding. Blind spots, curves, sun rays coming through the crowded trees. There were no other automobiles, no other signs of life.

The old abandoned depot suddenly appeared. And there was his station wagon – half off the overgrown parking area, into the tall grass. Tanner stamped on his brakes beside the wagon. There was no one in sight.

He jumped out of the Triumph and raced to the car.

In an instant his mind went out of control. The horror was real. The unbelievable had happened.

On the floor of the front seat was his wife. Slumped, motionless. In the back were little Janet and his son. Heads down. Bodies sprawled off the red seats.

Oh, Christ! Christ! It had happened! His eyes filled with tears. His body shook.

He pulled the door open, screaming in terror. And suddenly a wave of odor washed over him. The sickish odor he had smelled in his garage. He grabbed Ali's head and pulled her up, frightened beyond feeling.

'Ali! Ali! My God! *Please!* Ali!'

His wife opened her eyes slowly. Blinking. Conscious but not conscious. She moved her arms.

'Where . . . where? The *children!*' She drew out the word hysterically. The sound of her scream brought Tanner back to his senses. He leapt up and reached over the seat for his son and daughter.

They moved. They were alive! They *all* were *alive!*

Ali climbed out of the station wagon and stumbled to the ground. Her husband lifted his daughter out of the back seat and held her as she started to cry.

'What *happened?* What *happened?*' Alice Tanner pulled herself up.

'Don't talk, Ali. Breathe. As deeply as you can. Here!' He walked to her and handed her the sobbing Janet. 'I'll get Ray.'

'What *happened?* Don't tell me *not* to . . .'

'Be quiet! Just breathe. Breathe hard!'

He helped his son out of the back seat. The boy was sick and started to vomit. Tanner cupped his son's forehead with his hand, holding him around the waist with his left arm.

'John, you simply can't . . .'

'Walk around. Try to get Janet to walk! Do as I *say!*'

Obediently, dazedly, Alice Tanner did what her husband commanded. The boy began to shake his head in Tanner's hand.

'Feeling better, son?'

'Wow! . . . Wow! Where are we?' The boy was suddenly frightened.

'It's all right. It's all right . . . You're all . . . all right.'

Tanner looked over at his wife. She had put Janet's feet on the ground, holding her in her arms. The child was crying loudly now, and Tanner watched, filled with hatred and fear.

He walked to the station wagon to see if the keys were in the ignition.

They weren't. It didn't make sense.

He looked under the seats, in the glove compartment, in the back. Then he saw them. Wrapped in a piece of white paper, an elastic band holding the paper around the case. The packet was wedged between the collapsible seats, pushed far down, nearly out of sight.

His daughter was screaming now, and Alice Tanner picked the child up, trying to comfort her, repeating over and over again that everything was all right.

Making sure his wife could not see him, Tanner held the small package below the back seat, snapped the elastic band and opened the paper.

It was blank.

He crumpled the paper and stuffed it into his pocket. He would tell Ali what had happened now. They'd go away. Far away. But he would *not* tell her in front of the children.

'Get in the wagon.' Tanner spoke to his son softly and went to his wife, taking the hysterical child from her. 'Get the keys out of the Triumph, Ali. We're going home.'

His wife stood in front of him, her eyes wide with fright, the tears streaming down her face. She tried to control herself, tried with all her strength not to scream. 'What happened? What *happened* to us?'

The roar of an engine prevented Tanner from answering. In his anger, he was grateful. The Saddle Valley patrol car sped into the depot and came to a stop less than ten yards from them.

Jenkins and McDermott leapt out of the automobile. Jenkins had his revolver drawn.

'Is everything all right?' He ran up to Tanner. McDermott went rapidly to the station wagon and spoke quietly to the boy in the back seat.

'We found the note in your bedroom. Incidentally, we think we've recovered most of your property.'

'Our what?' Alice Tanner stared at the police officer.

'What property?'

'Two television sets, Mrs Tanner's jewelry, a box of silver, place settings, some cash. There's a list down at the station. We don't know if we've got everything. The car was abandoned several blocks from your house. They may have taken other things. You'll have to check.'

Tanner handed his daughter to Ali.

'What the hell are you talking about?'

'You were robbed. Your wife must have come back while they were in the process. She and the children were gassed in the garage . . . They were professionals, no doubt about it. Real professional methods . . .'

'You're a liar,' said Tanner softly. 'There was nothing . . .'

'Please!' interrupted Jenkins. 'The main thing now is your wife and children.'

As if on signal, McDermott called from inside the station wagon. 'I want to get this kid to the hospital! *Now!*'

'Oh, my God!' Alice Tanner ran to the automobile, carrying her daughter in her arms.

'Let McDermott take them,' said Jenkins.

'How can I trust you? You lied to me. There was nothing missing in my house. No television sets were gone, no signs of any robbery! Why did you lie?'

'There isn't time. I'm sending your wife and children with McDermott.' Jenkins spoke rapidly.

'They're going with *me!*'

'No they're not.' Jenkins raised his pistol slightly.

'I'll kill you, Jenkins.'

'Then what stands between you and Omega?' said Jenkins calmly. 'Be reasonable. Fassett's on his way out. He wants to see you.'

'I'm sorry. Truly, abjectly sorry. It won't, it *can't* happen again.'

'What *did* happen? Where was your infallible protection?'

'A logistical error on a surveillance schedule that hadn't been cross-checked. That's the truth. There's no point in lying to you. I'm the one responsible.'

'You weren't out here.'

'I'm still responsible. The Leather team's my responsibility. Omega saw that a post wasn't covered – for less than fifteen minutes, incidentally – and they moved in.'

'I can't tolerate that. You risked the lives of my wife and children!'

'I told you, there's no possibility of recurrence. Also – and in an inverted way, this should be comforting – this afternoon confirms the fact that Omega won't kill. Terror, yes. Murder, no.'

'Why? Because you say so? I don't buy it. The CIA track record reads like a disaster file. You're not making any more decisions for *me*, let's get that clear.'

'Oh? You are then?'

'Yes.'

'Don't be a fool. If not for yourself, for your family.'

Tanner got out of the chair. He saw through the Venetian blinds that two men were standing guard outside the motel window.

'I'm taking them away.'

'Where will you go?'

'I don't know. I just know I'm not staying here.'

'You think Omega won't follow you?'

'Why should it . . . they? I'm no part of you.'

'They won't believe that.'

'Then I'll make it clear!'

'Are you going to take out an ad in *The Times*?'

'No!' Tanner swung around and pointed a finger at the CIA man. 'You will! However you want to do it. Because if you don't, I'll tell the story of this operation and your inept, malicious handling of it on every network newscast in the country. You won't survive that.'

'Neither will you because you'll be dead. Your wife dead. Your son, your daughter . . . dead.'

'You can't threaten me . . .'

'For God's sake, look at history! Look at what's *really happened*!' Fassett exploded. Then suddenly he lowered his voice and raised his hand to his chest, speaking slowly. 'Take me . . . My wife was killed in East Berlin.

They murdered her for no earthly reason except that she was married to me. I was being . . . taught a lesson. And to teach me that lesson they took my wife. Don't make pronouncements to me. I've been there. You've been safe. Well, you're not safe now.'

Tanner was stunned. 'What are you trying to say?'

'I'm telling you that you'll do exactly what we've planned. We're too close now. I want Omega.'

'You can't force me and you know it!'

'Yes, I can . . . Because if you turn, if you run, I withdraw every agent in Saddle Valley. You'll be alone . . . and I don't think you can cope with the situation by yourself.'

'I'm taking my family away . . .'

'Don't be crazy! Omega raced in on a simple logistical error. That means they, whoever they are, are alert. Extremely alert, fast and thorough. What chance do you think you'll have? What chance do you give your family? We've admitted a mistake. We won't make any others.'

Tanner knew Fassett was right. If he was abandoned now, he didn't have the resources for control.

'You don't fool around, do you?'

'Did you ever – in a mine field?'

'I guess not . . . This afternoon. What was it?'

'Terror tactics. Without identification. That's in case you're clean. We realized what had happened and put out a counter-explanation. We'll withhold some of your property – small stuff, like jewelry, until it's over. More authentic.'

'Which means you expect me to go along with the "robbery".'

'Of course. It's safest.'

'Yes . . . Of course.' Tanner reached into his pocket for cigarettes. The telephone rang and Fassett picked it up.

He spoke quietly, then turned to the news director. 'Your family's back home. They're okay. Still scared, but okay. Some of our men are straightening up the place. It's a mess. They're trying to lift fingerprints. Naturally, it'll be found the thieves wore gloves. We've told your wife that you're still at headquarters making a statement.'

'I see.'

'You want us to drive you back?'

'No . . . No, I don't. I presume I'll be followed anyway.'

'Safety surveillance is the proper term.'

Tanner entered the Village Pub, Saddle Valley's one fashionable bar, and called the Tremaynes.

'Ginny, this is John. I'd like to talk to Dick. Is he there?'

'John *Tanner*?' Why did she say that? His name. She knew his voice.

'Yes. Is Dick there?'

'No . . . Of course not. He's at the office. What is it?'

'Nothing important.'

'Can't you tell me?'

'I just need a little legal advice. I'll try him at the office. Good-bye.'

Tanner knew he had done it badly. He had been awkward.

But then, so had Virginia Tremayne.

Tanner dialed New York.

'I'm sorry, Mr Tanner. Mr Tremayne's out on Long Island. In conference.'

'It's urgent. What's the number?'

Tremayne's secretary gave it to him reluctantly. He dialed it.

'I'm sorry, Mr Tremayne isn't here.'

'His office said he was in conference out there.'

'He called this morning and canceled. I'm sorry, sir.'

Tanner hung up the phone, then dialed the Cardones.

'Daddy and Mommy are out for the day, Uncle John. They said they'd be back after dinner. Do you want them to call you?'

'No . . . no, that's not necessary . . .'

There was an empty feeling in his stomach. He dialed the operator, gave her the information, including his credit card number, and three thousand four hundred miles away a telephone rang in Beverly Hills.

'Osterman residence.'

'Is Mr Osterman there?'

'No, he's not. May I ask who's calling, please?'

'Is Mrs Osterman there?'

'No.'

'When do you expect them back?'

'Next week. Who's calling, please?'

'The name's Cardone. Joseph Cardone.'

'C-A-R-D-O-N-E . . .'

'That's right. When did they go?'

'They left for New York last night. The ten o'clock flight, I believe.'

John Tanner hung up the receiver. The Ostermans were in New York! They'd gotten in by six o'clock that morning!

The Tremaynes, the Cardones, the Ostermans.

All there. None accounted for.

Any or all.

Omega!

14

Fassett had set a convincing scene. By the time Tanner returned home the rooms had been 'straightened up', but there was still disarray. Chairs were not in their proper places, rugs off center, lamps in different positions; the woman of the house hadn't yet put things to rights.

Ali told him how the police had helped her; if she suspected collusion she didn't let on.

But then Alice McCall had lived with violence as a child. The sight of policemen in her home was not unfamiliar to her. She was conditioned to react with a minimum of hysteria.

Her husband, on the other hand, was not conditioned at all for the role he had to play. For the second night, sleep was fitful, ultimately impossible. He looked at the dial on the clock radio. It was nearly three in the morning and his mind still raced, his eyes refused to stay shut.

It was no use. He had to get up, he had to walk around; perhaps eat something, read something, smoke.

Anything that would help him stop thinking.

He and Ali had had a number of brandies before going to bed – too many drinks for Ali; she was deep in sleep, as much from the alcohol as from exhaustion.

Tanner got out of bed and went downstairs. He wandered aimlessly around; he finished the remains of a cantaloupe in the kitchen, read the junk mail in the hallway, flipped through some magazines in the living room. Finally he went out to the garage. There was still the faint – ever so faint now – odor of the gas which had been used on his wife and children. He returned to the living room, forgetting to turn off the lights in the garage.

Extinguishing his last cigarette, he looked around for another pack; more for the security of knowing there was one than from any immediate need. There was a carton in the study. As he opened the top drawer of his desk, a noise made him look up.

There was a tapping on his study window and the beam of a flashlight waving in small circles against the pane.

'It's Jenkins, Mr Tanner,' said the muffled voice. 'Come to your back door.'

Tanner, relieved, nodded to the dark figure on the other side of the glass.

'This screen-door latch was broken,' said Jenkins softly as Tanner opened the kitchen door. 'We don't know how it happened.'

'I did it. What are you doing out there?'

'Making sure there's no repetition of this afternoon. There are four of us. We wondered what *you* were doing. The lights are on all over downstairs. Even in the garage. Is anything the matter? Has anyone phoned you?'

'Wouldn't you know if they had?'

Jenkins smiled as he stepped through the door. 'We're supposed to, I guess you know that. But there's no accounting for mechanical failures.'

'I suppose not. Care for a cup of coffee?'

'Only if you'd make enough for three other guys. They can't leave their posts.'

'Sure.' Tanner filled the hot water kettle. 'Instant be all right?'

'Be great. Thanks.' Jenkins sat down at the kitchen table, moving his large police holster so it hung free from the seat. He watched Tanner closely and then looked around the room.

'I'm glad you're outside. I appreciate it, really. I know it's a job, but still . . .'

'Not just a job. We're concerned.'

'That's nice to hear. You have a wife and kids?'

'No sir, I don't.'

'I thought you were married.'

'That's my partner, McDermott.'

'Oh, I see . . . You've been on the force here, let's see . . . a couple of years now, isn't it?'

'Just about.'

Tanner turned from the stove and looked at Jenkins. 'Are you one of them?'

'I beg your pardon?'

'I asked if you were one of them. This afternoon you used the name Omega. That means you're one of Fassett's men.'

'I was instructed what to tell you. I've met Mr Fassett, of course.'

'But you're not a small-town policeman, are you?'

Jenkins did not have time to answer. There was a cry from the grounds outside. Both men in the kitchen had heard that sound before, Tanner in France, Jenkins near the Yalu River. It was a scream in the instant of death.

Jenkins bolted to the screen door and raced outside, Tanner following at his heels. Two other men came out of the darkness.

'It's Ferguson! Ferguson!' They spoke harshly, but they did not yell. Jenkins rounded the pool and ran toward the woods beyond Tanner's property. The news editor stumbled and tried to keep up with him.

The mutilated body lay in a clump of weeds. The head was severed; its eyes were wide, as if the lids had been pierced and held with nails.

'Get back, Mr Tanner! Stay back! Don't look! Don't raise your voice!' Jenkins held the petrified news director by the shoulders, pushing him away from the corpse. The two other men ran into the woods, pistols drawn.

Tanner sank to the ground feeling sick, frightened beyond any fear he'd known.

'Listen to me,' whispered Jenkins, kneeling over the trembling man. 'That body in there wasn't meant for you to see. It has nothing to do with *you*! There are certain rules, certain signs we all know about. That man was killed for Fassett. It was meant for *him*.'

The body was wrapped in canvas and two men lifted it up to carry it away. Their moves were silent, efficient.

'Your wife's still sleeping,' said Fassett quietly. 'That's good . . . The boy got up and came downstairs. McDermott told him you were making coffee for the men.'

Tanner sat on the grass on the far side of the pool, trying to make sense out of the last hour. Fassett and Jenkins stood above him.

'For God's sake, how did it happen?' He watched the men carrying the body and his words could hardly be heard. Fassett knelt down.

'He was taken from behind.'

'From behind?'

'Someone who knew the woods behind your house.' Fassett's eyes bored into Tanner's and the news director understood the unspoken accusation.

'It's my fault, isn't it?'

'Possibly. Jenkins left his post. His position was adjacent . . . Why were you downstairs? Why were all the first-floor lights on?'

'I couldn't sleep. I got up.'

'The lights were on in the garage. Why were you in the garage?'

'I . . . I don't understand. I guess I was thinking about this afternoon.'

'You left the garage lights on . . . I can understand a man who's nervous getting up, going downstairs – having a cigarette, a drink. I can understand that. But I don't understand a man going into his garage and leaving the lights on . . . Were you going somewhere, Mr Tanner?'

'Going somewhere? . . . No. No, of course not. Where would I go?'

Fassett looked up at Jenkins, who was watching Tanner's face in the dim reflection of the light coming from the house.

'Are you sure?'

'My God . . . You thought I was running away. You thought I was running away and you came in to stop me!'

'Keep your voice down, please.' Fassett rose to his feet.

'Do you think I'd *do* that? Do you think for one minute I'd leave my family?'

'You could be taking your family with you,' answered Jenkins.

'Oh, Christ! That's why you came to the window. That's why you left your . . .' Tanner couldn't finish the sentence. He felt sick and wondered if he threw up where he could do it. He looked up at the two government men. 'Oh, Christ!'

'Chances are it would have happened anyway.' Fassett spoke calmly. 'It wasn't . . . wasn't part of any original plan. But you've *got* to understand. You behaved *abnormally*. It wasn't *normal* for you to do what you did. You've got to watch every move you make, everything you do or say. You can't forget that. *Ever.*'

Tanner awkwardly, unsteadily, got up. 'You're not going on with this? You've got to call it off.'

'Call it off? One of my men was just killed. We call it off now and you're also dead. So's the rest of your family.'

Tanner saw the sadness in the agent's eyes. One didn't argue with such men. They told the truth.

'Have you checked on the others?'

'Yes, we have.'

'Where are they?'

'The Cardones are at home. Tremayne stayed in New York; his wife's out here.'

'What about the Ostermans?'

'I'll go into that later. You'd better get back inside. We've doubled the patrol.'

'No you don't. What about the Ostermans? Aren't they in California?'

'You know they're not. You placed a call to them on your credit card at four-forty-six this afternoon.'

'Then where are they?'

Fassett looked at the news director and replied simply. 'They obviously made reservations under another name. We know they're in the New York area. We'll find them.'

'Then it could have been Osterman.'

'It could have been. You'd better get back. And don't worry. We've got an army out here.'

Tanner looked over at the woods where Fassett's man had been murdered. His whole body involuntarily shook for a moment. The proximity of such a brutal death appalled him. He nodded to the government men and started toward his house feeling only a sickening emptiness.

'Is it true about Tremayne?' asked Jenkins softly. 'He's in the city?'

'Yes. He had a fair amount to drink and took a room at the Biltmore.'

'Anyone check the room tonight?'

Fassett turned his attention from the figure of Tanner disappearing into the house. He looked at Jenkins. 'Earlier, yes. Our man reported that he went – probably staggered – to his room a little after midnight. We told him to pull out and pick Tremayne up again at seven. What's bothering you?'

'I'm not sure yet. It'll be clearer when we confirm Cardone's situation.'

'We did confirm it. He's at home.'

'We assume he's at home because we haven't had any reason to think otherwise up to now.'

'You'd better explain that.'

'The Cardones had dinner guests. Three couples. They all came together in a car with New York plates. Surveillance said they left in a hurry at twelve-thirty . . . I'm wondering now if Cardone was in that car. It was dark. He could have been.'

'Let's check it out. With both. The Biltmore'll be no problem. With Cardone we'll have Da Vinci make another phone call.'

Eighteen minutes later the two government men sat in the front seat of an automobile several hundred yards down the road from the Tanner house. The radio came in clearly.

'Information in, Mr Fassett. The Da Vinci call got us nowhere. Mrs Cardone said her husband wasn't feeling well; he was sleeping in a guest room and she didn't want to disturb him. Incidentally, she hung up on us. The Biltmore confirmed. There's no one in room ten-twenty-one. Tremayne didn't even sleep in his bed.'

'Thank you, New York,' said Laurence Fassett as he flipped the channel button to OFF. He looked over at Jenkins. 'Can you imagine a man like Cardone refusing a telephone call at four-thirty in the morning? From Da Vinci?'

'He's not there.'

'Neither's Tremayne.'

15

Fassett told him he could stay home on Thursday. Not that he had to be given permission; nothing could have dragged him away. Fassett also said that he'd contact him in the morning. The final plans for the total protection of the Tanner family would be made clear.

The news director put on a pair of khaki trousers and carried his sneakers and a sportshirt downstairs. He looked at the kitchen clock: twenty minutes to seven. The children wouldn't be up for at least an hour and a half. Ali, with luck, would sleep until nine-thirty or ten.

Tanner wondered how many men were outside. Fassett had said there was an army, but what good would an army be if Omega wanted him dead? What good had an army been for the government man in the woods at three-thirty in the morning? There were too many possibilities. Too many opportunities. Fassett had to understand that now. It had gone too far. If the preposterous were real, if the Ostermans, the Cardones or the Tremaynes really were a part of Omega, he couldn't simply greet them at his door as if nothing had happened. It was absurd!

He went to the kitchen door and quietly let himself out. He'd go toward the woods until he saw someone. He'd reach Fassett.

'Good morning.' It was Jenkins, dark circles of weariness under his eyes. He was sitting on the ground just beyond the edge of the woods. He couldn't be seen from the house or even the pool.

'Hello. Aren't you going to get any sleep?'

'I'm relieved at eight. I don't mind. What about you? You're exhausted.'

'Look, I want to see Fassett. I've got to see him before he makes any more plans.'

The patrolman looked at his wristwatch. 'He was going to call you after we gave him the word you were up. I don't think he expected it'd be so early. That may be good though. Wait a sec.' Jenkins walked a few feet into the woods and returned with a canvas-pack radio. 'Let's go. We'll drive over.'

'Why can't he come here?'

'Relax. Nobody could get near your house. Come on. You'll see.'

Jenkins picked up the radio by its shoulder strap and led Tanner through a newly created path in the woods surrounding his property. Every thirty to forty feet were men, kneeling, sitting, lying on their stomachs facing the house, unseen but seeing. As Jenkins and Tanner approached each man, weapons were drawn. Jenkins gave the radio to the patrol on the east flank.

'Call Fassett. Tell him we're on our way over,' he said.

'That agent was killed last night because the killer knew he'd been recognized. One part of Omega was identified and that was unacceptable.' Fassett sipped coffee, facing Tanner. 'It was also another sort of warning, but that doesn't concern you.'

'He was murdered fifty yards from my house, from my family! *Everything* concerns me!'

'All right! . . . Try to understand. We can assume the information on you has been returned; remember, you're just Tanner the newsman, nothing else. They're circling like hawks now, wary of each other. None knowing whether the others have accomplices, scouts of their own . . . The killer – *one* tentacle of Omega – ran a private surveillance. He collided with the agent; he had no choice but to kill. He didn't know him, he'd never seen him before. The only thing he *could* be sure of was that whoever posted the man would become concerned when he didn't report. Whoever was responsible for that man in the woods would come and find him. That was the warning; his death.'

'You can't be sure of that.'

'We're not dealing with amateurs. The killer knew the body would be removed before daylight. I told you in Washington, Omega's fanatic. A decapitated body fifty yards from your house is the kind of mistake that would call for an NKVD execution. *If* Omega was responsible. If not . . .'

'How do you know they're not working together? If the Ostermans or the Cardones or the Tremaynes are any part of it, they could have planned it together.'

'Impossible. They haven't been in contact since the harassment began. We've fed them all – each of them – contradictory stories, illogical suppositions, half truths. We've had cables routed through Zurich, telephone calls from Lisbon, messages delivered by strangers in dead-end streets. Each couple is in the dark. None know what the others are doing.'

The agent named Cole looked up at Fassett from the chair by the motel window. He knew that Fassett could not be absolutely sure of his last statement. They'd lost the Ostermans for nearly twelve hours. There was a surveillance lapse of three and three-and-a-half hours, respectively, with Tremayne and Cardone. Still, thought Cole, Fassett was right to say what he did.

'Where are the Ostermans? You said last night – this morning – that you didn't know where they were.'

'We found them. In a New York hotel. From what we've learned, it's doubtful Osterman was in the area last night.'

'But, again, you're not sure.'

'I said doubtful. Not beyond doubt.'

'And you're convinced it had to be one of them?'

'We think so. The killer was male almost certainly. It . . . took enormous strength . . . He knew the grounds around your property better than we did. And you should know we've studied your place for weeks.'

'For God's sake then, *stop* them! Confront them! You can't let it go on!'

'Which one?' Fassett asked quietly.

'*All* of them! A man was *killed*!'

Fassett put his coffee cup down. 'If we do as you suggest, which, I admit, is tempting – it was my man who was killed, remember – we not only wash out any chance we have to expose Omega, but we also take a risk with you and your family that I can't justify.'

'We couldn't be taking any greater risk and you know it.'

'You're in no danger. Not as long as you continue to act in a normal manner. If we walk in now we're admitting the weekend is a trap. That trap couldn't have been set without your assistance . . . We'd be signing your death warrants.'

'I don't understand that.'

'Then take my word for it,' said Fassett sharply. 'Omega *must* come to *us*. There's no other way.'

Tanner paused, watching Fassett carefully. 'That's not entirely true, is it? What you're saying is . . . it's too late.'

'You're very perceptive.'

Fassett picked up his cup and went to the table where there was a Thermos of coffee. 'There's only one more day. At the most two. Some part of Omega will break by then. All we need is one. One defection and it's over.'

'And one stick of dynamite in my house blows us to hell.'

'There'll be nothing like that. No violence. Not directed at you. Put simply, you're not important. Not any longer. They'll only be concerned about each other.'

'What about yesterday afternoon?'

'We've put out a police-blotter story. A robbery. Bizarre to be sure, but a robbery nevertheless. Just what your wife thinks happened, the way she thinks it happened. You don't have to deny anything.'

'They'll know it's a lie. They'll call it.'

Fassett looked calmly up from the Thermos. 'Then we'll have Omega, won't we? We'll know which one it is.'

'What am I supposed to do? Pick up a telephone and call you? They may have other ideas . . .'

'We'll hear every word said in your house starting with your first guest tomorrow afternoon. Later this morning two television repairmen will come to fix the sets damaged in the robbery. While tracing antenna wiring they'll also install miniaturized pick-ups throughout your home. Starting with the first arrival tomorrow, they'll be activated.'

'Are you trying to tell me you won't activate them until then?'

Cole interrupted. 'No, we won't. We're not interested in your privacy, only your safety.'

'You'd better get back,' said Fassett. 'Jenkins will drop you off at the south end of your property. You couldn't sleep so you went for a walk.'

Tanner crossed slowly to the door. He stopped and looked back at Fassett. 'It's just like it was in Washington, isn't it? You don't give me any alternative.'

Fassett turned away. 'We'll be in touch. If I were you I'd relax, go to the Club. Play tennis, swim. Get your mind off things. You'll feel better.'

Tanner looked at Fassett's back in disbelief. He was being dismissed, as a less-than-respected subordinate is dismissed before a high policy conference.

'Come on,' said Cole, standing up, 'I'll see you to the car.' As they walked, he added, 'I think you should know that that man's death last night complicates Fassett's job more than you'll ever realize. That killing was directed at him. It was *his* warning.'

The news director looked at Cole closely. 'What do you mean?'

'There are signs between old-line professionals and this is one of them. You're insignificant now . . . Fassett's brilliant. He's set the forces in motion and nothing can stop them. The people who conceived Omega realize what's happened. And they're beginning to see that they may be helpless. They want the man responsible to know they'll be back. Sometime. A severed head means a massacre, Mr Tanner. They took his wife. Now he's got three kids to worry about.'

Tanner felt the sickness coming upon him again.

'What kind of a world do you people live in?'

'The same one you do.'

16

When Alice awoke at ten-fifteen Thursday morning her immediate reaction was to remain in bed forever. She could hear the children arguing downstairs and the indistinguishable but patient words from her husband settling the dispute. She thought about his remarkable sense of small kindnesses that added up to major concern. That wasn't bad after so many years of marriage.

Perhaps her husband wasn't as quick or dramatic as Dick Tremayne, or as sheerly powerful as Joe Cardone, or as witty or bright as Bernie Osterman, but she wouldn't exchange places with Ginny, Betty, or Leila for anything in the world. Even if everything started all over again, she would wait for John Tanner, or *a* John Tanner. He was that rare man. He wanted to share, *had* to share. *Everything.* None of the others did. Not even Bernie, although he was the most like John. Even Bernie had quiet secrets, according to Leila.

In the beginning, Alice had wondered if her husband's need to share was merely the result of his pity for her. Because she was to be pitied, she realized without any sense of self-indulgence. Most of her life before she met John Tanner had been spent in flight or in pursuit of sanctuary. Her father, a self-professed rectifier of the world's ills, was never able to stay too long in one place. A contemporary John Brown.

The newspapers eventually labeled him . . . lunatic.

The Los Angeles police eventually killed him.

She remembered the words.

Los Angeles, February 10, 1945. Jason McCall, whom authorities believe to have been in the pay of the Communists, was shot down today outside his canyon headquarters when he emerged brandishing what appeared to be a weapon. The Los Angeles police and agents of the Federal Bureau of Investigation unearthed McCall's whereabouts after an extensive search . . .

The Los Angeles police and the agents of the Federal Bureau of Investigation, however, had not bothered to determine that Jason McCall's weapon was a bent piece of metal he called his 'plowshare'.

Mercifully, Alice had been with an aunt in Pasadena when the killing took place. She'd met the young journalism student, John Tanner, at the public inquest after her father's death. The Los Angeles authorities wanted the inquest public. There was no room for a martyr. They wanted it clear that under no circumstances was McCall's death a murder.

Which, of course, it was.

The young journalist – returned from the war – knew it and labeled it as such. And although his story did nothing for the McCall family, it did bring him closer to the sad and bewildered girl who became his wife.

Alice stopped thinking and rolled over on her stomach. It was all past. She was where she wanted to be.

Several minutes later she heard strange male voices downstairs in the hallway. She started to sit up when the door opened and her husband came in. He smiled and bent down, kissing her lightly on the forehead, but in spite of his casualness, there was something strained about him.

'Who's downstairs?' she asked.

'The TV men. They're rehooking the sets, but the outside antenna system's loused up. They have to locate the trouble.'

'Which means I get up.'

'It does. I'm not taking chances with you in bed in front of two well-proportioned men in overalls.'

'You once wore overalls. Remember? In your senior year you had that job at the gas station.'

'And when I got home I also remember they came off with alarming ease. Now, up you go.'

He *was* tense, she thought; he was imposing control on the situation, on himself. He announced that in spite of the pressures which descended on him on Thursdays, on this particular Thursday he was staying at home.

His explanation was simple. After yesterday afternoon, regardless of the continuing police investigation, he wasn't about to leave his family. Not until everything was cleared up.

He took them to the Club, where he and Ali played doubles with their neighbors, Dorothy and Tom Scanlan. Tom was reputed to be so rich he hadn't gone to work in a decade.

What struck Ali was her husband's determination to win. She was embarrassed when he accused Tom of miscalling a line shot and mortified when he made an unusually violent overhead, narrowly missing Dorothy's face.

They won the set, and the Scanlans turned down another. So they went to the pool, where John demanded what amounted to extraordinary service from the waiters. Late in the afternoon he spotted McDermott and insisted he join them for a drink. McDermott had come to the Club – so John told his wife – to tell a member that his car was long overdue at a parking meter in town.

And always, always, Tanner kept going to the telephone inside the Club. He could have had one brought to the poolside table but he wouldn't do so. He claimed that the Woodward conferences were getting heated and he'd rather not talk in public.

Alice didn't believe it. Her husband had many talents and perhaps the most finely honed was his ability to remain calm, even cold, under acute pressure. Yet today he was obviously close to panic.

They returned to Orchard Drive at eight o'clock. Tanner ordered the children to bed; Alice revolted.

'I've had it!' she said firmly. She pulled her husband into the living room and held his arm. 'You're being unreasonable, darling. I know how you felt. I felt it, too, but you've been barking orders all day long. Do this! Do that! It's not like you.'

Tanner remembered Fassett. He had to remain calm, normal. Even with Ali.

'I'm sorry. It's a delayed reaction, I guess. But you're right. Forgive me.'

'It's over and done with,' she added, not really accepting his quick apology. 'It was frightening, but everything's all right now. It's *over*.'

Oh Christ, thought Tanner. He wished to God it were that simple. 'It's over and I've behaved childishly and I want my wife to say she loves me so we can have a couple of drinks and go to bed together.' He kissed her lightly on the lips. 'And that, madam, is the best idea I've had all day.'

'You took a long time arriving at it,' she said as she smiled up at him. 'It'll take me a few minutes. I promised Janet I'd read her a story.'

'What are you going to read her?'

'"Beauty and the Beast". Ponder it.' She disengaged herself from his arms, touching his face with her fingers. 'Give me ten, fifteen minutes.'

Tanner watched her go back into the hall to the staircase. She'd been through so much, and now this. Now, Omega.

He looked at his watch. It was eight-twenty and Ali would be upstairs for at least ten minutes, probably twice as long. He decided to call Fassett at the motel.

It wasn't going to be the usual conversation with Fassett. No more condescending instructions, no more sermons. It was now the end of the third day; three days of harassment against the suspects of Omega.

John Tanner wanted specifics. He was entitled to them.

Fassett was alarmed, annoyed, at the news director's precise questions.

'I can't take time to phone you whenever someone crosses the street.'

'I need answers. The weekend starts tomorrow, and if you want me to go on with this, you'll tell me what's happened. Where are they now? What have their reactions been? I've *got* to know.'

For a few seconds there was silence. When Fassett spoke, his voice was resigned. 'Very well . . . Tremayne stayed in New York last night. I told you that, remember? While at the Biltmore he met a man named Townsend. Townsend's a known stock manipulator out of Zurich. Cardone and his wife went to Philadelphia this afternoon. She visited her family in Chestnut Hill and he went out to Bala Cynwyd to meet with a man we know is a high capo in the Mafia. They got back to Saddle Valley an hour ago. The Ostermans are at The Plaza. They're having dinner later tonight with a couple named Bronson. The Bronsons are friends from years ago. They're also on the Attorney General's subversive list.'

Fassett stopped and waited for Tanner to speak.

'And none of them have met? They haven't even called each other? They've made no plans? I want the truth!'

'If they've talked it hasn't been on any telephone we can control, which would mean they'd have to be at pay phones at simultaneous times, which they haven't. We know they haven't met – simple surveillance. If any of them has plans, they're individual, not coordinated . . . We're counting on that as I've told you. That's all there is.'

'There doesn't seem to be any relationship. With any of them?'

'That's right. That's what we've concluded.'

'But not what you expected. You said they'd panic. Omega would be in panic by now.'

'I think they are. Every one of them. Separately. Our projections are positive.'

'What the hell does that mean?'

'Think. One couple races to a powerful Mafioso. Another meets with a husband and wife who are as fanatic as anyone in the Presidium. And the lawyer has a sudden conference with an international securities thief out of Zurich. That's panic. The NKVD has many tentacles. Every one of them is on the brink. All we do is sit and wait.'

'Beginning tomorrow, sitting and waiting's not going to be so easy.'

'Be natural. You'll find yourself functioning on two levels really quite comfortably. It's always like that. There's no danger if you even *half* carry it off. They're too concerned with each other now. Remember, you don't have to hide yesterday afternoon. Talk about it. Be expansive. Do and say what comes naturally about it.'

'And you think they'll believe me?'

'They haven't got a choice! Don't you understand that? You made your reputation as an investigative reporter. Do I have to remind you that investigation ends when the subjects collide? That's the age-old wrap-up.'

'And I'm the innocent catalyst?'

'You better believe it. The more innocent, the better the wrap-up.'

Tanner lit a cigarette. He couldn't deny the government man any longer.

His logic was too sound. And the safety, the security, the all-holy well-being of Ali and the children was in this cold professional's hands.

'All right. I greet them all at the door as long-lost brothers and sisters.'

'That's the way. And if you feel like it, call them all in the morning, make sure they're coming over. Except the Ostermans, of course. Whatever you'd normally do . . . And remember, we're right there. The most sophisticated equipment the biggest corporation on earth owns is at work for you. Not even the smallest weapon could get through your front door.'

'Is that true?'

'We'd know it if a three-inch blade was in someone's pocket. A four-inch revolver would have you all out of there in sixty seconds.'

Tanner replaced the receiver and drew heavily on his cigarette. As he took his hand off the telephone he had the feeling – the physical feeling – of *leaving, jumping, going away*.

It was a strange sensation, an awesome sense of loneliness.

And then he realized what it was, and it disturbed him greatly.

His sanity was now dependent on a man named Fassett. He was utterly in his control.

PART THREE

The Weekend

17

The taxi drew up to the front of the Tanner house. John's dog, the stringy Welsh terrier, ran up and down the driveway, yapping with each advance and retreat, waiting for someone to acknowledge that the visitors were welcome. Janet raced across the front lawn. The taxi door opened; the Ostermans stepped out. Each carried gift-wrapped boxes. The driver brought out a single large suitcase.

From inside the house, Tanner looked at them both: Bernie, in an expensively cut Palm Beach jacket and light-blue slacks; Leila, in a white suit with a gold chain around her waist, the skirt well above her knees, and a wide-brimmed soft hat covering the left side of her face. They were the picture of California success. Yet somehow there was a trace of artifice with Bernie and Leila; they had moved into the real money barely nine years ago.

Or was their success itself a façade, wondered Tanner as he watched the couple bending down to embrace his daughter. Had they, instead, for years and years been inhabitants of a world where scripts and shooting schedules were only secondary – good *covers*, as Fassett might say?

Tanner looked at his watch. It was two minutes past five. The Ostermans were early – according to their original schedule. Perhaps it was their first mistake. Or perhaps they didn't expect him to be there. He always left the Woodward studio early when the Ostermans came, but not always in time to be home before five-thirty. Leila's letter had said plainly their flight from Los Angeles was due at Kennedy around five. A plane being late was understandable, normal. A flight that got in ahead of schedule was improbable.

They'd have to have an explanation. Would they bother?

'Johnny! For heaven's sake! I thought I heard the pup barking. It's Bernie and Leila. What are you standing there for?' Ali had come out of the kitchen.

'Oh, sorry . . . I just wanted to let Janet have her moment with them.'

'Go on out, silly. I'll just set the timer.' His wife walked back toward the kitchen as Tanner approached the front door. He stared at the brass knob and felt as he thought an actor might feel before making his first entrance in a difficult part. Unsure – totally unsure – of his reception.

He wet his lips and drew the back of his hand across his forehead. Deliberately he twisted the knob and pulled the door back swiftly. With his other hand he unlatched the aluminum screened panel and stepped outside.

The Osterman weekend had begun.

'Welcome, Schreibers!' he shouted with a wide grin. It was his usual greeting; Bernie considered it the most honorific.

'Johnny!'

'Hi, darling!'

Thirty yards away, they shouted back and smiled broad smiles. Yet even thirty yards away John Tanner could see their unsmiling eyes. Their eyes searched his – briefly, but unmistakably. For a split second Bernie even stopped smiling, stopped any motion whatsoever.

It was over in a moment. And there seemed to be a tacit agreement between them not to pursue the unspoken thoughts.

'Johnny, it's so awfully good to see you!' Leila ran across the lawn.

John Tanner accepted Leila's embrace and found himself responding with more overt affection than he thought he could muster. He knew why. He had passed the first test, the opening seconds of the Osterman weekend. He began to realize that Laurence Fassett could be right, after all. Perhaps he *could* carry it off.

Do as you normally do; behave as you'd normally behave. Don't think about anything else.

'John, you look great, just great, man!'

'Where's Ali, sweetie?' asked Leila, who stepped aside so Bernie could throw his long thin arms around Tanner.

'Inside. Casserole-doing-time. Come on in! Here, I'll grab the bag . . . No, Janet, honey, you can't lift Uncle Bernie's suitcase.'

'I don't know why not,' laughed Bernie. 'All it's filled with is towels from The Plaza.'

'The Plaza?' Tanner couldn't help himself. 'I thought your plane just got in.'

Osterman glanced at him. 'Uh uh. We flew in a couple of days ago. I'll tell you about it . . .'

In a strange way it was like old times, and Tanner was astonished that he found himself accepting the fact. There was still the sense of relief at physically seeing each other again, knowing that time and distance were meaningless to their friendship. There was still the feeling that they could take up conversations, continue anecdotes, finish stories begun months previously. And there was still Bernie; gentle, reflective Bernie with his quiet, devastating comments about the palm-lined drug store. Devastating but somehow never condescending; Bernie laughed at himself as well as his professional world, for it *was* his world.

Tanner remembered Fassett's words.

'. . . *you'll find yourself functioning on two levels quite comfortably. It's always like that.*'

Again, Fassett was right . . . In and out; in and out.

It struck Tanner as he watched Bernie that Leila kept shifting her eyes away from her husband to him. Once he returned her look; she lowered her eyes as a child might after a reprimand.

The telephone rang in the study. The sound was jarring to everyone but Alice. There was an extension phone on the table behind the sofa, but John ignored it as he crossed in front of the Ostermans toward the study door.

'I'll take it out here. It's probably the studio.'

As he entered the study he heard Leila speak to Ali, her voice lowered.

'Sweetie, Johnny seems tense. Is anything the matter? The way Bernie drawls on no one can get a word in.'

'Tense is understating it! You should have seen him yesterday!'

The telephone rang again; Tanner knew it wouldn't be normal to let it ring further. Yet he wanted so much to hear the Ostermans' reaction to Ali's story of the Wednesday terror.

He compromised. He picked the phone out of the cradle, held it to his side and listened for several seconds to the conversation.

Something caught his ear. Bernie and Leila reacted to Ali's words too quickly, with too much anticipation. They were asking questions before she finished sentences! They *did* know something.

'Hello? Hello! Hello, hello?' The anxious voice on the other end of the line belonged to Joe Cardone.

'Hello, Joe? Sorry, I dropped the phone . . .'

'I didn't hear it drop.'

'Very soft, very expensive carpets.'

'Where? In that study of yours with the parquet floor?'

'Hey, come on, Joe.'

'Sorry . . . The city was rotten hot today and the market's going to hell.'

'That's better. Now you sound like the cheerful fellow we're waiting for.'

'You mean everybody's there?'

'No. Just Bernie and Leila.'

'They're early. I thought the plane got in at five.'

'They flew in a couple of days ago.'

Cardone started to speak and then abruptly stopped. He seemed to catch his breath. 'Funny they didn't call. I mean, they didn't get in touch with me. Did they with you?'

'No, I guess they had business.'

'Sure, but you'd think . . .' Again Cardone stopped in the middle of a sentence. Tanner wondered whether this hesitation was meant for him; to convince him of the fact that Bernie and Joe hadn't met, hadn't spoken with each other.

'Bernie'll probably tell us all about it.'

'Yeah,' said Cardone, not really listening. 'Well, I just wanted to let you know we'd be late. I'll grab a quick shower; be there soon.'

'See you.' Tanner hung up the phone, surprised at his own calm. It occurred to him that he had controlled the conversation. *Controlled* it. He had to. Cardone was a nervous man and he hadn't called to say he'd be late. To begin with, he wasn't late.

Cardone had phoned to see if the others had come. Or if they were coming.

Tanner returned to the living room and sat down.

'Darling! Ali just told us! How dreadful! How simply terrifying!'

'My God, John! What an awful experience! The police said it was robbery?'

'So did *The New York Times*. Guess that makes it official.'

'I didn't see anything in *The Times*,' stated Bernie firmly.

'It was only a few lines near the back. We'll get better coverage in the local paper next week.'

'I've never heard of any robbery like that,' said Leila. 'I wouldn't settle for that, I really wouldn't.'

Bernie looked at her. 'I don't know. It's actually pretty smart. No identification, no harm to anyone.'

'What I don't understand is why they didn't just leave us in the garage.' Ali turned to her husband. It was a question he hadn't answered satisfactorily.

'Did the police say why?' asked Bernie.

'They said the gas was a low-yield variety. The thieves didn't want Ali or the kids to come to and see them. Very professional.'

'Very scary,' Leila said. 'How did the kids take it?'

'Ray's a neighborhood hero, of course,' said Ali. 'Janet's still not sure what happened.'

'Where *is* Ray?' Bernie pointed to a package in the hall. 'I hope he hasn't outgrown model airplanes. That's one of those remote-control things.'

'He'll love it,' said Ali. 'He's in the basement, I think. John's turning it over to him . . .'

'No, he's outside. In the pool.' Tanner realized that his interruption, his sharp correction of Ali, caused Bernie to look at him. Even Ali was startled by the abruptness of his statement.

So be it, thought Tanner. Let them all know the father was aware, every second, of the whereabouts of his own.

The dog began barking in front of the house; the sound of a car could be heard in the driveway. Alice walked to the window.

'It's Dick and Ginny. And Ray's *not* in the pool,' she added, smiling at John. 'He's in front saying hello.'

'He must have heard the car,' said Leila for no apparent reason.

Tanner wondered why she made the remark; it was as if she were defending him. He went to the front door and opened it. 'Come on in, son. Some other friends of yours are here.'

When he saw the Ostermans, the boy's eyes lit up. The Ostermans never arrived empty-handed. 'Hello, Aunt Leila. Uncle Bernie!' Raymond Tanner, age twelve, walked into the arms of Leila and then shook hands manfully, shyly, with Bernie.

'We brought you a little something. Actually your buddy Merv suggested it.' Bernie crossed to the hall and picked up the package. 'Hope you like it.'

'Thank you very much.' The boy took the gift and went into the dining room to unwrap it.

Virginia Tremayne came in, the picture of cool sensuality. She was dressed in a man-styled shirt with multicolored stripes and a tight knit skirt which accentuated the movements of her body. There were women in Saddle Valley who resented Ginny's appearance, but they weren't in these rooms. Ginny was a good friend.

'I told Dick you called Wednesday,' she said to Tanner, 'but he says you never reached him. The poor lamb's been holed up in a conference suite with some awful merger people from Cincinnatti or Cleveland or somewhere . . . Leila, darling! Bernie, love!' Ginny pecked Tanner's cheek and choreographed herself past him.

Richard Tremayne came in. He was watching Tanner and what he saw obviously pleased him.

Tanner, on the other hand, felt the look and whipped his head around too quickly. Tremayne didn't have time to shift his eyes away. The news director recognized in the lawyer's stare the look of a doctor studying a medical chart.

For a split second both men silently, unwillingly, acknowledged the tension. And then it passed, as it had passed with the Ostermans. Neither man dared sustain it.

'Hey, John! Sorry I didn't get your message. Ginny mentioned something legal.'

'I thought you might have read about it.'

'What, for God's sake?'

'We didn't get much coverage in the New York papers, but wait'll you read next Monday's weekly. We'll be celebrities.'

'What the hell are you talking about?'

'We were robbed Wednesday. Robbed and kidnapped and chloroformed and God knows what else!'

'You're joking!'

'The hell he is!' Osterman walked into the hallway. 'How are you, Dick?'

'Bernie! How are you, buddy?' The men grasped hands, but Tremayne could not seem to take his attention from John Tanner.

'Did you hear what he said? Did you hear that? What happened, for Christ's sake? I've been in town since Tuesday. Didn't even have time to get home.'

'We'll tell you all about it. Later. Let me get your drinks.' Tanner walked away rapidly. He couldn't fault Tremayne's reaction. The lawyer was not only shocked by what he'd heard, he was frightened. So much so that he had to make clear he had been gone since Tuesday.

Tanner made drinks for the Tremaynes and then went into the kitchen and looked out past his pool to the edge of the woods. Although there was no one in sight, he knew the men were there. With binoculars, with radios, probably with tiny speakers which magnified conversations taking place in any section of his house.

'Hey, John, I wasn't kidding!' It was Tremayne walking into the kitchen. 'Honest to God, I didn't know anything about it. About Wednesday, I mean. Why the hell didn't you reach me?'

'I tried. I even called a number on Long Island. Oyster Bay, I think.'

'Oh, shit! You know what I mean! You or Ali should have told Ginny. I'd have left the conference, you know that!'

'It's over with. Here's your drink.' Tremayne lifted the glass to his lips. He could drink any of them under the table.

'You can't leave it like that. Why did you call me in the first place?'

Tanner, stupidly, wasn't prepared for the question.

'I . . . I didn't like the way the police handled it.'

'The police? Fat-cap MacAuliff?'

'I never talked to Captain MacAuliff.'

'Didn't you give a statement?'

'Yes . . . yes, I did. To Jenkins and McDermott.'

'Where the hell was old law'n'order himself?'

'I don't know. He wasn't there.'

'Okay, Mac wasn't there. You say Jenkins and McDermott handled it. Ali told me they were the ones who found you . . .'

'Yes. Yes, that's what I was pissed-off about.'

'What?'

'I just didn't like the way they handled it. At least I didn't at the time. I've cooled it now. It was hot then, that's why I tried to reach you.'

'What are you figuring? Police negligence? Abridged rights? What?'

'I don't know, Dick! I just panicked, that's all. When you panic you want a lawyer.'

'I don't. I want a drink.' Tremayne held Tanner's eyes. Tanner blinked – as a small boy defeated in a game of stare.

'It's over with. Let's go back inside.'

'Maybe we ought to talk later. Maybe you have some kind of case and I don't see it.'

Tanner shrugged, knowing that Dick didn't really want to talk later at all. The lawyer was frightened, and his fear arrested his professional instinct to probe. As he walked away, Tanner had the feeling that Tremayne was telling the truth about one aspect of Wednesday afternoon. He hadn't been there himself.

But did he know who had been?

By six, the Cardones still hadn't arrived. No one asked why; the hour passed quickly and if anyone was concerned he hid it well. At ten minutes past, Tanner's eyes were drawn to a car driving slowly past his house. It was the Saddle Valley taxi, the sun causing intermittent, sharp flashes off the black enamel. In the rear window of the automobile he saw Joe Cardone's face for a moment. Joe was making sure all the guests had arrived. Or were still there, perhaps.

Forty-five minutes later the Cardones' Cadillac pulled into the driveway. When they entered the house it was obvious that Joe had had several drinks. Obvious because Joe was not a drinker, he didn't really approve of alcohol, and his voice was just a degree louder than it might have been.

'Bernie! Leila! Welcome to the heart of the eastern establishment!'

Betty Cardone, prim, stoutish, Anglican Betty, properly added to her husband's enthusiasm and the four of them exchanged embraces.

'Betty, you look adorable,' said Leila. 'Joe, my God, Joe! How can a man look so healthy? . . . Bernie built a gym and look what *I* got!'

'Don't you knock my Bernie!' said Joe, his arm around Osterman's shoulder.

'You tell her, Joe.' Bernie moved toward Cardone's wife and asked about the children.

Tanner started toward the kitchen, meeting Ali in the hallway. She carried a plate of hors d'oeuvres.

'Everything's ready. We can eat whenever we want, so I'll sit down for a while . . . Get me a drink, will you, dear?'

'Sure. Joe and Betty are here.'

Ali laughed. 'I gathered that . . . What's the matter, darling? You look funny.'

'No, nothing. I was just thinking I'd better call the studio.'

Ali looked at her husband. 'Please. Everybody's here now. Our best friends. Let's have fun. Forget about Wednesday, *please*, Johnny.'

Tanner leaned over the tray of hors d'oeuvres and kissed her. 'You're dramatizing,' he said, remembering Fassett's admonition. 'I really do have to call the studio.'

In the kitchen, Tanner walked again to the window. It was a little after seven o'clock and the sun had gone down behind the tall trees in the woods. Shadows lay across the backyard lawn and the pool. And beyond the shadows were Fassett's men.

That was the important thing.

As Ali had said, they were all there now. The best of friends.

The buffet of curry, with a dozen side dishes, was Ali's usual triumph. The wives asked the usual questions and Ali slightly embossed the culinary answers – as usual. The men fell into the normal arguments about the relative merits of the various baseball teams and, in between, Bernie revealed further the humorous – and extraordinary – working methods of Hollywood television.

While the women cleared out the dining room, Tremayne took the opportunity to press Tanner on the robbery. 'What the hell was it last Wednesday? Level with us. I don't buy the burglary story.'

'Why not?' asked Tanner.

'It doesn't make sense.'

'Nobody uses gas on anybody,' added Cardone. 'Blackjacks, blindfolds, a shot in the head, maybe. Not gas.'

'Advanced thinking, perhaps. I'd rather it was a harmless gas than a blackjack.'

'Johnny.' Osterman lowered his voice and looked toward the dining room. Betty came out the kitchen door and began removing several dishes and smiled. He smiled back. 'Are you working on something that might make you enemies?'

'I imagine I always am in one way or another.'

'I mean something like the San Diego thing.'

Joe Cardone watched Osterman carefully, wondering if he might elaborate. San Diego had been a Mafia operation.

'Not that I know of. I've got men digging in a lot of areas, but nothing

like that. At least I don't think so. Most of my best people have a free rein
. . . Are you trying to tie in Wednesday with something at work?'

'It hadn't struck you?' asked Tremayne.

'Hell, no! I'm a professional newsman. Do you get worried if you're
working on a sticky case?'

'Sometimes.'

'I read about that show of yours last Sunday.' Cardone sat down on the
couch next to Tremayne. 'Ralph Ashton has friends in high places.'

'That's crazy.'

'Not necessarily.' Cardone had trouble with 'necessarily'. 'I've met him.
He's a vindictive man.'

'He's not crazy,' interjected Osterman. 'No, it wouldn't be anything like
that.'

'Why should it be anything, period? Anything but a robbery?' Tanner lit
a cigarette and tried to watch the faces of the three men.

'Because, Goddamn it, it's not a natural way to get robbed,' exclaimed
Cardone.

'Oh?' Tremayne looked at Cardone, sitting next to him on the sofa. 'Are
you an expert on robbery?'

'No more than you are, counselor,' said Joe.

18

There was something artificial about the start of the weekend; Ali felt it.
Perhaps it was that the voices were louder than usual, the laughter more
pronounced.

Usually, when Bernie and Leila arrived, they all began calmly, catching
up with each family's affairs. Conversations about this or that child, this or
that career decision – these always occupied the first few hours. Her husband
called it the Osterman syndrome. Bernie and Leila brought out the best in
all of them. Made them talk, really *talk* with one another.

Yet no one had volunteered a single important personal experience. No
one had brought up a single vital part of their recent lives – except, of
course, the horrible thing on Wednesday afternoon.

On the other hand, Ali realized, she was still concerned about her husband
– concerned about his staying home from the office, his short temper, his
erratic behavior since Wednesday afternoon. Maybe she was imagining
things about everybody else.

The other women had rejoined their husbands; Alice had put away the left-overs. The children were in bed now. And she wouldn't listen to any more talk from Betty or Ginny about maids. She *could* afford a maid! *They* could afford a maid! But she wouldn't *have* one!

Her father had had maids. 'Disciples' he called them. 'Disciples' who cleaned and swept and brought-in and . . .

Her mother had called them 'maids'.

Ali stopped thinking and wondered if she'd had a drink she couldn't handle. She turned on the faucet and dabbed her face with cold water. Joe Cardone walked through the kitchen door.

'The boss-man told me if I wanted a drink, I pour it myself. Don't tell me where, I've been here before.'

'Go right ahead, Joe. Do you see everything you need?'

'Sure do. Lovely gin; beautiful tonic . . . Hey, what's the matter? You been crying?'

'Why should I be? I just splashed water on my face.'

'Your cheeks are all wet.'

'Water on the face does that.'

Joe put down the bottle of tonic and approached her. 'Are you and Johnny in any trouble? . . . This Wednesday afternoon . . . okay, it was a crazy type of robbery, Johnny told me . . . but if it was anything else, you'd let me know, wouldn't you? I mean, if he's playing around with sharks you wouldn't keep it a secret from me, would you?'

'Sharks?'

'Loan-sharks. I've got clients at Standard Mutual. Even a little stock. I know the company . . . You and Johnny live very well, but sixty thousand dollars after taxes isn't that much any more.'

Alice Tanner caught her breath. 'John does very well!'

'That's relative. In my opinion, John's in that big middle mess. He can't take over and he won't let go of his little kingdom to try for anything better. That's his business, and yours. But I want you to tell him for me . . . I'm his friend. His good friend. And I'm clean. Absolutely *clean*. If he needs anything, you tell him to call me, all right?'

'Joe, I'm touched. I really am. But I don't think it's necessary. I don't, really.'

'But you'll tell him?'

'Tell him yourself. John and I have an unspoken pact. We don't discuss his salary any more. Frankly because I agree with you.'

'Then you've got problems.'

'You're not being fair. Problems to you may not be problems for us.'

'I hope you're right. Tell him that, too.' Cardone walked rapidly back to the bar and picked up his glass. Before Ali could speak he walked through the door back into the living room.

Joe was telling her something and she didn't understand.

'Nobody appointed you or any other member of *any* news media to set yourselves up as infallible guardians of the truth! I'm sick and tired of it! I live with it every day.' Tremayne stood in front of the fireplace, his anger obvious to everyone.

'Not infallible, of course not,' answered Tanner. 'But no one gave the courts the right to stop us from looking for information as objectively as we can.'

'When that information is prejudicial to a client *or* his opponent you have no right to make it public. If it's factual, it'll be heard in court. Wait'll the verdict's rendered.'

'That's impossible and you know it.'

Tremayne paused, smiled thinly, and sighed. 'I know I do. Realistically, there's no solution.'

'Are you sure you want to find one?' asked Tanner.

'Of course.'

'Why? The advantage is yours. You win the verdict, fine. If you lose, you claim the court was corrupted by a biased press. You appeal.'

'It's the rare case that's won on appeal,' said Bernard Osterman, sitting on the floor in front of the sofa. 'Even I know that. They get the publicity, but they're rare.'

'Appeals cost money,' added Tremayne with a shrug. 'Most of the time for nothing. Especially corporate appeals.'

'Then force the press to restrain itself when there's a lot of heat. It's simple.' Joe finished his drink and looked pointedly at Tanner.

'It's not simple,' said Leila, sitting in an armchair opposite the sofa. 'It becomes judgment. Who defines restraint? That's what Dick means. There's no clear-cut definition.'

'At the risk of offending my husband, God forbid,' Virginia laughed as she spoke, 'I think an informed public is just as important as an unbiased courtroom. Perhaps they're even connected. I'm on your side, John.'

'Judgment, again,' said her husband. 'It's opinion. What's factual information and what's interpreted information?'

'One's truth,' said Betty off-handedly. She was watching her husband. He was drinking too much.

'Whose truth? Which truth? . . . Let's create a hypothetical situation. Between John and myself. Say I've been working for six months on a complicated merger. As an ethical attorney I'm dealing with men whose cause I believe in; by putting together a number of companies thousands of jobs are saved, firms which are going bankrupt suddenly have new lives. Then along come several people who are getting hurt – because of their own ineptness – and start shouting for injunctions. Suppose they reach John and start yelling "Foul!" Because they seem – seem, mind you – like underdogs, John gives their cause one *minute*, just one *minute* of network time across the country. Instantly my case is prejudiced. And don't let anyone tell you the courts aren't subject to media pressure. One *minute* as opposed to *six months*.'

'Do you think I'd allow that? Do you think any of us would?'

'You need copy. You always need copy! There are times when you don't understand!' Tremayne's voice grew louder.

Virginia stood up. 'Our John wouldn't do that, darling . . . I'm for another cup of coffee.'

'I'll get it,' said Alice, rising from the sofa. She'd been watching Tremayne, startled by his sudden vehemence.

'Don't be silly,' answered Ginny, going into the hallway.

'I'd like a drink.' Cardone held out his glass, expecting someone to take it.

'Sure, Joe.' Tanner took his glass. 'Gin and tonic?'

'That's what I've been drinking.'

'Too much of,' added his wife.

Tanner walked into the kitchen and began making Cardone's drink. Ginny was at the stove.

'I'm heating the Chemex; the candle burned out.'

'Thanks.'

'I always have the same problem. The damn candles go out and the coffee's cold.'

Tanner chuckled and poured the tonic. Then he realized that Ginny was making a comment, a rather unattractive comment. 'I told Ali to get an electric pot, but she refuses.'

'John?'

'Yes?'

'It's a beautiful night. Why don't we all take a swim?'

'Sure. Good idea. I'll backwash the filter. Let me get this to Joe.' Tanner returned to the living room in time to hear the opening bars of 'Tangerine'. Ali had put on an album called 'Hits of Yesterday'.

There were the proper responses, the laughs of recognition.

'Here you are, Joe. Anyone else for anything?'

There was a chorus of no-thanks. Betty had gotten up and was facing Dick Tremayne by the mantel. Tanner thought they looked as though they'd been arguing. Ali was at the stereo showing Bernie the back of the album cover; Leila Osterman sat opposite Cardone, watching him drink his gin and tonic, seemingly annoyed that he drank so quickly.

'Ginny and I are going to backwash the pool. We'll take a swim, okay? You've all got suits here; if not, there're a dozen extras in the garage.'

Dick looked at Tanner. It was a curious look, thought the news editor. 'Don't teach Ginny too much about that damned filter. I'm holding firm. No pool.'

'Why not?' asked Cardone.

'Too many kids around.'

'Build a fence,' said Joe with a degree of disdain.

Tanner started out toward the kitchen and the back door. He heard a sudden burst of laughter behind him, but it wasn't the laughter of people enjoying themselves. It was forced, somehow unkind.

Was Fassett right? Was Omega showing the signs? Were the hostilities slowly coming to the surface?

Outside he walked to the edge of the pool, to the filter box. 'Ginny?'

'I'm over here, by Ali's tomato plants. This stake fell down and I can't retie the vine.'

'Okay.' He turned and walked over to her. 'Which one? I can't see it.'

'Here,' said Ginny, pointing.

Tanner knelt down and saw the stake. It hadn't fallen over, it had been snapped. 'One of the kids must have run through here.' He pulled up the thin broken dowel and placed the tomato vine carefully on the ground. 'I'll fix it tomorrow.'

He got up. Ginny stood very close to him and put her hand on his arm. He realized they couldn't be seen from the house.

'I broke it,' Ginny said.

'Why?'

'I wanted to talk to you. Alone.'

She had undone several buttons of her blouse below the neckline. He could see the swell of her breasts. Tanner wondered if Ginny was drunk. But Ginny never got drunk, or if she did, no one ever knew it.

'What do you want to talk about?'

'Dick, for one thing. I apologize for him. He can become gross . . . rude, when he's upset.'

'Was he rude? Upset? I didn't notice.'

'Of course you did. I was watching you.'

'You were wrong.'

'I don't think so.'

'Let's get the pool done.'

'Wait a minute.' Ginny laughed softly. 'I don't frighten you, do I?'

'My friends don't frighten me,' Tanner said, smiling.

'We know a great deal about each other.'

Tanner watched Ginny's face closely, her eyes, the slight pinching of her lips. He wondered if this was the moment the unbelievable was about to be revealed to him. If it was, he'd help her say it. 'I suppose we always think we know our friends. I sometimes wonder if we ever do.'

'I'm very attracted . . . physically attracted to you. Did you know that?'

'No, I didn't,' said Tanner, surprised.

'It shouldn't bother you. I wouldn't hurt Ali for the world. I don't think physical attraction necessarily means a commitment, do you?'

'Everyone has fantasies.'

'You're sidestepping.'

'I certainly am.'

'I told you, I wouldn't harm your commitments.'

'I'm human. They'd be harmed.'

'I'm human, too. May I kiss you? At least I deserve a kiss.'

Ginny put her arms around the startled Tanner's neck and pressed her lips against his, opening her mouth. Tanner knew she was doing her best to arouse him. He couldn't understand it. If she meant what she was doing, there was nowhere to complete the act.

Then he did understand. She was promising.

She meant that.

'Oh, Johnny! Oh, God, Johnny!'

'All right, Ginny. All right. Don't . . .' Perhaps she really was drunk, thought Tanner. She'd feel like a fool tomorrow. 'We'll talk later.'

Ginny pulled slightly back. Her lips to the side of his. 'Of course, we'll talk later . . . Johnny? . . . Who is Blackstone?'

'Blackstone?'

'Please! I've got to know! Nothing will change, I promise you that! *Who is Blackstone?*'

Tanner held her shoulders, forcing her face in front of his own.

She was crying.

'I don't know any Blackstone.'

'Don't do this!' she whispered. 'Please, for God's sake, don't do this! Tell Blackstone to stop it!'

'Did Dick send you out here?'

'He'd kill me,' she said softly.

'Let me get it straight. You're offering me . . .'

'Anything you want! Just leave him *alone* . . . My husband's a good man. A very, very decent man. He's been a good friend to you! Please, don't hurt him!'

'You love him.'

'More than my life. So please, don't hurt him. And tell Blackstone to stop!'

She rushed off into the garage.

* * *

He wanted to go after her and be kind, but the specter of Omega prevented him. He kept wondering whether Ginny, who was capable of offering herself as a whore, was also capable of things far more dangerous.

But Ginny wasn't a whore. Careless, perhaps, even provocative in a humorous, harmless way, but it had never occurred to Tanner or anybody Tanner knew that she would share her bed with anyone but Dick. She wasn't like that.

Unless she was Omega's whore.

There was the forced laughter again from inside the house. Tanner heard the opening clarinet strains of 'Amapola'. He knelt down and picked the thermometer out of the water.

Suddenly he was aware that he wasn't alone. Leila Osterman was standing several feet behind him on the grass. She'd come outside silently; or perhaps he was too preoccupied to hear the kitchen door or the sound of her footsteps.

'Oh, hi! You startled me.'

'I thought Ginny was helping you.'

'She . . . spilled filter powder on her skirt . . . Look, the temperature's eighty-three. Joe'll say it's too warm.'

'If he can tell.'

'I see what you mean,' said Tanner, getting to his feet, smiling. 'Joe's no drinker.'

'He's trying.'

'Leila, how come you and Bernie got in a couple days ago?'

'He hasn't told you?' Leila was hesitant, seemingly annoyed that the explanation was left to her.

'No. Obviously.'

'He's looking around. He had conferences, lunches.'

'What's he looking for?'

'Oh, projects. You know Bernie; he goes through phases. He never forgets that *The New York Times* once called him exciting . . . or incisive, I never remember which. Unfortunately, he's acquired expensive tastes.'

'You've lost me.'

'He'd like to find a class series; you know, the old Omnibus type. There's a lot of talk around the agencies about upgrading.'

'Is there? I hadn't heard it.'

'You're in news, not programming.'

Tanner took out a pack of cigarettes and offered one to Leila. As he lit it he could see the concern, the strain, in her eyes. 'Bernie has a lot going for him. You and he have made the agencies a great deal of money. He won't have any trouble; he's persuasive as hell.'

'It takes more than persuasion, I'm afraid,' Leila said. 'Unless you want to work for a percentage of nonprofit culture . . . No, it takes influence. Enormous influence; enough to make the money people change their minds.' Leila drew heavily on her cigarette, avoiding Tanner's stare.

'Can he do that?'

'He might be able to. Bernie's word carries more weight than any other writer's on the coast. He has "clout", as they say . . . It extends to New York, take my word for it.'

Tanner found himself not wanting to talk. It hurt too much. Leila had all but told him, he thought. All but proclaimed the power of Omega. Of course Bernie was going to do what he wanted to do. Bernie was perfectly capable of making people change their minds, reverse decisions. Or Omega was, and he was part of it – part of them.

'Yes,' he said softly. 'I'll take your word for it. Bernie's a big man.'

They stood quietly for a moment, then Leila spoke sharply. 'Are you satisfied?'

'What?'

'I asked if you were satisfied. You've just questioned me like a cop. I can even furnish you with a list of his appointments, if you'd like. And there are hairdressers, department stores, shops – I'm sure they'd confirm my having been there.'

'What the hell are you talking about?'

'You know perfectly well! That's not a very nice party in there, in case you haven't noticed. We're all behaving as if we'd never met before, as if we really didn't like our new acquaintances.'

'That has nothing to do with me. Maybe you should look to yourselves.'

'Why?' Leila stepped back. Tanner thought she looked bewildered, but he didn't trust his appraisal. 'Why should we? What *is* it, John?'

'Can't *you* tell *me*?'

'Good Lord, you *are* after him, aren't you? You're after *Bernie*.'

'No, I'm not. I'm not after anyone.'

'You listen to me, John! Bernie would give his life for you! Don't you know that?'

Leila Osterman threw the cigarette on the ground and walked away.

As Tanner was about to carry the chlorine bucket to the garage, Ali came outside with Bernie Osterman. For a moment he wondered whether Leila had said anything. Obviously she hadn't. His wife and Bernie simply wanted to know where he kept the club soda and to tell him that everyone was getting into suits.

Tremayne stood in the kitchen doorway, glass in hand, watching the three of them talking. To Tanner he seemed nervous, uneasy.

Tanner walked into the garage and placed the plastic bucket in the corner next to the garage toilet. It was the coolest place. The kitchen door opened and Tremayne walked down the steps.

'I want to see you a minute.'

'Sure.'

Tremayne turned sideways and slid past the Triumph. 'I never see you driving this.'

'I hate it. Getting in and out of it's murder.'

'You're a big guy.'

'It's a small car.'

'I . . . I wanted to say I'm sorry about that bullshit I was peddling before. I have no argument with you. I got burned on a case several weeks ago by a reporter on *The Wall Street Journal*. Can you imagine? *The Journal*! My firm decided not to go ahead on the strength of it.'

'Free press or fair trial. A damned valid argument. I didn't take it personally.'

Tremayne leaned against the Triumph. He spoke cautiously. 'A couple of hours ago, Bernie asked you – he was talking about last Wednesday – if you were working on anything like that San Diego story. I never knew much about that except that it's still referred to in the newspapers . . .'

'It's been exaggerated out of proportion. A series of waterfront payoffs. Indigenous to the industry, I think.'

'Don't be so modest.'

'I'm not. It was a hell of a job and I damned near got the Pulitzer. It's been responsible for my whole career.'

'All right . . . Fine, good . . . Now, I'm going to stop playing games. Are you digging around something that affects me?'

'Not that I know of . . . It's what I said to Bernie; I've a staff of seventy-odd directly involved with news gathering. I don't ask for daily reports.'

'Are you telling me you don't know what they're doing?'

'I'm better than that,' said Tanner with a short laugh. 'I approve expenditures; nothing is aired without my clearing it.'

Tremayne pushed himself away from the Triumph. 'All right, let's level . . . Ginny came back inside fifteen minutes ago. I've lived with that girl for sixteen years. I know her . . . She'd been crying. She was outside with you and she came back crying. I want to know why.'

'I can't answer you.'

'I think you'd better try! . . . You resent the money I make, don't you?'

'That's not true.'

'Of course it is! You think I haven't heard Ali on your back! And now you subtly, off-handedly drop that nothing is *aired* without your *clearing* it! Is that what you told my wife? Am I supposed to hear the details from *her*? A wife can't testify; are you *protecting* us? What do you *want*?'

'Get hold of yourself! Are you into something so rotten you're getting paranoid? Is that it? You want to tell me about it?'

'No. No! Why was she *crying*?'

'Ask her yourself!'

Tremayne turned away and John Tanner could see the lawyer's body begin to shake as he passed his hands on the hood of the small sports car.

'We've known each other a long time; but you've never understood me at all . . . Don't make judgments unless you understand the men you're judging.'

So this was it, thought Tanner. Tremayne was admitting it. He was part of Omega.

And then Tremayne spoke again and the conclusion was destroyed. He turned around and the look on his face was pathetic.

'I may not be beyond reproach, I know that, but I'm within the law. That's the system. I may not like it all the time, but I respect that *system!*'

Tanner wondered if Fassett's men had placed one of their electronic pick-ups in the garage. If they had heard the words, spoken in such sorrow, with such a ring of truth. He looked at the broken man in front of him.

'Let's go into the kitchen. You need a drink and so do I.'

19

Alice flipped the switch under the living-room windowsill so the music would be heard on the patio speakers. They were all outside now on the pool deck. Even her husband and Dick Tremayne had finally gotten up from the kitchen table; they'd been sitting there for twenty minutes and Ali thought it strange they'd hardly spoken.

'Hello, gracious lady!' The voice was Joe's, and Alice felt herself grow tense. He walked from the hallway into view; he was in swimming trunks. There was something ugly about Joe's body; it dwarfed objects around it. 'You're out of ice, so I made a phone call to get some.'

'At this hour?'

'It's easier than one of us driving.'

'Who'd you call?'

'Rudy at the liquor store.'

'It's closed.'

Cardone walked toward her, weaving a bit. 'I got him at home; he wasn't in bed . . . He does little favors for me. I told him to leave a couple of bags on the front porch and charge it to me.'

'That wasn't necessary. I mean the charging.'

'Every little bit helps.'

'Please.' She walked toward the sofa if for no other reason than to get away from Cardone's gin-laden breath. He followed her.

'Did you think over what I told you?'

'You're very generous, but we don't need any help.'

'Is that what John said?'

'It's what he *would* say.'

'Then you haven't talked to him?'

'No.'

Cardone took her hand gently. She instinctively tried to pull it away, but he held it – firmly, with no trace of hostility, only warmth; but he held it nevertheless. 'I may be a little loaded but I want you to take me seriously . . . I've been a lucky man; it hasn't been hard at all, not really . . . Frankly, I even feel a little guilty, you know what I mean? I admire Johnny. I think the world of him because he *contributes* . . . I don't contribute much; I just take. I don't hurt anybody, but I take . . . You'd make me feel better if you'd let me *give* . . . for a change.'

He let her hand go and because she didn't expect it, her forearm snapped back against her waist. She was momentarily embarrassed. And perplexed. 'Why are you so determined to give us something? What brought it up?'

Cardone sat down heavily on the arm of the couch. 'You hear things. Rumors, gossip, maybe.'

'About us? About us and money?'

'Sort of.'

'Well, it's not true. It's simply not true.'

'Then let's put it another way. Three years ago when Dick and Ginny and Bernie and Leila went skiing with us at Gstaad, you and Johnny didn't want to go. Isn't that right?'

Alice blinked, trying to follow Joe's logic. 'Yes, I remember. We thought we'd rather take the children to Nassau.'

'But now John's very interested in Switzerland, isn't that right?' Joe's body was swaying slightly.

'Not that I know of. He hasn't told me about it.'

'Then if it's not Switzerland, maybe it's Italy. Maybe he's interested in Sicily; it's a very interesting place.'

'I simply don't understand you.'

Cardone got off the arm of the couch and steadied himself. 'You and I aren't so very different, are we? I mean, what credentials we have weren't exactly handed to us, were they? . . . We've earned them, after our own Goddamn fashion . . .'

'I think that's insulting.'

'I'm sorry, I don't mean to be insulting . . . I just want to be honest, and honesty starts with where you are . . . where you were.'

'You're drunk.'

'I certainly am. I'm drunk and I'm nervous. Lousy combination . . . You talk to John. You tell him to see me tomorrow or the next day. You tell him not to worry about Switzerland or Italy, all right? You tell him, no matter what, that I'm clean and I like people who contribute but don't hurt other people . . . That I'll pay.'

Cardone took two steps toward Ali and grabbed her left hand. Gently but insistently, he brought it to his lips, eyes closed, and kissed her palm. Ali had seen that type of kiss before; in her childhood she'd seen her father's fanatical adherents do the same. Then Joe turned and staggered into the hallway.

At the window a shifting of light, a reflection, a change of brightness caught Ali's eye. She turned her head. What she saw caused her to freeze. Outside on the lawn, no more than six feet from the glass, stood Betty Cardone in a white bathing suit, washed in the blue-green light of the swimming pool.

Betty had seen what had happened between Alice and her husband. Her eyes told Ali that.

Joe's wife stared through the window and her look was cruel.

The full tones of the young Sinatra filled the warm summer night as the four couples sat around the pool. Individually – it seemed never by twos to John Tanner – one or another would slip into the water and paddle lazily back and forth.

The women talked of schools and children while the men, on the opposite side of the deck, spoke less quietly of the market, politics, an inscrutable economy.

Tanner sat on the base of the diving board near Joe. He'd never seen him so drunk, and he bore watching. If any or all around the deck were part of Omega, Joe was the weakest link. He'd be the first to break.

Small arguments flared up, quickly subsiding. At one point, Joe's voice was loud and Betty reacted swiftly but quietly.

'You're drunk, husband-mine. Watch out.'

'Joe's all right, Betty,' said Bernie, clapping Cardone's knee. 'It was rotten-hot in New York today, remember?'

'You were in New York, too, Bernie,' answered Ginny Tremayne, stretching her legs over the side of the pool. 'Was it really that rotten-hot?'

'Rotten-hot, sweetheart.' It was Dick who spoke across the water to his wife.

Tanner saw Osterman and Tremayne exchange glances. Their unspoken communication referred to Cardone but it was not meant that he, Tanner, should understand or even notice. Then Dick got up and asked who'd like refills.

Only Joe answered yes.

'I'll get it,' said Tanner.

'Hell, no,' replied Dick. 'You watch the ballplayer. I want to call the kid anyway. We told her to be back by one; it's damn near two. These days you have to check.'

'You're a mean father,' said Leila.

'So long as I'm not a grandfather.' Tremayne walked across the grass to the kitchen door.

There was silence for several seconds, then the girls took up their relaxed conversation and Bernie lowered himself over the side into the pool.

Joe Cardone and Tanner did not speak.

Several minutes later, Dick came out of the kitchen door carrying two glasses. 'Hey, Ginny! Peg was teed off that I woke her up. What do you think of that?'

'I think she was bored with her date.'

Tremayne approached Cardone and handed him his glass. 'There you are, fullback.'

'I was a Goddamn halfback. I ran circles around your Goddamn Levi Jackson at the Yale Bowl!'

'Sure. But I talked to Levi. He said they could always get you. All they had to do was yell "tomato sauce" and you went for the sidelines!'

'Pretty Goddamn funny! I murdered that black son of a bitch!'

'He speaks well of you, too,' said Bernie, smiling over the side of the pool.

'And I speak well of *you*, Bernie! And big Dick, here!' Cardone clumsily got to his feet. 'I speak well of *all* of you!'

'Hey, Joe . . .' Tanner got off the board.

'Really, Joe, just sit down,' ordered Betty. 'You'll fall over.'

'Da Vinci!'

It was only a name but Cardone shouted it out. And then he shouted it again.

'*Da Vinci* . . .' He drew out the sound, making the dialect sharply Italian.

'What does *that* mean?' asked Tremayne.

'You tell me!' roared Cardone through the tense stillness around the pool.

'He's crazy,' said Leila.

'He's positively drunk, if nobody minds my saying so,' added Ginny.

'Since we can't – at least I can't – tell you what a Da Vinci is, maybe you'll explain.' Bernie spoke lightly.

'Cut it out! Just *cut it out!*' Cardone clenched and reclenched his fists.

Osterman climbed out of the water and approached Joe. His hands hung loosely at his sides. 'Cool it, Joe. Please . . . Cool it.'

'*Zurichchchch!*' The scream from Joe Cardone could be heard for miles, thought Tanner. It was happening! He'd said it!

'What do you mean, Joe?' Tremayne took a halting step toward Cardone.

'*Zurich!* That's what I mean!'

'It's a city in Switzerland! So what the hell else?' Osterman stood facing Cardone; he wasn't about to give quarter. 'You say what you mean!'

'No!' Tremayne took Osterman by the shoulder.

'Don't talk to me,' yelled Cardone. 'You're the one who . . .'

'*Stop it! All of you!*' Betty stood on the concrete deck at the end of the pool. Tanner would never have believed such strength could come from Cardone's wife.

But there it was. The three men parted from one another, as chastised dogs. The women looked up at Betty, and then Leila and Ginny walked away while Ali stood immobile, uncomprehending.

Betty continued, reverting now to the soft, suburban housewife she seemed to be. 'You're all behaving childishly and I know it's time for Joe to go home.'

'I . . . I think we can all have a nightcap, Betty,' said Tanner. 'How about it?'

'Make Joe's light,' answered Betty with a smile.

'No other way,' said Bernie.

'I'll get them.' Tanner started back toward the door. 'Everyone in?'

'Wait a minute, Johnny!' It was Cardone, a wide grin on his face. 'I'm the naughty boy so let me help. Also, I gotta go to the bathroom.'

Tanner went into the kitchen ahead of Cardone. He was confused, bewildered. He had expected that when Joe screamed the name 'Zurich' it would all be over. Zurich was the key that should have triggered the collapse. Yet it did not happen.

Instead, the opposite occurred.

A control was imposed; imposed by the most unlikely source imaginable, Betty Cardone.

Suddenly, from behind him came a crash. Tremayne was standing in the doorway, looking at the fallen Cardone.

'Well. A mountain of Princeton muscle just passed out! . . . Let's get him into my car. I'm chauffeur tonight.'

Passed out? Tanner didn't believe it. Cardone was drunk, yes. But he was nowhere near collapsing.

The three men dressed quickly and manhandled the lurching, incoherent Cardone into the front seat of Tremayne's car. Betty and Ginny were in the back. Tanner kept watching Joe's face, especially the eyes, for any signs of pretense. He could see none. And yet there was something false, he thought; there was too much precision in Cardone's exaggerated movements. Was Joe using silence to test the others, he wondered?

Or were his own observations being warped by the progressive tension?

'Damn it!' exclaimed Tremayne. 'I left my jacket inside.'

'I'll bring it to the Club in the morning,' said John. 'We're scheduled for eleven.'

'No, I'd better get it. I left some notes in the pocket; I may need them . . . Wait here with Bernie. I'll be back in a second.'

Dick ran inside and he grabbed his jacket from a hallway chair. He looked at Leila Osterman, who was polishing the top of a table in the living room.

'If I get these rings now maybe the Tanners'll have some furniture left,' she said.

'Where's Ali?'

'In the kitchen.' Leila continued rubbing the table top.

As Tremayne entered the kitchen, Alice was filling the dishwasher.

'Ali?'

'Oh! . . . Dick. Joe all right?'

'Joe's fine . . . How's John?'

'Isn't he out there with you?'

'I'm in here.'

'It's late; I'm too tired for jokes.'

'I couldn't feel less like joking . . . We've been good friends, Ali. You and Johnny mean a lot to us, to Ginny and me.'

'We feel the same; you know that.'

'I thought I did. I really believed it . . . Listen to me . . .' Tremayne's face was flushed; he swallowed repeatedly, unable to control the pronounced twitch over his left eye. 'Don't make judgments. Don't let John make . . . editorial judgments that hurt people unless he understands why they do what they do.'

'I don't understand what you're – '

'That's very important,' interrupted Tremayne. 'He should try to understand. That's one mistake I never commit in court. I always try to understand.'

Alice recognized the threat. 'I suggest that you say whatever it is you're saying to him.'

'I did and he wouldn't answer me. That's why I'm saying it to you . . . Remember, Ali. No one's ever completely what he seems. Only some of us are more resourceful. Remember that!'

Tremayne turned and left; a second later Ali heard the front door close. As she looked at the empty doorway, she was aware of someone else nearby. There was the unmistakable sound of a quiet footstep. Someone had walked through the dining room and was standing in her pantry, around the corner, out of sight. She walked slowly, silently to the arch. As she turned into the small narrow room she saw Leila standing motionless against the wall, staring straight ahead.

Leila had been listening to the conversation in the kitchen. She gasped when she saw Ali, then laughed with no trace of humor. She knew she'd been caught.

'I came for another cloth.' She held up a dustrag and went back inside the dining room without speaking further.

Alice stood in the center of the pantry wondering what dreadful thing was happening to all of them. Something was affecting the lives of everyone in the house.

They lay in bed; Ali on her back, John on his left side away from her. The Ostermans were across the hall in the guest room. It was the first time they'd been alone together all night.

Alice knew her husband was exhausted but she couldn't postpone the question – or was it a statement – any longer.

'There's some trouble between you and Dick and Joe, isn't there?'

Tanner rolled over; he looked up at the ceiling, almost relieved. He knew the question was coming and he had rehearsed his answer. It was another lie; he was getting used to the lies. But there was so little time left – Fassett had guaranteed that. He began slowly, trying to speak off-handedly.

'You're too damned smart.'

'I am?' She shifted to her side and looked at her husband.

'It's nasty, but it'll pass. You remember my telling you about that stock business Jim Loomis was peddling on the train?'

'Yes. You didn't want Janet to go over for lunch . . . to the Loomis', I mean.'

'That's right . . . Well, Joe and Dick jumped in with Loomis. I told them not to.'

'Why?'

'I checked on it.'

'What?'

'I checked on it . . . We've got a few thousand lying around drawing five percent. I figured why not? So I called Andy Harrison – he's head of Legal at Standard, you met him last Easter. He made inquiries.'

'What did he find out?'

'The whole thing smells. It's a boilerplate operation. It's rotten.'

'Is it illegal?'

'Probably will be by next week . . . Harrison suggested we do a feature on it. Make a hell of a show. I told that to Joe and Dick.'

'Oh, my God! That you'd do a program on it?'

'Don't worry. We're booked for months. There's no priority here. And even if we did, I'd tell them. They could get out in time.'

Ali heard Cardone and Tremayne again: '*Did you speak to him? What did he say?*' '*Don't let Johnny make judgments. . . .*' They had been panicked and now she understood why. 'Joe and Dick are worried sick, you know that, don't you?'

'Yeah. I gathered it.'

'You *gathered* it? For heaven's sake, these are your friends! . . . They're frightened! They're scared to death!'

'Okay. Okay. Tomorrow at the Club, I'll tell them to relax . . . The San Diego vulture isn't vulturing these days.'

'Really, that was cruel! No wonder they're all so upset! They think you're doing something terrible.' Ali recalled Leila's silent figure pressed against the pantry wall, listening to Tremayne alternately pleading and threatening in the kitchen. 'They've told the Ostermans.'

'Are you sure? How?'

'Never mind, it's not important. They must think you're a horror . . . Tomorrow morning, for heaven's sake, tell them not to worry.'

'I said I would.'

'It explains so much. That silly yelling at the pool, the arguments . . . I'm really very angry with you.' But Alice Tanner wasn't angry; the unknown was known to her. She could cope with it. She lay back, still concerned, still worried, but with a degree of calm she hadn't felt for several hours.

Tanner shut his eyes tight, and let his breath out. The lie had gone well. Better than he had thought it would. It was easier for him now, easier to alter the facts.

Fassett had been right, he could manage them all.

Even Ali.

He stood by the bedroom window. There was no moon in the sky, just clouds barely moving. He looked below at the side lawn and the woods beyond, and wondered suddenly if his eyes were playing tricks on him. There was the glow of a cigarette, distinctly seen. Someone was walking and smoking a cigarette in full view! Good Christ! he thought; did whoever it was realize that he was giving away the patrol?

And then he looked more closely. The figure was in a bathrobe. It was Osterman.

Had Bernie seen something? Heard something?

Tanner silently, rapidly went to the bedroom door and let himself out.

'I thought you might be up and around,' said Bernie sitting on a deck chair, looking at the water in the pool. 'This evening was a disaster.'

'I'm not so sure about that.'

'Then I assume you've given up your senses of sight and sound. It was a wet night at Malibu. If we all had had knives that pool would be deep red by now.'

'Your Hollywood mentality's working overtime.' Tanner sat down at the edge of the water.

'I'm a writer. I observe and distill.'

'I think you're wrong,' Tanner said. 'Dick was uptight about business; he told me. Joe got drunk. So what?'

Osterman swung his leg over the deck chair and sat forward. 'You're wondering what I'm doing here . . . It was a hunch, an instinct. I thought you might come down yourself. You didn't look like you could sleep any more than I could.'

'You intrigue me.'

'No jokes. It's time we talk.'

'About what?'

Osterman got up and stood above Tanner. He lit a fresh cigarette with the stub of his first. 'What do you want most? I mean for yourself and your family?'

Tanner couldn't believe he'd heard correctly. Osterman had begun with the tritest introduction imaginable. Still, he answered as though he took the question seriously.

'Peace, I guess. Peace, food, shelter, creature comforts. Are those the key words?'

'You've got all that. For your current purposes, anyway.'

'Then I *really* don't understand you.'

'Has it ever occurred to you that you have no right to select anything any more? Your whole life is programmed to fulfill a predetermined *function*; do you realize that?'

'It's universal, I imagine. I don't argue with it.'

'You can't argue. The system won't permit it. You're trained for something; you gain experience – that's what you do for the rest of your life. No arguments.'

'I'd be a rotten nuclear physicist; you'd be less than desirable in brain surgery . . .' Tanner said.

'Of course everything's relative; I'm not talking fantasy. I'm saying that we're controlled by forces we can't control any longer. We've reached the age of specialization, and that's the death knell. We live and work within our given circles; we're not allowed to cross the lines, even to look around. You more than me, I'm afraid. At least I have a degree of choice as to which piece of crap I'll handle. But crap, nevertheless . . . We're stifled.'

'I hold my own; I'm not complaining. Also, my risks are pretty well advertised.'

'But you have no back-ups! Nothing! You can't afford to stand up and say *this is me*! Not on the money-line, you can't! Not with *this* to pay for!' Osterman swung his arm to include Tanner's house and grounds.

'Perhaps I can't . . . on the money-line. But who can?'

Osterman drew up the chair and sat down. He held Tanner's eyes with his own and spoke softly. 'There's a way. And I'm willing to help.' He paused for a moment, as if searching for words, then started to speak again. 'Johnny . . .' Osterman stopped once more. Tanner was afraid he wouldn't continue, wouldn't find the courage.

'Go on.'

'I've got to have certain . . . assurances; that's very important!' Osterman spoke rapidly, the words tumbling forth on top of each other.

Suddenly both men's attention was drawn to the house. The light in Janet Tanner's bedroom had gone on.

'What's that?' asked Bernie, not bothering to disguise his apprehension.

'Just Janet. That's her room. We finally got it through her head that when she goes to the bathroom she should turn on the lights. Otherwise she bumps into everything and we're all up for twenty minutes.'

And then it pierced the air. Terrifyingly, with ear-shattering horror. A child's scream.

Tanner raced around the pool and in the kitchen door. The screams continued and lights went on in the other three bedrooms. Bernie Osterman nearly ran up Tanner's back as the two men raced to the little girl's room. Their speed had been such that Ali and Leila were just then coming out of their rooms.

John rushed against the door, not bothering about the doorknob. The door flew open and the four of them ran inside.

The child stood in the center of the room over the body of the Tanners' Welsh terrier. She could not stop screaming.

The dog lay in a pool of blood.

Its head had been severed from its body.

John Tanner picked up his daughter and ran back into the hallway. His mind stopped functioning. There was only the terrifying picture of the body in the woods alternating with the sight of the small dog. And the horrible words of the man in the parking lot at the Howard Johnson's motel.

'A severed head means a massacre.'

He had to get control, he *had* to.

He saw Ali whispering in Janet's ear, rocking her back and forth. He was aware of his son crying several feet away and the outline of Bernie Osterman comforting him.

And then he heard the words from Leila.

'I'll take Janet, Ali. Go to Johnny.'

Tanner leapt to his feet in fury. 'You touch her, I'll *kill* you! Do you hear me, I'll *kill* you!'

'*John!*' Ali yelled at him in disbelief. 'What are you *saying?*'

'*She* was across the hall! Can't you see that? She was *across the hall!*'

Osterman rushed toward Tanner, pushing him back, pinning his shoulders against the wall. Then he slapped him hard across the face.

'That dog's been dead for hours! Now, cut it out!'

For hours. It couldn't be for hours. It had just happened. The lights went on and the head was severed. The little dog's head was cut off . . . And Leila was across the hall. She and Bernie. Omega! A massacre!

Bernie cradled his head. 'I had to hit you. You went a little nuts . . . Come on, now. Pull yourself together. It's terrible, just terrible, I know. I got a daughter.'

Tanner tried to focus. First his eyes, then his thoughts. They were all looking at him, even Raymond, still sobbing by the door of his room.

'Isn't anybody here?' Tanner couldn't help himself. Where were Fassett's men? Where in God's name *were* they?

'Who, darling?' Ali put her arm around his waist in case he fell again.

'Nobody here.' It was a statement said softly.

'*We're* here. And we're calling the police. Right now!' Bernie put Tanner's hand on the staircase railing and walked him downstairs.

Tanner looked at the thin, strong man helping him down the steps. *Didn't Bernie understand? He was Omega. His wife was Omega! He couldn't phone the police!*

'The police? You want the police?'

'I certainly do. If that was a joke, it's the sickest I've ever seen. You're damned right I want them. Don't you?'

'Yes. Of course.'

They reached the living room; Osterman took command.

'Ali, you call the police! If you don't know the number, dial the operator!' And then he went into the kitchen.

Where were Fassett's men?

Alice crossed to the beige telephone behind the sofa. In an instant it was clear she didn't have to dial.

The beam of a searchlight darted back and forth through the front windows and danced against the wall of the living room. Fassett's men had arrived at last.

At the sound of the front door chimes, Tanner wrenched himself off the couch and into the hallway.

'We heard some yelling and saw the light on. Is everything all right?' It was Jenkins and he barely hid his anxiety.

'You're a little late!' Tanner said quietly. 'You'd better come on in! Omega's been here.'

'Take it easy.' Jenkins walked into the hallway, followed by McDermott.

Osterman came out of the kitchen.

'Jesus! You people are fast!'

'Twelve-to-eight shift, sir,' said Jenkins. 'Saw the lights on and people running around. That's unusual at this hour.'

'You're very alert and we're grateful . . .'

'Yes, sir,' Jenkins interrupted and walked into the living room. 'Is anything the matter, Mr Tanner? Can you tell us or would you rather speak privately?'

'There's nothing private here, officer.' Osterman followed the policemen and spoke before Tanner could answer. 'There's a dog upstairs in the first bedroom on the right. It's dead.'

'Oh?' Jenkins was confused. He turned back to Tanner.

'Its head was cut off. Severed. We don't know who did it.'

Jenkins spoke calmly. 'I see . . . We'll take care of it.' He looked over at his partner in the hallway. 'Get the casualty blanket, Mac.'

'Right.' McDermott went back outside.

'May I use your phone?'

'Of course.'

'Captain MacAuliff should be informed. I'll have to call him at home.'

Tanner didn't understand. This wasn't a police matter. It was Omega! What was Jenkins doing? Why was he calling MacAuliff? He should be reaching *Fassett*! MacAuliff was a local police officer; acceptable, perhaps, but fundamentally a political appointment. MacAuliff was responsible to the Saddle Valley town council, not to the United States government. 'Do you think that's necessary? At this hour? I mean, is Captain . . .'

Jenkins cut Tanner off abruptly. 'Captain MacAuliff is the Chief of Police. He'd consider it very abnormal if I didn't report this directly to him.'

In an instant Tanner understood. Jenkins had given him the key.

Whatever happened, whenever it happened, however it happened – there could be no deviation from the norm.

This was the Chasm of Leather.

And it struck Tanner further that Jenkins was making his phone call for the benefit of Bernard and Leila Osterman.

Captain Albert MacAuliff entered the Tanner house and immediately made his authority clear. Tanner watched him deliver his instructions to the police officers, in a low, commanding voice. He was a tall, obese man, with a thick neck which made his shirt collar bulge. His hands were thick, too, but strangely immobile, hanging at his sides as he walked – the mark of a man who'd spent years patrolling a beat on foot, shifting his heavy club from one hand to the other.

MacAuliff had been recruited from the New York police and he was a living example of the right man for the right job. Years ago the town council had gone on record that it wanted a no-nonsense man, someone who'd keep Saddle Valley clear of undesirable elements. And the best defense in these days of permissiveness was offense.

Saddle Valley had wanted a mercenary.

It had hired a bigot.

'All right, Mr Tanner, I'd like a statement. What happened here tonight?'

'We . . . we had a small party for friends.'

'How many?'

'Four couples. Eight people.'

'Any hired help?'

'No . . . No, no help.'

MacAuliff looked at Tanner, putting his notebook at his side. 'No maid?'

'No.'

'Did Mrs Tanner have anyone in during the afternoon? To help out?'

'No.'

'You're sure?'

'Ask her yourself.' Ali was in the study where they'd made makeshift beds for the children.

'It could be important. While you were at work she might have had some coloreds or PR's here.'

Tanner saw Bernie recoil. 'I was home all day.'

'Okay.'

'Captain.' Osterman stepped forward from Leila's side. 'Somebody broke into this house and slit that dog's throat. Isn't it possible that it was a thief? Mr and Mrs Tanner were robbed last Wednesday. Shouldn't we check . . .'

It was as far as he got. MacAuliff looked at the writer and scarcely disguised his contempt. 'I'll handle this, Mr . . .' The Police Chief glanced at his notebook. 'Mr Osterman. I'd like Mr Tanner to explain what happened here tonight. I'd appreciate it if you'd let *him* answer. We'll get to you in good time.'

Tanner kept trying to get Jenkins' attention, but the policeman avoided his eyes. The news director didn't know what to say – or what specifically *not* to say.

'Now then, Mr Tanner.' MacAuliff sat down and returned to his notebook, pencil poised. 'Let's start at the beginning. And don't forget things like deliveries.'

Tanner was about to speak when McDermott's voice could be heard from the second floor.

'Captain! Can I see you a minute? The guest room.'

Without saying anything, Bernie started up the stairs in front of Mac-Auliff, Leila following.

Instantly, Jenkins approached Tanner's chair and bent over. 'I've only got time to say this once. Listen and commit! Don't bring up any Omega business. None of it. Nothing! I couldn't say it before, the Ostermans were hovering over you.'

'Why not? For Christ's sake, this is Omega business! . . . What am I supposed to say? Why shouldn't I?'

'MacAuliff's not one of us. He's not cleared for anything. . . . Just tell him the truth about your party. That's *all!*'

'You mean he doesn't *know*?'

'He doesn't. I told you, he's not cleared.'

'What about the men outside, the patrols in the woods?'

'They're not his men . . . If you bring it up he'll think you're crazy. And the Ostermans will know. If you point at me I'll deny everything you say. You'll look like a psycho.'

'Do you people think that MacAuliff . . .'

'No. He's a good cop. He's also a small-time Napoleon so we can't use him. Not openly. But he's conscientious, he can help us. Get him to find where the Tremaynes and the Cardones went.'

'Cardone was drunk. Tremayne drove them all home.'

'Find out if they *went* straight home. MacAuliff loves interrogations; he'll nail them if they're lying.'

'How can I . . .'

'You're worried about them. That's good enough. And remember, it's nearly over.'

MacAuliff returned. McDermott had 'mistaken' the lateral catch in the guest room window as a possible sign of a break-in.

'All right, Mr Tanner. Let's start with when your guests arrived.'

And so John Tanner, functioning on two levels, related the blurred events of the evening. Bernie and Leila Osterman came downstairs and added very little of consequence. Ali came out of the study and contributed nothing.

'Very well, ladies and gentlemen.' MacAuliff got out of the chair.

'Aren't you going to question the others?' Tanner also rose and faced the police captain.

'I was going to ask you if we could use your telephone. We have procedures.'

'Certainly.'

'Jenkins, call the Cardones. We'll see them first.'

'Yes, sir.'

'What about the Tremaynes?'

'Procedures, Mr Tanner. After we speak to the Cardones we'll call the Tremaynes and *then* see them.'

'That way no one checks with anyone else, right?'

'That's right, Mr Osterman. You familiar with police work?'

'I write your guidelines every week.'

'My husband's a television writer,' said Leila.

'Captain.' Patrolman Jenkins spoke from the telephone. 'The Cardones aren't home. I've got the maid on the line.'

'Call the Tremaynes.'

The group remained silent while Jenkins dialed. After a brief conversation Jenkins put down the telephone.

'Same story, Captain. The daughter says they're not home either.'

Tanner sat up with his wife in the living room. The Ostermans had gone upstairs; the police departed in search of the missing couples. Neither John nor Ali was comfortable. Ali because she had decided in her own mind who had killed the dog, John because he couldn't get out of his mind the implications of the dog's death.

'It was Dick, wasn't it?' Alice asked.

'Dick?'

'He threatened me. He came into the kitchen and threatened me.'

'*Threatened* you?' If that was so, thought Tanner, why hadn't Fassett's men come sooner. 'When? How?'

'When they were leaving . . . I don't mean he threatened me personally. Just generally, all of us.'

'What did he say?' Tanner hoped Fassett's men were listening now. It would be a point he'd bring up later.

'He said you shouldn't make judgments. Editorial judgments.'

'What else?'

'That some . . . some people were more resourceful. That's what he said. That I should remember that people weren't always what they seemed . . . That some were more resourceful than others.'

'He could have meant several things.'

'It must be an awful lot of money.'

'What's a lot of money?'

'Whatever he and Joe are doing with Jim Loomis. The thing you had looked into.'

Oh, God, thought Tanner. The real and the unreal. He'd almost forgotten his lie.

'It's a lot of money,' he said softly, realizing he was on dangerous ground. It would occur to Ali that money itself was insufficient. He tried to anticipate her. 'More than just money, I think. Their reputations could go down the drain.'

Alice stared at the single lighted table lamp. 'Upstairs you . . . you thought Leila had done it, didn't you?'

'I was wrong.'

'She *was* across the hall . . .'

'That wouldn't make any difference; we went over that with MacAuliff.

He agreed. A lot of the blood had dried, congealed. The pup was killed hours ago.'

'I guess you're right.' Ali kept picturing Leila with her back pressed against the wall, staring straight ahead, listening to the conversation in the kitchen.

The clock on the mantel read five-twenty. They had agreed they would sleep in the living room, in front of the study, next to their children.

At five-thirty the telephone rang. MacAuliff had not found the Tremaynes or the Cardones. He told Tanner that he had decided to put out a missing persons bulletin.

'They may have decided to go into town, into New York,' said Tanner quickly. A missing persons bulletin might drive Omega underground, prolong the nightmare. 'Some of those Village spots stay open. Give them more time. They're friends, for heaven's sake!'

'Can't agree. No place stays open after four.'

'They may have decided to go to a hotel.'

'We'll know soon enough. Hotels and hospitals are the first places MPB's go to.'

Tanner's mind raced. 'You've searched the surrounding towns? I know a few private clubs . . .'

'So do we. Checked out.'

Tanner knew he had to think of something. Anything that would give Fassett enough time to control the situation. Fassett's men were listening on the line, there was no question about that; they'd see the danger instantly.

'Have you searched the area around the old depot? The one on Lassiter Road?'

'Who the hell would go out there? What for?'

'I found my wife and children there on Wednesday. Just a thought.'

The hint worked. 'Call you back,' MacAuliff said. 'I'll check that out.'

As he hung up the telephone, Ali spoke. 'No sign?'

'No . . . Honey, try to get some rest. I know of a couple of places – clubs – the police may not know about. I'll try them. I'll use the kitchen phone. I don't want to wake the kids.'

Fassett answered the phone quickly.

'It's Tanner. Do you know what's happened?'

'Yes. That was damned good thinking. You're hired.'

'That's the last thing I want. What are you going to do? You can't have an interstate search.'

'We know. Cole and Jenkins are in touch. We'll intercept.'

'And then what?'

'There are several alternate moves. I don't have time to explain. Also, I need this line. Thanks, again.' Fassett hung up.

'Tried two places,' said Tanner, coming back into the living room. 'No luck . . . Let's try to get some sleep. They probably found a party and dropped in. Lord knows we've done that.'

'Not in years,' said Ali.

Both of them pretended to sleep. The tick of the clock was like a metronome, hypnotic, exasperating. Finally, Tanner realized his wife was asleep. He closed his eyes, feeling the heavy weight of his lids, aware of the complete blackness in front of his mind. But his hearing would not rest. At six-forty he heard the sound of a car. It came from in front of his house. Tanner got out of the chair and went quickly to the window. MacAuliff walked up the path, and he was alone. Tanner went out to meet him.

'My wife's asleep. I don't want to wake her.'

'Doesn't matter,' said MacAuliff ominously. 'My business is with you.'

'What?'

'The Cardones and the Tremaynes were rendered unconscious by a massive dose of ether. They were left in their car off the road by the Lassiter depot. Now I want to know why you sent us there. How did you know?'

Tanner could only stare at MacAuliff in silence.

'Your answer?'

'So help me, I didn't know! I didn't know *anything* . . . I'll never forget Wednesday afternoon as long as I live. Neither would you if you were me. The depot just came to mind, I *swear* it!'

'It's one hell of a coincidence, isn't it?'

'Look, if I *had* known I would have told you hours ago! I wouldn't put my wife through this. For Christ's sake, be reasonable!'

MacAuliff looked at him questioningly. Tanner pressed on. 'How did it happen? What did they say? Where are they?'

'They're down at the Ridge Park Hospital. They won't be released until tomorrow morning at the earliest.'

'You must have talked with them.'

According to Tremayne, MacAuliff said, the four of them had driven down Orchard Drive less than half a mile when they saw a red flare in the road and an automobile parked on the shoulder. A man waved them down; a well-dressed man who looked like any resident of Saddle Valley. Only he wasn't. He'd been visiting friends and was on his way back to Westchester. His car had suddenly developed engine trouble and he was stuck. Tremayne offered to drive the man back to his friends' house. The man accepted.

That was the last Tremayne and the two wives remembered. Apparently Cardone had been unconscious throughout the incident.

At the deserted depot the police found an unmarked aerosol can on the floor of Tremayne's car. It would be examined in the morning, but MacAuliff had no doubt it was ether.

'There must be a connection with last Wednesday,' said Tanner.

'It's the obvious conclusion. Still, anyone who knows this neck of the woods knows that the old depot area is deserted. Especially anyone who read the papers or heard about Wednesday afternoon.'

'I suppose so. Were they robbed . . . too?'

'Not of money, or wallets or jewelry. Tremayne said he was missing some papers from his coat. He was very upset.'

'Papers?' Tanner remembered the lawyer saying he had left some notes in his jacket. Notes that he might need. 'Did he say which papers?'

'Not directly. He was hysterical – didn't make too much sense. He kept repeating the name "Zurich".'

John held his breath and, as he had learned to do, tensed the muscles of his stomach, trying with all his strength to suppress his surprise. It was so like Tremayne to arrive with written-down, pertinent data concerning the Zurich accounts. If there had been a confrontation, he was armed with the facts.

MacAuliff caught Tanner's reaction. 'Does Zurich mean something to you?'

'No, why should it?'

'You always answer a question with a question?'

'At the risk of offending you again, am I being officially questioned?'

'You certainly are.'

'Then, no. The name Zurich means nothing to me. I can't imagine why he'd say it. Of course, his law firm is international.'

MacAuliff made no attempt to conceal his anger. 'I don't know what's going on, but I'll tell you this much. I'm an experienced police officer and I've had some of the toughest beats a man can have. When I took this job I gave my word I'd keep this town clean. I meant that.'

Tanner was tired of him. 'I'm sure you did, Captain. I'm sure you always mean what you say.' He turned his back and started for the house.

It was MacAuliff's turn to be stunned. The suspect was walking away and there was nothing Saddle Valley's Police Chief could do about it.

Tanner stood on his front porch and watched MacAuliff drive off. The sky was brighter but there'd be no sun. The clouds were low, the rain would come, but not for a while.

No matter. Nothing mattered. It was over for him.

The covenant was broken now. The contract between John Tanner and Laurence Fassett was void.

For Fassett's guarantee had proven false. Omega did not stop with the

Tremaynes, the Cardones and the Ostermans. It went beyond the constituency of the weekend.

He was willing to play – *had* to play – under Fassett's rules as long as the other players were the men and women he knew.

Not now.

There was someone else now – someone who could stop a car on a dark road in the early morning hours and create terror.

Someone he didn't know. He couldn't accept that.

Tanner waited until noon before heading toward the woods. The Ostermans had decided to take a nap around eleven-thirty and it was a good time to suggest the same to Ali. They were all exhausted. The children were in the study watching the Saturday morning cartoons.

He walked casually around the pool, holding a six iron, pretending to practice his swing, but actually observing the windows on the rear of the house: the two children's rooms and the upstairs bathroom.

He approached the edge of the woods and lit a cigarette.

No one acknowledged his presence. There was no sign, nothing but silence from the small forest. Tanner spoke softly.

'I'd like to reach Fassett. Please answer. It's an emergency.'

He swung his golf club as he said the words.

'I repeat! It's urgent I talk with Fassett! Someone say where you are!'

Still no answer.

Tanner turned, made an improvised gesture toward nothing, and entered the woods. Once in the tall foliage he used his elbows and arms to push deeper into the small forest, toward the tree where Jenkins had gone for the portable radio.

No one!

He walked north; kicking, slashing, searching. Finally he reached the road.

There was no one there! No one was guarding his house! No one was watching the island!

No one!

Fassett's men were gone!

He raced from the road, skirting the edge of the woods, watching the windows fifty yards away on the front of his house.

Fassett's men were gone!

He ran across the back lawn, rounded the pool and let himself into the kitchen. Once inside he stopped at the sink for breath and turned on the cold water. He splashed it in his face and then stood up and arched his back, trying to find a moment of sanity.

No one! No one was guarding his house. No one guarding his wife and his children!

He turned off the water and then decided to let it run slowly, covering whatever footsteps he made. He walked through the kitchen door, hearing the laughter of his children from the study. Going upstairs, he silently turned the knob of his bedroom door. Ali was lying on top of their bed, her bathrobe fallen away, her nightgown rumpled. She was breathing deeply, steadily, asleep.

He closed the door and listened for any sound from the guest room. There was none.

He went back down into the kitchen, closed the door and walked through the archway into the small pantry to make sure that, too, was shut.

He returned to the telephone on the kitchen wall, lifting the receiver. He did not dial.

'Fassett! If you or any of your men are on this line, cut in and acknowledge! And I mean *now!*'

The dial tone continued; Tanner listened for the slightest break in the circuit.

There was none.

He dialed the motel. 'Room twenty-two, please.'

'I'm sorry, sir. Room twenty-two is not occupied.'

'Not occupied? You're wrong! I spoke to the party at five o'clock this morning!'

'I'm sorry, sir. They checked out.'

Tanner replaced the receiver, staring at it in disbelief.

The New York number! The emergency number!

He picked up the telephone, trying to keep his hand from trembling.

The beep of a recording preceded the flat-toned voice.

'The number you have reached is not in service. Please check the directory for the correct number. This is a recording. The number you have reached . . .'

John Tanner closed his eyes. It was inconceivable! Fassett couldn't be reached! Fassett's men had disappeared!

He was alone!

He tried to think. He *had* to think. Fassett had to be found! Some gargantuan error had taken place. The cold, professional government man with his myriad ruses and artifices had made some horrible mistake.

Yet Fassett's men were gone. Perhaps there was no mistake at all.

Tanner suddenly remembered that he, too, had resources. There existed for Standard Mutual Network necessary links to certain government agencies. He dialed Connecticut information and got the Greenwich number of Andrew Harrison, head of Standard's legal department.

'Hello, Andy? . . . John Tanner.' He tried to sound as composed as possible. 'Sorry as hell to bother you at home but the Asian Bureau just called. There's a story out of Hong Kong I want to clear . . . I'd rather not go into it now, I'll tell you Monday morning. It may be nothing, but I'd rather check . . . I guess CIA would be best. It's that kind of thing. They've cooperated with us before . . . Okay, I'll hold on.' The news editor cupped the telephone under his chin and lit a cigarette. Harrison came back with a number and Tanner wrote it down. 'That's Virginia, isn't it? . . . Thanks very much, Andy. I'll see you Monday morning.'

Once more he dialed.

'Central Intelligence. Mr Andrews' office.' It was a male voice.

'My name is Tanner. John Tanner. Director of News for Standard Mutual in New York.'

'Yes, Mr Tanner? Are you calling Mr Andrews?'

'Yes. Yes, I guess I am.'

'I'm sorry, he's not in today. May I help you?'

'Actually, I'm trying to locate Laurence Fassett.'

'Who?'

'Fassett. Laurence Fassett. He's with your agency. It's urgent I speak with him. I believe he's in the New York area.'

'Is he connected with this department?'

'I don't know. I only know he's with the Central Intelligence Agency. I told you, it's urgent! An emergency, to be exact!' Tanner was beginning to perspire. This was no time to be talking to a clerk.

'All right, Mr Tanner. I'll check our directory and locate him. Be right back.'

It was a full two minutes before he returned. The voice was hesitant but very precise.

'Are you sure you have the right name?'

'Of course I am.'

'I'm sorry, but there's no Laurence Fassett listed with the switchboard or in any index.'

'That's impossible! . . . Look, I've been working with Fassett! . . . Let me talk with your superior.' Tanner remembered how Fassett, even Jenkins, kept referring to those who had been 'cleared' for Omega.

'I don't think you understand, Mr Tanner. This is a priority office. You called for my associate . . . my subordinate, if you like. My name is Dwight. Mr Andrews refers decisions of this office to me.'

'I don't care who you are! I'm telling you this is an emergency! I think you'd better reach someone in much higher authority than yourself, Mr Dwight. I can't put it plainer. That's *all*! Do it *now*! I'll hold on!'

'Very well. It may take a few minutes . . .'

'I'll hold.'

It took seven minutes, an eternity of strain for Tanner, before Dwight returned to the line.

'Mr Tanner, I took the liberty of checking your own position so I assume you're responsible. However, I can assure you you've been misled. There's no Laurence Fassett with the Central Intelligence Agency. There never has been.'

23

Tanner hung up the telephone and supported himself on the edge of the sink. He pushed himself off and walked mindlessly out the kitchen door onto the backyard patio. The sky was dark. A breeze rustled the trees and caused ripples on the surface of the pool. There was going to be a storm, thought Tanner, as he looked up at the clouds. A July thunderstorm was closing in.

Omega was closing in.

With or without Fassett, Omega was real, that much was clear to Tanner. It was real because he had seen and sensed its power, the force it generated, capable of removing a Laurence Fassett, of manipulating the decisions and the personnel of the country's prime intelligence agency.

Tanner knew there was no point trying to reach Jenkins. What had Jenkins said in the living room during the early morning hours? . . . 'If you point at me, I'll deny everything . . .' If Omega could silence Fassett, silencing Jenkins would be like breaking a toy.

There had to be a starting point, a springboard that could propel him backward through the lies. He didn't care any longer; it just had to end, his family kept safe. It wasn't his war any more. His only concern was Ali and the children.

Tanner saw the figure of Osterman through the kitchen window.

That was it! Osterman was his point of departure, his break with Omega! He walked quickly back inside.

Leila sat at the table while Bernie stood by the stove boiling water for coffee.

'We're leaving,' Bernie said. 'Our bag's packed; I'll call for a taxi.'

'Why?'

'Something's terribly wrong,' said Leila, 'and it's none of our business. We're not involved and we don't care to be.'

'That's what I want to talk to you about. Both of you.'

Bernie and Leila exchanged looks.

'Go ahead,' said Bernie.

'Not here. Outside.'

'Why outside?'

'I don't want Ali to hear.'

'She's asleep.'

'It's got to be outside.'

The three of them walked past the pool to the rear of the lawn. Tanner turned and faced them.

'You don't have to lie any more. Either of you. I just want my part over with. I've stopped caring.' He paused for a moment. 'I know about Omega.'

'About what?' asked Leila.

'Omega . . . Omega!' Tanner's voice – his whisper – was pained. 'I don't *care*! So help me *God*, I *don't care*!'

'What are you talking about?' Bernie watched the news director, taking a step toward him. Tanner backed away. 'What's the matter?'

'For God's sake, don't do this!'

'Don't do what?'

'I told you! It doesn't make any difference to me! Just please! *Please!* Leave Ali and the kids alone. Do whatever you want with me! . . . Just leave *them* alone!'

Leila reached out and put her hand on Tanner's arm. 'You're hysterical, Johnny. I don't know what you're talking about.'

Tanner looked down at Leila's hand and blinked back his tears. 'How can you do this? Please! Don't lie any longer. I don't think I could stand that.'

'Lie about what?'

'You never heard about any bank accounts in Switzerland? In Zurich?'

Leila withdrew her hand and the Ostermans stood motionless. Finally, Bernie spoke quietly. 'Yes, I've heard of bank accounts in Zurich. We've got a couple.'

Leila looked at her husband.

'Where did you get the money?'

'We make a great deal of money,' answered Bernie cautiously. 'You know that. If it would ease whatever's troubling you, why don't you call our accountant. You've met Ed Marcum. There's no one better . . . or cleaner . . . in California.'

Tanner was confused. The simplicity of Osterman's reply puzzled him; it was so natural. 'The Cardones, the Tremaynes. They've got Zurich accounts, too?'

'I guess they have. So do fifty percent of the people I know on the coast.'

'Where did they get the money?'

'Why don't you ask them?' Osterman kept his voice quiet.

'*You* know!'

'You're being foolish,' said Leila. 'Both Dick and Joe are very successful men. Joe probably more than any of us.'

'But why *Zurich*? *What's in Zurich*?'

'A degree of freedom,' answered Bernie softly.

'That's it! That's what you were selling last night! "What do you want most?", you said. Those were your words!'

'There's a great deal of money to be made in Zurich, I won't deny that.'

'*With Omega*! That's how you make it, *isn't it? Isn't it?*'

'I don't know what that means,' said Bernie, now apprehensive himself.

'*Dick* and *Joe*! They're with *Omega*! So are *you*! The "Chasm of Leather"! Information for Zurich! *Money for information!*'

Leila grabbed her husband's hand. 'The phone calls, Bernie! The messages.'

'Leila, please . . . Listen, Johnny. I swear to you I don't know what you're talking about. Last night I offered to help you and I meant it. There are investments being made; I was offering you money for investments. That's all.'

'Not for information? Not for Omega?'

Leila clutched her husband's hand; Bernie responded by looking at her, silently commanding her to calm herself. He turned back to Tanner. 'I can't imagine any information you might have that I could want. I don't know any Omega. I don't know what it is.'

'Joe knows! Dick knows! They both came to Ali and me! They threatened us.'

'Then I'm no part of them. *We're* no part.'

'Oh, God, Bernie, something happened . . .' Leila couldn't help herself. Bernie reached over and took her in his arms.

'Whatever it is, it hasn't anything to do with us . . . Perhaps you'd better tell us what it's all about. Maybe we can help.'

Tanner watched them, holding each other gently. He wanted to believe them. He wanted friends; he desperately needed allies. And Fassett had said it; not *all* were Omega. 'You *really* don't know, do you? You *don't* know what Omega is. Or what "Chasm of Leather" means.'

'No,' said Leila simply.

Tanner believed them. He had to believe them, for it meant he wasn't alone any more. And so he told them.

Everything.

When he had finished the two writers stood staring at him, saying nothing. It had begun to drizzle lightly but none of them felt the rain. Finally, Bernie spoke.

'And you thought I was talking about . . . *we* had something to do with *this*?' Bernie narrowed his eyes in disbelief. 'My God! It's insane!'

'No, it's not. It's real. I've seen it.'

'You say Ali doesn't know?' asked Leila.

'I was told not to tell her, that's what they *told* me!'

'Who? Someone you can't even reach on the phone? A man Washington doesn't acknowledge? Someone who pumped you full of lies about us?'

'A man was *killed*! My family could have been killed last Wednesday! The Cardones and the Tremaynes were gassed last night!'

Osterman looked at his wife and then back at Tanner.

'*If* they really were gassed,' he said softly.

'You've got to tell Alice.' Leila was emphatic. 'You can't keep it from her any longer.'

'I know. I will.'

'And then we've got to get out of here,' said Osterman.

'Where to?'

'Washington. There are one or two Senators, a couple of Congressmen. They're friends of ours.'

'Bernie's right. We've got friends in Washington.'

The drizzle was beginning to turn into hard rain. 'Let's go inside,' said Leila, touching Tanner's shoulder gently.

'Wait! We can't talk in there. We can't say anything inside the house. It's wired.'

Bernie and Leila Osterman reacted as though they'd been slapped. 'Everywhere?' asked Bernie.

'I'm not sure . . . I'm not sure of anything any more.'

'Then we don't talk inside the house; or if we do we put on a radio loud and whisper.'

Tanner looked at his friends. Thank God! Thank *God*! It was the beginning of his journey back to sanity.

24

In less than an hour the July storm was upon them. The radio reports projected gale force winds; medium-craft warnings were up from Hatteras to Rhode Island, and the Village of Saddle Valley was neither so isolated nor inviolate as to escape the inundation.

Ali awoke with the first thunder and John told her – whispered to her –

through the sound of the loud radios, that they were to be prepared to leave with Bernie and Leila. He held her close to him and begged her not to ask questions, to trust him.

The children were brought into the living room; a television set moved in front of the fireplace. Ali packed two suitcases and placed them beside the garage entrance. Leila boiled eggs and wrapped celery and carrot sticks.

Bernie had said they might not stop driving for an hour or two.

Tanner watched the preparations and his mind went back a quarter of a century.

Evacuation!

The phone rang at two-thirty. It was a suppressed, hysterical Tremayne who – falsely, thought Tanner – recounted the events of the Lassiter depot and made it clear that he and Ginny were too shaken to come over for dinner. The Saturday evening dinner of an Osterman weekend.

'You've got to tell me what's going on!' Alice Tanner spoke to her husband in the pantry. There was a transistor radio at full volume and she tried to turn it down. He held her hand, preventing her, and pulled her to him.

'Trust me. Please *trust* me,' he whispered. 'I'll explain in the car.'

'In the car?' Ali's eyes widened in fright as she brought her hand to her mouth. 'Oh, my God! What you're saying is . . . you *can't* talk.'

'Trust me.' Tanner walked into the kitchen and spoke, gestured really, to Bernie. 'Let's load.' They went for the suitcases.

When Tanner and Osterman returned from the garage, Leila was at the kitchen window looking out on the backyard. 'It's becoming a regular gale out there.'

The phone rang and Tanner answered it.

Cardone was an angry man. He swore and swore again that he'd rip apart and rip apart once more the son of a bitch who'd gassed them. He was also confused, completely bewildered. His watch was worth eight hundred dollars and it wasn't taken. He'd had a couple of hundred in his wallet and it was left intact.

'The police said Dick had some papers stolen. Something about Zurich, Switzerland.'

There was a sharp intake of breath from Cardone and then silence. When Joe spoke he could hardly be heard. 'That's got nothing to do with *me!*' And then he rapidly told Tanner without much conviction that a call from Philadelphia had warned him that his father might be extremely ill. He and Betty would stay around home. Perhaps they'd see them all on Sunday. Tanner hung up the phone.

'Hey!' Leila was watching something out on the lawn. 'Look at those umbrellas. They're practically blowing away.'

Tanner looked out the window above the sink. The two large table umbrellas were bending under the force of the wind. The cloth of each was straining against the thin metal ribs. Soon they'd rip or invert themselves. Tanner knew it would appear strange if he didn't take care of them. It wouldn't be normal.

'I'll get them down. Take two minutes.'

'Want some help?'

'No sense both of us getting wet.'

'Your raincoat's in the hall closet.'

The wind was strong, the rain came down in torrents. He shielded his face with his hands and fought his way to the farthest table. He reached up under the flapping cloth and felt his fingers on the metal hasp. He started to push it in.

There was a shattering sound on the top of the wrought iron table. Pieces of metal flew up, searing his arm. Another report. Fragments of cement at his feet bounced off the base of the table. And then another shot, now on his other side.

Tanner flung himself under the metal table, crouching to the far side, away from the direction of the bullets.

Shots came in rapid succession, all around him, kicking up particles of metal and stone.

He started to crawl backwards onto the grass but the small eruptions of wet dirt paralysed him. He grabbed for a chair and held it, clutched it in front of him as though it were the last threads of a disintegrating rope and he were high above a chasm. He froze in panic, awaiting his death.

'Let go! Goddamn it! Let go!'

Osterman was pulling at him, slapping him in the face and wrenching his arms from the chair. They scrambled back toward the house; bullets thumped into the wooden shingles.

'Stay away! Stay away from the door!' Bernie screamed. But he wasn't in time, or his wife would not heed the command. Leila opened the door and Bernie Osterman threw Tanner inside, jumping on top of him as he did so. Leila crouched below the window and slammed the door shut.

The firing stopped.

Ali rushed to her husband and turned him over, cradling his head, wincing at the blood on his bare arms.

'Are you hit?' yelled Bernie.

'No . . . no, I'm all right.'

'You're not all right! Oh, God! Look at his arms!' Ali tried to wipe the blood away with her hand.

'Leila! Find some alcohol! Iodine! Ali, you got iodine?'

Tears were streaming down her cheeks, Alice could not answer the question. Leila grabbed her shoulders and spoke harshly.

'Stop it, Ali! *Stop* it! Where are some bandages, some antiseptic? Johnny needs help!'

'Some spray stuff . . . in the pantry. Cotton, too.' She would not let go of her husband. Leila crept toward the pantry.

Bernie examined Tanner's arms. 'This isn't bad. Just a bunch of scratches. I don't think anything's embedded . . .'

John looked up at Bernie, despising himself. 'You saved my life . . . I don't know what to say.'

'Kiss me on my next birthday . . . Good girl, Leila. Give me that stuff.' Osterman took a medicine can and held the spray steady on Tanner's arms. 'Ali, phone the police! Stay away from the window but get hold of that fat butcher you call a police captain!'

Alice reluctantly let her husband go and crawled past the kitchen sink. She reached up the side of the wall and removed the receiver.

'It's dead.'

Leila gasped. Bernie leapt toward Ali, grabbing the phone from her hand. 'She's right.'

John Tanner turned himself over and pressed his arms against the kitchen tile. He was all right. He could move.

'Let's find out where we stand,' he said slowly.

'What do you mean?' asked Bernie.

'You girls stay down on the floor . . . Bernie, the light switch is next to the telephone. Reach up and turn it on when I count to three.'

'What are you going to do?'

'Just do as I say.'

Tanner crept to the kitchen door, by the bar, and stood up out of sight of the window. The rain, the wind, the intermittent rumble of thunder were the only sounds.

'Ready? I'm going to start counting.'

'What's he going to do?' Ali started up, but Osterman grabbed her and held her to the floor.

'You've been here before, Bernie,' John said. 'Infantry Manual. Heading: Night Patrols. Nothing to worry about. The odds are a thousand to one on my side.'

'Not in any book I know.'

'Shut up! . . . One, two, *three*!'

Osterman flipped the switch and the overhead kitchen light went on. Tanner leapt toward the pantry.

It came. The signal. The sign that the enemy was there.

The shot was heard, the glass shattered, and the bullet smashed into the wall, sending pieces of plaster flying. Osterman turned off the light.

On the floor, John Tanner closed his eyes and spoke quietly. 'So, that's where we stand. The microphones were a lie . . . Everything, a lie.'

'*No! Stay back! Get back!*' screamed Leila before any of them knew what she meant. She lunged, followed by Alice, across the kitchen toward the doorway.

Tanner's children had not heard the shots outside; the sounds of the rain, the thunder, and the television set had covered them. But they'd heard the shot fired into the kitchen. Both women fell on them now, pulling them to the floor, shielding them with their bodies.

'Ali, get them into the dining room! Stay on the floor!' commanded Tanner. 'Bernie, you don't have a gun, do you?'

'Sorry, never owned one.'

'Me neither. Isn't it funny! I've always disapproved of anyone buying a gun. So Goddamned primitive.'

'What are we going to do?' Leila was trying to remain calm.

'We're going to get out of here,' answered Tanner. 'The shots are from the woods. Whoever is firing doesn't know whether we have weapons or not. He's not going to shoot from the front . . . at least I don't think so. Cars pass on Orchard pretty frequently . . . We'll pile into the wagon and get the hell out.'

'I'll open the door,' said Osterman.

'You've been hero enough for one afternoon. It's my turn . . . If we time it right, there's no problem. The door goes up fast.'

They crept into the garage.

The children lay in the back section of the wagon between the suitcases, cramped but protected. Leila and Ali crouched on the floor behind the front seat. Osterman was at the wheel and Tanner stood by the garage door, prepared to pull it up.

'Go ahead. Start it!' He would wait until the engine was full throttle then open the door and jump into the wagon. There were no obstructions. The station wagon would clear the small Triumph and swing around easily for the spurt forward down the driveway.

'Go ahead, Bernie! For Christ's sake, start it!'

Instead, Osterman opened his door and got out. He looked at Tanner.

'It's dead.'

Tanner turned the ignition key on the Triumph. The motor did not respond. Osterman opened the hood of the wagon and beckoned John over. The two men looked at the motor, Tanner holding a match.

Every wire had been cut.

'Does that door open from the outside?' asked Bernie.

'Yes. Unless it's locked.'

'Was it?'

'No.'

'Wouldn't we have heard it open?'

'Probably not with this rain.'

'Then it's possible someone's in here.'

The two men looked over at the small bathroom door. It was closed. The only hiding place in the garage. 'Let's get them out of here,' whispered Tanner.

Ali, Leila, and the two children went back into the house. Bernie and John looked around the walls of the garage for any objects which might serve as weapons. Tanner took a rusty axe; Osterman, a garden fork. Both men approached the closed door.

Tanner signaled Bernie to pull it open. Tanner rushed in, thrusting the blade of the axe in front of him.

It was empty. But on the wall, splotched in black spray paint, was the Greek letter Ω.

25

Tanner ordered them all into the basement. Ali and Leila took the children down the stairs, trying feebly to make a game of it. Tanner stopped Osterman at the staircase door.

'Let's put up a few obstacles, okay?'

'You think it's going to come to that?'

'I just don't want to take chances.'

The two men crept below the sight-lines of the windows and pushed three heavy armchairs, one on top of another, the third on its side, against the front door. Then they crawled to each window, standing out of sight, to make sure the locks were secure.

Tanner, in the kitchen, took a flashlight and put it in his pocket. Together they moved the vinyl table against the outside door. Tanner shoved the aluminum chairs to Osterman, who packed them under the table, one chair rim braced under the doorknob.

'This is no good,' Bernie said. 'You're sealing us up. We should be figuring out how to get away!'

'Have *you* figured that out?'

In the dim light Osterman could see only the outline of Tanner's body. Yet he could sense the desperation in his voice.

'No. No, I haven't. But we've got to *try*!'

'I know. In the meantime we should take every precaution . . . We don't know what's out there. How many or where they are.'

'Let's finish it, then.'

The two men crawled to the far end of the kitchen, beyond the pantry to the garage entrance. The outside garage door had been locked, but for additional security they propped the last kitchen chair under the knob and crept back into the hallway. They picked up their primitive weapons – the axe and the garden fork – and went down into the basement.

The sound of the heavy rain could be heard pounding on the small, rectangular windows, level with the ground outside the cellar. Intermittent flashes of lightning lit up the cinderblock walls.

Tanner spoke. 'It's dry in here. We're safe. Whoever's out there is soaked to the skin, he can't stay there all night . . . It's Saturday. You know how the police cars patrol the roads on weekends. They'll see there are no lights on and come investigate.'

'Why should they?' asked Ali. 'They'll simply think we went out to dinner . . .'

'Not after last night. MacAuliff made it clear he'd keep an eye on the house. His patrol cars can't see through to the back lawn but they'll notice the front. They're bound to . . . Look.' Tanner took his wife's elbow and led her to the single front window just above ground level to the side of the flagstone steps. The rain made rivulets on the panes of glass; it was hard to see. Even the street lamp on Orchard Drive was not always visible. Tanner took the flashlight out of his pocket and motioned Osterman over. 'I was telling Ali, MacAuliff said this morning that he'd have the house watched. He will, too. He doesn't want any more trouble . . . We'll take turns at this window. That way no one's eyes will get tired or start playing tricks. As soon as one of us sees the patrol car, we'll signal up and down with the flashlight. They'll see it. They'll stop.'

'That's good,' said Bernie. 'That's very good! I wish to hell you'd said that upstairs.'

'I wasn't sure. Funny, but I couldn't remember if you could see the street from this window. I've cleaned this basement a hundred times, but I couldn't remember for sure.' He smiled at them.

'I feel better,' said Leila, trying her best to instill John's confidence into the others.

'Ali, you take the first shift. Fifteen minutes apiece. Bernie, you and I will keep moving between the other windows. Leila, sort of stay with Janet, will you?'

'What can I do, Dad?' Raymond asked.

Tanner looked at his son, proud of him.

'Stay at the front window with your mother. You'll be permanent there. Keep watching for the police car.'

Tanner and Osterman paced between the two windows at the rear of the house and the one at the side. In fifteen minutes, Leila relieved Ali at the front window. Ali found an old blanket which she made into a small mattress so Janet could lie down. The boy remained at the window with Leila, peering out, intermittently rubbing his hand on the glass as if the action might wipe away the water outside.

No one spoke; the pounding rain and blasts of wind seemed to increase. It was Bernie's turn at the front. As he took the flashlight from his wife he held her close for several seconds.

Tanner's turn came and went, and Ali once again took her place. None of them said it out loud but they were losing hope. If MacAuliff was patrolling the area, with concentration on the Tanner property, it seemed illogical that a police car hadn't passed in over an hour.

'There it is! There it is, Dad! See the red light?'

Tanner, Bernie and Leila rushed to the window beside Alice and the boy. Ali had turned on the flashlight and was waving it back and forth. The patrol car had slowed down. It was barely moving, yet it did not stop.

'Give me the light!'

Tanner held the beam steady until he could see, dimly but surely, the blurred reflection of the white car through the downpour. Then he moved the beam vertically, rapidly.

Whoever was driving had to be aware of the light. The path of the beam had to cross the driver's window, hit the driver's eyes.

But the patrol car did not stop. It reached the line of the driveway and slowly drove away.

Tanner shut off the flashlight, not wanting to turn around, not wanting to see the faces of the others.

Bernie spoke softly. 'I don't like this.'

'He had to see it. He *had* to!' Ali was holding her son, who was still peering out the window.

'Not necessarily,' lied John Tanner. 'It's a mess out there. His windows are probably just as clouded as ours. Maybe more so. Car windows fog up. He'll be around again. Next time we'll make sure. Next time, I'll run out.'

'How?' asked Bernie. 'You'd never make it in time. We piled furniture in front of the door.'

'I'll get through this window.' Tanner mentally measured the space. It was far too small. How easily the lies came.

'I can crawl out of there, Dad!' The boy was right. It might be necessary to send him.

But he knew he wouldn't. He couldn't.

Whoever was in the patrol car had seen the beam of light and hadn't stopped.

'Let's get back to the windows. Leila, you take over here. Ali, check Janet. I think she's fallen asleep.'

Tanner knew he had to keep them doing something, even if the action meant nothing. Each would have his private thoughts, his private panic.

There was a shattering crack of thunder. A flash of lightning lit up the basement.

'Johnny!' Osterman's face was against the left rear window. 'Come here.'

Tanner ran to Osterman's side and looked out. Through the whipping patterns of the downpour he saw a short, vertical beam of light rising from the ground. It was moving from far back on the lawn, beyond the pool, near the woods. The beam swayed slowly, jerkily. Then a flash of lightning revealed the figure holding the flashlight. Someone was coming toward the house.

'Someone's worried he's going to fall into the pool,' whispered Bernie.

'What is it?' Ali's intense voice came from the makeshift mattress where she sat with her daughter.

'There's somebody out there,' answered Tanner. 'Everybody stay absolutely still . . . It could be . . . all right. It might be the police.'

'Or the person who shot at us! Oh, God!'

'Ssh! Be quiet.'

Leila left the front window and went over to Alice.

'Get your face away from the glass, Bernie.'

'He's getting nearer. He's going around the pool.'

The two men moved back and stood at the side of the window. The man in the downpour wore a large poncho, his head sheltered by a rain hat. He extinguished the light as he approached the house.

Above them, the prisoners could hear the kitchen door rattling, then the sound of a body crashing against the wood. Soon the banging stopped and except for the storm there was silence. The figure left the area of the kitchen door, and Tanner could see from his side of the window the beam of light darting up and down. And then it disappeared around the far end of the house by the garage.

'Bernie!' Leila stood up beside Alice and the child. 'Look! Over there!'

Through her side window came the intermittent shafts of another beam of light. Although it was quite far away, the beam was bright; it danced closer. Whoever was carrying that light was racing toward the house.

Suddenly it went out and again there was only the rain and the lightning. Tanner and Osterman went to the side window, one on each side, and cautiously looked out. They could see no one, no figure, nothing but rain, forced into diagonal sheets by the wind.

There was a loud crash from upstairs. And then another, this one sharper, wood slamming against wood. Tanner went toward the stairs. He had locked the cellar door, but it was thin; a good kick would break it from its hinges. He held the axe level, prepared to swing at anything descending those stairs.

Silence.

There were no more sounds from the house.

Suddenly, Alice Tanner screamed. A large hand was rubbing the pane of glass in the front window. The beam of a powerful flashlight pierced the darkness. Someone was squatting behind the light, the face hidden under a rain hood.

Tanner rushed to his wife and daughter, picking up the child from the blanket.

'Get back! Get back against the wall!'

The glass shattered and flew in all directions under the force of the outsider's boot. The kicking continued. Mud and glass and fragments of wood came flying into the basement. Rain swept through the broken window. The six prisoners huddled by the front wall as the beam of light flashed about the floor, the opposite wall and the stairs.

What followed paralysed them.

The barrel of a rifle appeared at the edge of the window frame and a volley of ear-shattering shots struck the floor and rear wall. Silence. Cinderblock dust whirled about the basement; in the glare of the powerful flashlight it looked like swirling clouds of stone mist. The firing began again, wildly, indiscriminately. The infantryman in Tanner told him what was happening. A second magazine had been inserted into the loading clip of an automatic rifle.

And then another rifle butt smashed the glass of the left rear window directly opposite them. A wide beam of light scanned the row of human beings against the wall. Tanner saw his wife clutching their daughter, shielding the small body with her own, and his mind cracked with fury.

He raced to the window, swinging the axe toward the shattered glass and the crouching figure behind it. The form jumped back; shots pounded into the ceiling above Tanner's head. The shaft of light from the front window caught him now. It's over, Tanner thought. It was going to be over for him. Instead, Bernie was swinging the garden fork at the rifle barrel, deflecting shots away from Tanner. The news director crawled back to his wife and children.

'Get over here!' he yelled, pushing them to the far wall, the garage side of the basement. Janet could not stop screaming.

Bernie grabbed his wife's wrist and pulled her toward the basement corner. The beams of light crisscrossed each other. More shots were fired; dust filled the air; it became impossible to breathe.

The light from the rear window suddenly disappeared; the one from the front continued its awkward search. The second rifle was changing its position. And then from the far side window came another crash and the sound of breaking glass. The wide beam of light shone through again, now blinding them. Tanner shoved his wife and son toward the rear corner next to the stairs. Shots poured in; Tanner could feel the vibration as the bullets spiraled into the wall above and around him.

Crossfire!

He held the axe tightly, then he lunged forward, through the fire, fully understanding that any one bullet might end his life. But none could end it until he reached his target. Nothing could prevent that!

He reached the side window and swung the axe diagonally into it. An anguished scream followed; blood gushed through the opening. Tanner's face and arms were covered with blood.

The rifle in the front window tried to aim in Tanner's direction, but it was impossible. The bullets hit the floor.

Osterman rushed toward the remaining rifle, holding the garden fork at his shoulder. At the last instant he flung it through the outline of the broken glass as if it were a javelin. A cry of pain; the firing stopped.

Tanner supported himself against the wall under the window. In the flashes of lightning he could see the blood rolling down over the cinderblock.

He was alive, and that was remarkable.

He turned and went back toward his wife and children. Ali held the still screaming Janet. The boy had turned his face into the wall and was weeping uncontrollably.

'Leila! Jesus, God! *Leila!*' Bernie's hysterical roar portended the worst. '*Leila, where are you?*'

'I'm here,' Leila said quietly. 'I'm all right, darling.'

Tanner found Leila against the front wall. She had not followed his command to move.

And then Tanner saw something which struck his exhausted mind. Leila wore a large greenish brooch – he hadn't noticed it before. He saw it clearly now, for it shone in the dark. It was iridescent, one of those mod creations sold in fashionable boutiques. It was impossible to miss in the darkness.

A dim flash of lightning lit up the wall around her. Tanner wasn't sure but he was close to being sure: there were no bullet markings near her.

Tanner held his wife and daughter with one arm and cradled his son's head with the other. Bernie ran to Leila and embraced her. The wail of a siren was heard through the sounds of the outside storm, carried by the blasts of wind through the smashed windows.

They remained motionless, spent beyond human endurance. Several minutes later they heard the voices and the knocking upstairs.

'Tanner! Tanner! Open the door!'
He released his wife and son and walked to the broken front window.
'We're here. We're here, you Goddamned filthy pricks.'

26

Tanner had seen these two patrolmen numerous times in the Village, directing traffic and cruising in radio cars, but he didn't know their names. They had been recruited less than a year ago and were younger than Jenkins and McDermott.

Now he attacked. He pushed the first policeman violently against the hallway wall. The blood on his hands was smudged over the officer's raincoat. The second patrolman had dashed down the basement stairs for the others.

'For Christ's sake, let go!'

'You dirty *bastard*! You *fucking punk*! We could have been . . . *would* have been *killed* down there! All of us! My wife! My children! *Why did you do that?* You give me an answer and give it to me quick!'

'Goddamn it, let go! Do *what*? *What* answer, for God's sake?'

'You passed this house a half hour ago! You saw the Goddamn flashlight and you beat it! You raced out of here!'

'You're crazy! Me and Ronnie been in the north end! We got a transmission to get over here not five minutes ago. People named Scanlan reported shots . . .'

'Who's in the other car? I want to know who's in the other *car*!'

'If you'll take your Goddamned hands off me I'll go out and bring in the route sheet. I forget who – but I know *where* they are. They're over on Apple Drive. There was a robbery.'

'The Cardones live on Apple Drive!'

'It wasn't the Cardones' house. I know that one. It was Needham. An old couple.'

Ali came into the hall from the stairs, holding Janet in her arms. The child was retching, gasping for air. Ali was crying softly, rocking her daughter back and forth in her arms.

Their son followed, his face filthy from the dust, smudged with his tears. The Ostermans were next. Bernie held on to Leila's waist, supporting her up the stairs. He held on to her as though he would never let her go.

The second patrolman came slowly through the doorway. His expression startled the other officer.

'Holy Mary Mother of God,' he said softly. 'It's a human slaughterhouse down there . . . I swear to Christ I don't see how any of 'em are alive.'

'Call MacAuliff, Get him over here.'

'The line's dead,' said Tanner, gently leading Ali to the couch in the living room.

'I'll go radio in.' The patrolman named Ronnie went to the front door. 'He won't believe this,' he said quietly.

The remaining patrolman got an armchair for Leila. She collapsed into it and for the first time started to weep. Bernie leaned over behind his wife and caressed her hair. Raymond crouched beside his father, in front of his mother and sister. He was so terrified he could do nothing but stare into his father's face.

The policeman wandered toward the basement stairs. It was obvious he wanted to go down, not only out of curiosity, but because the scene in the living room was somehow so private.

The door opened and the second patrolman leaned in. 'I told Mac. He picked up the radio call on his car frequency. Jesus, you should have heard him. He's on his way.'

'How long will it be?' asked Tanner from the couch.

'Not long, sir. He lives about eight miles out and the roads are rotten. But the way he sounded he'll be here faster than anyone else could.'

'I've stationed a dozen deputies around the grounds and two men in the house. One will stay downstairs, the other in the upper hallway. I don't know what else I can do.' MacAuliff was in the basement with Tanner. The others were upstairs. Tanner wanted the police captain to himself.

'Listen to me! Someone, one of *your* men, passed this house and refused to stop! I know damned well he saw the flashlight! He saw it and drove away!'

'I don't believe that. I checked. Nobody in the cars spotted anything around here. You saw the route sheet. This place is marked for extra concentration.'

'I *saw* the patrol car *leave*! . . . Where's Jenkins? McDermott?'

'It's their day off. I'm thinking of calling them back on duty.'

'It's funny they're off on weekends, isn't it?'

'I alternate my men on weekends. The weekends are very well covered. Just like the council ordered.'

Tanner caught the tone of self-justification in MacAuliff's voice.

'You've got to do one other thing.'

MacAuliff wasn't paying attention. He was inspecting the walls of the cinderblock cage. He stooped his immense frame down and picked up several lead slugs from the floor.

'I want every piece of evidence picked up here and sent down for analysis. I'll use the FBI if Newark can't do it . . . What did you say?'

'I said you've got to do one more thing. It's imperative, but you've got to do it with me alone. Nobody else.'

'What's that?'

'You and I are going to find a phone, and you're going to get on it and make two calls.'

'Who to?' MacAuliff asked the question because Tanner had taken several steps toward the cellar staircase to make sure no one was there.

'The Cardones and the Tremaynes. I want to know where they are. Where they *were*.'

'What the hell . . .'

'Just do as I say!'

'You think . . .'

'I don't think *anything*! I just want to know where they are . . . Let's say I'm still worried about them.' Tanner started for the stairs, but MacAuliff stood motionless in the center of the room.

'Wait a minute! You want me to make the calls and then follow up with verification. Okay, I'll do it . . . Now, it's my turn. You give me a pain. You aggravate my ulcer. What the hell's going on? There's too much crap here to suit me! If you and your friends are in some kind of trouble, come clean and tell me. I can't do a thing if I don't know who to go after. And I'll tell you this,' MacAuliff lowered his voice and pointed his finger at the news director, his other hand on his ulcerated stomach, 'I'm not going to have my record loused up because you play games. I'm not going to have mass homicide on my beat because you don't tell me what I should know so I can prevent it!'

Tanner stood where he was, one foot on the bottom step. He looked and wondered. He could tell in a minute, he thought.

'All right . . . Omega . . . You've heard of Omega?' Tanner stared into MacAuliff's eyes, watching for the slightest betrayal.

'I forgot. You're not cleared for Omega, are you?'

'What the hell are you talking about?'

'Ask Jenkins. Maybe he'll tell you . . . Come on, let's go.'

Three telephone calls were made from MacAuliff's police car. The information received was clear, precise. The Tremaynes and the Cardones were neither at home nor in the vicinity.

The Cardones were in Rockland County, across the New York line. Dining out, the maid said; and if the police officer reached them would he be so kind as to ask them to call home. There was an urgent message from Philadelphia.

The Tremaynes, Virginia sick again, had returned to their doctor in Ridge Park.

The doctor confirmed the Tremaynes' visit to his office. He was quite sure they'd gone into New York City. As a matter of fact, he had prescribed dinner and a show. Mrs Tremayne's relapse was primarily psychological. She had to get her mind on things other than the Lassiter depot.

It was all so specific, thought Tanner. So well established through second and third parties.

Yet neither couple was really accounted for.

For as Tanner reconstructed the events in the basement, he realized that one of the figures intent on killing them could have been a woman.

Fassett had said Omega was killers and fanatics. Men *and* women.

'There's your answer.' MacAuliff's words intruded on Tanner's thoughts. 'We'll check them out when they return. Easy enough to verify whatever they tell us . . . as you know.'

'Yes . . . Yes, of course. You'll call me after you talk to them.'

'I won't promise that. I will if I think you should know.'

The mechanic arrived to repair the automobiles. Tanner took him through the kitchen into the garage and watched the expression on his face as he inspected the severed wires.

'You were right, Mr Tanner. Every lead. I'll splice in temporary connections and we'll make them permanent down at the shop. Somebody played you a rotten joke.'

Back in the kitchen Tanner rejoined his wife and the Ostermans. The children were upstairs in Raymond's room where one of MacAuliff's policemen had volunteered to stay with them, play whatever games they liked, try to keep them calm while the adults talked.

Osterman was adamant. They *had* to get out of Saddle Valley, they had to get to Washington. Once the station wagon was repaired they'd leave, but instead of driving they'd go to Kennedy Airport and take a plane. They'd trust no taxis, no limousines. They'd give MacAuliff no explanations; they'd simply get in the car and go. MacAuliff had no legal right to hold them.

Tanner sat next to Ali, across from the Ostermans, and held her hand. Twice Bernie and Leila had tried to force him to explain everything to his wife and both times Tanner had said he would do so privately.

The Ostermans thought they understood.

Ali didn't and so he held her hand.

And each time Leila spoke Tanner remembered her shining brooch in the darkness of the basement – and the unmarked wall behind her.

The front door chimed and Tanner went to answer it. He came back smiling.

'Sounds from reality. The telephone repair crew.' Tanner did not return to his seat. The blurred outlines of a plan were slowly coming into focus. He'd need Ali.

His wife turned and looked at him, reading his thoughts. 'I'm going up to see the children.'

She left and Tanner walked to the table. He reached down for his pack of cigarettes and put them in his shirt pocket.

'You're going to tell her now?' asked Leila.

'Yes.'

'Tell her everything. Maybe she'll make some sense out of this . . . Omega.' Bernie still looked unbelieving. 'Christ knows, I can't.'

'You saw the mark on the wall.'

Bernie looked strangely at Tanner. 'I saw a mark on the wall.'

'Excuse me, Mr Tanner.' It was the downstairs policeman at the kitchen door. 'The telephone men want to see you. They're in your study.'

'Okay. Be right out.' He turned back to Bernie Osterman. 'To refresh your memory, the mark you saw was the Greek letter Omega.'

He walked rapidly out the kitchen door and went to the study. Outside the windows, the storm clouds hovered, the rain, though letting up, was still strong. It was dark in the room; only the desk lamp was on.

'Mr Tanner.' The voice came from behind and he swung around. There was the man named Cole, dressed in the blue jacket of the telephone company, looking at him intently. Another man stood next to him. 'Please don't raise your voice.'

Tanner's shock was such that he lost control of himself. He lunged at the agent. 'You son of a bitch . . .'

He was stopped by both men. They held his arms tightly behind him, pressed against the small of his back. Cole gripped his shoulders and spoke rapidly, with great intensity.

'Please! We know what you've been through! We can't change that, but we can tell you it's over! It's *over*, Mr Tanner. Omega's cracked!'

'Don't you tell me anything! You bastards! You filthy bastards! You don't exist! They never heard of Fassett! Your phones are disconnected! Your . . .'

'We had to get out fast!' interrupted the agent. 'We had to abandon both posts. It was mandatory. It will all be explained to you.'

'I don't believe a thing you say!'

'Just listen! Make up your mind later, but *listen*. Fassett's not two miles from here putting the last pieces together. He and Washington are closing in. We'll have Omega by morning.'

'What Omega? What Fassett? I called Washington! I talked to McLean, Virginia!'

'You spoke with a man named Dwight. In title, he's Andrews' superior, but not in fact. Dwight was never cleared for Omega. He checked with Clandestine Services, and the call came to the Director. There was no alternative but to deny, Mr Tanner. In these cases we always deny. We *have* to.'

'Where are the guards outside? What happened to all your Goddamned taps? Your shock troops who wouldn't let us be touched?'

'It will all be explained to you . . . I won't lie. Mistakes are made. One massive error, if you like. We can never make up for them, we know that. But we've never been faced with an Omega before. The main point is – the objective is right in front of us. We're on target now!'

'That's horseshit! The *main point* is my wife and children were almost killed!'

'Look. Look at this.' Cole took a small metal disk from his pocket. His colleague let go of Tanner's arms. 'Go on, take it. Look at it closely.'

Tanner took the object in his hand, and turned it to catch the light. He saw that the tiny object was corroded, pockmarked.

'So?'

'That's one of the miniaturized pick-ups. The corrosion is acid. Acid dropped on it, to ruin it. The pick-ups have been messed up in every room. We're not getting any transmissions.'

'How could anyone find them?'

'It's easy enough with the proper equipment. There's no evidence on any of these, no fingerprints. That's Omega, Mr Tanner.'

'Who is it?'

'Even I don't know that. Only Fassett does. He's got everything under control. He's the best man in three continents. If you won't take my word ask the Secretary of State. The President, if you like. Nothing more will happen in this house.'

John Tanner took several deep breaths and looked at the agent. 'You realize you haven't explained anything.'

'I told you. Later.'

'That's not good enough!'

Cole returned Tanner's questioning look. 'What choice have you got?'

'Call that policeman in here and start yelling.'

'What good would that do you? Buy you a couple of hours of peace. How long would it last?'

Tanner would ask him one further question. Whatever the answer, it would make no difference. The plan in John Tanner's mind was crystallizing. But Cole would never know it.

'What's left for me to do?'

'Do nothing. Absolutely nothing.'

'Whenever you people say that, the mortars start pounding the beach.'

'No mortars now. That's over with.'

'I see. It's over with . . . All right. I . . . do . . . nothing. May I go back to my wife now?'

'Of course.'

'Incidentally, is the telephone really fixed?'

'Yes, it is.'

The news editor turned, his arms aching, and walked slowly into the hallway.

No one could be trusted any longer.

He would force Omega's hand himself.

27

Ali sat on the edge of the bed and listened to her husband's story. There were moments when she wondered if he were sane. She knew that men like her husband, men who functioned a great deal of the time under pressure, were subject to breakdowns. She could understand maniacs in the night, lawyers and stockbrokers in the panic of impending destruction, even John's compelling drive to reform the unreformable. Yet what he was telling her now was beyond her comprehension.

'Why did you agree?' she asked him.

'It sounds crazy, but I was trapped. I didn't have a choice. I had to go through with it.'

'You volunteered!' said Ali.

'Not really. Once I agreed to let Fassett reveal the names, I signed an affidavit which made me indictable under the National Security Act. Once I knew who they were I was hung. Fassett knew I would be. It was impossible to continue normal relationships with them. And if I didn't, I might step over the line and be prosecuted.'

'How awful,' said Ali softly.

'Filthy is more to the point.'

He told her about the succeeding episodes with Ginny and Leila outside by the pool. And how Dick Tremayne had followed him into the garage. Finally how Bernie had started to tell him something just before Janet's screams had wakened the household.

'He never told you what it was?'

'He said he was only offering me money for investments. I accused them both of being part of Omega . . . Then he saved my life.'

'No. Wait a minute.' Ali sat forward. 'When you went out for the umbrellas and we all watched you in the rain . . . and then the shots started and we all panicked . . . I tried to go out and Leila and Bernie stopped me. So I screamed and tried to break away. Leila – not Bernie – held me against the wall. Suddenly she looked at Bernie and said, "You can go, Bernie! It's all right, Bernie!" . . . I didn't understand, but she ordered him.'

'A woman doesn't send her husband in front of a firing squad.'

'That's what I wondered about. I wondered if I'd have the courage to send you out . . . for Bernie.'

And so Tanner told his wife about the brooch; and the wall with no bullet marks.

'But they were *in* the basement, darling. They weren't *outside*. They weren't the ones who shot at us.' Ali stopped. The memory of the horror was too much. She couldn't bring herself to speak further of it. Instead, she told him about Joe's hysterics in the living room and the fact that Betty Cardone had watched them through the window.

'So here we are,' he said when she had finished. 'And I'm not sure where that is.'

'But the man downstairs said it would be over. He told you that.'

'They've told me a lot of things . . . But which one is it? Or is it all three?'

'Who?' she asked.

'Omega. It has to be in couples. They have to operate in couples . . . But the Tremaynes and the Cardones were gassed in the car. They *were* left on Lassiter . . . Or were they?'

Tanner put his hands in his pockets and paced the floor. He went to the window and leaned against the sill, looking out on the front lawn.

'There are a lot of cops outside. They're bored to death. I bet they haven't seen the basement. I wonder – '

The glass shattered. Tanner spun around and blood spurted out of his shirt. Ali screamed, running to her husband as he fell to the floor.

More shots were fired but none came through the window. They were outside.

The patrolman in the hallway crashed through the door and raced to the fallen Tanner. No more than three seconds later the downstairs guard rushed into the room, his pistol drawn. Voices were heard yelling outside on the grounds. Leila entered, gasped, and ran to Ali and her fallen husband.

'Bernie! For God's sake, *Bernie!*'

But Osterman did not appear.

'Get him on the bed!' roared the patrolman from the upstairs hallway. 'Please, ma'am, let go! Let me get him on the bed!'

Osterman could be heard yelling on the staircase. 'What the hell happened?' He came into the room. 'Oh, *Jesus*! Oh, Jesus *Christ*!'

Tanner regained consciousness and looked around. MacAuliff stood next to the doctor; Ali sat on the bed. Bernie and Leila were at the footrail, trying to smile at him reassuringly.

'You're going to be fine. Very superficial,' said the doctor. 'Painful, but not serious. Shoulder cartilage, that's what it is.'

'I was shot?'

'You were shot.' MacAuliff agreed.

'Who shot me?'

'We don't know that.' MacAuliff tried to conceal his anger, but it surfaced. The captain was obviously convinced he was being ignored; that vital information was being withheld from him. 'But I tell you this, I intend to question each one of you if it takes all night to find out what's happening here. You're all being damned fools and I won't permit it!'

'The wound is dressed,' said the doctor, putting on his jacket. 'You can get up and around as soon as you feel like it, only take it easy, Mr Tanner. Not much more than a deep cut. Very little loss of blood.' The doctor smiled and left rapidly. He had no reason to remain.

The moment the door was closed, MacAuliff made his abrupt statement. 'Would you all wait downstairs, please? I want to be left alone with Mr Tanner.'

'Captain, he was just shot,' said Bernie firmly. 'You can't question him now; I won't let you.'

'I'm a police officer on official business; I don't need your permission. You heard the doctor. He's not seriously hurt.'

'He's been through enough!' Ali stared at MacAuliff.

'I'm sorry, Mrs Tanner. This is necessary. Now will you all please . . .'

'No, we will *not*!' Osterman left his wife's side and approached the police chief. 'He's not the one who should be questioned. *You* are. Your whole Goddamn police force should be put on the carpet . . . I'd like to know why that patrol car didn't stop, Captain! I heard your explanation and I don't accept it!'

'You continue this, Mr Osterman, I'll call in an officer and have you locked up!'

'I wouldn't try that . . .'

'Don't tempt me! I've dealt with your kind before! I *worked* New York, sheenie!'

Osterman had grown very still. 'What did you say?'

'Don't provoke me. You're provoking me!'

'Forget it!' said Tanner from the bed. 'I don't mind, really.'

Alone with MacAuliff, Tanner sat up. His shoulder hurt, but he could move it freely.

MacAuliff walked to the end of the bed and held the footrail with both hands. He spoke calmly. 'You talk now. You tell me what you know or I'll book you for withholding information in attempted murder.'

'They were trying to kill *me*.'

'That's still murder. M-u-r-d-e-r. It doesn't make any difference whether it's yours or that big Jew bastard's!'

'Why are you so hostile?' Tanner asked. 'Tell me. You should be begging at my feet. I'm a taxpayer and you haven't protected my house.'

MacAuliff made several attempts to speak but he was choking on his own anger. Finally he controlled himself.

'Okay. I know a lot of you don't like the way I run things. You bastards want to put me out and get some fucking hippie from a half-assed law school! Well, the only way you can do that is if I louse up. And I'm not *gonna* louse up! My record stays clean! This town stays clean! So you tell me what's going on and if I need help, I'll call it in! I can't do that without something to go on!'

Tanner rose from the bed, at first unsteadily, and then, to his surprise, firmly.

'I believe you. You're too frantic to lie . . . And you're right. A lot of us *don't* like you. But that may be chemical, so let's let it go . . . Still, I'm not answering questions. Instead, I'm giving you an order. You'll keep this house guarded night and day until I tell you to stop! Do you understand that?'

'I don't *take* orders!'

'You'll take them from me. If you don't, I'll plaster you across sixty million television screens as the typical example of the outdated, uneducated, unenlightened threat to real law enforcement! You're obsolete. Get that pension and run.'

'You couldn't do that . . .'

'Couldn't I? Check around.'

MacAuliff stood facing Tanner. The veins in his neck were so apparent the news director thought they would burst. 'I hate you bastards!' he said coldly. 'I hate your guts.'

'As I do yours . . . I've seen you in action . . . But that doesn't matter now. Sit down.'

Ten minutes later MacAuliff rushed out of the house into the diminishing July storm. He slammed the front door behind him and gave cursory orders to several police deputies on the lawn. The men acknowledged with feeble salutes, and MacAuliff climbed into his car.

Tanner took a shirt from his bureau drawer and awkwardly put it on. He went out of the bedroom and started down the stairs.

Ali was in the hallway talking to the police officer and saw him. She rushed up to meet him on the staircase landing.

'There are police crawling all over the place. I wish it were an army . . . Oh, Lord! I'm trying to be calm. I really am! But I can't!' She embraced him, conscious of the bandage beneath his shirt. 'What are we going to do? Who are we going to *turn* to?'

'Everything's going to be all right . . . We just have to wait a little longer.'

'What for?'

'MacAuliff is getting me information.'

'What information?'

Tanner moved Ali against the wall. He spoke quietly, making sure the policeman wasn't watching them. 'Whoever was outside those basement windows is hurt. One I know is badly wounded – in the leg. The other we can't be sure of, but Bernie thinks he hit him in the shoulder or the chest. MacAuliff's going out to see the Cardones and the Tremaynes. He'll phone me then. It may take quite a while, but he'll get back to me.'

'Did you tell him what to look for?'

'No. Nothing. I simply asked him to follow up their stories about where they were. That's all. I don't want MacAuliff making decisions. That's for Fassett.'

But it wasn't for Fassett, thought Tanner. It wasn't for anyone but him any longer. He'd tell Ali when he had to. At the last minute. So he smiled at her and put his arm around her waist and wished he could be free to love her again.

The telephone rang at ten-forty-seven.

'John? It's Dick. MacAuliff was over to see me.' Tremayne was breathing hard into the telephone, but was keeping his voice reasonably calm. His control was stretched very thin, however.

'. . . I have no idea what you're involved with – intended murder, for God's sake! – and I don't *want* to know, but it's more than I can take! I'm sorry, John, but I'm getting the family out of here. I've got reservations on Pan Am at ten in the morning.'

'Where are you going?'

Tremayne did not reply. Tanner spoke again. 'I asked you where you were going.'

'Sorry, John . . . this may sound rotten, but I don't want to tell you.'

'I think I understand . . . Do us a favor, though. Drop by on the way to the airport.'

'I can't promise that. Good-bye.'

Tanner held his finger down on the phone and then released it. He dialed the Saddle Valley police station.

'Police headquarters. Sergeant Dale.'

'Captain MacAuliff, please. John Tanner calling.'

'He's not here, Mr Tanner.'

'Can you reach him? It's urgent.'

'I can try on the car radio; do you want to hold?'

'No, just have him call me as soon as possible.' Tanner gave his telephone number and hung up. MacAuliff was probably on his way to the Cardones. He should have arrived by now. He'd call soon. Tanner returned to the living room. He wanted to unnerve the Ostermans.

It was part of his plan.

'Who called?' asked Bernie.

'Dick. He heard what happened . . . He's taking the family and leaving.'

The Ostermans exchanged looks.

'Where?'

'He didn't say. They've got a flight in the morning.'

'He didn't say where he was going?' Bernie stood up casually but couldn't hide his anxiety.

'I told you. He wouldn't tell me.'

'That's not what you said.' Osterman looked at Tanner. 'You said "didn't say". That's different from not telling you.'

'I suppose it is . . . You still think we should head down to Washington?'

'What?' Osterman was looking at his wife. He hadn't heard Tanner's question.

'Do you still think we should go to Washington?'

'Yes.' Bernie stared at Tanner. 'Now more than ever. You need protection. Real protection . . . They're trying to kill you, John.'

'I wonder. I wonder if it's me they're trying to kill.'

'What do you mean?' Leila stood up, facing Tanner.

The telephone rang.

Tanner returned quickly to the study and picked up the receiver. It was MacAuliff.

'Listen,' said Tanner quietly. 'I want you to describe exactly – *exactly* – where Tremayne was during your interrogation.'

'In his study.'

'*Where* in his study?'

'At his desk. Why?'

'Did he get up? Did he walk around? To shake your hand, for instance?'

'No . . . No, I don't think so. No, he didn't.'

'What about his wife? She let you in?'

'No. The maid. Tremayne's wife was upstairs. She was sick. We verified that; called the doctor, remember?'

'All right. Now tell me about the Cardones. Where did you find them?'

'Spoke first with his wife. One of the kids let me in. She was lying on the sofa, her husband was in the garage.'

'Where did you talk with him?'

'I just told you. In the garage. I didn't get there too soon either. He's on his way to Philadelphia. His father's sick. They gave him the last rites.'

'Philadelphia? . . . Where exactly was he?'

'In the *garage*, I said! His bags were packed. He was in the car. He told me to be quick. He wanted to take off.'

'He was *in* the car?'

'That's right.'

'Didn't that seem strange to you?'

'Why should it? For Christ's sake, his father's dying! He wanted to get the hell to Philadelphia. I'll check it out.'

Tanner hung up the phone.

Neither couple was seen by MacAuliff under normal conditions. None stood, none walked. Both had reasons not to be at his house on Sunday.

Tremayne behind a desk, frightened, immobile.

Cardone seated in an automobile, anxious only to drive away.

One or both *wounded*.

One or both, perhaps, Omega.

The time had come. Outside the rain had stopped; his traveling would be easier now, although the woods would still be wet.

In the kitchen, he changed into the clothes he'd carried down from the bedroom: black trousers, a black long-sleeved sweater, and sneakers. He put money in his pocket, making sure that his change included at least six dimes. Finally, he clipped a pencil-light to the top of his sweater.

Then he went to the hallway door and called Ali into the kitchen. He dreaded this moment far more than anything which lay before him. Yet there was no other way. He knew he had to tell her.

'What are you doing? Why – '

Tanner held his fingers to his lips and drew her close to him. They had walked to the far end of the kitchen by the garage door, the furthest point from the hallway. He whispered calmly to her.

'Remember I asked you to trust me?'

Ali nodded her head slowly.

'I'm going out for a while; just for a little while. I'm meeting a couple of men who can help us. MacAuliff made contact.'

'Why can't they come here? I don't want you to go outside. You can't go outside!'

'There's no other practical way. It's been arranged,' he lied, knowing she suspected the lie. 'I'll phone you in a little while. You'll know everything's all right then. But until I do, I want you to tell the Ostermans I went for a walk . . . I'm upset, anything you like. It's important they think *you* believe I went for a walk. That I'll be back any minute. Maybe I'm talking to some of the men outside.'

'Who *are* you going to meet? You've got to tell me.'

'Fassett's men.'

She held his gaze. The lie was established between them now and she searched his eyes. 'You have to do this?' she asked quietly.

'Yes.' He embraced her roughly, anxious to leave, and walked rapidly to the kitchen door.

Outside he strolled about his property, establishing his presence with the police deputies in front and back of his house, to the point where he guessed he was no longer really watched. And then, when he felt no one was looking at him, he disappeared into the woods.

He made a wide circle toward the west, using the tiny beam of the pencil light to avoid obstacles. The wetness, the softness of the earth, made the going difficult, but eventually he saw the backyard lights of his neighbors the Scanlans, three hundred feet from his property line. He was soaked as he approached the Scanlans' back porch and rang the bell.

Fifteen minutes later – again longer than Tanner had anticipated – he climbed into Scanlan's Mercedes coupé and started the engine. Scanlan's Smith & Wesson magazine-clip pistol was in his belt, three extra clips of ammunition in his pocket.

Tanner swung left down Orchard Drive toward the center of the Village. It was past midnight; he was behind the schedule he had set.

He took momentary stock of himself and his actions. He had never considered himself an exceptionally brave man. Whatever courage he had ever displayed was always born of the moment. And he wasn't feeling courageous now. He was desperate.

It was strange. His fear – the profound, deeply felt terror he had lived with for days – now created its own balance, gave birth to its own anger. Anger at being manipulated. He could accept it no longer.

Saddle Valley was quiet, the main street softly lit by replicas of gas lamps, the storefronts in keeping with the town's image of quiet wealth. No neons, no floodlights, everything subdued.

Tanner drove past The Village Pub and the taxi stand, made a U-turn, and parked. The public telephone was directly across from the Mercedes. He wanted the car positioned far enough away so he could see the whole area. He walked across the street and made his first call.

'It's Tanner, Tremayne. Be quiet and listen to me . . . Omega's finished. It's being disbanded. I'm calling it off. Zurich's calling it off. We've put you through the final test and you've failed. The stupidity displayed by everyone is beyond belief! I'm issuing the phase-out orders tonight. Be at the Lassiter depot at two-thirty. And don't try to call my home. I'm phoning from the Village. I'll take a taxi to the area. My house is being watched, thanks to *all* of you! Be at the depot at two-thirty and bring Virginia. Omega's collapsed! If you want to get out alive, be there . . . Two-thirty!'

Tanner pressed down the receiver. The Cardones next.

'Betty? It's Tanner. Listen closely. You get hold of Joe and tell him Omega is finished. I don't care how you do it, but get him back here. That's an order from Zurich. Tell him that! . . . Omega's collapsed. You've all been damn fools. Disabling my cars was stupid. I'm issuing phase-out orders tonight at the Lassiter depot at two-thirty. You and Joe be there! Zurich expects you. And *don't* try to phone me back. I'm calling from the Village. My house is watched. I'll take a taxi. Remember. The Lassiter depot – tell Joe.'

Once more Tanner pressed the receiver down. His third call was to his own home.

'Ali? Everything's fine, darling. There's nothing to worry about. Now, don't talk! Put Bernie on the phone right away . . . Ali, not *now*! Put Bernie on the *phone*! . . . Bernie, it's John. I'm sorry I took off but I had to. I know who Omega is but I need your help. I'm calling from the Village. I'll need a car later . . . not now; later. I don't want mine seen in the Village. I'll use a taxi. Meet me out at the Lassiter depot at two-thirty. Turn right out of the driveway and go east on Orchard – it curves north – for about a mile. You'll see a large pond, there's a white fence around it. On the other side is Lassiter Road. Go down Lassiter a couple of miles and you'll see the depot . . . It's over, Bernie. I'll have Omega at the depot at two-thirty. For Christ's sake *don't, don't blow it*! Trust me! *Don't* call anybody or *do* anything! Just *be* there!'

Tanner hung up the telephone, opened the door and ran toward the Mercedes coupé.

He stood in the darkened doorway of a toy store. It occurred to him that Scanlan's Mercedes was a familiar car in the Village and the Tremaynes, the Cardones, and perhaps even the Ostermans knew Scanlan was his nearest neighbor. That might be to his advantage, he considered. If the assumption were made that he'd borrowed the automobile, it would be further assumed that he remained in the area. The hunt, then, would be thorough. There was nothing to do but wait now. Wait until a little after two o'clock before driving out to the Lassiter depot.

Wait in the center of the Village to see who came after him; who tried to stop him from making the rendezvous. Which couple? Or would it be all three? For Omega had to be frightened now. The unutterable had been said; the mystery brought out into the open.

Omega would have to try to stop him now. If anything Fassett had said was true, that was their only course of action. To intercept him before he reached the depot.

He counted on it. They wouldn't stop him – he'd make sure of that, but he wanted to know in advance who the enemy was.

He looked up and down the street. There were only four people visible. A couple walking a Dalmatian, a man emerging from the Pub, and the driver asleep in the front seat of his taxi.

From the east end of town Tanner saw the headlights of a car approaching slowly. Soon he saw it was his own station wagon. He pressed back into the recessed, unlit doorway.

The driver was Leila Osterman. Alone.

Tanner's pulse quickened. What had he done? It had never occurred to him that any of the couples would separate in a crisis! Yet Leila was alone! And there was nothing to prevent Osterman from holding his family as hostages! Osterman was one of those being protected, not one of the hunted. He could move about freely, leave the premises if he wished. Force Ali and the children to go with him if he thought it necessary!

Leila parked the station wagon in front of the Pub, got out, and walked rapidly over to the taxi driver, shaking him awake. They talked quietly for a moment; Tanner couldn't hear the voices. Eventually Leila turned back to the Pub and went in. Tanner remained in the doorway, fingering the dimes in his pocket, waiting for her to come out. The waiting was agony. He had to get to the phone. He had to get through to the police! He had to make sure his family was safe!

Finally she appeared, got in the wagon, and drove off. Five or six blocks west she turned right; the car disappeared.

Tanner raced across the street to the telephone booth. He dropped in a dime and dialed.

'Hello?'

Thank God! It was Ali!

'It's me.'

'Where are you . . .'

'Never mind that now. Everything's fine . . . Are you all right?' He listened carefully for any false note.

'Of course, I am. We're worried sick about you. What are you doing?'

She sounded natural. It was all right.

'I don't have time. I want . . .'

She interrupted him. 'Leila went out looking for you. You've made an awful mistake . . . We've talked. You and I were wrong, darling. Very *wrong*. Bernie got so worried he thought . . .'

He cut her off. He didn't have the seconds to waste; not on the Ostermans, not now. 'I've got to get off the phone. Stay with the guards. Do as I say. Don't let them out of your sight!'

He hung up before she could speak. He had to reach the police. Every moment counted now.

'Headquarters. Jenkins speaking.'

So the one man on the Saddle Valley police force cleared for Omega was back. MacAuliff had recalled him.

'Headquarters,' repeated the patrolman testily.

'This is John Tanner . . .'

'Jesus Christ, where have you been? We've been looking all over for you!'

'You won't find me. Not until I want you to . . . Now, listen to me! The two policemen in the house – I want them to stay with my wife. She's never to be left alone! The children either! Never! None of them can be alone with Osterman!'

'Of course! We know that! Now, where are you? Don't be a damned fool!'

'I'll phone you later. Don't bother to trace this call. I'll be gone.'

He slammed down the receiver and opened the door, looking for a better vantage point than the storefront. He couldn't run unobserved from the doorway. He started back across the street. The taxi driver was asleep again.

Suddenly, without warning, Tanner heard the roar of an engine. The blurred outline of a car without headlights sped toward him. It came out of nowhere at enormous speed; he was its target. He raced toward the opposite sidewalk only feet ahead of the rushing car. He threw himself toward the curb, twisting his body away from the automobile.

At the same instant he felt a great blow on his left leg. There was a piercing sound of tires braking on asphalt. Tanner fell, rolling with his plunge, and saw the black car narrowly miss the Mercedes, then speed away down Valley Road.

The pain in his leg was excruciating; his shoulder was throbbing. He hoped to Christ he could walk! He had to be able to *walk*!

The cab driver was running toward him.

'Jesus! What happened?'

'Help me up, will you, please?'

'Sure! Sure! You okay? . . . That guy must've had a load on! Jesus! You could've been killed. You want me to get a doctor?'

'No. No. I don't think so.'

'I got a telephone right over there! I'll call the cops! They'll have a doctor here in no time!'

'No! No, don't! I'm all right . . . Just help me walk around a bit.' It was painful for him, but Tanner found he could move. That was the important fact. The pain didn't matter now. Nothing mattered but Omega. And Omega was out in the open!

'I better call the police anyway,' said the driver, holding on to Tanner's arm. 'That clown should get yanked off the road.'

'No . . . I mean, I didn't get the license. I didn't even see what kind of car. It wouldn't do any good.'

'I guess not. Serve the bastard right, though, if he plows himself into a tree.'

'Yeah. That's right.' Tanner was walking by himself now. He'd be all right.

The telephone at the taxi stand rang across the street.

'There goes my phone . . . You okay?'

'Sure. Thanks.'

'Saturday night. Probably the only call I'll get on the whole shift. Only keep one cab on duty Saturday night. That's one too many.' The driver moved away. 'Good luck, buddy. You sure you don't want a doctor?'

'No, really. Thanks.'

He watched the driver take down an address, then heard his voice as he repeated it.

'Tremayne. Sixteen Peachtree. Be there in five minutes, ma'am.' He hung up and saw Tanner watching him. 'How d'you like that? She wants to go to a motel at Kennedy. Who do you suppose she's shacking up with out there?'

Tanner was bewildered. The Tremaynes had two cars of their own . . . Had Tremayne intended to ignore the command to meet at the Lassiter depot? Or, by making sure the single Saturday night taxi was away, was Tremayne hoping to isolate him in the Village?

Either was possible.

Tanner hobbled toward an alley running alongside of the Pub, used primarily for deliveries. From there, since it led to a municipal parking lot, he could escape undetected if it were necessary. He stood in the alley and massaged his leg. He'd have a huge welt in an hour or so. He looked at his watch. It was twelve-forty-nine. Another hour before he would drive to the depot. Perhaps the black car would return. Perhaps others would come.

He wanted a cigarette, but did not want to strike a match near the street. He could cup the glow of a cigarette, not the flame of a match. He walked ten yards into the alley and lit up. He heard something. Footsteps?

He inched his way back toward the Valley Road entrance. The Village was deserted. The only sounds were muted, coming from the Pub. Then the Pub's door opened and three people came out. Jim and Nancy Loomis with a man he didn't recognize. He laughed sadly to himself.

Here he was, John Tanner, the respected Director of News for Standard Mutual, hiding in a darkened alley – filthy, soaked, a bullet crease in his shoulder and a welling bruise on his leg from a driver intent on murder – silently watching Jim and Nancy come out of the Pub. Jim Loomis. He had been touched by Omega and he'd never know it.

From the west end of Valley Road – the direction of Route Five – came an automobile traveling quietly at no more than ten miles an hour. The driver seemed to be looking for someone or something on Valley Road.

It was Joe.

He hadn't gone to Philadelphia. There was no dying father in Philadelphia. The Cardones had lied.

It was no surprise to Tanner.

He pressed his back against the alley wall and made himself as inconspicuous as he could, but he was a large man. For no other reason than that it gave him security, Tanner withdrew the pistol from his belt. He'd kill Cardone if he had to.

When the car was within forty feet of him, two short blasts from a second automobile, coming from the other direction, made Cardone stop.

The second car approached rapidly.

It was Tremayne. As he passed the alley, Tanner could see the look of panic on his face.

The lawyer pulled up beside Cardone and the two men spoke quickly, softly. Tanner couldn't make out the words, but he could tell they were spoken rapidly and with great agitation. Tremayne made a U-turn, and the automobiles raced off in the same direction.

Tanner relaxed and stretched his pained body. All were accounted for now. All he knew about and one more he didn't. Omega plus one, he considered. Who was in the black automobile? Who had tried to run him down?

There was no point in putting it off any longer. He'd seen what he had to see. He'd drive to within a few hundred yards of the Lassiter depot and wait for Omega to declare themselves.

He walked out of the alley and started for the car. And then he stopped.

There was something wrong with the car. In the subdued light of the gas lamps he could see that the automobile's rear end had settled down to the surface of the street. The chrome bumper was inches above the pavement.

He ran to the car and unclipped his pencil light. Both back tires were flat, the metal rims supporting the weight of the automobile. He crouched down and saw two knives protruding from the deflated rubber.

How? When? He was within twenty yards every second! The street was deserted! No one! No one could have crept behind the Mercedes without being seen!

Except, perhaps, those few moments in the alley. Those moments when he lit a cigarette and crouched by the wall watching Tremayne and Cardone. Those seconds when he'd thought he'd heard footsteps.

The tires had been slashed not five minutes ago!

Oh Christ! thought Tanner. The manipulation hadn't stopped at all! Omega was at his heels. Knowing. Knowing every move he made. Every second!

What had Ali started to say on the phone? Bernie had . . . what? He started toward the booth, taking the last dime out of his pocket. He pulled the pistol out of his belt and looked around as he crossed the street. Whoever punctured the tires might be waiting, watching.

'Ali?'

'Darling, for God's sake come home!'

'In a little while, hon. Honest, no problems. No problems at all . . . I just want to ask you a question. It's important.'

'It's just as important that you get *home!*'

'You said before that Bernie had decided something. What was it?'

'Oh . . . when you called the first time. Leila went out after you; Bernie didn't want to leave us alone. But he was worried that you might not listen to her and since the police were here, he decided to go find you himself.'

'Did he take the Triumph?'

'No. He borrowed a car from one of the police.'

'Oh, Christ!' Tanner didn't mean to explode into the phone but he couldn't help it. The black automobile out of nowhere! The *plus-one* was really part of the three! 'Is he back?'

'No. Leila is, though. She thinks he may have gotten lost.'

'I'll call you.' Tanner hung up. Of course Bernie was 'lost'. There hadn't been time for him to get back. Not since Tanner had been in the alley, not since the tires were slashed.

And now he realized that somehow he had to reach the Lassiter depot. Reach it and position himself before any part of Omega could stop him, or know where he was.

Lassiter Road was diagonally northwest, about three miles from the center of the Village. The depot perhaps another mile or two beyond. He'd walk it. It was all he could do.

He started as quickly as he could, his limp diminishing with movement, then ducked into a doorway. No one followed him.

He kept up a zigzag pattern northwest until he reached the outskirts of town – where there were no sidewalks, only large expanses of lawn. Lassiter wasn't far away now. Twice he lay on the ground while automobiles raced past him, drivers oblivious to anything but the road in front of them.

Finally, through a back stretch of woods behind a well-trimmed lawn, neither unlike his own, he reached Lassiter Road.

On the rough tarred surface he turned left and started the final part of his journey. It wasn't any farther than a mile or a mile and a half by his calculations. He could reach the deserted depot in fifteen minutes if his leg held out. If it didn't, he'd simply slow down, but he'd get there. His watch read one-forty-one. There was time.

Omega wouldn't arrive early. It couldn't afford to. It – or they – didn't know what was waiting for them.

Tanner limped along the road and found he felt better – more secure – holding Scanlan's pistol in his hand. He saw a flicker of light behind him. Headlights, three or four hundred yards away. He crossed into the woods bordering on the road and lay flat on the muddy ground.

The car passed him traveling slowly. It was the same black car that had run him down on Valley Road. He couldn't see the driver; the absence of street lights made any identification impossible.

When it was out of sight, Tanner went back to the road. He had considered walking in the woods but it wasn't feasible. He could make better time on the cleared surface. He went on, hobbling now, wondering whether the black automobile belonged to a policeman currently stationed at 22 Orchard Drive. Whether the driver was a writer named Osterman.

He had gone nearly half a mile when the lights appeared again, only now in front of him. He dove into the brush, hoping to God he hadn't been seen, unlatching the safety of his pistol as he lay there.

The automobile approached at incredible speed. Whoever was driving was racing back to find someone.

Was it to find him?

Or Leila Osterman?

Or was it to reach Cardone, who had *no* dying father in Philadelphia. Or Tremayne, who *wasn't* on his way to the motel at Kennedy Airport.

Tanner got up and kept going, his leg about to collapse under him, the pistol gripped tightly in his hand.

He rounded a bend in the road and there it was. A single sagging street lamp lit the crumbling station house. The old stucco depot was boarded up, giant weed drooping ominously from the cracks in the rotted wood. Small ugly leaves grew out of the foundation.

There was no wind, no rain, no sound but the rhythmic drip of water from thousands of branches and leaves – the last exhausted effects of the storm.

He stood on the outskirts of the decayed, overgrown parking area trying to decide where to position himself. It was nearly two o'clock and a secluded place had to be found. The station house itself! Perhaps he could get inside. He started across the gravel and weeds.

A blinding light flashed in his eyes; his reflexes lurched him forward. He rolled over on his wounded shoulder, yet felt no pain. A powerful searchlight had pierced the dimness of the depot grounds, and gunshots echoed throughout the deserted area. Bullets thumped into the earth around him and whistled over his head. He kept rolling, over and over, knowing that one of the bullets had hit his left arm.

He reached the edge of the sunken gravel and raised his pistol toward the blinding light. He fired rapidly in the direction of the enemy. The searchlight exploded; a scream followed. Tanner kept pulling the trigger until the clip was empty. He tried to reach into his pocket with his left hand for a second clip and found he couldn't move his arm.

There was silence again. He put down the pistol and awkwardly extracted another clip with his right hand. He twisted the pistol on its back and with his teeth holding the hot barrel, pushed the fresh clip into the chamber, burning his lips as he did so.

He waited for his enemy to move. To make any sound at all. Nothing stirred.

Slowly he rose, his left arm now completely immobile. He held the pistol in front of him, ready to pull the trigger at the slightest movement in the grass.

None came.

Tanner backed his way toward the door of the depot, holding his weapon up, probing the ground carefully with his feet so that no unexpected obstacle would cause him to fall. He reached the boarded-up door, knowing he couldn't possibly break it down if it was nailed shut. Most of his body was inoperative. He had little strength left.

Still, he pushed his back against the door and the heavy wood gave slightly, creaking loudly as it did so. Tanner turned his head just enough to see that the opening was no more than three or four inches. The ancient hinges were caked with rust. He slammed his right shoulder against the edge of the door and it gave way, plunging Tanner into the darkness, onto the rotted floor of the station.

He lay where he was for several seconds. The station house door was three-quarters open, the upper section snapped away from its hinges. The street lamp fifty yards away provided a dull wash of illumination. Broken and missing boards from the roof were a second, inadequate source of light.

Suddenly Tanner heard a creaking behind him. The unmistakable sound of a footstep on the rotted floor. He tried to turn around, tried to rise. He was too late. Something crashed into the base of his skull. He felt himself grow dizzy, but he saw the foot. A foot encased in bandages.

As he collapsed on the rotted floor, blackness sweeping over him, he looked upward into a face.

Tanner knew he had found Omega.

It was Laurence Fassett.

29

He couldn't know how long he'd been unconscious. Five minutes? An hour? There was no way to tell. He couldn't see his watch, he couldn't move his left arm. His face was against the rough splintered floor of the crumbling station house. He could feel the blood slowly trickling from his wounded arm; his head ached.

Fassett!

The manipulator.

Omega.

As he lay there, isolated fragments of past conversations raced through his mind.

'. . . we should get together . . . our wives should get together . . .'

But Laurence Fassett's wife had been killed in East Berlin. Murdered in East Berlin. That fact had been his most moving entreaty.

And there was something else. Something to do with a Woodward broadcast . . . The broadcast about the CIA a year ago.

'. . . I was in the States then. I saw that one.'

But he wasn't 'in the States' then. In Washington Fassett had said he'd been on the Albanian border a year ago. '. . . forty-five days of haggling.' In the field. It was why he'd contacted John Tanner, the solid, clean news director of Standard Mutual, a resident of the target, Chasm of Leather.

There were other contradictions – none as obvious, but they were there. They wouldn't do him any good now. His life was about to end in the ruins of the Lassiter depot.

He moved his head and saw Fassett standing above him.

'We've got a great deal to thank you for. If you are as good a shot as I think you are you've created the perfect martyr out there. A dead hero. If he's only wounded, he'll soon be dead at any rate . . . Oh, he's the other part of us, but even he'd recognize the perfect contribution of his sacrifice . . . You see, I didn't lie to you. We are fanatics. We have to be.'

'What now?'

'We wait for the others. One or two are bound to show up. Then it'll be over. Their lives and yours, I'm afraid. And Washington will have its Omega. Then, perhaps, a field agent named Fassett will be given another commendation. If they're not careful, they'll make me Director of Operations one day.'

'You're a traitor.' Tanner found something in the dark shadows by his right hand. It was a loose piece of flooring about two feet long, an inch or so wide. He awkwardly, painfully, sat up, pulling the plank to his side.

'Not by my lights. A defector, perhaps. Not a traitor. Let's not go into that. You wouldn't understand or appreciate the viewpoint. Let's just say in my opinion you're the traitor. *All* of you. Look around you . . .'

Tanner lashed out with the piece of wood and crashed it with all his might across the bandaged foot in front of him. Blood erupted instantly, spreading through the gauze. Tanner flung himself upward into Fassett's groin, trying desperately to reach the hand with the gun. Fassett screamed in anguish. Tanner found the agent's wrist with his right hand, his left arm immobile, serving only as a limp tentacle. He drove Fassett back against the wall and ground his heel into Fassett's wounded foot, stamping it over and over again.

Tanner wrenched the gun free and it fell to the floor, sliding toward the open door and the dim shaft of light. Fassett's screams shattered the stillness of the station house as he slumped against the wall.

John lunged for the pistol, picked it up and held it tightly in his hand. He got up, every part of his body in pain, the blood flowing now out of his arm.

Fassett was barely conscious, gasping in agony. Tanner wanted this man alive, wanted Omega alive. But he thought of the basement, of Ali and the children, and so he took careful aim and fired twice, once into the mass of blood and flesh which was Fassett's wound, once into the knee cap of the leg.

He lurched back toward the doorway, supporting himself in the frame. Painfully, he looked at his watch: two-thirty-seven. Seven minutes after Omega's appointed time.

No one else would come now. Half of Omega lay in agony in the station house; the rest in the tall, wet grass beyond the parking lot.

He wondered who it was.

Tremayne?

Cardone?

Osterman?

Tanner tore off part of his sleeve and tried to wrap it around the wound in his arm. If only he could stop the bleeding, even a bit. If he could do that perhaps he could make it across the old parking area to where the searchlight was.

But he couldn't, and, off balance, fell backwards to the floor. He was no better off than Fassett. Both their lives would ebb away right there. Inside the ancient depot.

A wailing began; Tanner wasn't sure if it was a trick of his brain or if it was real. Real! It was growing louder.

Sirens, then the roar of engines. Then the screeching of brakes against the loose gravel and wet dirt.

Tanner rose to his elbow. He tried with all his strength to get up – only to his knees, that would be good enough. That would be sufficient to crawl. Crawl to the doorway.

The beams of searchlights filtered through the loose boards and cracked stucco, one light remaining on the entrance. Then a voice, amplified by a bull horn.

'This is the police! We are accompanied by federal authorities! If you have weapons, throw them out and follow with your hands up! . . . If you are holding Tanner hostage, release him! You are surrounded. There's no way for you to escape!'

Tanner tried to speak as he crawled toward the door. The voice sounded once again.

'We repeat. Throw out your weapons . . .'

Tanner could hear another voice – yelling, this one not on a horn.

'Over here! Throw a light over here! By this automobile! Over here in the grass!'

Someone had found the rest of Omega.

'Tanner! John Tanner! Are you inside!?'

Tanner reached the entrance and pulled himself up by the edge of the door into the spill of light.

'There he is! Jesus, *look* at him!'

Tanner fell forward. Jenkins raced to his side.

* * *

'There you are, Mr Tanner. We've tied you up as best we can. It'll hold till the ambulance gets here. See if you can walk.' Jenkins braced Tanner around the waist and pulled him to his feet. Two other policemen were carrying out Fassett.

'That's him . . . That's Omega.'

'We know. You're a very impressive fellow. You did what no one else was able to do in five years of trying. You got Omega for us.'

'There's someone else. Over there . . . Fassett said he was the other part of them.'

'We found him. He's dead. He's still there. You want to go over and see who it is? Tell your grandchildren some day.'

Tanner looked at Jenkins and replied haltingly. 'Yes. Yes, I would. I guess I'd better know.'

The two men walked over into the grass. Tanner was both fascinated and repelled by the moment that approached, the moment when he would see for himself the second face of Omega. He sensed that Jenkins understood. The revelation had to be of his own observation, not second hand. He had to bear witness to the most terrible part of Omega.

The betrayal of love.

Dick. Joe. Bernie.

Several men were examining the black automobile with the ruined searchlight. The body lay face down by the sedan's door. In the dark, Tanner could see it was a large man.

Jenkins turned on his flashlight and kicked the body over. The beam of light shone into his face.

Tanner froze.

The riddled body in the grass was Captain Albert MacAuliff.

A police officer approached and spoke to Jenkins from the edge of the parking area.

'They want to come over.'

'Why not? It goes with their territories. The beach is secured.' Jenkins spoke with more than a trace of contempt.

'Come on!' yelled McDermott to some men in the shadows on the other side of the parking lot.

Tanner could see the three tall figures walking across the gravel, walking slowly, reluctantly.

Bernie Osterman, Joe Cardone. Dick Tremayne.

He limped with Jenkins' help out of the grass, away from Omega. The four friends faced each other; none knew what to say.

'Let's go,' said Tanner to Jenkins.

'Pardon us, gentlemen.'

PART FOUR

Sunday Afternoon

30

Sunday afternoon in the Village of Saddle Valley, New Jersey. The two patrol cars roamed up and down the streets as usual, but they remained at cruising speeds, lazily turning into the shady roads. The drivers smiled at the children and waved at the residents doing their Sunday chores. Golf bags and tennis rackets could be seen in small foreign convertibles and in gleaming station wagons. The sun was bright; the trees and the lawns glistened, refreshed by the July storm.

Saddle Valley was awake, preparing for a perfect Sunday afternoon. Telephones were dialed, plans made, a number of apologies offered for last evening's behavior. They were laughed off – what the hell, last evening was Saturday night. In Saddle Valley, New Jersey, Saturday nights were quickly forgiven.

A late model dark blue sedan with whitewall tires drove into the Tanner driveway. Inside the house John Tanner got up from the couch and walked painfully to the window. His upper chest and his entire left arm was encased in bandages. So, too, was his left leg, from thigh to ankle.

Tanner looked out the window at the two men walking up the path. One he recognized as Patrolman Jenkins – but only on second glance. Jenkins was not in his police uniform. Now he looked like a Saddle Valley commuter – a banker or an advertising executive. Tanner didn't know the second man. He'd never seen him before.

'They're here,' he called toward the kitchen. Ali came out and stood in the hallway. She was dressed casually in slacks and a shirt, but the look in her eyes wasn't casual at all.

'I suppose we've got to get it over with. The sitter's out with Janet. Ray's at the club . . . I suppose Bernie and Leila are at the airport by now.'

'If they made it in time. There were statements, papers to sign. Dick's acting as everyone's attorney.'

The chimes rang and Ali went to the door. 'Sit down, darling. Just a little at a time, the doctor said.'

'Okay.'

Jenkins and his unfamiliar partner came in. Alice brought coffee and the four of them sat across from each other, the Tanners on the couch, Jenkins and the man he introduced as Grover in the armchairs.

'You're the one I talked to in New York, aren't you?' John asked.

'Yes, I am. I'm with the Agency. Incidentally, so is Jenkins. He's been assigned here for the past year and a half.'

'You were a very convincing policeman, Mr Jenkins,' said Ali.

'It wasn't difficult. It's a pleasant place, nice people.'

'I thought it was the Chasm of Leather.' Tanner's hostility was apparent. It was time for explanations. He had demanded them.

'That, too, of course,' added Jenkins softly.

'Then we'd better talk about it.'

'Very well,' said Grover. 'I'll summarize in a few words. "Divide and kill". That was Fassett's premiss. Omega's premiss.'

'Then there really was a Fassett. That was his name, I mean.'

'There certainly was. For ten years Laurence Fassett was one of the finest operatives in the Agency. Excellent record, dedicated. And then things happened to him.'

'He sold out.'

'It's never that simple,' said Jenkins. 'Let's say his commitments changed. They altered drastically. He became the enemy.'

'And you didn't know it?'

Grover hesitated before replying. He seemed to be searching for the least painful words. His head nodded, imperceptibly. 'We knew . . . We found out gradually, over a period of years. Defectors of Fassett's caliber are never revealed overnight. It's a slow process; a series of assignments with conflicting objectives. Sooner or later a pattern emerges. When it does, you make the most of it . . . Which is exactly what we did.'

'That seems to me awfully dangerous, complicated.'

'A degree of danger, perhaps; not complicated, really. Fassett was maneuvered, just as he maneuvered you and your friends. He was brought into the Omega operation because his credentials warranted it. He was brilliant and this was an explosive situation . . . Certain laws of espionage are fundamental. We correctly assumed that the enemy would give Fassett the responsibility of keeping Omega *intact*, not *allowing* its destruction. He was at once the defending general and the attacking force. The strategy was well thought out, take my word for it. Do you begin to see?'

'Yes.' Tanner was barely audible.

'"Divide and kill". Omega existed. Chasm of Leather *was* Saddle Valley.

The checks on residents *did* uncover the Swiss accounts of the Cardones and the Tremaynes. When Osterman appeared, he, too, was found to have an account in Zurich. The circumstances were perfect for Fassett. He had found three couples allied with each other in an illegal or at least highly questionable financial venture in Switzerland.'

'Zurich. That's why the name Zurich made them all nervous. Cardone was petrified.'

'He had every reason to be. He and Tremayne. One the partner in a highly speculative brokerage house with a lot of Mafia financing; and the other an attorney with a firm engaged in unethical mergers – Tremayne, the specialist. They could have been ruined. Osterman had the least to lose, but, nevertheless, as part of the public media, an indictment might have had disastrous effects. As you know better than we do, networks are sensitive.'

'Yes,' said Tanner again without feeling.

'If, during the weekend, Fassett could so intensify mistrust between the three couples that they began hurling accusations at each other – the next step would be violence. Once *that possibility* was established, the real Omega intended to murder at least two of the couples, and Fassett could then present us with a substitute Omega. Who could refuse him? The subjects would be dead. It . . . was brilliant.'

Tanner rose painfully from the couch and limped to the fireplace. He gripped the mantel angrily.

'I'm glad you can sit there and make professional judgments.' He turned on the government men. 'You had no right, *no* right! My *wife*, my *children* were damn near *killed*! Where were your men outside on the grounds? What happened to all that protective equipment from the biggest corporation in the world? Who listened on those electronic . . . *things* which were supposedly installed all over the house? *Where was everybody? We were left in that cellar to die!'*

Grover and Jenkins let the moment subside. They accepted Tanner's hostility calmly, with understanding. They'd been through such moments before. Grover spoke quietly, in counterpoint to Tanner's anger.

'In operations such as these, we anticipate that errors – I'll be honest, generally one massive error – occur. It's unavoidable when you consider the logistics.'

'What error?'

Jenkins spoke. 'I'd like to answer that . . . The error was mine. I was the senior officer at "Leather" and the only one who knew about Fassett's defection. The only one. Saturday afternoon McDermott told me that Cole had unearthed extraordinary information and had to see me right away. I didn't check it out with Washington, I didn't confirm it. I just accepted it and drove into the city as fast as I could . . . I thought that Cole, or someone here at "Leather", had discovered who Fassett really was. If that had been the case a whole new set of instructions would have to come from Washington . . .'

'We were prepared,' interrupted Grover. 'Alternate plans were ready to be implemented.'

'I got into New York, went up to the hotel suite . . . and Cole wasn't there. I know it sounds incredible, but he was out to dinner. He was simply *out to dinner*. He left the name of the restaurant, so I went there. This all took time. Taxis, traffic. I couldn't use the phone; all conversations were recorded. Fassett might have been tipped. Finally I got to Cole. He didn't know what I was talking about. He'd sent no message.'

Jenkins stopped, the telling of the story angered and embarrassed him.

'That was the error?' asked Ali.

'Yes. It gave Fassett the time he needed. *I* gave him the time.'

'Wasn't Fassett risking too much? Trapping himself? Cole denied the message.'

'He calculated the risk. Timed it. Since Cole was constantly in touch with "Leather", a single message, especially second hand, could be garbled. The fact that I fell for the ruse also told him something. Put simply, I was to be killed.'

'That doesn't explain the guards outside. Your going to New York doesn't explain their not being there.'

'We said Fassett was brilliant,' continued Grover. 'When we tell you why they weren't there, why there wasn't a single patrol within miles, you'll understand just how brilliant he was . . . He systematically withdrew all the men from your property on the grounds that *you were Omega*. The man they were guarding with their lives was, in reality, the enemy.'

'*What?*'

'Think about it. Once you were dead, who could disprove it?'

'Why would they believe it?'

'The electronic pick-ups. They'd stopped functioning throughout your house. One by one they stopped transmitting. You were the only one here who knew they existed. Therefore, *you* were eliminating them.'

'But I wasn't! I didn't know where they were! I still don't!'

'It wouldn't make any difference if you did.' It was Jenkins who spoke. 'Those transmitters had operating capacities of anywhere from thirty-six to forty-eight hours only. No more. I showed you one last night. It was treated with acid. They all were. The acid gradually ate through the miniature plates and shorted out the transmissions . . . But all the men in the field knew was that they weren't functioning. Fassett then announced that he'd made the error. *You* were Omega and he hadn't realized it. I'm told he did it very effectively. There's something awesome about a man like Fassett admitting a major mistake. He withdrew the patrols and then he and MacAuliff moved in for the kill. They were able to do it because I wasn't there to stop them. He'd removed me from the scene.'

'Did you know about MacAuliff?'

'No,' answered Jenkins. 'He wasn't even a suspect. His cover was pure genius. A bigoted small-town cop, veteran of the New York police, and a right-winger to boot. Frankly, the first hint we had of his involvement was when you said the police car didn't stop when you signaled from the basement. Neither patrol car was in the vicinity at the time; MacAuliff made sure of that. However, he carries a red signal light in his trunk. Simple clamp device that can be mounted on top. He was circling your house, trying to draw you out . . . When he finally got here, two things struck us. The first was that he'd been reached by car radio. Not at home. The second was a general description supplied by those on duty. That MacAuliff kept holding his stomach, claimed to be having a severe ulcer attack. MacAuliff had no history of ulcers. It was possible that he'd been wounded. It turned out to be correct. His "ulcer" was a gash in his stomach. Courtesy of Mr Osterman.'

Tanner reached for a cigarette. Ali lit it for him.

'Who killed the man in the woods?'

'MacAuliff. And don't hold yourself responsible. He would have killed him whether you got up and turned on the light or not. He also gassed your family last Wednesday. He used the police riot supply.'

'What about our dog? In my daughter's bedroom.'

'Fassett,' said Grover. 'You had ice cubes delivered at one-forty-five; they were left on the front porch. Fassett saw the chance to create further panic and so he simply took them in. You were all at the pool. Once he got inside, he could maneuver; he's a pro. He was just a man delivering ice cubes. Even if you saw him, he could have told you it was extra precaution on his part. You certainly couldn't have argued. And Fassett obviously was the man on the road who gassed the Cardones and the Tremaynes.'

'Everything was calculated to keep us *all* in a constant state of panic. With no let up. Force my husband to think it was each of them.' Ali stared at Tanner and spoke quietly. 'What have we done? What did we say to them?'

'At one time or another I was convinced each person had given himself . . . or herself . . . away. I was positive.'

'You were looking for that desperately. The relationships in this house, during the weekend, were intensely personal. Fassett knew that.' Grover looked over at Jenkins. 'Of course, you must realize that they were all frightened. They had good reason to be. Regardless of their own personal, professional guilts, they shared a major one.'

'Zurich?'

'Precisely. It accounted for their final actions. Cardone wasn't going to a dying father in Philadelphia last night. He'd called his partner Bennett to come out. He didn't want to talk on the phone and he thought his house might be watched. Yet he wasn't about to go far away from his family. They met at a diner on Route Five . . . Cardone told Bennett about the Zurich manipulation and offered his resignation for a settlement. His idea was to turn state's evidence for the Justice Department in return for immunity.'

'Tremayne said he was leaving this morning . . .'

'Lufthansa. Straight through to Zurich. He's a good attorney, very agile in these sorts of negotiations. He was getting out with what he could salvage.'

'Then they both – separately – were leaving Bernie with the mess.'

'Mr and Mrs Osterman had their own plans. A syndicate in Paris was prepared to assume their investment. All it would have taken was a cablegram to the French attorneys.'

Tanner rose from the couch and limped toward the windows overlooking his backyard. He wasn't sure he wanted to hear any more. The sickness was everywhere. It left no one, it seemed, untouched. Fassett had said it.

It's a spiral, Mr Tanner. No one lives in a deep freeze any more.

He turned slowly back to the government men. 'There are still questions.'

'We'll never be able to give you all the answers,' said Jenkins. 'No matter what we tell you now, the questions will be around for a long time. You'll find inconsistencies, seeming contradictions, and they'll turn into doubts. The questions will become real again . . . That's the difficult part. Everything was too subjective for you. Too personal. You operated for five days in a state of exhaustion, with little or no sleep. Fassett counted on that too.'

'I don't mean that. I mean physical things . . . Leila wore a brooch that could be seen in the dark. There were no bullet marks in the wall around her . . . Her husband wasn't here when I was in the Village last night. Someone slashed the tires then and tried to run me down . . . The rendezvous at the Lassiter depot was my idea. How could Fassett have known if one of them hadn't told him? . . . How can you be so sure? You didn't know about MacAuliff. How do you know they aren't . . .' John Tanner stopped as he realized what he was about to say. He looked at Jenkins, who was staring at him.

Jenkins had spoken the truth. The questions were real again, the deceptions too personal.

Grover leaned forward in his chair. 'In time everything will be answered. Those questions aren't difficult. Fassett and MacAuliff worked as a team. Fassett had the telephone taps moved to his new location once he left the motel. He easily could have radioed MacAuliff in the Village to kill you and then gone out to the depot when MacAuliff told him he'd failed. Obtaining other automobiles is no problem, slashing tires no feat . . . Mrs Osterman's brooch? An accident of dress. The unmarked wall? Its location, as I understand it, makes direct fire almost impossible.'

'"Almost", "could have" . . . oh, God.' Tanner walked back to the sofa and awkwardly sat down. He took Ali's hand. 'Wait a minute.' He spoke haltingly. 'Something happened in the kitchen yesterday afternoon . . .'

'We know,' interrupted Jenkins gently. 'Your wife told us.'

Ali looked at John and nodded. Her eyes were sad.

'Your friends, the Ostermans, are remarkable people,' continued Jenkins. 'Mrs Osterman saw that her husband wanted to, *had* to go out and help you. He couldn't stand by and watch you killed . . . They're very close to each other. She was giving him permission to risk his life for you.'

John Tanner closed his eyes.

'Don't dwell on it,' said Jenkins.

Tanner looked at Jenkins and understood.

Grover got out of his chair. It was a signal for Jenkins, who did the same.

'We'll go now. We don't want to tire you out. There'll be plenty of time later. We owe you that . . . Oh, by the way. This belongs to you.' Grover reached into his pocket and withdrew an envelope.

'What is it?'

'The affidavit you signed for Fassett. Your agreement with Omega. You'll have to take my word that the recording is buried in the archives. Lost for a millennium that way. For the sake of both countries.'

'I understand . . . One last thing.' Tanner paused, afraid of his question.

'What is it?'

'Which of them called you? Which of them told you about the Lassiter depot?'

'They did it together. They all met back here and decided to phone the police.'

'Just like that?'

'That's the irony, Mr Tanner,' said Jenkins. 'If they had done what they should have done earlier, none of this would have happened. But it was only last night that they got together and told each other the truth.'

Saddle Valley was filled with whispers. In the dimly lit Village Pub men gathered in small groups and talked quietly. At the Club, couples sat around the pool and spoke softly of the strange rumors circulated – the Cardones had taken a long vacation, no one knew where; there was trouble in his firm, some said. Richard Tremayne was drinking more than usual, and his usual was too much. There were other stories about the Tremaynes, too. The maid was no longer there, the house a far cry from what it had been. Virginia's garden was going to seed.

But soon the stories stopped. Saddle Valley was nothing if not resilient.

People forgot to ask about the Cardones and the Tremaynes after a while. They never fitted in, really. Their friends were hardly the kind a person wanted at the Club. There simply wasn't the time for much concern. There was so much to do. Saddle Valley, in summer, was glorious. Why shouldn't it be?

Isolated, secure, inviolate.

And John Tanner knew there'd never be another Osterman weekend.

Divide and kill.

Omega had won, after all.

THE MATLOCK PAPER

One

Loring walked out the side entrance of the Justice Department and looked for a taxi. It was nearly five-thirty, a spring Friday, and the congestion in the Washington streets was awful. Loring stood by the curb and held up his left hand, hoping for the best. He was about to abandon the effort when a cab that had picked up a fare thirty feet down the block stopped in front of him.

'Going east, mister? It's O.K. This gentleman said he wouldn't mind.'

Loring was always embarrassed when these incidents occurred. He unconsciously drew back his right forearm, allowing his sleeve to cover as much of his hand as possible – to conceal the thin black chain looped around his wrist, locked to the briefcase handle.

'Thanks, anyway. I'm heading south at the next corner.'

He waited until the taxi re-entered the flow of traffic and then resumed his futile signaling.

Usually, under such conditions, his mind was alert, his feelings competitive. He would normally dart his eyes in both directions, ferreting out cabs about to disgorge passengers, watching the corners for those dimly lit roof signs that meant this particular vehicle was for hire if you ran fast enough.

Today, however, Ralph Loring did not feel like running. On this particular Friday, his mind was obsessed with a terrible reality. He had just borne witness to a man's being sentenced to death. A man he'd never met but knew a great deal about. An unknowing man of thirty-three who lived and worked in a small New England town four hundred miles away and who had no idea of Loring's existence, much less of the Justice Department's interest in him.

Loring's memory kept returning to the large conference room with the huge rectangular table around which sat the men who'd pronounced the sentence.

He had objected strenuously. It was the least he could do for the man he'd never met, the man who was being maneuvered with such precision into such an untenable position.

'May I remind you, Mr. Loring,' said an assistant attorney general who'd once been a judge advocate in the navy, 'that in any combat situation basic risks are assumed. A percentage of casualties is anticipated.'

'The circumstances are different. This man isn't trained. He won't know who or where the enemy is. How could he? We don't know ourselves.'

'Just the point.' The speaker then had been another assistant AG, this one a recruit from some corporation law office, fond of committee meetings, and, Loring suspected, incapable of decisions without them. 'Our subject is highly mobile. Look at the psychological profile, "flawed but mobile in the extreme." That's exactly what it says. He's a logical choice.'

'"Flawed but mobile"! What in heaven's name does that mean? May *I* remind this committee that I've worked in the field for fifteen years. Psychological profiles are only screening guidelines, hit-and-miss judgments. I would no more send a man into an infiltration problem without knowing him thoroughly than I would assume the responsibility for NASA mathematics.'

The chairman of the committee, a career professional, had answered Loring.

'I understand your reservations; normally, I'd agree. However, these aren't normal conditions. We have barely three weeks. The time factor overrides the usual precautions.'

'It's the risk we have to assume,' said the former judge advocate pontifically.

'*You're* not assuming it,' Loring replied.

'Do you wish to be relieved of the contact?' The chairman made the offer in complete sincerity.

'No, sir. I'll make it. Reluctantly. I want that on the record.'

'One thing before we adjourn.' The corporation lawyer leaned forward on the table. 'And this comes right from the top. We've all agreed that our subject is motivated. The profile makes that clear. What must also be made clear is that any assistance given this committee by the subject is given freely and on a voluntary basis. We're vulnerable here. We cannot, repeat *cannot*, be responsible. If it's possible, we'd like the record to indicate that the subject came to *us*.'

Ralph Loring had turned away from the man in disgust.

If anything, the traffic was heavier now. Loring had about made up his mind to start walking the twenty-odd blocks to his apartment when a white Volvo pulled up in front of him.

'Get in! You look silly with your hand up like that.'

'Oh, it's you. Thanks very much.' Loring opened the door and slid into the small front seat, holding his briefcase on his lap. There was no need to hide the thin black chain around his wrist. Cranston was a field man, too; an overseas route specialist. Cranston had done most of the background work on the assignment which was now Loring's responsibility.

'That was a long meeting. Accomplish anything?'

'The green light.'

'It's about time.'

'Two assistant AGs and a concerned message from the White House were responsible.'

'Good. Geo division got the latest reports from Force-Mediterranean this morning. It's a regular mass conversion of source routes. It's confirmed. The fields in Ankara and Konya in the north, the projects in Sidi Barrani and Rashid, even the Algerian contingents are systematically cutting production. It's going to make things very difficult.'

'What the hell do you want? I thought the objective was to rip them out. You people are never satisfied.'

'Neither would you be. We can exert controls over routes we know about; what in God's name do we know about places like . . . Porto Belocruz, Pilcomayo, a half dozen unpronounceable names in Paraguay, Brazil, Guiana? It's a whole goddamn new ballgame, Ralph.'

'Bring in the SA specialists. CIA's crawling with them.'

'No way. We're not even allowed to ask for maps.'

'That's asinine.'

'That's espionage. We stay clean. We're strictly according to Interpol-Hoyle; no funny business. I thought you knew that.'

'I do,' replied Loring wearily. 'It's still asinine.'

'You worry about New England, USA. We'll handle the pampas, or whatever they are – it is.'

'New England, USA, is a goddamn microcosm. That's what's frightening. What happened to all those poetic descriptions of rustic fences and Yankee spirit and ivied brick walls?'

'New poetry. Get with it.'

'Your sympathy is overwhelming. Thanks.'

'You sound discouraged.'

'There isn't enough time . . .'

'There never is.' Cranston steered the small car into a faster lane only to find it bottlenecked at Nebraska and Eighteenth. With a sigh, he shoved the gearshift into neutral and shrugged his shoulders. He looked at Loring, who was staring blankly at the windshield. 'At least you got the green light. That's something.'

'Sure. With the wrong personnel.'

'Oh . . . I see. Is that him?' Cranston gestured his head toward Loring's briefcase.

'That's him. From the day he was born.'

'What's his name?'

'Matlock. James B. Matlock II. The *B* is for Barbour, very old family – two very old families. James Matlock, B.A., M.A., Ph.D. A leading authority in the field of social and political influences on Elizabethan literature. How about that?'

'Jesus! Are those his qualifications? Where does he start asking questions? At faculty teas for retired professors?'

'No. That part of it's all right; he's young enough. His qualifications are included in what Security calls "flawed but mobile in the extreme." Isn't that a lovely phrase?'

'Inspiring. What does it mean?'

'It's supposed to describe a man who isn't very nice. Probably because of a loused-up army record, or a divorce – I'm sure it's the army thing – but in spite of that insurmountable handicap, is very well liked.'

'I like him already.'

'That's my problem. I do, too.'

The two men fell into silence. It was clear that Cranston had been in the field long enough to realize when a fellow professional had to think by himself. Reach certain conclusions – or rationalizations – by himself. Most of the time, it was easy.

Ralph Loring thought about the man whose life was detailed so completely in his briefcase, culled from a score of data-bank sources. James Barbour Matlock was the name, but the person behind the name refused to come into focus. And that bothered Loring; Matlock's life had been shaped by disturbing, even violent, inconsistencies.

He was the surviving son of two elderly, immensely wealthy parents who lived in handsome retirement in Scarsdale, New York. His education had been properly Eastern Establishment: Andover and Amherst, with the proper expectations of a Manhattan-based profession – banking, brokerage, advertising. There was nothing in his precollege or undergraduate record to indicate a deviation from this pattern. Indeed, marriage to a socially prominent girl from Greenwich seemed to confirm it.

And then things happened to James Barbour Matlock, and Loring wished he understood. First came the army.

It was the early sixties, and by the simple expedient of agreeing to a six-month extension of service, Matlock could have sat comfortably behind a desk as a supply officer somewhere – most likely, with his family's connections, in Washington or New York. Instead, his service file read like a hoodlum's: a series of infractions and insubordinations that guaranteed him the least desirable of assignments – Vietnam and its escalating hostilities. While in the Mekong Delta, his military behavior also guaranteed him two summary courts-martial.

Yet there appeared to be no ideological motivation behind his actions, merely poor, if any, adjustment.

His return to civilian life was marked by continuing difficulties, first with his parents and then with his wife. Inexplicably, James Barbour Matlock, whose academic record had been gentlemanly but hardly superior, took a small apartment in Morningside Heights and attended Columbia University's graduate school.

The wife lasted three and a half months, opting for a quiet divorce and a rapid exit from Matlock's life.

The following several years were monotonous intelligence material. Matlock, the incorrigible, was in the process of becoming Matlock, the scholar. He worked around the calendar, receiving his master's degree in fourteen months, his doctorate two years later. There was a reconciliation of sorts with his parents, and a position with the English department at Carlyle University in Connecticut. Since then Matlock had published a number of books and articles and acquired an enviable reputation in the academic community. He was obviously popular – 'mobile in the extreme' (silly goddamn expression); he was moderately well-off and apparently possessed none of the antagonistic traits he'd displayed during the hostile years. Of course, there was damn little reason for him to be discontented, thought Loring. James Barbour Matlock II had his life nicely routined; he was covered on all flanks, thank you, including a girl. He was currently, with discretion, involved with a graduate student named Patricia Ballantyne. They kept separate residences, but according to the data, were lovers. As near as could be determined, however, there was no marriage in sight. The girl was completing her doctoral studies in archeology, and a dozen foundation grants awaited her. Grants that led to distant lands and unfamiliar facts. Patricia Ballantyne was not for marriage; not according to the data banks.

But what of Matlock? wondered Ralph Loring. What did the facts tell him? How could they possibly justify the choice?

They didn't. They couldn't. Only a trained professional could carry out the demands of the current situation. The problems were far too complex, too filled with traps for an amateur.

The terrible irony was that if this Matlock made errors, fell into traps, he might accomplish far more far quicker than any professional.

And lose his life doing so.

'What makes you all think he'll accept?' Cranston was nearing Loring's apartment and his curiosity was piqued.

'What? I'm sorry, what did you say?'

'What's the motive for the subject's acceptance? Why would he agree?'

'A younger brother. Ten years younger, as a matter of fact. The parents are quite old. Very rich, very detached. This Matlock holds himself responsible.'

'For what?'

'The brother. He killed himself three years ago with an overdose of heroin.'

Ralph Loring drove his rented car slowly down the wide, tree-lined street past the large old houses set back beyond manicured lawns. Some were fraternity houses, but there were far fewer than had existed a decade ago. The social exclusivity of the fifties and early sixties was being replaced. A few of the huge structures had other identifications now. *The House, Aquarius* (naturally), *Afro-Commons, Warwick, Lumumba Hall.*

Connecticut's Carlyle University was one of those medium-sized 'prestige' campuses that dot the New England landscape. An administration, under the guidance of its brilliant president, Dr. Adrian Sealfont, was restructuring the college, trying to bring it into the second half of the twentieth century. There were inevitable protests, proliferation of beards, and African studies balanced against the quiet wealth, club blazers, and alumni-sponsored regattas. Hard rock and faculty tea dances were groping for ways to coexist.

Loring reflected, as he looked at the peaceful campus in the bright spring sunlight, that it seemed inconceivable that such a community harbored any real problems.

Certainly not the problem that had brought him there.

Yet it did.

Carlyle was a time bomb which, when detonated, would claim extraordinary victims in its fallout. That it *would* explode, Loring knew, was inevitable. What happened before then was unpredictable. It was up to him to engineer the best possible probabilities. The key was James Barbour Matlock, B.A., M.A., Ph.D.

Loring drove past the attractive two-story faculty residence that held four apartments, each with a separate entrance. It was considered one of the better faculty houses and was usually occupied by bright young families before they'd reached the tenure necessary for outlying homes of their own. Matlock's quarters were on the first floor, west section.

Loring drove around the block and parked diagonally across the street from Matlock's door. He couldn't stay long; he kept turning in the seat, scanning the cars and Sunday morning pedestrians, satisfied that he himself wasn't being observed. That was vital. On Sunday, according to Matlock's surveillance file, the young professor usually read the papers till around noon and then drove to the north end of Carlyle where Patricia Ballantyne lived in one of the efficiency apartments reserved for graduate students. That is, he drove over if she hadn't spent the night with him. Then the two generally went out into the country for lunch and returned to Matlock's apartment or went south into Hartford or New Haven. There were variations, of course. Often the Ballantyne girl and Matlock took weekends together, registering as man and wife. Not this weekend, however. Surveillance had confirmed that.

Loring looked at his watch. It was twelve-forty, but Matlock was still in his apartment. Time was running short. In a few minutes, Loring was expected to be at Crescent Street. 217 Crescent. It was where he would make cover-contact for his second vehicle transfer.

He knew it wasn't necessary for him to physically watch Matlock. After all, he'd read the file thoroughly, looked at scores of photographs, and even talked briefly with Dr. Sealfont, Carlyle's president. Nevertheless, each agent had his own working methods, and his included watching subjects for a period of hours before making contact. Several colleagues at Justice claimed it gave him a sense of power. Loring knew only that it gave him a sense of confidence.

Matlock's front door opened and a tall man walked out into the sunlight. He was dressed in khaki trousers, loafers, and a tan turtleneck sweater. Loring saw that he was modestly good looking with sharp features and fairly long blond hair. He checked the lock on his door, put on a pair of sunglasses, and walked around the sidewalk to what Loring presumed was a small parking area. Several minutes later, James Matlock drove out of the driveway in a Triumph sportscar.

The government man reflected that his subject seemed to have the best of a pleasant life. Sufficient income, no responsibilities, work he enjoyed, even a convenient relationship with an attractive girl.

Loring wondered if it would all be the same for James Barbour Matlock three weeks from then. For Matlock's world was about to be plunged into an abyss.

Two

Matlock pressed the Triumph's accelerator to the floor and the low-slung automobile vibrated as the speedometer reached sixty-two miles per hour. It wasn't that he was in a hurry – Pat Ballantyne wasn't going anywhere – just that he was angry. Well, not angry, really; just irritated. He was usually irritated after a phone call from home. Time would never eliminate that. Nor money, if ever he made any to speak of – amounts his father considered respectable. What caused his irritation was the infuriating condescension. It grew worse as his mother and father advanced in years. Instead of making peace with the situation, they dwelled on it. They insisted that he spend the spring midterm vacation in Scarsdale so that he and his father could make daily trips into the city. To the banks, to the attorneys. To make ready for the inevitable, when and if it ever happened.

'. . . There's a lot you'll have to digest, son,' his father had said sepulchrally. 'You're not exactly prepared, you know. . . .'

'. . . You're all that's left, darling,' his mother had said with obvious pain.

Matlock knew they enjoyed their anticipated, martyred leave-taking of this world. They'd made their mark – or at least his father had. The amusing part was that his parents were as strong as pack mules, as healthy as wild horses. They'd no doubt outlast him by decades.

The truth was that they wanted him with them far more than he wished to be there. It had been that way for the past three years, since David's death at the Cape. Perhaps, thought Matlock, as he drew up in front of Pat's apartment, the roots of his irritation were in his own guilt. He'd never quite made peace with himself about David. He never would.

And he didn't want to be in Scarsdale during the midterm holidays. He didn't want the memories. He had someone now who was helping him forget the awful years – of death, no love, and indecision. He'd promised to take Pat to St. Thomas.

The name of the country inn was the Cheshire Cat, and, as its title implied, it was Englishy and pubbish. The food was decent, the drinks generous, and those factors made it a favorite spot of Connecticut's exurbia. They'd finished their second Bloody Mary and had ordered roast beef and Yorkshire pudding. There were perhaps a dozen couples and several families in the spacious dining area. In the corner sat a single man reading *The New York Times* with the pages folded vertically, commuter fashion.

'He's probably an irate father waiting for a son who's about to splash out. I know the type. They take the Scarsdale train every morning.'

'He's too relaxed.'

'They learn to hide tension. Only their druggists know. All that Gelusil.'

'There are always signs, and he hasn't any. He looks positively self-satisfied. You're wrong.'

'You just don't know Scarsdale. Self-satisfaction is a registered trademark. You can't buy a house without it.'

'Speaking of such things, what are you going to do? I really think we should cancel St. Thomas.'

'I don't. It's been a rough winter; we deserve a little sun. Anyway, they're being unreasonable. There's nothing I want to learn about the Matlock manipulations; it's a waste of time. In the unlikely event that they ever *do* go, others'll be in charge.'

'I thought we agreed that was only an excuse. They want you around for a while. I think it's touching they do it this way.'

'It's not touching, it's my father's transparent attempt at bribery. . . . Look. Our commuter's given up.' The single man with the newspaper finished his drink and was explaining to the waitress that he wasn't ordering lunch. 'Five'll get you ten he pictured his son's hair and leather jacket – maybe bare feet – and just panicked.'

'I think you're wishing it on the poor man.'

'No, I'm not. I'm too sympathetic. I can't stand the aggravation that goes with rebellion. Makes me self-conscious.'

'You're a very funny man, Private Matlock,' said Pat, alluding to Matlock's inglorious army career. 'When we finish, let's go down to Hartford. There's a good movie.'

'Oh, I'm sorry, I forgot to tell you. We can't today. . . . Sealfont called me this morning for an early evening conference. Said it was important.'

'About what?'

'I'm not sure. The African studies may be in trouble. That "Tom" I recruited from Howard turned out to be a beaut. I think he's a little to the right of Louis XIV.'

She smiled. 'Really, you're terrible.'

Matlock took her hand.

The residence of Dr. Adrian Sealfont was imposingly appropriate. It was a large white colonial mansion with wide marble steps leading up to thick double doors carved in relief. Along the front were Ionic pillars spanning the width of the building. Floodlights from the lawn were turned on at sundown.

Matlock walked up the stairs to the door and rang the bell. Thirty seconds later he was admitted by a maid, who ushered him through the hallway toward the rear of the house, into Dr. Sealfont's huge library.

Adrian Sealfont stood in the center of the room with two other men. Matlock, as always, was struck by the presence of the man. A shade over six feet, thin, with aquiline features, he radiated a warmth that touched all who were near him. There was about him a genuine humility which concealed his brilliance from those who did not know him. Matlock liked him immensely.

'Hello, James.' Sealfont extended his hand to Matlock. 'Mr. Loring, may I present Dr. Matlock?'

'How do you do? Hi, Sam,' Matlock addressed this last to the third man, Samuel Kressel, dean of colleges at Carlyle.

'Hello, Jim.'

'We've met before, haven't we?' asked Matlock, looking at Loring. 'I'm trying to remember.'

'I'm going to be very embarrassed if you do.'

'I'll bet you will!' laughed Kressel with his sardonic, slightly offensive, humor. Matlock also liked Sam Kressel, more because he knew the pain of Kressel's job – what he had to contend with – than for the man himself.

'What do you mean, Sam?'

'I'll answer you,' interrupted Adrian Sealfont. 'Mr. Loring is with the federal government, the Justice Department. I agreed to arrange a meeting between the three of you, but I did not agree to what Sam and Mr. Loring have just referred to. Apparently Mr. Loring has seen fit to have you – what is the term – under surveillance. I've registered my strong objections.' Sealfont looked directly at Loring.

'You've had me *what?*' asked Matlock quietly.

'I apologize,' said Loring persuasively. 'It's a personal idiosyncrasy and has nothing to do with our business.'

'You're the commuter in the Cheshire Cat.'

'The what?' asked Sam Kressel.

'The man with the newspaper.'

'That's right. I knew you'd noticed me this afternoon. I thought you'd recognize me the minute you saw me again. I didn't know I looked like a commuter.'

'It was the newspaper. We called you an irate father.'

'Sometimes I am. Not often, though. My daughter's only seven.'

'I think we should begin,' Sealfont said. 'Incidentally, James, I'm relieved your reaction is so understanding.'

'My only reaction is curiosity. And a healthy degree of fear. To tell you the truth, I'm scared to death.' Matlock smiled haltingly. 'What's it all about?'

'Let's have a drink while we talk.' Adrian Sealfont smiled back and walked to his copper-topped dry bar in the corner of the room. 'You're a bourbon and water man, aren't you, James? And Sam, a double Scotch over ice, correct? What's yours, Mr. Loring?'

'Scotch'll be fine. Just water.'

'Here, James, give me a hand.' Matlock crossed to Sealfont and helped him.

'You amaze me, Adrian,' said Kressel, sitting down in a leather armchair. 'What in heaven's name prompts you to remember your subordinates' choice of liquor?'

Sealfont laughed. 'The most logical reason of all. And it certainly isn't confined to my . . . colleagues. I've raised more money for this institution with alcohol than with hundreds of reports prepared by the best analytic minds in fund-raising circles.' Here Adrian Sealfont paused and chuckled – as much to himself as to those in the room. 'I once gave a speech to the

Organization of University Presidents. In the question and answer period, I was asked to what I attributed Carlyle's endowment. . . . I'm afraid I replied, "To those ancient peoples who developed the art of fermenting the vineyards." . . . My late wife roared but told me later I'd set the fund back a decade.'

The three men laughed; Matlock distributed the drinks.

'Your health,' said the president of Carlyle, raising his glass modestly. The toast, however, was brief. 'This is a bit awkward, James . . . Sam. Several weeks ago I was contacted by Mr. Loring's superior. He asked me to come to Washington on a matter of utmost importance, relative to Carlyle. I did so and was briefed on a situation I still refuse to accept. Certain information which Mr. Loring will impart to you seems incontrovertible on the surface. But that is the surface: rumor; out-of-context statements, written and verbal; constructed evidence which may be meaningless. On the other hand, there might well be a degree of substance. It is on that possibility that I've agreed to this meeting. I must make it clear, however, that I cannot be a party to it. Carlyle *will not* be a party to it. Whatever may take place in this room has my unacknowledged approval but not my official sanction. You act as individuals, not as members of the faculty or staff of Carlyle. If, indeed, you decide to act at all. . . . Now, James, if that doesn't "scare you," I don't know what will.' Sealfont smiled again, but his message was clear.

'It scares me,' said Matlock without emphasis.

Kressel put down his glass and leaned forward on the chair. 'Are we to assume from what you've said that you don't endorse Loring's presence here? Or whatever it is he wants?'

'It's a gray area. If there's substance to his charges, I certainly cannot turn my back. On the other hand, no university president these days will openly collaborate with a government agency on speculation. You'll forgive me, Mr. Loring, but too many people in Washington have taken advantage of the academic communities. I refer specifically to Michigan, Columbia, Berkeley . . . among others. Simple police matters are one thing, infiltration . . . well, that's something else again.'

'Infiltration? That's a pretty strong word,' said Matlock.

'Perhaps too strong. I'll leave the terms to Mr. Loring.'

Kressel picked up his glass. 'May I ask why we – Matlock and I – have been chosen?'

'That, again, will be covered in Mr. Loring's discussion. However, since I'm responsible for *you* being here, Sam, I'll tell you *my* reasons. As dean, you're more closely attuned to campus affairs than anyone else. . . . You will also be aware of it if Mr. Loring or his associates overstep their bounds. . . . I think that's all I have to say. I'm going over to the assembly.

That filmmaker, Strauss, is speaking tonight and I've got to put in an appearance.' Sealfont walked back to the bar and put his glass on the tray. The three other men rose.

'One thing before you go,' said Kressel, his brow wrinkled. 'Suppose one or both of us decide we want no part of Mr. Loring's . . . business?'

'Then refuse.' Adrian Sealfont crossed to the library door. 'You are under no obligation whatsoever; I want that perfectly clear. Mr. Loring understands. Good evening, gentlemen.' Sealfont walked out into the hallway, closing the door behind him.

Three

The three men remained silent, standing motionless. They could hear the front entrance open and close. Kressel turned and looked at Loring.

'It seems to me you've been put on the spot.'

'I usually am in these situations. Let me clarify my position; it will partly explain this meeting. The first thing you should know is that I'm with the Justice Department, *Narcotics* Bureau.'

Kressel sat down and sipped at his drink. 'You haven't traveled up here to tell us forty percent of the student body is on pot and a few other items, have you? Because if so, it's nothing we don't know.'

'No, I haven't. I assume you *do* know about such things. Everyone does. I'm not sure about the percentage, though. It could be a low estimate.'

Matlock finished his bourbon and decided to have another. He spoke as he crossed to the copper bar table. 'It may be low or high, but comparatively speaking – in relation to other campuses – we're not in a panic.'

'There's no reason for you to be. Not about that.'

'There's something else?'

'Very much so.' Loring walked to Sealfont's desk and bent down to pick up his briefcase from the floor. It was apparent that the government man and Carlyle's president had talked before Matlock and Kressel arrived. Loring put the briefcase on the desk and opened it. Matlock walked back to his chair and sat down.

'I'd like to show you something.' Loring reached into the briefcase and withdrew a thick page of silver-colored stationery, cut diagonally as if with pinking shears. The silver coating was now filthy with repeated handling and blotches of grease or dirt. He approached Matlock's chair and handed it to him. Kressel got up and came over.

'It's some kind of letter. Or announcement. With numbers,' said Matlock. 'It's in French; no, Italian, I think. I can't make it out.'

'Very good, professor,' said Loring. 'A lot of both and not a predominance of either. Actually, it's a Corsican dialect, written out. It's called the Oltremontan strain, used in the southern hill country. Like Etruscan, it's not entirely translatable. But what codes are used are simple to the point of not being codes at all. I don't think they were meant to be; there aren't too many of these. So there's enough here to tell us what we need to know.'

'Which is?' asked Kressel, taking the strange-looking paper from Matlock.

'First I'd like to explain how we got it. Without that explanation, the information is meaningless.'

'Go ahead.' Kressel handed the filthy silver paper back to the government agent, who carried it to the desk and carefully returned it to his briefcase.

'A narcotics courier – that it, a man who goes into a specific source territory carrying instructions, money, messages – left the country six weeks ago. He was more than a courier, actually; he was quite powerful in the distribution hierarchy; you might say he was on a busman's holiday, Mediterranean style. Or perhaps he was checking investments. . . . At any rate, he was killed by some mountain people in the Toros Daglari – that's Turkey, a growing district. The story is, he canceled operations there and the violence followed. We accept that; the Mediterranean fields are closing down right and left, moving into South America. . . . The paper was found on his body, in a skin belt. As you saw, it's been handed around a bit. It brought a succession of prices from Ankara to Marrakesh. An Interpol undercover man finally made the purchase and it was turned over to us.'

'From Toros Dag-whatever-it-is to Washington. That paper's had quite a journey,' said Matlock.

'And an expensive one,' added Loring. 'Only it's not in Washington now, it's here. From Toros Daglari to Carlyle, Connecticut.'

'I assume that means something.' Sam Kressel sat down, apprehensively watching the government man.

'It means the information in that paper concerns Carlyle.' Loring leaned back against the desk and spoke calmly, with no sense of urgency at all. He could have been an instructor in front of a class explaining a dry but necessary mathematics theorem. 'The paper says there'll be a conference on the tenth of May, three weeks from tomorrow. The numbers are the map coordinates of the Carlyle area – precision decimals of longitude and latitude in Greenwich units. The paper itself identifies the holder to be one of those summoned. Each paper has either a matching half or is cut from a pattern that can be matched – simple additional security. What's missing is the precise location.'

'Wait a minute.' Kressel's voice was controlled but sharp; he was upset.

'Aren't you ahead of yourself, Loring? You're giving us information – obviously restricted – before you state your request. This university administration isn't interested in being an investigative arm of the government. Before you go into facts, you'd better say what you want.'

'I'm sorry, Mr. Kressel. You said I was on the spot and I am. I'm handling it badly.'

'Like hell. You're an expert.'

'Hold it, Sam.' Matlock raised his hand off the arm of the chair. Kressel's sudden antagonism seemed uncalled for. 'Sealfont said we had the option to refuse whatever he wants. If we exercise that option – and we probably will – I'd like to think we did so out of judgement, not blind reaction.'

'Don't be naïve, Jim. You receive restricted or classified information and instantly, *post facto*, you're involved. You can't deny receiving it; you can't say it didn't happen.'

Matlock looked up at Loring. 'Is that true?'

'To a degree, yes. I won't lie about it.'

'Then why should we listen to you?'

'Because Carlyle University *is* involved; has been for years. And the situation is critical. So critical that there are only three weeks left to act on the information we have.'

Kressel got out of his chair, took a deep breath, and exhaled slowly. 'Create the crisis – without proof – and force the involvement. The crisis fades but the records show the university was a silent participant in a federal investigation. That was the pattern at the University of Wisconsin.' Kressel turned to Matlock. 'Do you remember that one, Jim? Six days of riots on campus. Half a semester lost on teach-ins.'

'That was Pentagon oriented,' said Loring. 'The circumstances were entirely different.'

'You think the Justice Department makes it more palatable? Read a few campus newspapers.'

'For Christ's sake, Sam, let the man talk. If you don't want to listen, go home. I want to hear what he has to say.'

Kressel looked down at Matlock. 'All right. I think I understand. Go ahead, Loring. Just remember, no obligations. And we're not bound to respect any conditions of confidence.'

'I'll gamble on your common sense.'

'That may be a mistake.' Kressel walked to the bar and replenished his drink.

Loring sat on the edge of the desk. 'I'll start by asking both of you if you've ever heard of the word *nimrod?*'

'Nimrod is a Hebrew name,' Matlock answered. 'Old Testament. A descendant of Noah, ruler of Babylon and Nineveh. Legendary prowess as a hunter, which obscures the more important fact that he founded, or built, the great cities in Assyria and Mesopotamia.'

Loring smiled. 'Very good again, professor. A *hunter* and a *builder*. I'm speaking in more contemporary terms, however.'

'Then, no, I haven't. Have you, Sam?'

Kressel walked back to his chair, carrying his glass. 'I didn't even know what you just said. I thought a nimrod was a casting fly. Very good for trout.'

'Then I'll fill in some background. . . . I don't mean to bore you with narcotics statistics. I'm sure you're bombarded with them constantly.'

'Constantly,' said Kressel.

'But there's an isolated geographical statistic you may not be aware of. The concentration of drug traffic in the New England states is growing at a rate exceeding that of any other section of the country. It's a startling pattern. Since 1968, there's been a systematic erosion of enforcement procedures. . . . Let me put it into perspective, geographically. In California, Illinois, Louisiana, narcotics controls have improved to the point of at least curtailing the growth curves. It's really the best we can hope for until the international agreements have teeth. But not in the New England area. Throughout this section, the expansion has gone wild. It's hit the colleges hard.'

'How do you know that?' asked Matlock.

'Dozens of ways and always too late to prevent distribution. Informers, marked inventories from Mediterranean, Asian, and Latin American sources, traceable Swiss deposits; that *is* restricted data.' Loring looked at Kressel and smiled.

'Now I know you people are crazy.' Kressel spoke disagreeably. 'It seems to me that if you can substantiate those charges, you should do so publicly. And loud.'

'We have our reasons.'

'Also restricted, I assume,' said Kressel with faint disgust.

'There's a side issue,' continued the government man, disregarding him. 'The eastern prestige campuses – large and small, Princeton, Amherst, Harvard, Vassar, Williams, Carlyle – a good percentage of their enrollments include VIP kids. Sons and daughters of very important people, especially in government and industry. There's a blackmail potential, and we think it's been used. Such people are painfully sensitive to drug scandals.'

Kressel interrupted. 'Granting what you say is true, and I don't, we've had less trouble here than most other colleges in the northeast area.'

'We're aware of that. We even think we know why.'

'That's esoteric, Mr. Loring. Say what you want to say.' Matlock didn't like the games some people played.

'Any distribution network which is capable of systematically servicing, expanding, and controlling an entire section of the country has got to have a base of operations. A clearing house – you might say, a command post. Believe me when I tell you that this base of operations, the command post for the narcotics traffic throughout the New England states, is Carlyle University.'

Samuel Kressel, dean of the colleges, dropped his glass on Adrian Sealfont's parquet floor.

Ralph Loring continued his incredible story. Matlock and Kressel remained in their chairs. Several times during his calm, methodical explanation, Kressel began to interrupt, to object, but Loring's persuasive narrative cut him short. There was nothing to argue.

The investigation of Carlyle University had begun eighteen months ago. It had been triggered by an accounts ledger uncovered by the French Sureté during one of its frequent narcotics investigations in the port of Marseilles. Once the ledger's American origins were established, it was sent to Washington under Interpol agreement. Throughout the ledger's entries were references to 'C-22°-59°' consistently followed by the name *Nimrod*. The numbered degree marks were found to be map co-ordinates of northern Connecticut, but not decimally definitive. After tracing hundreds of possible trucking routes from Atlantic seaboard piers and airports relative to the Marseilles operation, the vicinity of Carlyle was placed under maximum surveillance.

As part of the surveillance, telephone taps were ordered on persons known to be involved with narcotics distribution from such points as New York, Hartford, Boston, and New Haven. Tapes were made of conversations of underworld figures. All calls regarding narcotics to and from the Carlyle area were placed to and from public telephone booths. It made the intercepts difficult, but not impossible. Again, restricted methods.

As the information files grew, a startling fact became apparent. The Carlyle group was independent. It had no formal ties with structured organized crime; it was beholden to no one. It *used* known criminal elements, was not used *by* them. It was a tightly knit unit, reaching into the majority of New England universities. And it did not – apparently – stop at drugs.

There was evidence of the Carlyle unit's infiltration into gambling, prostitution, even postgraduate employment placement. Too, there seemed to be a purpose, an objective beyond the inherent profits of the illegal activities. The Carlyle unit could have made far greater profit with less complications by dealing outright with known criminals, acknowledged suppliers in all areas. Instead, it spent its own money to set up its organization. It was its own master, controlling its own sources, its own distribution. But what its ultimate objectives were was unclear.

It had become so powerful that it threatened the leadership of organized crime in the Northeast. For this reason, leading figures of the underworld had demanded a conference with those in charge of the Carlyle operation. The key here was a group, or an individual, referred to as *Nimrod*.

The purpose of the conference, as far as could be determined, was for an accommodation to be reached between Nimrod and the overlords of crime who felt threatened by Nimrod's extraordinary growth. The conference would be attended by dozens of known and unknown criminals throughout the New England states.

'Mr Kressel.' Loring turned to Carlyle's dean and seemed to hesitate. 'I suppose you have lists – students, faculty, staff – people you know or have reason to suspect are into the drug scene. I can't assume it because I don't know, but most colleges do have.'

'I won't answer that question.'

'Which, of course, gives me my answer,' said Loring quietly, even sympathetically.

'Not for a minute! You people have a habit of assuming exactly what you want to assume.'

'All right, I stand rebuked. But even if you'd said yes, it wasn't my purpose to ask for them. It was merely by way of telling you that we *do* have such a list. I wanted you to know that.'

Sam Kressel realized he'd been trapped; Loring's ingenuousness only annoyed him further. 'I'm sure you do.'

'Needless to say, we'd have no objection to giving you a copy.'

'That won't be necessary.'

'You're pretty obstinate, Sam,' said Matlock. 'You burying your head?'

Before Kressel could reply, Loring spoke. 'The dean knows he can change his mind. And we've agreed, there's no crisis here. You'd be surprised how many people wait for the roof to cave in before asking for help. Or accepting it.'

'But there aren't many surprises in your organization's proclivity for turning difficult situations into disasters, are there?' countered Sam Kressel antagonistically.

'We've made mistakes.'

'Since you have names,' continued Sam, 'why don't you go after them? Leave us out of it; do your own dirty work. Make arrests, press charges. Don't try to deputize *us*.'

'We don't want to do that. . . . Besides, most of our evidence is inadmissible.'

'That occurred to me,' interjected Kressel.

'And what do we gain? What do *you* gain?' Loring leaned forward, returning Sam's stare. 'We pick up a couple of hundred potheads, a few dozen speedfreaks; users and low-level pushers. Don't you understand, that doesn't *solve* anything.'

'Which brings us to what you really want, doesn't it?' Matlock sank back into the chair; he watched the persuasive agent closely.

'Yes,' answered Loring softly. 'We want Nimrod. We want to know the location of that conference on May 10. It could be anywhere within a radius of fifty to a hundred miles. We want to be prepared for it. We want to break the back of the Nimrod operation, for reasons that go way beyond Carlyle University. As well as narcotics.'

'How?' asked James Matlock.

'Dr. Sealfont said it. Infiltration. . . . Professor Matlock, you are what's known in intelligence circles as a highly mobile person within your environment. You're widely accepted by diverse, even conflicting factions – within both the faculty and the student body. We have the names, you have the mobility.' Loring reached into his briefcase and withdrew the scissored page of filthy stationery. 'Somewhere out there is the information we need. Somewhere there's someone who has a paper like this; someone who knows what we have to know.'

James Barbour Matlock remained motionless in his chair, staring at the government man. Neither Loring nor Kressel could be sure what he was thinking but both had an idea. If thoughts were audible, there would have been full agreement in that room at that moment. James Matlock's mind had wandered back three, almost four years ago. He was remembering a blond-haired boy of nineteen. Immature for his age, perhaps, but good, kind. A boy with problems.

They'd found him as they'd found thousands like him in thousands of cities and towns across the country. Other times, other Nimrods.

James Matlock's brother, David, had inserted a needle in his right arm and had shot up thirty mg. of white fluid. He had performed the act in a catboat in the calm waters of a Cape Cod inlet. The small sailboat had drifted into the reeds near shore. When they found it, James Matlock's brother was dead.

Matlock made his decision.

'Can you get me the names?'

'I have them with me.'

'Just hold it.' Kressel stood up, and when he spoke, it wasn't in the tone of an angry man – it was with fear. 'Do you realize what you're asking him to do? He has no experience in this kind of work. He's not trained. Use one of your *own* men.'

'There isn't time. There's no time for one of our men. He'll be protected; you can help.'

'I can *stop* you!'

'No, you can't, Sam,' said Matlock from the chair.

'Jim, for Christ's sake, do you know what he's asking? If there's *any* truth to what he's said, he's placing you in the worst position a man can be in. An informer.'

'You don't have to stay. My decision doesn't have to be your decision. Why don't you go home?' Matlock rose and walked slowly to the bar, carrying his glass.

'That's impossible now,' said Kressel, turning toward the government agent. 'And *he knows it.*'

Loring felt a touch of sadness. This Matlock was a good man; he was doing what he was doing because he felt he owed a debt. And it was coldly, professionally projected that by accepting the assignment, James Matlock was very possibly going to his death. It was a terrible price, that possibility. But the objective was worth it. The conference was worth it.

Nimrod was worth it.

That was Loring's conclusion.

It made his assignment bearable.

Four

Nothing could be written down; the briefing was slow, repetition constant. But Loring was a professional and knew the value of taking breaks from the pressures of trying to absorb too much too rapidly. During these periods, he attempted to draw Matlock out, learn more about this man whose life was so easily expendable. It was nearly midnight; Sam Kressel had left before eight o'clock. It was neither necessary nor advisable that the dean be present during the detailing of the specifics. He was a liaison, not an activist. Kressel was not averse to the decision.

Ralph Loring learned quickly that Matlock was a private man. His answers to innocuously phrased questions were brief, thrown-away replies constituting no more than self-denigrating explanations. After a while, Loring gave up. Matlock had agreed to do a job, not make public his thoughts or his motives. It wasn't necessary; Loring understood the latter. That was all that mattered. He was just as happy not to know the man too well.

Matlock, in turn – while memorizing the complicated information – was, on another level, reflecting on his own life, wondering in his own way why he'd been selected. He was intrigued by an evaluation that could describe him as being *mobile*; what an awful word to have applied!

Yet he knew he was precisely what the term signified. He *was* mobile. The professional researchers, or psychologists, or whatever they were, were accurate. But he doubted they understood the reasons behind his . . . 'mobility.'

The academic world had been a refuge, a sanctuary. Not an objective of long-standing ambition. He had fled into it in order to buy time, to organize a life that was falling apart, to understand. To get his *head straight*, as the kids said these days.

He had tried to explain it to his wife, his lovely, quick, bright, ultimately hollow wife, who thought he'd lost his senses. What was there to understand but an *awfully* good job, an *awfully* nice house, an *awfully* pleasant club, and a *good* life with an *awfully* rewarding social and financial world? For her, there *was* nothing more to understand. And he understood that.

But for him that world had lost its meaning. He had begun to drift away from its core in his early twenties, during his last year at Amherst. The separation became complete with his army experience.

It was no one single thing that had triggered his rejection. And the rejection itself was not a violent act, although violence played its role in the early days of the Saigon mess. It had begun at home, where most life-styles are accepted or rejected, during a series of disagreeable confrontations with his father. The old gentleman – too old, too gentlemanly – felt justified in demanding a better performance from his first son. A direction, a sense of purpose not at all in evidence. The senior Matlock belonged to another era – if not another century – and believed the gap between father and son a desirable thing, the lower element being dismissible until it had proved itself in the marketplace. Dismissible but, of course, malleable. In ways, the father was like a benign ruler who, after generations of power, was loathe to have the throne abandoned by his rightful issue. It was inconceivable to the elder Matlock that his son would not assume the leadership of the family business. Businesses.

But for the younger Matlock, it was all *too* conceivable. And preferable. He was not only uncomfortable thinking about a future in his father's *marketplace*, he was also afraid. For him there was no joy in the regimented pressures of the financial world; instead, there was an awesome fear of inadequacy, emphasized by his father's strong – overpowering – competence. The closer he came to entering that world, the more pronounced was his fear. And it occurred to him that along with the delights of extravagant shelter and unnecessary creature comforts had to come the justification for doing what was expected in order to possess these things. He could not find that justification. Better the shelter should be less extravagant, the creature comforts somewhat limited, than face the prospects of continuing fear and discomfort.

He had tried to explain *that* to his father. Whereas his wife had claimed he'd lost his senses, the old gentleman pronounced him a misfit.

Which didn't exactly refute the army's judgment of him.

The army.

A disaster. Made worse by the knowledge that it was of his own making. He found that blind physical discipline and unquestioned authority were abhorrent to him. And he was large enough and strong enough and had a sufficient vocabulary to make his unadjustable, immature objections known – to his disadvantage.

Discreet manipulations by an uncle resulted in a discharge before his tour of service was officially completed; for that he *was* grateful to an influential family.

And at this juncture of his life, James Barbour Matlock II was a mess. Separated from the service less than gloriously, divorced by his wife, dispossessed – symbolically if not actually – by his family, he felt the panic of belonging nowhere, of being without motive or purpose.

So he'd fled into the secure confines of graduate school, hoping to find an answer. And as in a love affair begun on a sexual basis but growing into psychological dependence, he had married that world; he'd found what had eluded him for nearly five vital years. It was the first real commitment he'd ever experienced.

He was free.

Free to enjoy the excitement of a meaningful challenge; free to revel in the confidence that he was equal to it. He plunged into his new world with the enthusiasm of a convert but without the blindness. He chose a period of history and literature that teemed with energy and conflict and contradictory evaluations. The apprentice years passed swiftly; he was consumed and pleasantly surprised by his own talents. When he emerged on the professional plateau, he brought fresh air into the musty archives. He made startling innovations in long-unquestioned methods of research. His doctoral thesis on court interference with English Renaissance literature – news management – blew into the historical ashcan several holy theories about one benefactress named Elizabeth.

He was the new breed of scholar: restless, sceptical, unsatisfied, always searching while imparting what he'd learned to others. Two and a half years after receiving his doctorate, he was elevated to the tenured position of associate professor, the youngest instructor at Carlyle to be so contracted.

James Barbour Matlock II made up for the lost years, the awful years.

Perhaps best of all was the knowledge that he could communicate his excitement to others. He was young enough to enjoy sharing his enthusiasm, old enough to direct the inquiries.

Yes, he was *mobile*; God, was he! He couldn't, *wouldn't* turn anyone off, shut anyone out because of disagreement – even dislike. The depth of his own gratitude, the profoundness of his relief was such that he unconsciously promised himself never to discount the concerns of another human being.

'Any surprises?' Loring had completed a section of the material that dealt with narcotics purchases as they'd been traced.

'More a clarification, I'd say,' replied Matlock. 'The old-line fraternities or clubs – mostly white, mostly rich – get their stuff from Hartford. The black units like Lumumba Hall go to New Haven. Different sources.'

'Exactly; that's student orientation. The point being that none buy from the Carlyle suppliers. From Nimrod.'

'You explained that. The Nimrod people don't want to be advertised.'

'But they're here. They're used.'

'By whom?'

'Faculty and staff,' answered Loring calmly, flipping over a page. 'This *may* be a surprise. Mr. and Mrs. Archer Beeson . . .'

Matlock immediately pictured the young history instructor and his wife. They were Ivy League conformity itself – falsely arrogant, aesthetically precious. Archer Beeson was a young man in an academic hurry; his wife, the perfect faculty ingenue, carelessly sexy, always in awe.

'They're with LSD and the methedrines. Acid and speed.'

'Good Lord! They fooled the hell out of me. How do you know?'

'It's too complicated to go into, also restricted. To over-simplify: they, he, used to purchase heavily from a distributor in Bridgeport. The contact was terminated and he didn't show up on any other lists. But he's not off. We think he made the Carlyle connection. No proof, though . . . Here's another.'

It was the coach of varsity soccer, a jock who worked in physical education. His items were marijuana and amphetamines; his previous source, Hartford. He was considered a pusher on campus, not a user. Although the Hartford source was no longer employed, the man's varied and dummied bank accounts continued to grow. Assumption: Nimrod.

And another. This one frightening to Matlock. The assistant dean of admissions. An alumnus of Carlyle who returned to the campus after a brief career as a salesman. He was a flamboyant, open-handed man; a proselytizer for the cause of Carlyle. A popular enthusiast in these days of cynicism. He, too, was considered a distributor, not a user. He covered himself well through second- and third-level pushers.

'We think he came back here through the Nimrod organization. Good positioning on Nimrod's part.'

'Goddamn scarey. That son of a bitch makes parents think he's a combination of astronaut and chaplain.'

'Good positioning, as I said. Remember? I told you and Kressel: the Nimrod people have interests that go beyond drugs.'

'But you don't know what they are.'

'We'd better find out. . . . Here's the breakdown of the kids.'

The names of the students seemed endless to Matlock. There were 563 out of a total enrollment of 1200 plus. The government man admitted that many were included not because of confirmation of individual use, but due to their campus affiliations. Clubs and fraternities were known to pool resources for the purchase of narcotics.

'We haven't the time to ascertain the validity of every name. We're looking for relationships; any, no matter how remote. You've got to have all kinds of avenues; we can't restrict them. . . . And there's one aspect to this list; I don't know whether you see it or not.'

'I certainly do. At least, I think I do. Twenty or thirty names here ring loud bells in several high places. Some very influential parents. Industry, government. Here.' Matlock pointed. 'The president's cabinet, if I'm not mistaken. And I'm not.'

'You see.' Loring smiled.

'Has any of this had any effect?'

'We don't know. Could have, could be. The Nimrod tentacles are spreading out fast. That's why the alarms are sounding; louder than your bells. Speaking unofficially, there could be repercussions no one's dreamed of . . . Defense overruns, union contracts, forced installations. You name it. It *could* be related.'

'Jesus Christ,' said Matlock softly.

'Exactly.'

The two men heard the front door of Sealfont's mansion open and shut. As if by reflex, Loring calmly took the papers from Matlock's hand and quickly replaced them in his briefcase. He closed the case and then did an unexpected thing. He silently, almost unobtrusively, whipped back his jacket and curled his fingers around the handle of a revolver in a small holster strapped to his chest. The action startled Matlock. He stared at the hidden hand.

The library door opened and Adrian Sealfont walked in. Loring casually removed his hand from inside his coat. Sealfont spoke kindly.

'I *do try*. I honestly do. I understand the words and the pictures and take no offense whatsoever at the braided hair. What confuses me is the hostility. Anyone past thirty is the natural enemy of these fellows.'

'That was Strauss, wasn't it?' asked Matlock.

'Yes. Someone inquired about the New Wave influence. He replied that the New Wave was ancient history. Prehistoric, was his word. . . . I won't interrupt you gentlemen. I would, however, like to know Kressel's status, Mr. Loring. Obviously, James has accepted.'

'So has Mr. Kressel, sir. He'll act as liaison between us.'

'I see.' Sealfont looked at Matlock. There was a sense of relief in his eyes. 'James, I can tell you now. I'm extremely grateful you've decided to help.'

'I don't think there's an alternative.'

'There isn't. What's frightening is the possibility of such total involvement. Mr. Loring, I'll want to be advised the minute you have anything concrete. At that point, I shall do whatever you wish, follow any instructions. All I ask is that you supply me with proof and you'll have my complete, my official cooperation.'

'I understand, sir. You've been very helpful. More than we had a right to expect. We appreciate it.'

'As James said, there is no alternative. But I must impose limits; my first obligation is to this institution. The campuses these days might appear dormant; I think that's a surface evaluation. . . . You have work to do and I have some reading to finish. Good night, Mr. Loring. James.'

Matlock and the government man nodded their good nights as Adrian Sealfont closed the library door.

By one o'clock, Matlock could absorb no more. The main elements – names, sources, conjectures – were locked in; he would never forget them. Not that he could recite everything by rote; that wasn't expected. But the sight of any particular individual on the lists would trigger a memory response. He knew Loring was right about that. It was why the agent insisted that he say the names out loud, repeating them several times each. It would be enough.

What he needed now was a night's sleep, if sleep would come. Let everything fall into some kind of perspective. Then in the morning he could begin to make initial decisions, determine which individuals should be approached, selecting those least likely to come in contact with one another. And this meant familiarizing himself with immediate friends, faculty or student body status – dozens of isolated fragments of information beyond the data supplied by Loring. Kressel's files – the ones he disclaimed having – would help.

Once in conversations he'd have to make his way carefully – thrusting, parrying, watching for signs, looks, betrayals.

Somewhere, with someone, it would happen.

'I'd like to go back to something,' said Loring. 'Background material.'

'We've covered an awful lot. Maybe I should digest what I've got.'

'This won't take a minute. It's important.' The agent reached into his briefcase and withdrew the filthy, scissored paper. 'Here, this is yours.'

'Thanks for I-don't-know-what.' Matlock took the once-shining silver paper and looked at the strange script.

'I told you it was written in Oltremontan-Corsican and, except for two words, that's correct. At the bottom, on a single line, you'll see the phrase *Venerare Omerta*. That's not Corsican, it's Sicilian. Or a Sicilian contraction, to be precise.'

'I've seen it before.'

'I'm sure you have. It's been given wide distribution in newspapers, movies, fiction. But that doesn't lessen its impact on those concerned by it. It's very real.'

'What does it mean?'

'Roughly translated: Respect the law of Omerta. Omerta is an oath of allegiance *and* silence. To betray either is asking to be killed.'

'Mafia?'

'It's involved. You might say it's the party of the second part. Bear in mind that this little announcement was issued jointly by two factions trying to reach an accommodation. "Omerta" goes across the board; it's understood by both.'

'I'll bear it in mind, but I don't know what I'm supposed to do with it.'

'Just know about it.'

'O.K.'

'One last item. Everything we've covered here tonight is related to narcotics. But if our information is correct, the Nimrod people are involved in other fields. Sharking, prostitution, gambling . . . perhaps, and it's only perhaps, municipal controls, state legislatures, even the federal government. . . . Experience tells us that narcotics is the weakest action, the highest rate of collapse among these activities, and that's why we've centered on it. In other words, concentrate on the drug situation but be aware that other avenues exist.'

'It's no secret.'

'Maybe not to you. Let's call it a night.'

'Shouldn't you give me a number where I can reach you?'

'Negative. Use Kressel. We'll check with him several times a day. Once you start asking questions, you may be put under a microscope. Don't call Washington. And *don't* lose our Corsican invitation. It's your ultimate clout. Just find another one.'

'I'll try.'

Matlock watched as Loring closed his briefcase, looped the thin black chain around his wrist, and snapped the built-in lock.

'Looks very cloak-and-daggerish, doesn't it?' Loring laughed.

'I'm impressed.'

'Don't be. The custom began with diplomatic couriers who'd take their pouches to hell with them, but today it's simply a protection against purse-snatching. . . . So help me, that's what they think of us.'

'I don't believe a word you say. That's one of those cases that make smoke screens, send out radio signals, and trigger bombs.'

'You're right. It does all those things and more. It's got secret compartments for sandwiches, laundry, and God knows what else.' Loring swung the briefcase off the desk. 'I think it'd be a good idea if we left separately. Preferably one from the front, one from the rear. Ten minutes apart.'

'You think that's necessary?'

'Frankly, no, but that's the way my superiors want it.'

'O.K. I know the house. I'll leave ten minutes after you do, from the kitchen.'

'Fine.' Loring extended his right hand by steadying the bottom of his case with his left. 'I don't have to tell you how much we appreciate what you're doing.'

'I think you know why I'm doing it.'

'Yes, we do. Frankly, we counted on it.'

Loring let himself out of the library and Matlock waited until he heard the outer door open and close. He looked at his watch. He'd have one more drink before he left.

By one-twenty Matlock was several blocks away from the house. He walked slowly west toward his apartment, debating whether to detour around the campus. It often helped him to walk out a problem; he knew sleep would come fitfully. He passed a number of students and several faculty members, exchanging low-keyed, end of the weekend greetings with those he recognized. He'd about made up his mind to turn north on High Street, away from the direction of his apartment, when he heard the footsteps behind him. First the footsteps, then the harshly whispered voice.

'Matlock! Don't turn around. It's Loring. Just keep walking and listen to me.'

'What is it?'

'Someone knows I'm here. My car was searched . . .'

'Christ! How do you know?'

'Field threads, preset markings. All over the car. Front, back, trunk. A very thorough, very professional job.'

'You're sure?'

'So goddamn sure I'm not going to start that engine!'

'Jesus!' Matlock nearly stopped.

'Keep walking. If anyone was watching me – and you can be damned sure someone was – I made it clear I'd lost my ignition key. Asked several people who passed by where a pay phone was and waited till I saw you far enough away.'

'What do you want me to do? There's a phone booth on the next corner. . . .'

'I know. I don't think you'll have to do anything, and for both our sakes, I hope I'm right. I'm going to jostle you as I pass – pretty hard. Lose your balance, I'll shout my apologies. Pretend you twisted an ankle, a wrist, anything you like; *but buy time!* Keep me in sight until a car comes for me and *I nod that* it's *O.K.* Do you have all that? I'll get to the booth in a hurry.'

'Suppose you're still phoning when I get there?'

'Keep walking but *keep checking.* The car's cruising.'

'What's the point?'

'This briefcase. That's the point. There's only one thing Nimrod – if it *is* Nimrod – would like more than this briefcase. And that's the paper in your coat pocket. So be careful.'

Without warning, he rushed up beside Matlock and pushed him off the sidewalk.

'Sorry, fella! I'm in an awful hurry!'

Matlock looked up from the ground, reflecting that he'd had no reason to *pretend* to fall. The force of Loring's push eliminated that necessity. He swore and rose awkwardly. Once on his feet, he limped slowly toward the phone booth several hundred yards away. He wasted nearly a minute lighting a cigarette. Loring was inside the booth now, sitting on the plastic seat, hunched over the phone.

Any second, Matlock expected Loring's car to drive up the street.

Yet none came.

Instead, there was the tiniest break in the spring noises. A rush of air through the new leaves. Or was it the crush of a stone beneath a foot, or a small twig unable to take the weight of the new growth in the trees? Or was it Matlock's imagination? He couldn't be sure.

He approached the booth and remembered Loring's orders. *Walk by and pay no attention.* Loring was still huddled over the phone, his briefcase resting on the floor, its chain visible. But Matlock could hear no conversation, could see no movement from the man within. Instead, again, there was a sound: now, the sound of a dial tone.

Despite his instructions, Matlock approached the booth and opened the door. There was nothing else he could do. The government man had not even *begun* his call.

And in an instant, he understood why.

Loring had fallen into the gleaming gray metal of the telephone. He was dead. His eyes wide, blood trickling out of his forehead. A small circular hole no larger than a shirt button, surrounded by a spray of cracked glass, was ample evidence of what had happened.

Matlock stared at the man who had briefed him for hours and left him minutes ago. The dead man who had thanked him, joked with him, then finally warned him. He was petrified, unsure of what he should do, *could* do.

He backed away from the booth toward the steps of the nearest house. Instinct told him to stay away but not to run away. Someone was out there in the street. Someone with a rifle.

When the words came, he realized they were his, but he didn't know when he'd decided to shout them. They just emerged involuntarily.

'Help . . . *Help!* There's a man out here! He's been *shot!*'

Matlock raced up the steps of the corner house and began pounding on the door with all his strength. Several lights went on in several different homes. Matlock continued shouting.

'For God's *sake*, someone call the *police! There's a dead man out here!*'

Suddenly, from the shadows underneath the full trees in the middle of the block, Matlock heard the roar of an automobile engine, then the sound of swerving tires as the vehicle pulled out into the middle of the street and started forward. He rushed to the edge of the porch. The long black automobile plunged out of the darkness and sped to the corner. Matlock tried to see the license plates and, realizing that was impossible, took a step down to identify the make of the car. Suddenly he was blinded. The beam of a searchlight pierced the dimly lit spring night and focused itself on him. He pulled his hands up to shield his eyes and then heard the quiet slap, the instant rush of air he had heard minutes ago.

A rifle was being fired at him. A rifle with a silencer.

He dove off the porch into the shrubbery. The black car sped away.

Five

He waited alone. The room was small, the window glass meshed with wire. The Carlyle Police Station was filled with officers and plainclothesmen called back on duty; no one could be sure what the killing signified. And none discounted the possibility that others might follow.

Alert. It was the particular syndrome of midcentury America, thought Matlock.

The gun.

He'd had the presence of mind after reaching the police to call Sam

Kressel. Kressel, in shock, told him he would somehow contact the appropriate men in Washington and then drive down to the station house.

Until further instructions, they both agreed Matlock would restrict himself to a simple statement on finding the body and seeing the automobile. He had been out for a late night walk, that was all.

Nothing more.

His statement was typed out; questions as to time, his reasons for being in the vicinity, descriptions of the 'alleged perpetrator's vehicle,' direction, estimated speed – all were asked routinely and accepted without comment.

Matlock was bothered by his unequivocal negative to one question.

'Did you ever see the deceased before?'

'No.'

That hurt. Loring deserved more than a considered, deliberate lie. Matlock recalled that the agent said he had a seven-year-old daughter. A wife and a child; the husband and father killed and he could not admit he knew his name.

He wasn't sure why it bothered him, but it did. Perhaps, he thought, because he knew it was the beginning of a great many lies.

He signed the short deposition and was about to be released when he heard a telephone ring inside an office beyond the desk. Not *on* the desk, beyond it. Seconds later, a uniformed policeman emerged and said his name in a loud voice, as if to make sure he had not left the building.

'Yes, officer?'

'We'll have to ask you to wait. If you'll follow me, please.'

Matlock had been in the small room for nearly an hour; it was 2:45 A.M. and he had run out of cigarettes. It was no time to run out of cigarettes.

The door opened and a tall, thin man with large, serious eyes walked in. He was carrying Loring's briefcase. 'Sorry to detain you, Dr. Matlock. It is "Doctor," isn't it?'

'"Mister" is fine.'

'My identification. Name's Greenberg, Jason Greenberg. Federal Bureau of Investigation. I had to confirm your situation. . . . It's a hell of a note, isn't it?'

'"A hell of a note"? Is that all you can say?'

The agent looked at Matlock quizzically. 'It's all I care to share,' he said quietly. 'If Ralph Loring had completed his call, he would have reached me.'

'I'm sorry.'

'Forget it. I'm out-briefed – that is, I know something but not much about the Nimrod situation; I'll get filled in before morning. Incidentally, this fellow Kressel is on his way over. He knows I'm here.'

'Does this change anything? . . . That sounds stupid, doesn't it? A man is killed and I ask you if it changes anything. I apologize again.'

'No need to; you've had a terrible experience. . . . Any change is up to you. We accept the fact that Ralph's death could alter tonight's decision. We ask only that you keep your own counsel in what was revealed to you.'

'You're offering me a chance to renege?'

'Of course. You're under no obligation to us.'

Matlock walked to the small, rectangular window with the wire-enclosed glass. The police station was at the south end of the town of Carlyle, about half a mile from the campus, the section of town considered industrialized. Still, there were trees along the streets. Carlyle was a very clean town, a neat town. The trees by the station house were pruned and shaped.

And Carlyle was also something else.

'Let me ask you a question,' he said. 'Does the fact that I found Loring's body associate me with him? I mean, would I be considered a part of whatever he was doing?'

'We don't think so. The way you behaved tends to remove you from any association.'

'What do you mean?' Matlock turned to face the agent.

'Frankly, you panicked. You didn't run, you didn't take yourself out of the area; you flipped out and started shouting your head off. Someone who's programmed for an assignment wouldn't react like that.'

'I wasn't programmed for *this*.'

'Same results. You just found him and lost your head. If this Nimrod even *suspects* we're involved . . .'

'Suspects!' interrupted Matlock. 'They *killed* him!'

'*Someone* killed him. It's unlikely that it's any part of Nimrod. Other factions, maybe. No cover's absolutely foolproof, even Loring's. But his was the closest.'

'I don't understand you.'

Greenberg leaned against the wall and folded his arms, his large, sad eyes reflective. 'Ralph's field cover was the best at Justice. For damn near fifteen years.' The agent looked down at the floor. His voice was deep, with faint bitterness. 'The kind of goddamn cover that works best when it doesn't matter to a man anymore. When it's finally used, it throws everyone off balance. And insults his family.'

Greenberg looked up and tried to smile, but no smile would come.

'I still don't understand you.'

'It's not necessary. The main point is that you simply stumbled on the scene, went into panic, and had the scare of your life. You're dismissible, Mr. Matlock . . . So?'

Before Matlock could respond, the door swung open and Sam Kressel entered, his expression nervous and frightened.

'Oh, Christ! This is terrible! Simply terrible. You're Greenberg?'

'And you're Mr. Kressel.'

'Yes. What's going to happen?' Kressel turned to Matlock, speaking in the same breath. 'Are you all right, Jim?'

'Sure.'

'Well, Greenberg, what's *happening*!?' They told me in Washington that you'd let us know.'

'I've been talking to Mr. Matlock and . . .'

'Listen to me,' interrupted Kressel suddenly. 'I called Sealfont and we're of the same opinion. What happened was terrible . . . tragic. We express our sympathies to the man's family, but we're most anxious that any use of the Carlyle name be cleared with us. We assume this puts everything in a different light and, therefore, we insist we be kept out of it. I think that's understandable.'

Greenberg's face betrayed his distaste. 'You race in here, ask me what's happening, and before you give me a chance to answer, you tell me what *must* happen. Now, how do you want it? Do I call Washington and let them have *your* version or do you want to listen first? Doesn't make a particle of difference to me.'

'There's no reason for antagonism. We never asked to be involved.'

'Nobody does.' Greenberg smiled. 'Just please let me finish. I've offered Matlock his out. He hasn't given me his answer, so I can't give you mine. However, if he says what I think he's going to say, Loring's cover will be activated immediately. It'll be activated anyway, but if the professor's in, we'll blow it up a bit.'

'What the hell are you talking about?' Kressel stared at the agent.

'For years Ralph was a partner in just about the most disreputable law firm in Washington. Its clients read like a cross section of a Mafia index. . . . Early this morning, there was the first of two vehicle transfers. It took place in a Hartford suburb, Elmwood. Loring's car with the D.C. plates was left near the home of a well-advertised capo. A rented automobile was waiting for him a couple of blocks away. He used that to drive to Carlyle and parked it in front of 217 Crescent Street, five blocks from Sealfont's place. 217 Crescent is the residence of a Dr. Ralston. . . .'

'I've met him,' interjected Matlock. 'I've heard he's . . .'

'. . . an abortionist,' completed Greenberg.

'He's in no way associated with this university!' said Kressel emphatically.

'You've had worse,' countered Greenberg quietly. 'And the doctor is still a Mafia referral. At any rate, Ralph positioned the car and walked into town for the second transfer. I covered him; this briefcase is prime material. He

was picked up by a Bell Telephone truck which made routine stops –
including one at a restaurant called the Cheshire Cat – and finally delivered
him to Sealfont's. No one could have known he was there. If they had, they
would have intercepted him outside; they were watching the car on
Crescent.'

'That's what he told me,' said Matlock.

'He knew it was possible; the trace to Crescent was intentionally left open.
When he confirmed it, to his satisfaction, he acted fast. I don't know what
he did, but he probably used whatever stragglers he could find until he
spotted you.'

'That's what he did.'

'He wasn't fast enough.'

'What in God's name does this have to do with *us*? What *possible* bearing
can it have?' Kressel was close to shouting.

'If Mr. Matlock wants to go on, Loring's death will be publicized as an
underworld killing. Disreputable lawyer, maybe a bag man; undesirable
clients. The capo and the doctor will be hauled in; they're expendable. The
smoke screen's so thick everyone's off balance. Even the killers. Matlock's
forgotten. It'll work; it's worked before.'

Kressel seemed astonished at Greenberg's assured glibness, his confidence,
his calm professionalism. 'You talk awfully fast, don't you?'

'I'm very bright.'

Matlock couldn't help but smile. He liked Greenberg; even in – perhaps
because of – the sadly disagreeable circumstances. The agent used the
language well; his mind was fast. He was, indeed, bright.

'And if Jim says he washes his hands of it?'

Greenberg shrugged. 'I don't like to waste words. Let's hear him say it.'

Both the men looked at Matlock.

'I'm afraid I'm not going to, Sam. I'm still in.'

'You can't be serious! That man was killed!'

'I know. I found him.'

Kressel put his hand on Matlock's arm. It was the gesture of a friend. 'I'm
not an hysterical shepherd watching over a flock. I'm concerned. I'm
frightened. I see a man being manipulated into a situation he's not qualified
to handle.'

'That's subjective,' broke in Greenberg quietly. 'We're concerned, too. If
we didn't think he was capable, we never would have approached him.'

'I think you would,' said Kressel. 'I don't for a minute believe such a
consideration would stop you. You use the word *expendable* too easily, Mr.
Greenberg.'

'I'm sorry you think so. Because I don't. We don't. . . . I haven't gotten
the detailed briefing, Kressel, but aren't you supposed to act as liaison?

Because if that's true, I suggest you remove yourself. We'll have someone else assigned to the job.'

'And give you a clear field? Let you run roughshod over this campus? Not on your life.'

'Then we work together. As disagreeable as that may be for both of us . . . You're hostile; perhaps that's good. You'll keep me on my toes. You protest too much.'

Matlock was startled by Greenberg's statement. It was one thing to form an antagonistic coalition, quite another to make veiled accusations; insulting to use a literary cliché.

'That remark requires an explanation,' said Kressel, his face flushed with anger.

When Greenberg replied, his voice was soft and reasonable, belying the words he spoke. 'Pound sand, mister. I lost a very good friend tonight. Twenty minutes ago I spoke with his wife. I don't give explanations under those conditions. That's where my employers and me part company. Now, shut up and I'll write out the hours of contact and give you the emergency telephone numbers. If you don't want them, get the hell out of here.'

Greenberg lifted the briefcase onto a small table and opened it. Sam Kressel, stunned, approached the agent silently.

Matlock stared at the worn leather briefcase, only hours ago chained to the wrist of a dead man. He knew the deadly pavanne had begun. The first steps of the dance had been taken violently.

There were decisions to make, people to confront.

Six

The implausible name below the door bell on the two-family faculty house read: Mr. and Mrs. Archer Beeson. Matlock had elicited the dinner invitation easily. History instructor Beeson had been flattered by his interest in coordinating a seminar between two of their courses. Beeson would have been flattered if a faculty member of Matlock's attainments had asked him how his wife was in bed (and most wondered). And since Matlock was very clearly male, Archer Beeson felt that 'drinks and din' with his wife wriggling around in a short skirt might help cement a relationship with the highly regarded professor of English literature.

Matlock heard the breathless shout from the second-floor landing. 'Just a sec!'

It was Beeson's wife, and her broad accent, overcultivated at Miss Porter's and Finch, sounded caricatured. Matlock pictured the girl racing around checking the plates of cheese and dip – very unusual cheese and dip, conversation pieces, really – while her husband put the final touches on the visual aspects of his bookcases – perhaps several obscure tomes carelessly, carefully, placed on tables, impossible for a visitor to miss.

Matlock wondered if these two were also secreting small tablets of lysergic acid or capsules of methedrine.

The door opened and Beeson's petite wife, dressed in the expected short skirt and translucent silk blouse that loosely covered her large breasts, smiled ingenuously.

'Hi! I'm Ginny Beeson. We met at several *mad* cocktail parties. I'm *so* glad you could come. Archie's just finishing a paper. Come on up.' She preceded Matlock up the stairs, hardly giving him a chance to acknowledge. 'These stairs are *horrendous*! Oh, well, the price of starting at the bottom.'

'I'm sure it won't be for long,' said Matlock.

'That's what Archie keeps saying. He'd better be right or I'll have muscles all over my legs!'

'I'm sure he is,' said Matlock looking at the soft, unmuscular, large expanse of legs in front of him.

Inside the Beeson apartment, the cheese and dip were prominently displayed on an odd-shaped coffee table, and the anticipated showcase volume was one of Matlock's own. It was titled *Interpolations in Richard II* and it resided on a table underneath a fringed lamp. Impossible for a visitor to miss.

The minute Ginny closed the door, Archie burst into the small living room from what Matlock presumed was Beeson's study – also small. He carried a sheaf of papers in his left hand; his right was extended.

'Good-oh! Glad you could make it, old man! . . . Sit, sit. Drinks are due and overdue! Good! I'm flaked out for one! . . . Just spent three hours reading twenty versions of the Thirty Years' War!'

'It happens. Yesterday I got a theme on *Volpone* with the strangest ending I ever heard of. Turned out the kid never read it but saw the film in Hartford.'

'With a new ending?'

'Totally.'

'God! That's marvy!' injected Ginny semihysterically. 'What's your drink preference, Jim? I may call you Jim, mayn't I, Doctor?'

'Bourbon and a touch of water, and you certainly better, Ginny. I've never gotten used to the "doctor." My father calls it fraud. Doctors carry stethoscopes, not books.' Matlock sat in an easy chair covered with an Indian serape.

'Speaking of doctors, I'm working on my dissertation now. That and two more hectic summers'll do the trick.' Beeson took the ice bucket from his wife and walked to a long table underneath a window where bottles and glasses were carelessly arranged.

'It's worth it,' said Ginny Beeson emphatically. 'Isn't it worth it, Jim?'

'Almost essential. It'll pay off.'

'That and *publishing*.' Ginny Beeson picked up the cheese and crackers and carried them to Matlock. 'This is an interesting little Irish *fromage*. Would you believe, it's called "Blarney"? Found it in a little shop in New York two weeks ago.'

'Looks great. Never heard of it.'

'Speaking of publishing. I picked up your *Interpolations* book the other day. *Damned fascinating!* Really!'

'Lord, I've almost forgotten it. Wrote it four years ago.'

'It should be a *required text!* That's what Archie said, isn't it, Archie?'

'Damned right! Here's the poison, old man,' said Beeson, bringing Matlock his drink. 'Do you work through an agent, Jim? Not that I'm nosy. I'm years from writing anything.'

'That's not true, and you know it,' Ginny pouted vocally.

'Yes, I do. Irving Block in Boston. If you're working on something, perhaps I could show it to him.'

'Oh, no, I wouldn't . . . that'd be awfully presumptuous of me. . . .' Beeson retreated with feigned humility to the couch with his drink. He sat next to his wife and they – involuntarily, thought Matlock – exchanged satisfied looks.

'Come on, Archie. You're a bright fellow. A real comer on this campus. Why do you think I asked you about the seminar! *You* could be doing *me* the favor. I might be bringing Block a winner. That rubs off, you know.'

Beeson's expression had the honesty of gratitude. It embarrassed Matlock to return the instructor's gaze until he saw something else in Beeson's eyes. He couldn't define it, but it was there. A slight wildness, a trace of panic.

The look of a man whose mind and body knew drugs.

'That's *damned* good-oh of you, Jim. I'm touched, *really*.'

The cheese, drinks, and dinner somehow passed. There were moments when Matlock had the feeling he was outside himself, watching three characters in a scene from some old movie. Perhaps on board ship or in a sloppily elegant New York apartment with the three of them wearing tightly fitted formal clothes. He wondered why he visualized the scene in such fashion – and then he knew. The Beesons had a thirties quality about them. The thirties that he had observed on the late night television films. They were somehow an anachronism, of this time but not of the time. It was either more than camp or less than put-on; he couldn't be sure. They were not artificial in themselves, but there was a falseness in their emphatic small talk, their dated expressions. Yet the truth was that they were the *now* of the present generation.

Lysergic acid and methedrine.

Acid heads. Pill poppers.

The Beesons were somehow forcing themselves to show themselves as part of a past and carefree era. Perhaps to deny the times and conditions in which they found themselves.

Archie Beeson and his wife were frightening.

By eleven, after considerable wine with the 'interesting-little-veal-dish-from-a-recipe-in-an-old-Italian-cookbook,' the three of them sat down in the living room. The last of the proposed seminar problems was ironed out. Matlock knew it was time to begin; the awful, awkward moment. He wasn't sure how; the best he could do was to trust his amateur instincts.

'Look, you two . . . I hope to hell this won't come as too great a shock, but I've been a long time without a stick.' He withdrew a thin cigarette case from his pocket and opened it. He felt foolish, uncomfortably clumsy. But he knew he could not show those feelings. 'Before you make any judgments, I should tell you I don't go along with the pot laws and I never have.'

Matlock selected a cigarette from the dozen in the case and left the case open on the table. Was that the proper thing to do? He wasn't sure; he didn't know. Archie and his wife looked at each other. Through the flame in front of his face, Matlock watched their reaction. It was cautious yet positive. Perhaps it was the alcohol in Ginny, but she smiled hesitantly, as if she was relieved to find a friend. Her husband wasn't quite so responsive.

'Go right ahead, old man,' said the young instructor with a trace of condescension. 'We're hardly on the attorney general's payroll.'

'Hardly!' giggled the wife.

'The laws are archaic,' continued Matlock, inhaling deeply. 'In all areas. Control and an abiding sense of discretion – self-discretion – are all that matter. To deny experience is the real crime. To prohibit any intelligent individual's right to fulfillment is . . . goddamn it, it's repressive.'

'Well, I think the key word is *intelligent*, Jim. *In*discriminate use among the *un*intelligent leads to chaos.'

'Socratically, you're only half right. The other half is "control." Effective control among the "iron" and "bronze" then frees the "gold" – to borrow from *The Republic*. If the intellectually superior were continually kept from thinking, experimenting, because their thought processes were beyond the comprehension of their fellow citizens, there'd be no great works – artistically, technically, politically. We'd still be in the Dark Ages.'

Matlock inhaled his cigarette and closed his eyes. Had he been too strong, too positive? Had he sounded too much the false proselytizer? He waited, and the wait was not long. Archie spoke quietly, but urgently nevertheless.

'Progress is being made every day, old man. Believe that. It's the truth.'

Matlock half opened his eyes in relief and looked at Beeson through the cigarette smoke. He held his gaze steady without blinking and then shifted his stare to Beeson's wife. He spoke only two words.

'You're children.'

'That's a relative supposition under the circumstances,' answered Beeson still keeping his voice low, his speech precise.

'And that's talk.'

'Oh, don't be so sure about that!' Ginny Beeson had had enough alcohol in her to be careless. Her husband reached for her arm and held it. It was a warning. He spoke again, taking his eyes off Matlock, looking at nothing.

'I'm not at all sure we're on the same wavelength . . .'

'No, probably not. Forget it. . . . I'll finish this and shove off. Be in touch with you about the seminar.' Matlock made sure his reference to the seminar was offhanded, almost disinterested.

Archie Beeson, the young man in an academic hurry, could not stand that disinterest.

'Would you mind if I had one of those?'

'If it's your first, yes, I would. . . . Don't try to impress me. It doesn't really matter.'

'My first? . . . Of what?' Beeson rose from the couch and walked to the table where the cigarette case lay open. He reached down, picked it up, and held it to his nostrils. 'That's passable grass. I might add, just passable. I'll try one . . . for openers.'

'For openers?'

'You seem to be very sincere but, if you'll forgive me, you're a bit out of touch.'

'From what?'

'From where it's at.' Beeson withdrew two cigarettes and lit them in *Now, Voyager* fashion. He inhaled deeply, nodding and shrugging a reserved approval, and handed one to his wife. 'Let's call this an hors d'oeuvre. An appetizer.'

He went into his study and returned with a Chinese lacquered box, then showed Matlock the tiny peg which, when pushed, enabled the holder to flip up a thin layer of wood on the floor of the box, revealing a false bottom. Beneath were two dozen or so white tablets wrapped in transparent plastic.

'This is the main course . . . the entrée, if you're up to it.'

Matlock was grateful for what knowledge he possessed and the intensive homework he'd undertaken during the past forty-eight hours. He smiled but his tone of voice was firm.

'I only take white trips under two conditions. The first is at *my* home with very good, very old friends. The second is with very good, very old friends at *their* homes. I don't know you well enough, Archie. Self-destruction. . . . I'm not averse to a small red journey, however. Only I didn't come prepared.'

'Say no more. I just may be.' Beeson took the Chinese box back into his study and returned with a small leather pouch, the sort pipe smokers use for tobacco, and approached Matlock's chair. Ginny Beeson's eyes grew wide; she undid a button on her half-unbuttoned blouse and stretched her legs.

'Dunhill's best.' Beeson opened the top flap and held the pouch down for Matlock to see inside. Again there was the clear plastic wrapped around tablets. However, these were deep red and slightly larger than the white pills in the Chinese box. There were at least fifty to sixty doses of Seconal.

Ginny jumped out of the chair and squealed. 'I *love* it! It's the pinky-groovy!'

'Beats the hell out of brandy,' added Matlock.

'We'll trip. Not too much, old man. Limit's five. That's the house rules for new old friends.'

The next two hours were blurred for James Matlock, but not as blurred as they were for the Beesons. The history instructor and his wife quickly reached their 'highs' with the five pills – as would have Matlock had he not been able to pocket the final three while pretending to have swallowed them. Once on the first plateau, it wasn't hard for Matlock to imitate his companions and then convince Beeson to go for another dosage.

'Where's the almighty discretion, Doctor?' chuckled Beeson, sitting on the floor in front of the couch, reaching occasionally for one of his wife's legs.

'You're better friends than I thought you were.'

'Just the *beginning* of a beautiful, *beautiful* friendship.' The young wife slowly reclined on the couch and giggled. She seemed to writhe and put her right hand on her husband's head, pushing his hair forward.

Beeson laughed with less control than he had shown earlier and rose from the floor. 'I'll get the magic then.'

When Beeson walked into his study, Matlock watched his wife. There was no mistaking her action. She looked at Matlock, opened her mouth slowly, and pushed her tongue out at him. Matlock realized that one of Seconal's side effects was showing. As was most of Virginia Beeson.

The second dosage was agreed to be three, and Matlock was now easily able to fake it. Beeson turned on his stereo and played a recording of 'Carmina Burana.' In fifteen minutes Ginny Beeson was sitting on Matlock's lap, intermittently rubbing herself against his groin. Her husband was spread out in front of the stereo speakers, which were on either side of the turntable.

Matlock spoke as though exhaling, just loud enough to be heard over the music.

'These are some of the best I've had, Archie. . . . Where? Where's the supply from?'

'Probably the same as yours, old man.' Beeson turned over and looked at Matlock and his wife. He laughed. 'Now, I don't know what you mean. The magic or the girl on your lap. Watch her, Doctor. She's a minx.'

'No kidding. Your pills are a better grade than mine and my grass barely passed inspection. Where? Be a good friend.'

'You're funny, man. You keep asking. Do I ask you? No. . . . It's not polite. . . . Play with Ginny. Let me listen.' Beeson rolled back over face down on the floor.

The girl on Matlock's lap suddenly put her arms around his neck and pressed her breasts against his chest. She put her head to the side of his face and began kissing his ears. Matlock wondered what would happen if he lifted her out of the chair and carried her into the bedroom. He wondered, but he didn't want to find out. Not then. Ralph Loring had not been murdered to increase his, Matlock's, sex life.

'Let me try one of your joints. Let me see just how advanced your taste is. You may be a phony, Archie.'

Suddenly Beeson sat up and stared at Matlock. He wasn't concerned with his wife. Something in Matlock's voice seemed to trigger an instinctive doubt. Or was it the words? Or was it the too normal pattern of speech Matlock used? The English professor thought of all these things as he returned Beeson's look over the girl's shoulder. Archie Beeson was suddenly a man warned, and Matlock wasn't sure why. Beeson spoke haltingly.

'Certainly, old man. . . . Ginny, don't annoy Jim.' He began to rise.

'Pinky groovy . . .'

'I've got several in the kitchen. . . . I'm not sure where but I'll look. Ginny, I told you not to tease Jim. . . . Be nice to him, be good to him.' Beeson kept staring at Matlock, his eyes wide from the Seconal, his lips parted, the muscles of his face beyond relaxation. He backed away toward the kitchen door, which was open. Once inside, Archie Beeson did a strange thing. Or so it appeared to James Matlock.

He slowly closed the swing-hinged door and held it shut.

Matlock quickly eased the drugged girl off his lap and she quietly stretched out on the floor. She smiled angelically and reached her arms up for him. He smiled down, stepping over her.

'Be right back,' he whispered. 'I want to ask Archie something.' The girl rolled over on her stomach as Matlock walked cautiously toward the kitchen door. He ruffled his hair and purposely, silently, lurched, holding onto the dining room table as he neared the entrance. If Beeson suddenly came out, he wanted to appear irrational, drugged. The stereo was a little louder now, but through it Matlock could hear the sound of Archie's voice talking quietly, excitedly on the kitchen telephone.

He leaned against the wall next to the kitchen door and tried to analyse the disjointed moments that caused Archie Beeson to panic, to find it so imperative to reach someone on the telephone.

Why? What?

Had the grand impersonation been so obvious? Had he blown his first encounter?

If he had, the least he could do was try to find out who was on the other end of the line, who it was that Beeson ran to in his disjointed state of anxiety.

One fact seemed clear: whoever it was had to be more important than Archer Beeson. A man – even a drug addict – did not panic and contact a lesser figure on his own particular totem.

Perhaps the evening wasn't a failure; or his failure – conversely – a necessity. In Beeson's desperation, he might let slip information he never would have revealed if he *hadn't* been desperate. It wasn't preposterous to force it out of the frightened, drugged instructor. On the other hand, that was the least desirable method. If he failed in that, too, he was finished before he'd begun. Loring's meticulous briefing would have been for nothing; his death a rather macabre joke, his terrible cover – so painful to his family, so inhuman somehow – made fruitless by a bumbling amateur.

There was no other way, thought Matlock, but to try. Try to find out who Beeson had reached *and* try to put the pieces of the evening back where Beeson might accept him again. For some insane reason, he pictured Loring's briefcase and the thin black chain dangling from the handle. For an even crazier reason, it gave him confidence; not much, but some.

He assumed a stance as close to the appearance of collapse as he could imagine, then moved his head to the door frame and slowly, quarter inch by quarter inch, pushed it inward. He fully expected to be met by Beeson's staring eyes. Instead, the instructor's back was to him; he was hunched over like a small boy trying to control his bladder, the phone clutched to his thin scrunched neck, his head bent to the side. It was obvious that Beeson thought his voice was muffled, indistinguishable beneath the sporadic crescendos of the 'Carmina Burana.' But the Seconal had played one of its tricks. Beeson's ear and his speech were no longer synchronized. His words were not only clear. They were emphasized by being spaced out and repeated.

'. . . You *do not* understand me. I want you to understand me. *Please*, understand. He keeps asking questions. He's not *with* it. He *is not with it*. I swear to Christ he's a plant. Get hold of Herron. Tell Herron to reach him for *God's* sake. Reach him, *please*! I could lose everything! . . . No. No, I can tell! I *see* what I *see*, *man*! When that bitch turns horny I have *problems*. I mean there are appearances, old man. . . . Get Lucas. . . . For Christ's sake *get* to him! I'm in *trouble* and I can't. . . .'

Matlock let the door swing slowly back into the frame. His shock was such that thought and feeling were suspended; he saw his hand still on the kitchen door, yet he felt no wood against his fingers. What he had just heard was no less horrible than the sight of Ralph Loring's lifeless body in the telephone booth.

Herron. *Lucas Herron!*

A seventy-year-old legend. A quiet scholar who was as much revered for his perceptions of the human condition as he was for his brilliance. A lovely man, an honored man. There had to be a mistake, an explanation.

There was no time to ponder the inexplicable.

Archer Beeson thought he was a 'plant.' And now, someone else thought so, too. He couldn't allow that. He had to think, force himself to *act*.

Suddenly he understood. Beeson himself had told him what to do.

No informer – no one not narcotized – would attempt it.

Matlock looked over at the girl lying face down on the living room floor. He crossed rapidly around the dining table and ran to her side, unbuckling his belt as he did so. In swift movements, he took off his trousers and reached down, rolling her over on her back. He lay down beside her and undid the remaining two buttons on her blouse, pulling her brassiere until the hasp broke. She moaned and giggled, and when he touched her exposed breasts, she moaned again and lifted one leg over Matlock's hip.

'Pinky groovy, pinky groovy . . .' She began breathing through her mouth, pushing her pelvis into Matlock's groin; her eyes half open, her hands reaching down, stroking his leg, her fingers clutching at his skin.

Matlock kept his eyes toward the kitchen door, praying it would open.

And then it did, and he shut his eyes.

Archie Beeson stood in the dining area looking down at his wife and guest. Matlock, at the sound of Beeson's footsteps, snapped his head back and feigned terrified confusion. He rose from the floor and immediately fell back down again. He grabbed his trousers and held them in front of his shorts, rising once more unsteadily and finally falling onto the couch.

'Oh, Jesus! Oh, sweet Jesus, Archie! Christ, young fella! I didn't think I was this freaked out! . . . I'm far out, Archie! What the hell, what do I *do*? I'm *gone*, man, I'm sorry! Christ, I'm sorry!'

Beeson approached the couch, his half-naked wife at his feet. From his expression it was impossible to tell what he was thinking. Or the extent of his anger.

Or was it anger?

His audible reaction was totally unexpected. He started to laugh. At first softly, and then with gathering momentum, until he became nearly hysterical.

'Oh, *God*, old man! I said it! I *said* she was a minx! . . . Don't worry. No tattle tales. No rapes, no dirty-old-man-on-the-faculty. But we'll have our *seminar*. Oh, Christ, yes! That'll be some *seminar*! And you'll tell them all you picked *me*! Won't you? Oh, yes! That's what you'll tell them, isn't it?'

Matlock looked into the wild eyes of the addict above him.

'Sure. Sure, Archie. Whatever you say.'

'You better believe it, old man! And don't apologize. No apologies are necessary! The apologies are mine!' Archer Beeson collapsed on the floor in laughter. He reached over and cupped his wife's left breast; she moaned and giggled her maddening, high-pitched giggle.

And Matlock knew he had won.

Seven

He was exhausted, both by the hour and by the tensions of the night. It was ten minutes past three and the choral strains of the 'Carmina Burana' were still hammering in his ears. The image of the bare-breasted wife and the jackal-sounding husband – both writhing on the floor in front of him – added revulsion to the sickening taste in his mouth.

But what bothered him most was the knowledge that Lucas Herron's name was used within the context of such an evening.

It was inconceivable.

Lucas Herron. The 'grand old bird,' as he was called. A reticent but obvious fixture of the Carlyle campus. The chairman of the Romance languages department and the embodiment of the quiet scholar with a deep and abiding compassion. There was always a glint in his eyes, a look of bemusement mixed with tolerance.

To associate him – regardless of how remotely – with the narcotics world was unbelievable. To have heard him sought after by an hysterical addict – for essentially, Archer Beeson *was* an addict, psychologically if not chemically – as though Lucas were some sort of power under the circumstances was beyond rational comprehension.

The explanation had to lie somewhere in Lucas Herron's immense capacity for sympathy. He was a friend to many, a dependable refuge for the troubled, often the deeply troubled. And beneath his placid, aged, unruffled surface, Herron was a strong man, a leader. A quarter of a century ago, he had spent countless months of hell in the Solomon Islands as a middle-aged infantry officer. A lifetime ago, Lucas Herron had been an authentic hero in a vicious moment of time during a savage war in the Pacific. Now over seventy, Herron was an institution.

Matlock rounded the corner and saw his apartment half a block away. The campus was dark; aside from the street lamps, the only light came from one of his rooms. Had he left one on? He couldn't remember.

He walked up the path to his door and inserted his key. Simultaneously with the click of the lock, there was a loud crash from within. Although it startled him, his first reaction was amusement. His clumsy, long-haired house cat had knocked over a stray glass or one of those pottery creations Patricia Ballantyne had inflicted on him. Then he realized such a thought was ridiculous, the product of an exhausted mind. The crash was too loud for pottery, the shattering of glass too violent.

He rushed into the small foyer, and what he saw pushed fatigue out of his brain. He stood immobile in disbelief.

The entire room was in shambles. Tables were overturned; books pulled from the shelves, their pages torn from the bindings, scattered over the floor, his stereo turntable and speakers smashed. Cushions from his couch and armchairs were slashed, the stuffing and foam rubber strewn everywhere; the rugs upended, lumped in folds; the curtains ripped from their rods, thrown over the upturned furniture.

He saw the reason for the crash. His large casement window, on the far right wall bordering the street, was a mass of twisted lead and broken glass. The window consisted of two panels; he remembered clearly that he had opened both before leaving for the Beesons. He liked the spring breezes, and it was too early in the season for screens. So there was no reason for the window to be smashed; the ground was perhaps four or five feet below the casement, sufficient to dissuade an intruder, low enough for a panicked burglar to negotiate easily.

The smashing of the window, therefore, was not for escape. It was intended.

He had been watched, and a signal had been given.

It was a warning.

And Matlock knew he could not acknowledge that warning. To do so was to acknowledge more than a robbery; he was not prepared to do that.

He crossed rapidly to his bedroom door and looked inside. If possible, his bedroom was in more of a mess than the living room. The mattress was thrown against the wall, ripped to shreds. Every drawer of his bureau was dislodged, lying on the floor, the contents scattered all around the room. His closet was like the rest – suits and jackets pulled from the clothes rod, shoes yanked from their recesses.

Even before he looked he knew his kitchen would be no better off than the rest of his apartment. The foodstuffs in cans and boxes had not been thrown on the floor, simply moved around, but the soft items had been torn to pieces. Matlock understood again. One or two crashes from the other rooms were tolerable noise levels; a continuation of the racket from his kitchen might arouse one of the other families in the building. As it was, he could hear the faint sounds of footsteps above him. The final crash of the window had gotten someone up.

The warning was explicit, but the act itself was a search.

He thought he knew the object of that search, and again he realized he could not acknowledge it. Conclusions were being made as they had been made at Beeson's; he had to ride them out with the most convincing denials he could manufacture. That much he knew instinctively.

But before he began that pretense, he had to find out if the search was successful.

He shook the stammering lethargy out of his mind and body. He looked once again at his living room; he studied it. All the windows were bare, and the light was sufficient for someone with a pair of powerful binoculars stationed in a nearby building or standing on the inclining lawn of the campus beyond the street to observe every move he made. If he turned off the lights, would such an unnatural action lend credence to the conclusions he wanted denied?

Without question. A man didn't walk into a house in shambles and proceed to turn off lights.

Yet he had to reach his bathroom, at that moment the most important room in the apartment. He had to spend less than thirty seconds inside to determine the success or failure of the ransacking, and do so in such a way as to seem innocent of any abnormal concerns. If anyone *was* watching.

It was a question of appearance, of gesture, he thought. He saw that the stereo turntable was the nearest object to the bathroom door, no more than five feet away. He walked over and bent down, picking up several pieces, including the metal arm. He looked at it, then suddenly dropped the arm and brought his finger to his mouth, feigning an imagined puncture on his skin. He walked into the bathroom rapidly.

Once inside, he quickly opened the medicine cabinet and grabbed a tin of Band-Aids from the glass shelf. He then swiftly reached down to the left of the toilet bowl where the cat's yellow plastic box was placed and picked up a corner of the newspaper underneath the granules of litter. Beneath the newspaper he felt the coarse grain of the two layers of canvas he had inserted and lifted up an edge.

The scissored page was still intact. The silver Corsican paper that ended in the deadly phrase *Venerare Omerta* had not been found.

He replaced the newspaper, scattered the litter, and stood up. He saw that the frosted glass of the small window above the toilet was partially opened, and he swore.

There was no time to think of that.

He walked back into the living room, ripping the plastic off a Band-Aid.

The search had failed. Now the warning had to be ignored, the conclusions denied. He crossed to the telephone and called the police.

'Can you give me a list of what's missing?' A uniformed patrolman stood in the middle of the debris. A second policeman wandered about the apartment making notes.

'I'm not sure yet. I haven't really checked.'

'That's understandable. It's a mess. You'd better look, though. The quicker we get a list, the better.'

'I don't think anything *is* missing, officer. What I mean is, I don't have anything particularly valuable to anyone else. Except perhaps the stereo . . . and that's smashed. There's a television set in the bedroom, that's okay. Some of the books could bring a price, but look at them.'

'No cash, jewelry, watches?'

'I keep money in the bank and cash in my wallet. I wear my watch and haven't any jewelry.'

'How about exam papers? We've been getting a lot of that.'

'In my office. In the English department.'

The patrolman wrote in a small black notebook and called to his partner, who had gone into the bedroom. 'Hey, Lou, did the station confirm the print man?'

'They're getting him up. He'll be over in a few minutes.'

'Have you touched anything, Mr. Matlock?'

'I don't know. I may have. It was a shock.'

'Particularly any of the broken items, like that record player? It'd be good if we could show the fingerprint man specific things you haven't touched.'

'I picked up the arm, not the casing.'

'Good. It's a place to start.'

The police stayed for an hour and a half. The fingerprint specialist arrived, did his work, and departed. Matlock thought of phoning Sam Kressel, but reasoned that there wasn't anything Kressel could do at that hour. And in the event someone outside *was* watching the building, Kressel shouldn't be seen. Various people from the other apartments had wakened and had come down offering sympathy, help, and coffee.

As the police were leaving, a large patrolman turned in the doorway. 'Sorry to take so much time, Mr. Matlock. We don't usually lift prints in a break and entry unless there's injury or loss of property, but there's been a lot of this sort of thing recently. Personally, I think it's those weirdos with the hair and the beads. Or the niggers. We never had trouble like this before the weirdos and the niggers got here.'

Matlock looked at the uniformed officer, who was so confident of his analysis. There was no point in objecting; it would be useless, and Matlock was too tired. 'Thanks for helping me straighten up.'

'Sure thing.' The patrolman started down the cement path, then turned again. 'Oh, Mr. Matlock.'

'Yes?' Matlock pulled the door back.

'It struck us that maybe someone was looking for something. What with all the slashing and books and everything . . . you know what I mean?'

'Yes.'

'You'd tell us if that was the case, wouldn't you?'

'Of course.'

'Yeah. It'd be stupid to withhold information like that.'

'I'm not stupid.'

'No offense. Just that sometimes you guys get all involved and forget things.'

'I'm not absentminded. Very few of us are.'

'Yeah.' The patrolman laughed somewhat derisively. 'I just wanted to bring it up. I mean, we can't do our jobs unless we got all the facts, you know?'

'I understand.'

'Yeah. Good.'

'Good night.'

'Good night, Doctor.'

He closed the door and walked into his living room. He wondered if his insurance would cover the disputable value of his rarer books and prints. He sat down on the ruined couch and surveyed the room. It was still a mess; the carnage had been thorough. It would take more than picking up debris and righting furniture. The warning had been clear, violent.

The startling fact was that the warning existed at all.

Why? From whom?

Archer Beeson's hysterical telephone call? That was possible, even preferable, perhaps. It might encompass a motive unrelated to Nimrod. It could mean that Beeson's circle of users and pushers wanted to frighten him enough to leave Archie alone. Leave them all alone; and Loring had specifically said there was no proof that the Beesons were involved with the Nimrod unit.

There was no proof that they weren't, either.

Nevertheless, if it *was* Beeson, the alarm would be called off in the morning. There was no mistaking the conclusion of the night's engagement. The 'near-rape' by a dirty, drugged 'old man.' He was Beeson's academic ladder.

On the other hand, and far less preferable, there was the possibility that the warning *and* the search were centered on the Corsican paper. What had Loring whispered behind him on the sidewalk?

'. . . There's only one thing they want more than this briefcase; that's the paper in your pocket.'

It was then reasonable to assume that he'd been linked to Ralph Loring.

Washington's assessment that his panic at finding Loring dissociated him from the agent was in error, Jason Greenberg's confidence misplaced.

Still again, as Greenberg had suggested, they might test him. Press him before issuing a clean bill of health.

Might, could, possible, still again.

Conjectures.

He had to keep his head; he couldn't allow himself to overreact. If he was to be of *any* value, he had to play the innocent.

Might have, could have, it was possible.

His body ached. His eyes were swollen and his mouth still had the terrible aftertaste of the combined dosages of Seconal, wine, and marijuana. He was exhausted; the pressures of trying to reach unreachable conclusions were overtaking him. His memory wandered back to the early days in 'Nam and he recalled the best advice he'd ever been given in those weeks of unexpected combat. That was to rest whenever he could, to sleep if it was at all possible. The advice had come from a line sergeant who, it had been rumored, had survived more assaults than any man in the Mekong Delta. Who, it was also rumored, had slept through an ambush which had taken most of his company.

Matlock stretched out on the barely recognizable couch. There was no point in going into the bedroom – his mattress was destroyed. He unbuckled his belt and kicked off his shoes. He could sleep for a few hours; then he'd talk to Kressel. Ask Kressel and Greenberg to work out a story for him to use about the invasion of his apartment. A story approved by Washington and, perhaps, the Carlyle police.

The police.

Suddenly he sat up. It hadn't struck him at the time, but now he considered it. The crass but imperiously polite patrolman whose primitive detection powers had centered on the 'weirdos and niggers' had addressed him as 'Mister' throughout the nearly two hours of police investigation. Yet when he was leaving, when he insultingly referred to the possibility of

Matlock's withholding information, he had called him 'Doctor.' The 'mister' was normal. The 'doctor' was most unusual. No one outside the campus community – and rarely there – ever called him 'Doctor,' ever called *any* Ph.D. 'Doctor.' It struck most holders of such degrees as fatuous, and only the fatuous expected it.

Why had the patrolman used it? He didn't know him, he had never seen him to his knowledge. How would the patrolman know he was even entitled to the name 'doctor'?

As he sat there, Matlock wondered if the combined efforts and pressures of the last hours were taking their toll. Was he now finding unreasonable meanings where no meanings existed? Was it not entirely plausible that the Carlyle police had a list of the Carlyle faculty and that a desk sergeant, or whoever took emergency calls, had checked his name against the list and casually stated his title? Was he not, perhaps, consigning the patrolman to a plateau of ignorance because he disliked the officer's prejudices?

A lot of things were possible.

And disturbing.

Matlock fell back onto the couch and closed his eyes.

At first the noise reached him as a faint echo might from the far end of a long, narrow tunnel. Then the noise became identifiable as rapid, incessant tapping. Tapping which would not stop, tapping which became louder and louder.

Matlock opened his eyes and saw the blurred light coming from two table lamps across from the couch. His feet were drawn up under him, his neck perspiring against the rough surface of the sofa's corduroy cover. Yet there was a cool breeze coming through the smashed, lead-framed window.

The tapping continued, the sound of flesh against wood. It came from the foyer, from his front door. He flung his legs over the side onto the floor and found that they both were filled with pins and needles. He struggled to stand.

The tapping and the knocking became louder. Then the voice. 'Jamie! Jamie!'

He walked awkwardly toward the door.

'Coming!' He reached the door and opened it swiftly. Patricia Ballantyne, dressed in a raincoat, silk pajamas evident underneath, walked rapidly inside.

'Jamie, for God's sake, I've been trying to call you.'

'I've been here. The phone didn't ring.'

'I know it didn't. I finally got an operator and she said it was out of order. I borrowed a car and drove over as fast as I could and . . .'

'It's not out of order, Pat. The police – the police were here and a quick look around will explain why – they used it a dozen times.'

'Oh, good Lord!' The girl walked past him into the still-disheveled room. Matlock crossed to the telephone and picked it up from the table. He quickly held it away from his ear as the piercing tone of a disengaged instrument whistled out of the receiver.

'The bedroom,' he said, replacing the telephone and going to his bedroom door.

On his bed, on top of the slashed remains of his mattress, was his bedside phone. The receiver was off the hook, *underneath* the pillow, muffling the harsh sound of the broken connection so it would not be heard. Someone had not wanted it to ring.

Matlock tried to remember everyone who'd been there. All told, more than a dozen people. Five or six policemen – in and out of uniform; husbands and wives from other apartments; several late-night passersby who had seen the police cars and wandered up to the front door. It had been cumulatively blurred. He couldn't remember all the faces.

He put the telephone back on the bedside table and was aware that Pat stood in the doorway. He gambled that she hadn't seen him remove the pillow.

'Someone must have knocked it over straightening out things,' he said, pretending irritation. 'That's rotten; I mean your having to borrow a car. . . . Why did you? What's the matter?'

She didn't reply. Instead, she turned and looked back into the living room. 'What happened?'

Matlock remembered the patrolman's language. 'They call it "break and entry." A police phrase covering human tornadoes, as I understand it. . . . Robbery. I got myself robbed for the first time in my life. It's quite an experience. I think the poor bastards were angry because there wasn't anything of any value so they ripped the place apart. . . . Why'd you come over?'

She spoke softly, but the intensity of her voice made Matlock realize that she was close to panic. As always, she imposed a control on herself when she became emotional. It was an essential part of the girl.

'A couple of hours ago – at quarter to four to be exact – my phone rang. The man, it was a man, asked for you. I was asleep, and I suppose I didn't make much sense, but I pretended to be upset that anyone would think you were there. . . . I didn't know what to do. I was confused. . . .'

'Okay, I understand that. So?'

'He said he didn't believe me. I was a liar. I . . . I was so surprised that anyone would phone then – at quarter to four – and called me a liar . . . I was confused. . . .'

'What did you say?'

'It's not what *I* said. It's what *he* said. He told me to tell you to . . . not to stay "behind the globe" or "light the lower world." He said it *twice*! He said it was an awful joke but you'd understand. It was frightening! . . . Do you? Do you understand?'

Matlock walked past her into the living room. He looked for his cigarettes and tried to remain calm. She followed him. 'What did he mean?'

'I'm not sure.'

'Has it anything to do with . . . this?' She gestured her hand over the apartment.

'I don't think so.' He lit his cigarette and wondered what he should tell her. The Nimrod people hadn't wasted any time finding associations. If it *was* Nimrod.

'What did he mean by . . . "standing behind the globe"? It sounds like a riddle.'

'It's a quote, I think.' But Matlock did not have to think. He knew. He recalled Shakespeare's words precisely: *Knowest thou not that when the searching eye of heaven is hid behind the globe and lights the lower world . . . then thieves and robbers range abroad unseen . . . in murders and in outrage bloody here.*

'What does it mean?'

'I don't *know*! I can't remember it. . . . Somebody's confusing me with someone else. That's the only thing I can imagine. . . . What did he sound like?'

'Normal. He was angry but he didn't shout or anything.'

'No one you recognized? Not specifically, but did you ever hear the voice before?'

'I'm not sure. I don't think so. No one I could pick out, but . . .'

'But what?'

'Well, it was a . . . cultivated voice. A little actorish, I think.'

'A man used to lecturing.' Matlock made a statement, he did not ask a question. His cigarette tasted sour so he crushed it out.

'Yes, I guess that would describe it.'

'And probably not in a science lab. . . . That reduces the possibilities to roughly eighty people on campus.'

'You're making assumptions I don't understand! That phone call *did* have something to do with what happened here.'

He knew he was talking too much. He didn't want to involve Pat; he *couldn't* involve her. Yet someone else had – and that fact was a profound complication. 'It might have. According to the best sources – naturally I refer to television detectives – thieves make sure people aren't home before they rob a place. They were probably checking me out.'

The girl held his wavering eyes with her gaze. 'Weren't you home then?

At quarter to four? . . . The question is not inquisitorial, my darling, simply a point of information.'

He swore at himself silently. It was the exhaustion, the Beeson episode, the shock of the apartment. Of course the question wasn't inquisitorial. He was a free agent. And, of course, he was at home at quarter to four.

'I'm not sure. I wasn't that concerned with the time. It was one hell of a long evening.' He laughed feebly. 'I was at Archie Beeson's. Proposed seminars with young instructors promote a lot of booze.'

She smiled. 'I don't think you understand me. I really don't mind what Poppa Bear was doing. . . . Well, of course, I do, but right now I don't understand why you're lying to me. . . . You were *here* two hours ago, and that phone call wasn't any thief checking your whereabouts and you *know* it.'

'Momma Bear's reaching. That doesn't go with the territory.' Matlock was rude. It, too, like the lying, was obviously false. Whatever his past rebellions, whatever his toughness, he was a kind person and she knew that.

'All right. I apologize. I'll ask one more question and then I'll leave. . . . What does *Omerta* mean?'

Matlock froze. 'What did you say?'

'The man on the phone. He used the word *Omerta*.'

'How?'

'Very casually. Just a reminder, he said.'

Eight

Field Agent Jason Greenberg walked through the borderless door of the squash court. 'You're working up quite a sweat there, Dr. Matlock.'

'I'd hate to have it analysed. . . . Anyway, it was your idea. I would have been just as happy at Kressel's office or even downtown somewhere.'

'This is better. . . . We've got to talk quickly, though. The gym registry has me listed as an insurance surveyor. I'm checking the extinguishers in the corridors.'

'They probably need checking.' Matlock walked to a corner where a gray sweatshirt was wrapped in a towel. He unwound it and slipped it over his head. 'What have you come up with? Last night was a little hairy.'

'If you discount confusion, we haven't come up with a thing. At least nothing specific. A couple of theories, that's all. . . . We think you handled yourself very well.'

'Thanks. I was confused. What are the theories? You sound academic, and I'm not sure I like that.'

Greenberg's head suddenly shifted. From the right wall there could be heard a dull thumping. 'Is that another court?'

'Yes. There are six of them on this side. They're practice courts, no balconies. But you know that.'

Greenberg picked up the ball and threw it hard against the front wall. Matlock understood and caught it on the bounce. He threw it back; Greenberg returned it. They maintained a slow rhythm, neither man moving more than a foot or two, each taking his turn to throw. Greenberg spoke softly, in a monotone.

'We think you're being tested. That's the most logical explanation. You *did* find Ralph. You made a statement about seeing the car. Your reasons for being in the area were weak; so weak we thought they were plausible. They want to make sure, that's why they brought in the girl. They're being thorough.'

'Okay. Theory number one. What's number two?'

'I said that was the most logical. . . . It's the only one, really.'

'What about Beeson?'

'What about him? You were there.'

Matlock held the squash ball in his hand for a few seconds before lobbing it against the side wall. The wall away from Greenberg's stare.

'Could Beeson have been smarter than I thought and sent out an alarm?'

'He could have. We think it's doubtful. . . . The way you described the evening.'

But Matlock had *not* described the *entire* evening. He had not told Greenberg or anyone of Beeson's telephone call. His reasons weren't rational, they were emotional. Lucas Herron was an old man, a gentle man. His sympathy for troubled students was legendary; his concern for young, untried, often arrogant new instructors was a welcomed sedative in faculty crises. Matlock had convinced himself that the 'grand old bird' had befriended a desperate young man, helping him in a desperate situation. He had no right to surface Herron's name on the basis of a phone call made by a panicked drug user. There were too many possible explanations. Somehow he'd speak with Herron, perhaps over coffee at the Commons, or in the bleachers at a baseball game – Herron loved baseball – talk to him, tell him he should back away from Archer Beeson.

' – about Beeson?'

'What?' Matlock had not heard Greenberg.

'I asked you if you had second thoughts about Beeson.'

'No. No, I haven't. He's not important. As a matter of fact, he'll probably throw away the grass and the pills – except for *my* benefit – if he thinks he can use me.'

'I won't try to follow that.'

'Don't. I just had momentary doubts. . . . I can't believe you arrived at only one theory. Come on. What else?'

'All right. Two others and they're not even plausible – both from the same egg. The first is that there might be a leak in Washington. The second – a leak here at Carlyle.'

'Why not plausible?'

'Washington first. There are fewer than a dozen men who know about this operation, and that includes Justice, Treasury, and the White House. They're the caliber of men who exchange secret messages with the Kremlin. Impossible.'

'And Carlyle?'

'You, Adrian Sealfont, and the obnoxious Samuel Kressel. . . . I'd like nothing better than pointing at Kressel – he's a prick – but, again, impossible. I'd also take a certain ethnic delight in knocking a venerated WASP like Sealfont off his pedestal, but there, too – no sense. That leaves you. Are you the one?'

'Your wit is staggering.' Matlock had to run to catch the ball which Greenberg threw into a corner. He held it in his hand and looked at the agent. 'Don't misunderstand me – I like Sam, or at least I think I do – but why is he "impossible"?'

'Same as Sealfont. . . . In an operation like this we start at the beginning. And I *mean* the *beginning*. We don't give a goddamn about positions, status, or reputation – good or bad. We use every trick in the books to prove someone guilty, not innocent. We try to find even the flimsiest reason *not* to clear him. Kressel's as clean as John the Baptist. Still a prick, but clean. Sealfont's worse. He's everything they say. A goddamn saint – Church of England, of course. So, again, that leaves you.'

Matlock whipped the ball up in a spinning reverse shot into the rear left ceiling. Greenberg stepped back and slashed the ball in midair into the right wall. It bulleted back between Matlock's legs.

'I gather you've played the game,' said Matlock with an embarrassed grin.

'The bandit of Brandeis. What about the girl? Where is she?'

'In my apartment. I made her promise not to leave till I got back. Outside of safety, it's one way to get the place cleaned up.'

'I'm assigning a man to her. I don't think it's necessary, but it'll make *you* feel better.' Greenberg looked at his watch.

'It will and thanks.'

'We'd better hurry. . . . Now, listen. We're letting everything take its normal course. Police blotter, newspapers, everything. No covers, no counter stories, nothing to obstruct normal curiosity or your perfectly normal reactions. Someone broke into your apartment and smashed up the place. That's all you know. . . . And there's something else. You may not like it, but we think it's best – and safest.'

'What?'

'We think Miss Ballantyne should report the phone call she received to the police.'

'Hey, come on! The caller expected to find me there at four o'clock in the morning. You don't spell that kind of thing out. Not if you're on a fellowship and expect to work for museum foundations. They still revere McKinley.'

'The eye of the beholder, Dr. Matlock . . . She just received a phone call; some man asked for you, quoted Shakespeare, and made an unintelligible reference to some foreign word or city. She was goddamn mad. It wouldn't rate five lines in a newspaper, but since your apartment was broken into, it's logical she'd report it.'

Matlock was silent. He walked over to the corner of the squash court where the ball had settled and picked it up. 'We're a couple of ciphers who got pushed around. We don't know what happened; just that we don't like it.'

'That's the idea. Nothing is so convincing as someone who's a bewildered injured party and lets everybody know it. Make an insurance issue about those old books of yours. . . . I've got to go. There aren't that many extinguishers in the building. Anything else? What are you doing next?'

Matlock bounced the ball on the floor. 'A fortuitous invitation. Fortuitously received over a number of beers at the Afro-Commons. I'm invited to a staged version of the original puberty rites of the Mau Mau tribes. Tonight at ten o'clock in the cellars of Lumumba Hall. . . . It used to be the Alpha Delta fraternity house. I can tell you there are a lot of white Episcopalians spinning in hell over that one.'

'Again, I'm not following, Doctor.'

'You don't do your homework, either. . . . Lumumba Hall is very large on your list.'

'Sorry. You'll phone me in the morning?'

'In the morning.'

'I'll call you Jim if you'll call me Jason.'

'No kiss, but agreed.'

'O.K. Practice some more in here. I'll take you when this is over.'

'You're on.'

Greenberg let himself out. He looked up and down the narrow corridor, satisfied that no one was there; no one had seen him enter or leave the court. Continuous thumping could be heard within the walls. All the courts were in use. Greenberg wondered, as he was about to turn the corner into the main hallway, why the Carlyle gymnasium was so heavily attended at eleven o'clock in the morning. It was never the case at Brandeis; not fifteen years ago. Eleven o'clock in the morning was a time for class.

He heard a strange noise that was not the sound of a hard ball against thick wood and turned quickly.

No one.

He entered the main hall and turned once again. No one. He left quickly.

The sound he heard was that of a stubborn latch. It came from the door next to Matlock's court. Out of that door a man emerged. He, too, as Greenberg had done less than a minute before, looked up and down the narrow corridor. But instead of being satisfied that no one was there, he was annoyed. The obstinate latch had caused him to miss seeing the man who'd met with James Matlock.

Now the door of court four opened and Matlock himself stepped into the corridor. The man ten feet away was startled, pulled his towel up to his face, and walked away, coughing.

But the man wasn't quick enough. Matlock knew that face.

It was the patrolman from his apartment at four o'clock in the morning.

The patrolman who had called him 'Doctor.' The man in uniform who knew beyond a doubt that the campus troubles were caused by the 'weirdos and the niggers.'

Matlock stared at the retreating figure.

Nine

Over the large cathedral doors one could see – if one looked closely, or the sun was shining at a certain angle – the faded imprint of the Greek letters AΔφ. They had been there in bas-relief for decades, and no amount of sand blasting or student damage could eradicate them completely. The fraternity house of Alpha Delta Phi had gone the way of other such buildings at Carlyle. Its holy order of directors could not find it within themselves to accept the inevitable. The house had been sold – lock, stock, leaking roof, and bad mortgage – to the blacks.

The blacks had done well, even extremely well, with what they had to work with. The decrepit old house had been totally refurbished inside and out. All past associations with its former owners were obliterated wherever possible. The scores of faded photographs of venerated alumni were replaced with wildly theatrical portraits of the new revolutionaries – African, Latin

American, Black Panther. Throughout the ancient halls were the new commands, screeched in posters and psychedelic art: *Death to the Pigs! Up Whitey! Malcolm Lives! Lumumba the Black Christ!*

Between these screams for recognition were replicas of primitive African artifacts – fertility masks, spears, shields, animal skins dipped in red paint, shrunken heads suspended by hair with complexions unmistakably white.

Lumumba Hall wasn't trying to fool anyone. It reflected anger. It reflected fury.

Matlock didn't have to use the brass knocker set beside the grotesque iron mask at the edge of the door frame. The large door opened as he approached it, and a student greeted him with a bright smile.

'I was hoping you'd make it! It's gonna be a groove!'

'Thanks, Johnny. Wouldn't miss it.' Matlock walked in, struck by the proliferation of lighted candles throughout the hallway and adjoining rooms. 'Looks like a wake. Where's the casket?'

'That's later. Wait'll you see!'

A black Matlock recognized as one of the campus extremists walked up to them. Adam Williams' hair was long – African style and clipped in a perfect semicircle above his head. His features were sharp; Matlock had the feeling that if they met in the veldt, Williams would be assumed to be a tribal chief.

'Good evening,' Williams said with an infectious grin. 'Welcome to the seat of revolution.'

'Thanks very much.' They shook hands. 'You don't look so revolutionary as you do funereal. I was asking Johnny where the casket was.'

Williams laughed. His eyes were intelligent, his smile genuine, without guile or arrogance. In close quarters, the black radical had little of the firebrand quality he displayed on the podium in front of cheering supporters. Matlock wasn't surprised. Those of the faculty who had Williams in their courses often remarked on his subdued, good-humored approach. So different from the image he projected in campus – rapidly becoming national – politics.

'Oh, Lord! We're lousing up the picture then! This is a happy occasion. A little gruesome, I suppose, but essentially joyful.'

'I'm not sure I understand,' Matlock smiled.

'A youngster from the tribe reaches the age of manhood, the brink of an active, responsible life. A jungle Bar Mitzvah. It's a time for rejoicing. No caskets, no weeping shrouds.'

'That's right! That's right, Adam!' said the boy named Johnny enthusiastically.

'Why don't you get Mr. Matlock a drink, brother.' And then he turned to Matlock. 'It's all the same drink until after the ceremony – it's called Swahili punch. Is that O.K.?'

'Of course.'

'Right.' Johnny disappeared into the crowd toward the dining room and the punch bowl. Adam smiled as he spoke.

'It's a light rum drink with lemonade and cranberry juice. Not bad, really. . . . Thank you for coming. I mean that.'

'I was surprised to be invited. I thought this was a very "in" thing. Restricted to the tribe. . . . That didn't come out the way I meant it.'

Williams laughed. 'No offense. I used the word. It's good to think in terms of tribes. Good for the brothers.'

'Yes, I imagine it is. . . .'

'The collective, protective social group. Possessing an identity of its own.'

'If that's the purpose – the constructive purpose – I indorse it.'

'Oh, it is. Tribes in the bush don't always make war on each other, you know. It's not all stealing, looting, carrying away women. That's a Robert Ruark hang-up. They trade, share hunting and farming lands together, coexist in the main probably better than nations or even political subdivisions.'

It was Matlock's turn to laugh. 'All right, professor. I'll make notes *after* the lecture.'

'Sorry. Avocational hazard.'

'Avocational or occupational?'

'Time will tell, won't it? . . . One thing I should make clear, however. We don't need your endorsement.'

Johnny returned with Matlock's cup of Swahili punch. 'Hey, you know what? Brother Davis, that's Bill Davis, says you told him you were going to flunk him, then at midterm you gave him a High Pass!'

'Brother Davis got off his fat ass and did a little work.' Matlock looked at Adam Williams. 'You don't object to that kind of endorsement, do you?'

Williams smiled broadly and placed his hand on Matlock's arm. 'No, sir, bwana. . . . In that area you run King Solomon's Mines. Brother Davis is here to work as hard as he can and go as far as his potential will let him. No argument there. Bear down on the brother.'

'You're positively frightening.' Matlock spoke with a lightness he did not feel.

'Not at all. Just pragmatic. . . . I've got some last-minute preparations to look after. See you later.' Williams hailed a passing student and walked through the crowd toward the staircase.

'Come on, Mr. Matlock. I'll show you the new alterations.' Johnny led Matlock into what used to be Alpha Delta's common room.

In the sea of dark faces, Matlock saw a minimum of guarded, hostile looks. There were, perhaps, less overt greetings than he might expect outside on the campus, but by and large, his presence was accepted. He thought for a moment that if the brothers knew why he had come, the inhabitants of Lumumba Hall might turn on him angrily. He was the only white person there.

The alterations in the common room were drastic. Gone were the wide moldings of dark wood, the thick oak window seats beneath the huge cathedral windows, the solid, heavy furniture with the dark red leather. Instead, the room was transformed into something else entirely. The arched windows were no longer. They were now squared at the top, bordered by jet-black dowels an inch or two in diameter, which looked like long, rectangular slits. Spreading out from the windows into the walls was a textured pattern of tiny wooden bamboo strips shellacked to a high polish. This same wall covering was duplicated on the ceiling, thousands of highly glossed reeds converging towards the center. In the middle of the ceiling was a large circle, perhaps three feet in width, in which there was placed a thick pane of rippled glass. Beyond the glass shone a bright yellowish white light, its flood diffused in ripples over the room. What furniture he could see through the mass of bodies was not really furniture at all. There were various low-cut slabs of thick wood in different shapes on short legs – these Matlock assumed were tables. Instead of chairs, there were dozens of pillows in vibrant colors scattered about the edge of the walls.

It didn't take Matlock long to realize the effect.

Alpha Delta Phi's common room had been transformed brilliantly into the replica of a large thatched African hut. Even to the point of the blazing equatorial sun streaming through the enclosure's vent to the skies.

'This is remarkable! Really remarkable. It must have taken months.'

'Almost a year and a half,' Johnny said. 'It's very comfortable, very relaxing. Did you know that lots of top designers are going in for this sort of thing now? I mean the back-to-nature look. It's very functional and easy to maintain.'

'That sounds dangerously like an apology. You don't have to apologize. It's terrific.'

'Oh, I'm *not* apologizing.' Johnny retreated from his explanation. 'Adam says there's a certain majesty in the primitive. A very proud heritage.'

'Adam's right. Only he's not the first person to make that observation.'

'Please don't put us down, Mr. Matlock. . . .'

Matlock looked at Johnny over the rim of his cup of Swahili punch. Oh, Christ, he thought, the more things change, the more they remain the same.

The high-ceilinged chapter room of Alpha Delta Phi had been carved out of the cellars at the farthest end of the fraternity house. It had been built shortly after the turn of the century when impressive alumni had poured impressive sums into such hobbies as secret societies and debutante cotillions. Such activities promulgated and propagandized a way of life, yet assuredly kept it selective.

Thousands of starched young men had been initiated in this chapel-like enclosure, whispering the secret pledges, exchanging the unfamiliar handshakes explained to them by stern-faced older children, vowing till death to keep the selected faith. And afterward, getting drunk and vomiting in corners.

Matlock thought these thoughts as he watched the Mau Mau ritual unfold before him. It was no less childish, no less absurd than the preceding scenes in this room, he considered. Perhaps the physical aspects – the simulated physical aspects – were more brutal in what they conveyed, but then the roots of the ceremony were not based in the delicate steps of a cotillion's pavanne but, instead, in harsh, animal-like pleas to primitive gods. Pleas for strength and survival. Not supplications for continued exclusivity.

The tribal rite itself was a series of unintelligible chants, each one growing in intensity, over the body of a black student – obviously the youngest brother in Lumumba Hall – stretched out on the concrete floor, naked except for a red loincloth strapped around his waist and legs, covering his genitals. At the finish of each chant, signifying the end of one canto and the commencement of the succeeding song, the boy's body was raised above the crowd by four extremely tall students, themselves naked to the waist, wearing jet-black dance belts, their legs encased in spirals of rawhide strips. The room was lighted by dozens of thick candles mounted on stands, causing shadows to dance across the upper wall and the ceiling. Adding to this theatrical effect was the fact that the five active participants in the ritual had their skins covered with oil, their faces streaked in diabolical patterns. As the singing grew wilder, the young boy's rigid body was thrown higher and higher until it left the hands of its four supporters, returning split seconds later into the outstretched arms. Each time the black body with the red loincloth was flung into the air, the crowd responded with growing volumes of guttural shouts.

And then Matlock, who had been watching with a degree of detachment, suddenly found himself frightened. Frightened for the small Negro whose stiff, oiled body was being flung into air with such abandon. For two additional blacks, dressed like the others, had joined the four in the center of the floor. However, instead of helping toss the now soaring figure, the two blacks crouched between the rectangular foursome – beneath the body – and withdrew long-bladed knives, one in each hand. Once in their squatting positions, they stretched out their arms so that the blades were held upright, as rigid, as stiff as the body above them. Each time the small Negro descended, the four blades inched closer to the falling flesh. One slip, one oily miscalculation on the part of just one of the four blacks, and the ritual would end in death for the small student. In murder.

Matlock, feeling that the ritual had gone as far as he could allow, began scanning the crowd for Adam Williams. He saw him in front, on the edge of the circle, and started pushing his way toward him. He was stopped – quietly but firmly – by the blacks around him. He looked angrily at a Negro who held his arm. The black didn't acknowledge his stare; he was hypnotized by the action now taking place in the center of the room.

Matlock saw why instantly. For the body of the small boy was now being *spun*, alternately face up and face down with each elevation. The danger of error was increased tenfold. Matlock grabbed the hand on his arm, twisted it inward, and flung it off him. He looked once more in the direction of Adam Williams.

He wasn't there. He was nowhere in sight! Matlock stood still, undecided. If he raised his voice between the crowd's roaring crescendos, it was entirely possible that he might cause a break in the concentration of those handling the body. He couldn't risk that, and yet he couldn't allow the dangerous absurdity to continue.

Suddenly Matlock felt another hand, this one on his shoulder. He turned and saw the face of Adam Williams behind him. It startled him. Had some primitive tribal signal been transmitted to Williams? The black radical gestured with his head for Matlock to follow him through the shouting crowd to the outer edge of the circle. Williams spoke between the roars.

'You look worried. Don't be.'

'Look! This crap's gone far enough! That kid could be killed!'

'No chance. The brothers have rehearsed for months. . . . It's really the most simplistic of the Mau Mau rites. The symbolism is fundamental. . . . See? The child's eyes remain open. First to the sky, then facing the blades. He is constantly aware – every second – that his life is in the hands of his brother warriors. He cannot, he *must* not show fear. To do so would betray his peers. Betray the confidence he must place in their hands – as they will some day place their lives in *his* hands.'

'It's childish, *dangerous stupidity*, and you *know* it!' cut in Matlock. 'Now, I'm telling you, Williams, you put a stop to it or I will!'

'Of course,' continued the black radical, as if Matlock had not spoken, 'there are anthropologists who insist that the ceremony is essentially one of fertility. The unsheathed knives representing erections, the four protectors guarding the child through its formative years. Frankly, I think that's reaching. Also, it strikes me as contradictory even for the primitive mind. . . .'

'Goddamn you!' Matlock grabbed Williams by the front of his shirt. Immediately other blacks closed in on him.

Suddenly there was total silence in the eerily lit room. The silence lasted only a moment. It was followed by a series of mind-shattering screams from the mouths of the four Negroes in the center of the crowd in whose hands the life of the young student depended. Matlock whipped around and saw the shining black body descending downward from an incredible height above the outstretched hands.

It couldn't be true! It wasn't happening! Yet it was!

The four blacks suddenly, in unison, crouched into kneeling positions *away* from the center, their arms slashed to their sides. The young student came crashing down, *face toward the blades*. Two further screams followed. In a fraction of a second, the students holding the huge knives swung their weapons across one another and in an unbelievable display of wrist strength, *caught* the body on the flat of the blades.

The crowd of blacks went wild.

The ceremony was over.

'Do you believe me now?' Williams asked, speaking in a corner with Matlock.

'Whether I do or not doesn't change what I said. You can't *do* this sort of thing! It's too goddamn dangerous!'

'You exaggerate. . . . Here, let me introduce another guest.' Williams raised his hand and a tall thin black with close-cropped hair and glasses, dressed in an expensively cut tan suit, joined them. 'This is Julian Dunois, Mr. Matlock. Brother Julian is our expert. Our choreographer, if you like.'

'A pleasure.' Dunois extended his hand, speaking with a slight accent.

'Brother Julian is from Haiti. . . . Harvard Law out of Haiti. A most unusual progression, I think you'll agree.'

'It certainly is. . . .'

'Many Haitians, even the Ton Ton Macoute, still get upset when they hear his name.'

'You exaggerate, Adam,' said Julian Dunois with a smile.

'That's what I just said to Mr. Matlock. *He* exaggerates. About the danger of the ceremony.'

'Oh, there's danger – as there's danger if one crosses the Boston Commons wearing a blindfold. The petcock of safety, Mr. Matlock, is that those holding the knives watch closely. In the training there is as much emphasis on being able to drop the knives instantly as there is in holding them up.'

'That may be so,' Matlock acknowledged. 'But the margin for error terrifies me.'

'It's not as narrow as you think.' The lilt in the Haitian's voice was as reassuring as it was attractive. 'Incidentally, I'm a fan of yours. I've enjoyed your works on the Elizabethans. May I add, you're not exactly what I expected. I mean, you're far, far younger.'

'You flatter me. I didn't think I was known in law schools.'

'My undergraduate major was English literature.'

Adam interrupted politely. 'You two enjoy yourselves. There'll be drinks upstairs in a few minutes; just follow the crowd. I've got things to do. . . . I'm glad you've met. You're both strangers, in a way. Strangers should meet in unfamiliar areas. It's comforting.'

He gave Dunois an enigmatic look and walked rapidly away through the crowd.

'Why does Adam feel he has to talk in what I'm sure he considers are profound riddles?' Matlock asked.

'He's very young. He strives constantly to make emphasis. Very bright, but very young.'

'You'll pardon me, but you're not exactly ancient. I doubt more than a year or two older than Adam.'

The black in the expensively cut tan suit looked into Matlock's eyes and laughed gently.

'Now you flatter *me*,' he said. 'If the truth were known – and why shouldn't it be? – and if my tropic color did not disguise the years so well, you'd know that I was precisely one year, four months, and sixteen days *older* than *you*.'

Matlock stared at the Negro, speechless. It took him nearly a full minute to assimilate the lawyer's words and the meaning behind those words. The black's eyes did not waver. He returned Matlock's stare in equal measure. Finally, Matlock found his voice.

'I'm not sure I like this game.'

'Oh, come, we're both here for the same reason, are we not? You from your vantage point, I from mine. . . . Let's go upstairs and have a drink. . . . Bourbon and soda, isn't it? Sour mash, if it's available, I understand.'

Dunois preceded Matlock through the crowd, and Matlock had no other course but to follow.

Dunois leaned against the brick wall.

'All right,' Matlock said, 'the amenities are over. Everyone's acknowledged your show downstairs, and there's no one left for me to impress my white skin on. I think it's time you started explaining.'

They were alone now, outside on the porch. Both held drinks.

'My, aren't we professional? Would you care for a cigar? I can assure you it's Havana.'

'No cigar. Just talk. I came here tonight because these are my friends. I felt privileged to be invited. . . . Now, you've attached something else and I don't like it.'

'Bravo! Bravo!' said Dunois, raising his glass. 'You do that very well. . . . Don't worry, they know nothing. Perhaps they suspect, but believe me, only in the vaguest terms.'

'What the hell are you talking about?'

'Finish your drink and let's walk out on the lawn.' Dunois drained his rum and, as if by reflex, Matlock drank the remainder of his bourbon. The two men walked down the steps of the Lumumba Hall, Matlock following the black to the base of a large elm tree. Dunois turned suddenly and grabbed Matlock by the shoulders.

'Take your goddamn hands off me!'

'Listen to me! I want that paper! I *must have* that paper! And you must tell me *where it is!*'

Matlock flung his hands up to break Dunois's grip. But his arms did not respond. They were suddenly heavy, terribly heavy. And there was a whistling. A growing, piercing whistling in his head.

'What? What?. . . . What paper? I don't have any paper. . . .'

'Don't be difficult! We'll get it, you know! . . . Now, just tell me where it is!'

Matlock realized that he was being lowered to the ground. The outline of the huge tree above him began to spin, and the whistling in his brain became louder and louder. It was unendurable. He fought to find his mind again.

'What are you doing? What are you doing to me!?'

'The paper, Matlock! Where is the Corsican *paper?*'

'Get *off* me!' Matlock tried to yell. But nothing came from his lips.

'The silver paper, goddamn you to hell!'

'No paper.. . . . no. Haven't paper! No!'

'Listen to me! You just had a drink, remember the drink? . . . You just finished that drink. Remember? . . . You can't be alone now! You don't *dare* be alone!'

'What? . . . What? Get off me! You're crushing me!'

'I'm not even *touching* you. The drink is! You just consumed three tabs of *lysergic acid*! You're in trouble, Doctor! . . . *Now! You tell me where that paper is!*'

From his inner recesses he found an instant of clarity. From the spinning, turning, whirling spirals of mind-blasting colors, he saw the form of the man above him and he lashed out. He grabbed at the white shirt between the dark borders of the jacket and pulled it down with all the strength he could summon. He brought his fist up and hit the descending face as hard as he could. Once the face was jarred, he began hammering at the throat beneath it mercilessly. He could feel the shattering of the glasses and he knew his fist had found the eyes and crushed the glass into the rolling head.

It was over in a period of time he could never ascertain. Dunois's body was beside him, unconscious.

And he knew he had to run. Run furiously away! What had Dunois said? . . . Don't dare be alone. Don't *dare*! He had to find Pat! Pat would know what to do. He had to find her! The chemical in his body was going to take full effect soon and he knew it. Run, for Christ's sake!

But where?! Which way?! He didn't know *the way*! *The goddamn, fucking way*! The street was there, he raced along the street, but was it the *right way*?! Was it the *right street*?!

Then he heard a car. It *was* a car, and it was coming close to the curb and the driver was looking at him. Looking at him, so he ran faster, tripping once over the curb and falling into the pavement and rising again. Running, for Christ Almighty's sake, running till the breath in his lungs was gone and he could no longer control the movement of his feet. He felt himself swerve, unable to stop himself, toward the wide gulf of the street, which suddenly became a river, a black putrid river in which he would drown.

He vaguely heard the screech of the brakes. The lights blinded him, and the figure of a man reached down and poked at his eyes. He didn't care any longer. Instead, he laughed. Laughed through the blood which flowed into his mouth and over his face.

He laughed hysterically as Jason Greenberg carried him to the car.

And then the earth, the world, the planet, the galaxy, and the entire solar system went crazy.

Ten

The night was agony.

The morning brought a degree of reality, less so for Matlock than for the two people sitting beside him, one on either side of the bed. Jason Greenberg, his large, sad eyes drooping, his hands calmly crossed on his lap, leaned forward. Patricia Ballantyne, her arm stretched out, held a cool washcloth on Matlock's forehead.

'The schvugs gave you one hell of a party, friend.'

'Shh!' whispered the girl. 'Leave him alone.'

Matlock's eyes wandered as best they could around the room. He was in Pat's apartment, in her bedroom, her bed.

'They gave me acid.'

'You're telling *us* . . . We had a doctor – a real doctor – brought in from Litchfield. He's the nice fella you kept trying to take the eyeballs from. . . . Don't worry, he's federal. No names.'

'Pat? How come . . .'

'You're a very sweet acid head, Jamie. You kept yelling my name.'

'It also made the best sense,' interrupted Greenberg. 'No hospitals. No out-patient records. Nice and private; good thinking. Also, you're very persuasive when you're violent. You're a hell of a lot stronger than I thought. Especially for such a lousy handball player.'

'You shouldn't have brought me here. Goddamn it, Greenberg, you shouldn't have *brought* me here!'

'Forgetting for the moment that it was your idea . . .'

'I was drugged!'

'It was a *good* idea. What would you have preferred? The emergency clinic? . . . "Who's that on the stretcher, Doctor? The one screaming." . . . "Oh, just Associate Professor Matlock, Nurse. He's on an acid trip."'

'You know what I mean! You could have taken me home. Strapped me down.'

'I'm relieved to see you don't know much about acid,' said Greenberg.

'What he means, Jamie . . .,' Pat took his hand, '. . . if it's bad, you should be with someone you know awfully well. The reassurance is necessary.'

Matlock looked at the girl. And then at Greenberg. 'What have you told her?'

'That you volunteered to help us; that we're grateful. With your help we may be able to prevent a serious situation from getting worse.' Greenberg spoke in a monotone; it was obvious that he didn't wish to expand.

'It was a very cryptic explanation,' Pat said. 'He wouldn't have given me that if I hadn't threatened him.'

'She was going to call the police.' Greenberg sighed, his sad eyes sadder. 'She was going to have me locked up for dosing you. I had no choice.'

Matlock smiled.

'Why are you doing this, Jamie?' Pat found nothing amusing.

'The man said it: the situation's serious.'

'But why *you*?'

'Because I can.'

'What? Turn in kids?'

'I told you,' said Jason. 'We're not interested in students. . . .'

'What's Lumumba Hall, then? A branch of General Motors?'

'It's one contact point; there are others. Frankly, we'd rather *not* have gotten involved with that crowd; it's ticklish. Unfortunately, we can't choose.'

'That's offensive.'

'I don't think there's much I could say that wouldn't be offensive to you, Miss Ballantyne.'

'Perhaps not. Because I thought the FBI had more important work to do than harassing young blacks. Obviously, you don't.'

'Hey, come on.' Matlock squeezed the girl's hand. She took it from him.

'No, I mean that, Jamie! No games, no radical chic. There are drugs all over this place. Some of it's a bad scene, most of it's pretty standard. We *both* know that. Why all of a sudden are the kids at Lumumba singled out?'

'We wouldn't *touch* those kids. Except to help them.' Greenberg was weary from the long night. His irritation showed.

'I don't like the way you people help people and I don't like what happened to Jamie! Why did you send him there?'

'He didn't *send* me. I maneuvered that myself.'

'Why?'

'It's too complicated and I'm too washed out to explain it.'

'Oh, Mr. Greenberg did that. He explained all right. They've given you a badge, haven't they? They can't do it themselves so they pick a nice, easygoing fellow to do it for them. You take all the risks; and when it's over, you'll never be trusted on this campus again. Jamie, for God's sake, this is your *home*, your *work*!'

Matlock held the girl's eyes with his own, doing his best to calm her. 'I know that better than you do. My home needs to be helped – and that's no game either, Pat. I think the risks are worth it.'

'I won't pretend to understand that.'

'You can't understand it, Miss Ballantyne, because we can't tell you enough to make it reasonable. You'll have to accept that.'

'Do I?'

'I'm asking you to,' said Matlock. 'He saved my life.'

'I wouldn't go that far, Professor.' Greenberg shrugged as he spoke.

Pat stood up. 'I think he threw you overboard and tossed you a rope as an afterthought. . . . Are you all right?'

'Yes,' answered Matlock.

'I have to go; I won't if you don't want me to.'

'No, you go ahead. I'll call you later. Thanks for the ministrations.'

The girl looked briefly at Greenberg – it was not a pleasant look – and crossed to her dresser. She picked up a brush and rapidly stroked her hair, slipping an orange headband into place. She watched Greenberg through the mirror. He returned the stare.

'The man who's been following me, Mr. Greenberg. Is he one of your men?'

'Yes.'

'I don't like it.'

'I'm sorry.'

Pat turned. 'Will you remove him, please?'

'I can't do that. I'll tell him to be less obvious.'

'I see.' She took her purse from the dresser top and reached down to the floor, picking up her accordion briefcase. Without speaking further, the girl walked out of the bedroom. Several seconds later, the two men could hear the apartment door open and shut firmly.

'That is one very strong-willed young lady,' said Jason.

'There's a good reason.'

'What do you mean?'

'I thought you fellows were so familiar with the people you had to deal with. . . .'

'I'm still getting briefed. I'm the back-up, remember?'

'Then I'll save you time. In the late fifties her father got McCarthyized out of the State Department. Of course, he was very dangerous. He was a language consultant. He was cleared for translating newspapers.'

'Shit.'

'That's the word, brother. He never made it back. She's had scholarships all her life; the cupboard's bare. She's a little sensitive to your type.'

'Boy, do you pick 'em!'

'You picked *me*, remember?'

Matlock opened the door to his apartment and walked into the foyer. Pat had done a good job putting the rooms in order – as he knew she would. Even the curtains were rehung. It was a little after three – most of the day wasted. Greenberg had insisted that the two of them drive over to Litchfield for a re-examination by the doctor. Shaken but operable, was the verdict.

They stopped for lunch at the Cheshire Cat. During the meal, Matlock kept looking over at the small table where four days ago Ralph Loring had sat with his folded newspaper. The lunch was quiet. Not strained – the two men were comfortable in each other's company – but quiet, as if each had too much to think about.

On the road back to Carlyle, Greenberg told him to stay in his apartment until he contacted him. Washington hadn't issued any new instructions. They were evaluating the new information, and until they confirmed any further involvement, Matlock was to remain 'OOS' – a term the English professor found hard to equate with grownups: *out of strategy*.

It was just as well, he thought. He had his own strategy to think about –

Lucas Herron. The 'grand old bird,' the campus elder statesman. It was time to reach him, to warn him. The old man was out of his element, and the quicker he retreated, the better for everyone – Carlyle included. Yet he didn't want to telephone him, he didn't want to arrange a formal meeting – he had to be subtler than that. He didn't want to alarm old Lucas, have him talking to the wrong people.

It occurred to Matlock that he was acting as some sort of protector for Herron. That presumed Lucas was innocent of any serious involvement. He wondered if he had the right to make that assumption. On the other hand, by civilized standards, he had no right to make any other.

The telephone rang. It couldn't be Greenberg, he thought. He'd just left him at the curb. He hoped it wasn't Pat; he wasn't ready to talk to her yet. Reluctantly he lifted the instrument to his ear. 'Hello!'

'Jim! Where have you *been*!? I've been calling since eight this morning! I was so goddamn worried I went over there twice. Got your key from maintenance.' It was Sam Kressel. He sounded as though Carlyle had lost its accreditation.

'It's too involved to go into now, Sam. Let's get together later. I'll come over to your place after dinner.'

'I don't know if it can wait that long. Jesus! What the hell got *into* you?'

'I don't understand.'

'At Lumumba last night!'

'What are you talking about? What have you heard?'

'That black bastard, Adam Williams, handed in a report to my office accusing you of just about everything short of advocating slavery! He claims the only reason he's not filing police charges is that you were blind drunk! Of course, the alcohol stripped you of your pretenses and showed clearly what a racist you are!'

'What?!'

'You broke up furniture, slapped around some kids, smashed windows. . . .'

'You know damned well that's bullshit!'

'I figured as much.' Kressel lowered his voice. He was calming down. 'But my knowing it doesn't help, can't you see that? This is the kind of thing we've got to *avoid*. Polarization! The government walks onto a campus, polarization follows.'

'Listen to me. Williams' statement is a decoy – if that's the word. It's camouflage. They drugged me last night. If it hadn't been for Greenberg, I don't know where I'd be right now.'

'Oh, God! . . . Lumumba's on your list, isn't it? That's all we *need*! The blacks'll scream persecution. Christ knows what'll happen.'

Matlock tried to speak calmly. 'I'll come over around seven. Don't do anything, don't say anything. I've got to get off the phone. Greenberg's supposed to call.'

'Wait a minute, Jim! One thing. This Greenberg . . . I don't trust him. I don't trust any of them. Just remember. Your loyalty's to Carlyle. . . .'

Kressel stopped, but he had not finished. Matlock realized he was at a loss for words.

'That's a strange thing to say.'

'I think you know what I mean.'

'I'm not sure I do. I thought the idea was to work together. . . .'

'*Not at the expense of ripping this campus apart!*' The dean of colleges sounded nearly hysterical.

'Don't worry,' Matlock said. 'It won't tear. I'll see you later.' Matlock hung up the phone before Kressel could speak again. His mind needed a short rest, and Kressel never let anyone rest where his domain was concerned. Sam Kressel, in his own way, was as militant as any extremist, and, perhaps, quicker to cry 'foul.'

These thoughts led Matlock to another consideration – two considerations. Four days ago, he had told Pat that he didn't want to change their plans for St. Thomas. Carlyle's midterm holiday, a short ten days at the end of April, would start after classes on Saturday, in three days. Under the circumstances, St. Thomas was out – unless Washington decided to retire him, and he doubted that. He'd use his parents as the excuse. Pat would understand, even be sympathetic. The other thought was his own classes. He had fallen behind. His desk was piled with papers – mostly themes and essay exams. He had also missed his two classes earlier in the day. He was not so much concerned for his students – his method was to accelerate in the fall and winter and relax in the spring – but he didn't want to add any fuel to such fires as Williams' false complaint. An absentee associate professor was a target for gossip. His class load for the next three days was medium – three, two, and two. He'd organize the work later. Between now and seven o'clock, however, he had to find Lucas Herron. If Greenberg called while he was out, he'd blame it on a forgotten graduate conference.

He decided to shower, shave, and change clothes. Once in the bathroom, he checked the litter box. The Corsican paper was there – he knew it would be.

The shave and shower completed, Matlock walked into his bedroom, selecting clothes and a course of action. He didn't know Herron's daily schedule, although it would be a simple matter to find out if Lucas had any late afternoon classes or seminars. If he didn't, Matlock knew Herron's house; it would take about fifteen minutes to get there by car. Herron lived eight miles from the campus, on a rarely traveled back road in a section once a part of the old Carlyle family estate. Herron's home had been a carriage house. It was out of the way, but as Lucas kept saying, 'Once there, it's worth it.'

The rapid tapping of the door knocker broke his concentration. It also frightened him – he felt himself gasping for breath; that was disturbing.

'Be right there,' he yelled, slipping a white sport shirt over his head. He walked barefoot to the front door and opened it. It was impossible for him to conceal his shock. In the doorframe stood Adam Williams – alone.

'Afternoon.'

'Jesus! . . . I don't know whether to hit you in the mouth right now or first call the police! What the hell do you want? Kressel's already called me, if that's what you're checking on.'

'Please let me talk to you. I'll be quick.' The black spoke with urgency, trying, thought Matlock, to conceal his fear.

'Come on in. And *make* it quick.' Matlock slammed the door as Williams passed by him into the foyer. The black turned and tried to smile, but there was no humour in his eyes.

'I'm sorry about that report. Truly sorry. It was an unpleasant necessity.'

'I don't buy that and you can't sell it! What did you want Kressel to do? Bring me up before the board and burn me out of here? Did you think I'd just sit down and play doormat? You're a goddamn maniac!'

'We didn't think *anything* would happen. That's precisely why we did it. . . . We couldn't be sure where you went. You disappeared, you know. You might say we had to take the offensive and then later agree that it was all a disagreeable misunderstanding. . . . It's not a new tactic. I'll send Kressel another report, backing off – but not entirely. In a couple of weeks, it'll be forgotten.'

Matlock raged, as much against Williams' attitude as his conscienceless pragmatism. But when he spoke he did not raise his voice. 'Get out. You disgust me.'

'Oh, come off it, man! Haven't we *always disgusted* you?!' Matlock had hit a nerve and Williams responded in kind. But just as suddenly, he took hold of himself. 'Let's not argue theoretical practicalities. Let me get to the point and leave.'

'By all means.'

'All right. Listen to me. Whatever Dunois wanted from you, *give* it to him! . . . That is, give it to me and I'll send it on. No forked tongue; it's last-extremity language!'

'Too pat a phrase. No sale. Why would I have anything Brother Julian wanted? Did he say so? Why doesn't he come over himself?'

'Brother Julian doesn't stay long in any one place. His talents are in great demand.'

'Staging Mau Mau puberty rituals?'

'He really does that, you know. It's a hobby.'

'Send him to me.' Matlock crossed in front of Williams and went to the coffee table. He reached down and picked up a half-empty pack of cigarettes. 'We'll compare notes on associative body movements. I've a hell of a collection of sixteenth-century folk dances.'

'Talk seriously. There's no *time*!'

Matlock lit a cigarette. 'I've got all the time in the world. I just want to see Brother Julian again; I want to put him in jail.'

'No chance! No chance. I'm here for *your* benefit! If I leave without it, I can't *control* it!'

'Two pronouns signifying the same or different objects?'

'Oh, you're too much! You're really too much! Do you know who Julian Dunois *is*?'

'Part of the Borgia family? Ethiopian branch?'

'*Stop it, Matlock!* Do what he says! People could be hurt. Nobody wants that.'

'I *don't* know who Dunois is and I don't much give a damn. I just know he drugged me and assaulted me and is exercising a dangerous influence on a bunch of children. Beyond this, I suspect he had my apartment broken into and many of my personal belongings destroyed. I want him put away. From you *and* from me.'

'Be reasonable, *please*!'

Matlock walked swiftly to the curtains in front of his casement window and with a flourish, yanked them down, displaying the shattered glass and twisted lead.

'Is this one of Brother Julian's calling cards?'

Adam Williams stared, obviously shocked, at the mass of destruction. 'No, man. Absolutely, no. That's not Julian's style. . . . That's not even my style. That's someone else.'

Eleven

The road to Lucas Herron's house was dotted with the potholes of winter. Matlock doubted that the town of Carlyle would fill them in; there were too many other commercially traveled streets still showing the effects of the New England freeze. As he approached the old carriage house, he slowed his Triumph to barely ten miles an hour. The bumps were jarring, and he wanted to reach Herron's house with little noise.

Thinking that Jason Greenberg might have had him followed, Matlock took the long route to Herron's, driving four miles north on a parallel road and then doubling back on Herron's street. There was no one behind him. The nearest houses to Herron's were a hundred yards away on either side, none in front. There'd been talk of turning the area into a housing development just as there'd been talk of enlarging Carlyle University, but nothing came of either project. Actually, the first depended upon the second, and there was strong alumni opposition to any substantial physical change at Carlyle. The alumni were Adrian Sealfont's personal cross.

Matlock was struck by the serenity of Herron's home. He'd never really looked at the house before. A dozen times, more or less, he'd driven Lucas home after faculty meetings, but he'd always been in a hurry. He'd never accepted Lucas's invitations for a drink and, as a result, he had never been inside the house.

He got out of the car and approached the old brick structure. It was tall and narrow; the faded stone covered with thousands of strands of ivy heightened the feeling of isolation. In front, on the large expanse of lawn, were two Japanese willow trees in full spring bloom, their purple flowers cascading toward the earth in large arcs. The grass was cut, the shrubbery pruned, and the white gravel on the various paths was gleaming. It was a house and grounds which were loved and cared for, yet one had the feeling that they were not shared. It was the work of and for one person, not two or a family. And then Matlock remembered that Lucas Herron had never married. There were the inevitable stories of a lost love, a tragic death, even a runaway bride-to-be, but whenever Lucas Herron heard about such youthful romanticizing he countered with a chuckle and a statement about being 'too damned selfish.'

Matlock walked up the short steps to the door and rang the bell. He tried practicing an opening smile, but it was false; he wouldn't be able to carry it off. He was afraid.

The door swung back and the tall, white-haired Lucas Herron, dressed in wrinkled trousers and a half-unbuttoned, oxford-blue shirt, stared at him.

It was less than a second before Herron spoke, but in that brief instant, Matlock knew that he'd been wrong. Lucas Herron knew why he had come.

'Well, Jim! Come in, come in, my boy. A pleasant surprise.'

'Thank you, Lucas. I hope I'm not interrupting anything.'

'Not a thing. You're just in time, as a matter of fact. I'm dabbling in alchemy. A fresh fruit gin Collins. Now I won't have to dabble alone.'

'Sounds good to me.'

The inside of Herron's house was precisely as Matlock thought it would be – as his own might be in thirty-odd years, if he lived that long alone. It was a mixed bag, an accumulated total of nearly half a century of unrelated gatherings from a hundred unrelated sources. The only common theme was comfort; there was no concern for style or period or coordination. Several walls were lined with books, and those which were not were filled with enlarged photographs of places visited abroad – one suspected during sabbaticals. The armchairs were thick and soft, the tables within arm's reach – the sign of practiced bachelorhood, thought Matlock.

'I don't think you've ever been here – inside, I mean.'

'No, I haven't. It's very attractive. Very comfortable.'

'Yes, it's that. It's comfortable. Here, sit down, I'll finish the formula and bring us a drink.' Herron started across the living room toward what Matlock presumed was the door to the kitchen and then stopped and turned. 'I know perfectly well that you haven't come all the way out here to liven up an old man's cocktail hour. However, I have a house rule: at least one drink – religion and strong principles permitting – before any serious discussion.' He smiled and the myriad lines around his eyes and temples became more pronounced. He was an *old*, old man. 'Besides, you look terribly serious. The Collins'll lessen the degree, I promise you.'

Before Matlock could answer, Herron walked rapidly through the door. Instead of sitting, Matlock walked to the wall nearest him, against which was a small writing desk, above it a half-dozen photographs that hung in no discernible pattern. Several were of Stonehenge taken from the same position, the setting sun at dramatically different angles. Another was of a rock-bound coast, mountains in the distance, fishing boats moored offshore. It looked Mediterranean, possibly Greece or the Thracian Islands. Then there was a surprise. On the lower right side of the wall, only inches above the desk, was a small photograph of a tall, slender army officer standing by the trunk of a tree. Behind him the foliage was profuse, junglelike; to the sides were the shadows of other figures. The officer was helmetless, his shirt drenched with sweat, his large right hand holding the stock of a submachine gun. In his left hand the officer held a folded piece of paper – it looked like a map – and the man had obviously just made a decision. He was looking upward, as though toward some high terrain. The face was taut but not excited. It was a good face, a strong face. It was a dark-haired, middle-aged Lucas Herron.

'I keep that old photograph to remind me that time was not always so devastating.'

Matlock snapped up, startled. Lucas had re-entered and had taken him off guard. 'It's a good picture. Now I know who really won that war.'

'No doubt about it. Unfortunately, I never heard of that particular island either before or since. Someone said it was one of the Solomons. I think they blew it up in the fifties. Wouldn't take much. Couple of fire crackers'd do it. Here.' Herron crossed to Matlock, handing him his drink.

'Thanks. You're too modest. I've heard the stories.'

'So have I. Impressed the hell out of me. They grow better as I grow older. . . . What do you say we sit in the back yard. Too nice to stay indoors.' Without waiting for a reply, Herron started out and Matlock followed.

Like the front of the house, the back was precisely manicured. On a flagstone patio, there were comfortable-looking, rubber-stranded beach chairs, each with a small table by its side. A large wrought-iron table with a sun umbrella was centered in the middle of the flagstones. Beyond, the lawn was close cropped and full. Dogwood trees were dotted about, each spaded around its trunk, and two lines of flowers – mostly roses – stretched lengthwise to the end of the lawn, about a hundred feet away. At the end of the lawn, however, the pastoral effect abruptly stopped. Suddenly there were huge trees, the underbrush thick, mangled, growing within itself. The side borders were the same. Around the perimeters of the sculptured back lawn was an undisciplined, overgrown forest.

Lucas Herron was surrounded by a forbidding green wall.

'It *is* a good drink, you'll admit.' The two men were seated.

'It certainly is. You'll convert me to gin.'

'Only in spring and summer. Gin's not for the rest of the year. . . . All right, young fellow, the house rule's been observed. What brings you to Herron's Nest?'

'I think you have an idea.'

'Do I?'

'Archie Beeson.' Matlock watched the old man, but Herron's concentration was on his glass. He showed no reaction.

'The young history man?'

'Yes.'

'He'll make a fine teacher one day. Nice little filly of a wife, too.'

'Nice . . . and promiscuous, I think.'

'*Appearances*, Jim.' Herron chuckled. 'Never thought of you as Victorian. . . . One grows infinitely more tolerant of the appetites as one gets older. And the innocent whetting of them. You'll see.'

'Is that the key? The tolerance of appetites?'

'Key to what?'

'Come on. He wanted to reach you the other night.'

'Yes, he did. And you were there. . . . I understand your behavior left something to be desired.'

'My behavior was calculated to leave that impression.' For the first time Herron betrayed a trace of concern. It was a small reaction, the blinking of his eyes in rapid succession.

'That was reprehensible.' Herron spoke softly and looked up at his imposing green wall. The sun was going below the line of tall trees; long shadows were cast across the lawn and patio.

'It was necessary.' Matlock saw the old man's face wince in pain. And then he recalled his own reaction to Adam Williams' description of the 'unpleasant necessity' of sending Sam Kressel the false report of his actions at Lumumba Hall. The parallel hurt.

'The boy's in trouble. He's sick. It's a disease and he's trying to cure himself. That takes courage. . . . This is no time for campus Gestapo tactics.' Herron took a long drink from his glass while his free hand gripped the arm of the chair.

'How did you know about it?'

'That might be privileged information. Let's say I heard from a respected co-worker of ours – in the medical line – who ran across the symptoms and became concerned. What difference does it make? I tried to help the boy and I'd do it again.'

'I'd like to believe that. It's what I wanted to believe.'

'Why is that difficult for you?'

'I don't know. . . . Something at the front door a few minutes ago. Perhaps this house. I can't put my finger on it. . . . I'm being completely honest with you.'

Herron laughed but still avoided Matlock's eyes. 'You're too wound up in the Elizabethans. The plots and counterplots of *The Spanish Tragedy*. . . . You young faculty crusaders should stop trying to be an amateur Scotland Yard. Not too long ago it was fashionable around here to have Red Dogs for breakfast. You're just magnifying the situation out of proportion.'

'That's not true. I'm not a faculty crusader. I'm no part of that crowd, and I think you know it.'

'What was it then? Personal interest? In the boy. Or his wife? . . . I'm sorry, I shouldn't have said that.'

'I'm glad you did. I have no interest in Virginia Beeson – sexual or otherwise. Although I can't imagine what else there would be.'

'Then you put on quite an act.'

'I certainly did. I took extreme measures to keep Beeson from knowing why I was there. It was that important.'

'To whom?' Herron slowly put his glass down with his right hand, his left still gripped the arm of the chair.

'To people beyond this campus. Washington people. The federal authorities . . .'

Lucas Herron took a sudden, sustained intake of breath through his nostrils. In front of Matlock's eyes, Herron's face began to drain itself of color. When he spoke, he did so barely above a whisper.

'What are you saying?'

'That I was approached by a man from the Justice Department. The information he showed me was frightening. Nothing was trumped up, nothing overdramatized. It was straight data. I was given a free choice whether to cooperate or not.'

'And you accepted?' Herron's words were uttered softly in disbelief.

'I didn't feel there was an alternative. My younger brother . . .'

'You didn't feel there was an *alternative?*' Herron rose from his chair, his hands began to shake, his voice grew in intensity. 'You didn't *feel* there was an *alternative?!*'

'No, I didn't,' Matlock remained calm. 'That's why I came out here. To warn you, old friend. It's much deeper – far more dangerous . . .'

'*You* came out here to warn *me?!* What have you *done?* What in the name of everything sacred *have you done?* . . . Now, you listen to me! You listen to what I say!' Herron backed off, bumping into the small side table. In one whip of his left arm, he sent it crashing onto the flagstones. 'You let it go, do you hear me! You go back and tell them *nothing! Nothing exists!* It's all . . . all in their imaginations! *Don't touch it! Let it go!*'

'I can't do that,' said Matlock gently, suddenly afraid for the old man. 'Even Sealfont will have to agree. He can't fight it any longer. It's there, Lucas. . . .'

'Adrian! Adrian's been told? . . . Oh, my God, do you know what you're doing? *You'll destroy so much.* So many, many . . . Get out of here! *Get out!* I don't know you! Oh, *Jesus! Jesus!*'

'Lucas, what is it?' Matlock got up and took several steps toward the old man. Herron continued backing away, an old man in panic.

'Don't come near me! Don't you *touch me!*'

Herron turned and started running as well as his ancient legs could carry him across the lawn. He stumbled, falling to the ground, and picked himself up. He didn't look back. Instead he ran with all his might toward the rear of the yard, toward the overgrown woods. And then he disappeared through his huge green wall.

'Lucas! For Christ's sake!' Matlock raced after the old man, reaching the edge of the woods only seconds behind him. Yet he was nowhere in sight. Matlock whipped at the overgrowth in front of him and stepped into the tangled mass of foliage. Branches slashed back at him, and the intricate webbings of giant weeds ensnared his feet as he kicked his way into the dense woods.

Herron was gone.

'Lucas! Where are you?!'

There was no answer, only the rustling of the disturbed growth behind him. Matlock went farther into the forest, ducking, crouching, sidling by the green barriers in front of him. There was no sign of Lucas Herron, no sound.

'Lucas! For God's sake, Lucas, answer me!'

Still no reply, no hint of presence.

Matlock tried to look around him, tried to spot a break in the patterns of foliage, a route to follow. He could see none. It was as if Lucas were matter one moment, vapor the next.

And then he heard it. Indistinct, from all sides of him, echoing softly from some unknown place. It was a deep-throated moan, a wail. Near, yet far in the dense distance. And then the wail diminished and became a plaintive sob. A single sob, punctuated by a single word – clear, and spoken in hatred.

The word was –

'Nimrod . . .'

Twelve

'Goddamn it, Matlock! I told you to stay put until I contacted you!'

'Goddamn it, Greenberg! How did you get into my apartment?!'

'You didn't get your window fixed.'

'You haven't offered to pay for it.'

'We're even. Where have you been?'

Matlock threw his car keys on the coffee table and looked at his broken stereo set in the corner. 'It's an involved story and I suspect . . . pathetic. I'll tell you all about it after I've had a drink. My last one was interrupted.'

'Get me one, too. I've also got a story and mine's *definitely* pathetic.'

'What do you drink?'

'Very little, so whatever you're having is fine.'

Matlock looked out his front window. The curtains were strewn on the floor where he had torn them in front of Adam Williams. The sun was almost down now. The spring day was over. 'I'm going to squeeze some lemons and have a fresh fruit Tom Collins.'

'Your file says you drink bourbon. Sour mash.'

Matlock looked at the federal agent. 'Does it?'

Greenberg followed Matlock into the kitchen and watched in silence as he fixed their drinks. Matlock handed the federal man his glass.

'Looks fancy.'

'It's not. . . . Whose pathetic story gets first telling?'

'I'll want to hear yours, of course, but under the circumstances, mine has priority.'

'You sound ominous.'

'No. Just pathetic. . . . I'll start by asking you if you'd care to know where I've been since I dropped you off.' Greenberg leaned against the counter.

'Not particularly, but you'll tell me anyway.'

'Yes, I will. It's part of the pathos. I was out at your local airport – Bradley Field – waiting for a jet dispatched by Justice a few hours ago from Dulles. There was a man on the plane who brought me two sealed envelopes which I had to sign for. Here they are.' Greenberg reached into his jacket pocket and took out two long business envelopes. He put one on the counter and began to open the second.

'They look very official,' said Matlock, edging himself up so that he sat next to the sink, his long legs dangling over the side in front of the cabinets.

'They couldn't be more official. . . . This envelope contains the summary of our conclusions based on information you gave us – gave me. It ends with a specific recommendation. I'm allowed to convey this information in my own words as long as I cover all the facts. . . .'

'Jason Greenberg gets two points.'

'However,' continued the federal man without acknowledging Matlock's interruption, 'the contents of the second envelope must be delivered verbatim. You are to read it thoroughly – *should it be necessary* – and if it's acceptable, you've got to acknowledge that by your signature.'

'This gets better and better. Am I running for the Senate?'

'No, you're just running. . . . I'll start as instructed.' Greenberg glanced at the unfolded paper and then looked across at Matlock. 'The man at Lumumba Hall named Julian Dunois – alias Jacques Devereaux, Jésus Dambert, and probably several others we don't know about – is a legal strategist for the Black Left militants. The term *legal strategist* covers everything from court manipulations to agent provocateur. When involved with the former, he uses the name of Dunois, the latter – any number of aliases. He operates out of unusual places geographically. Algiers, Marseilles, the Caribbean – including Cuba – and, we suspect, Hanoi and probably Moscow. Perhaps even Peking. In the States he has a regular, bona fide law office in upper Harlem and a West Coast affiliate in San Francisco. . . . He's generally in the background, but wherever he's in evidence, bad news usually follows. Needless to say, he's on the attorney general's list of undesirables, and these days that's not respectable any longer. . . .'

'These days,' broke in Matlock, 'that includes almost everyone to the left of AT&T.'

'No comment. To continue. The surfacing of Dunois in this operation adds a dimension not anticipated – a new aspect not considered before. It goes beyond domestic lawbreakers and enters the area of international crime and/or subversion. *Or* a combination of both. In light of the fact that drugs were used on you, your apartment broken into and ripped apart, your friend, Miss Ballantyne, indirectly threatened – and don't kid yourself, that's what it was – in light of all this, the recommendation is as follows. You withdraw from any further participation in this investigation. Your involvement is beyond the realm of reasonable risk.' Greenberg dropped the paper on the counter and took several swallows of his drink. Matlock swung his legs slowly back and forth in front of the cabinet beneath him. 'What say you, in the docket?' asked Greenberg.

'I'm not sure. It seems to me you're not finished.'

'I'd like to be. Right here. The summary's accurate, and I think you should agree with the recommendation. Pull out, Jim.'

'Finish first. What's the other letter? The one I'm supposed to read verbatim?'

'It's only necessary if you reject the recommendation. Don't reject it. I'm not instructed to lean that way, so that's off the record.'

'You know damned well I'm going to reject it, so why waste time?'

'I *don't* know that. I don't want to *believe* that.'

'There's no way out.'

'There are counter explanations I can activate in an hour. Get you off the hook, out of the picture.'

'Not any longer.'

'What? Why?'

'That's *my* pathetic story. So you'd better continue.'

Greenberg searched Matlock's eyes for an explanation, found none, and so picked up the second envelope and opened it.

'In the unlikely and ill-advised event that you reject our recommendation to cease and desist, you must understand that you do so against the express wishes of the Justice Department. Although we will offer whatever protection we can – as we would any citizen – you act under your own responsibility. We cannot be held liable for any injuries or inconveniences of any nature.'

'Is that what it says?'

'No, that's *not* what it says, but that's what it means,' said Greenberg, unfolding the paper. 'It's much simpler and even more inclusive. Here.' The federal agent handed Matlock the letter.

It was a statement signed by an assistant attorney general with a separate line on the left for Matlock's signature.

'An investigative office of the Department of Justice accepted the offer of James B. Matlock to make inquiries of a minor nature with regard to certain illegal acts alleged to have occurred within the vicinity of Carlyle University. However, the Department of Justice now considers the situation to be a professional matter, and any further participation on the part of Professor Matlock is deemed unwarranted and against the policies of the Department. Therefore, the Department of Justice hereby informs James B. Matlock that it appreciates his previous cooperation but requests him to remove himself from any further involvement in the interest of safety and investigatory progress. It is the opinion of the Department that further actions on the part of Professor Matlock might tend to interfere with the aims of the Investigation in the Carlyle area. Mr. Matlock has received the original of this letter and so signifies by his signature below.'

'What the hell are you talking about? This says that I agree to pull out.'

'You'd make a lousy lawyer. Don't buy a bicycle on time before talking to me.'

'What?'

'Nowhere! No*where* does your signing this little stinkpot say you *agree* to retire from the scene. Only that Justice *requested* you to.'

'Then why in hell should I sign it?'

'Excellent question. You may buy a bicycle. . . . You sign it if, as you say, you reject the recommendation to pull out.'

'Oh, for Christ's sake!' Matlock slipped down from the edge of the sink and threw the paper across the counter next to Greenberg. 'I may not know law but I know language. You're talking in contradictions!'

'Only on the surface. . . . Let me ask you a question. Say you continue playing undercover agent. Is it conceivable that you may want to ask for help? An emergency, perhaps?'

'Of course. Inevitable.'

'You get no help whatsoever without that letter going back signed. . . . Don't look at *me*! I'll be replaced in a matter of days. I've been in the area too long already.'

'Kind of hypocritical, isn't it? The only way I can count on any assistance – any protection – is to sign a statement that says I won't need it.'

'It's enough to send me into private practice. . . . There's a new term for this sort of thing these days. It's called 'hazardless progress.' Use whatever – who*ever* – you can. But don't take the blame if a *game plan* gets fucked up. Don't be responsible.'

'And I jump without a parachute if I don't sign.'

'I told you. Take some free advice – I'm a good lawyer. Quit. Forget it. But *forget it.*'

'And I told *you* – I can't.'

Greenberg reached for his drink and spoke softly. 'No matter what you do, it's not going to bring your brother out of his grave.'

'I know that.' Matlock was touched, but he answered firmly.

'You might prevent other younger brothers but you probably won't. In either case, someone else can be recruited from professional ranks. I hate like hell to admit it, but Kressel was right. And if we don't get this conference – this convocation of peddlers in a couple of weeks – there'll be others.'

'I agree with everything you say.'

'Then why hesitate? Pull out.'

'Why? . . . I haven't told you *my* pathetic little story, that's why. Remember? You had priority, but I've still got my turn.'

'So tell.'

And Matlock told him. Everything he knew about Lucas Herron – legend, giant, the 'grand old bird' of Carlyle. The terror-stricken skeleton who had run into his personal forest. The wail of the single word: 'Nimrod.' Greenberg listened, and the longer Matlock talked, the sadder Jason Greenberg's eyes became. When Matlock finished, the federal agent drank the last of his drink and morosely nodded his head in slow motion.

'You spelled out everything for him, didn't you? You couldn't come to *me*, you had to go to *him*. Your campus saint with a bucket of blood in his hands. . . . Loring was right. We had to reach a conscience-stricken amateur. . . . Amateurs in front of us and amateurs behind us. At least I'll say this for you. You got a conscience. That's more than I can say for the rear flank.'

'What should I do?'

'Sign the stinkpot.' Greenberg picked up the Justice Department letter from the counter and handed it to Matlock. 'You're going to need help.'

Patricia Ballantyne preceded Matlock to the small side table at the far end of the Cheshire Cat. The drive out had been strained. The girl had hammered away – quietly, acidly – at Matlock's cooperating with the government, in particular and specifically the Federal Bureau of Investigation. She claimed not to be reacting to a programmed liberal response; there was simply too much overwhelming evidence that such organizations had brought the country ten steps from its own particular police state.

She knew firsthand. She'd witnessed the anguished aftermath of one FBI exercise and knew it wasn't isolated.

Matlock held her chair as she sat down, touching her shoulders as she did so. Touching, reaffirming, lessening the imagined hurt. The table was small, next to a window, several feet from a terrace that soon – in late May – would be in use for outside dining. He sat across from her and took her hand.

'I'm not going to apologize for what I'm doing. I think it has to be done. I'm not a hero and I'm not a fink. I'm not asked to be heroic, and the information they want ultimately will help a lot of people. People who need help – desperately.'

'Will those people *get* help? Or will they simply be prosecuted? Instead of hospitals and clinics . . . will they find themselves in jail?'

'They're not interested in sick kids. They want the ones who make them sick. So do I.'

'But in the process, the kids get hurt.' A statement.

'Some may be. As few as possible.'

'That's contemptible.' The girl took her hand away from Matlock's. 'It's so condescending. Who makes *those* decisions? You?'

'You're beginning to sound like a one-track tape.'

'I've *been* there. It's not pleasant.'

'This is entirely different. I've met just two men; one . . . left. The other's Greenberg. They're not your nightmares from the fifties. Take my word for that.'

'I'd like to.'

The manager of the Cheshire Cat approached the table. 'There's a telephone call for you, Mr. Matlock.'

Matlock felt a twinge of pain in his stomach. It was the nerves of fear. Only one person knew where he was – Jason Greenberg.

'Thanks, Harry.'

'You can take it by the reservations desk. The phone's off the hook.'

Matlock got out of his chair and looked briefly at Pat. In the months and months of their going out together, from restaurants to parties to dinners, he had never received a telephone call, had never been interrupted that way. He saw that realization in her eyes. He walked rapidly away from the table to the reservations desk.

'Hello?'

'Jim?' It *was* Greenberg, of course.

'Jason?'

'Sorry to bother you. I wouldn't if I didn't have to.'

'What is it, for heaven's sake?'

'Lucas Herron's dead. He committed suicide about an hour ago.'

The pain in Matlock's stomach suddenly returned. It wasn't a twinge this time, but instead a sharp blow that left him unable to breathe. All he could see in front of his eyes was the picture of the staggering, panicked old man running across the manicured lawn and disappearing into the dense foliage bordering his property. And then the wailing sound of a sob and the name of Nimrod whispered in hatred.

'Are you all right?'

'Yes. Yes, I'm all right.' For reasons he could not fathom, Matlock's memory focused on a small, black-framed photograph. It was an enlarged snapshot of a dark-haired, middle-aged infantry officer with a weapon in one hand, a map in the other, the face lean and strong, looking up toward the high ground.

A quarter of a century ago.

'You'd better get back to your apartment. . . .' Greenberg was issuing an order, but he had the sense to be gentle about it.

'Who found him?'

'My man. No one else knows yet.'

'Your man?'

'After our talk, I put Herron under surveillance. You get to spot the signs. He broke in and found him.'

'How?'

'Cut his wrists in the shower.'

'Oh, Christ! What have I done?'

'Cut that out! Get back here. We've got people to reach. . . . Come on, Jim.'

'What can I tell Pat?' Matlock tried to find his mind but it kept wandering back to a helpless, frightened old man.

'As little as possible. But hurry.'

Matlock replaced the receiver and took several deep breaths. He searched his pockets for cigarettes and remembered that he'd left them at the table.

The table. Pat. He had to go back to the table and think of something to say.

The truth. Goddamn it, the *truth*.

He made his way around two antique pillars toward the far end of the room and the small side table by the window. In spite of his panic, he felt a degree of relief and knew it was because he had decided to be honest with Pat. God knew he had to have someone other than Greenberg and Kressel to talk to.

Kressel! He was supposed to have gone to Kressel's house at seven. He'd forgotten all about it!

But in an instant Sam Kressel went out of his thoughts. He saw the small side table by the window and there was no one there.

Pat was gone.

Thirteen

'No one saw her leave?' Greenberg followed a frustrated Matlock into the living room from the foyer. Sam Kressel's voice could be heard from the bedroom, shouting excitedly into a telephone. Matlock took notice of it, his attention split in too many areas.

'That's Sam in there, isn't it?' he asked. 'Does he know about Herron?'

'Yes. I called him after I talked to you. . . . What about the waitresses? Did you ask them?'

'Of course, I did. None of them were sure. It was busy. One said she thought she might have gone to the ladies' room. Another hinted, s'help me, hinted, that she might have been the girl who left with a couple from another table.'

'Wouldn't they have had to pass you on the way out? Wouldn't you have seen her?'

'Not necessarily. We were in the back. There are two or three doors which lead to a terrace. In summer, especially when it's crowded, they put tables on the terrace.'

'You drove out in your car?'

'Naturally.'

'And you didn't see her outside, walking on the road, on the grounds?'

'No.'

'Did you recognize any of the other people there?'

'I didn't really look. I was . . . preoccupied.' Matlock lit a cigarette. His hand shook as he held the match.

'If you want my opinion, I think she spotted someone she knew and asked for a lift home. A girl like that doesn't go anywhere she doesn't want to go without a fight.'

'I know. That's occurred to me.'

'Have a fight?'

'You might say it was diminishing but not over. The phone call probably set her off again. Old English teachers rarely get calls while out at restaurants.'

'I'm sorry.'

'It's not your fault. I told you, she's uptight. She keeps thinking about her father. I'll try her apartment when Sam gets off the phone.'

'*He's* a funny man. I tell him about Herron – naturally he goes off the deep end. He says he's got to talk privately with Sealfont so he goes into the bedroom and shouts so loud they can hear him in Poughkeepsie.'

Matlock's thoughts shifted quickly to Herron. 'His death – his *suicide* – is going to be the biggest shock this campus has had in twenty years. Men like Lucas simply don't die. They certainly don't die like *this*. . . . Does Sam know I saw him?'

'He does. I couldn't withhold that. I told him pretty much what you told me – shorter version, of course. He refuses to believe it. The implications, I mean.'

'I don't blame him. They're not easy to believe. What do we do now?'

'We wait. I've made a report. Two lab men from the Hartford Bureau are out there now. The local police have been called in.'

At the mention of the police, Matlock suddenly remembered the patrolman out of uniform in the squash court corridor, who had walked rapidly away at the moment of recognition. He'd told Greenberg and Greenberg had never given him an explanation – if there was one. He asked again.

'What about the cop in the gym?'

'The story's reasonable. At least so far. The Carlyle police are assigned three mornings a week for limited use of the facilities. Town-gown relations. Coincidence.'

'You're settling for that?'

'I said, "so far." We're running a check on the man. Nothing's turned up but an excellent record.'

'He's a bigot, a nasty bastard.'

'This may surprise you, but that's no crime. It's guaranteed in the Bill of Rights.'

Sam Kressel walked through the bedroom door quickly, emphatically. Matlock saw that he was as close to pure fear as he'd ever seen a man. There was an uncomfortable similarity between Sam's face and the bloodless expression of Lucas Herron before the old man had raced into the woods.

'I heard you come in,' Kressel said. 'What are we going to *do*? What in hell are we *going to do*? . . . Adrian doesn't believe that absurd story any more than *I* do! *Lucas Herron! It's insane!*'

'Maybe. But it's true.'

'Because *you* say so? How can you be sure? You're no professional in these matters. As I understand it, Lucas admitted he was helping a student through a drug problem.'

'He . . . they aren't students.'

'I see.' Kressel stopped briefly and looked back and forth between Matlock and Greenberg. 'Under the circumstances, I demand to know the identities.'

'You'll get them,' said Greenberg quietly. 'Go on. I want to hear why Matlock's so wrong, the story so absurd.'

'Because Lucas Herron isn't . . . wasn't the only member of the faculty concerned with these problems. There are dozens of us giving aid, helping wherever we can!'

'I don't follow you.' Greenberg stared at Kressel. 'So you help. You don't go and kill yourself when a fellow member of the faculty finds out about it.'

Sam Kressel removed his glasses and looked momentarily reflective, sad. 'There's something else neither of you know about. I've been aware of it for some time but not so knowledgeably as Sealfont. . . . Lucas Herron was a very sick man. One kidney was removed last summer. The other was also cancerous and he knew it. The pain must have been unbearable for him. He hadn't long.'

Greenberg watched closely as Kressel returned his glasses to his face. Matlock bent down and crushed out his cigarette in an ashtray on the coffee table. Finally, Greenberg spoke.

'Are you suggesting that there's no relationship between Herron's suicide and Matlock's seeing him this afternoon?'

'I'm not suggesting any such thing. I'm sure there's a relationship. . . . But you didn't know Lucas. His whole life for nearly half a century, except for the war years, was Carlyle University. It's been his total, complete existence. He loved this place more than any man could love a woman, more than any parent a child. I'm sure Jim's told you. If he thought for a moment that his world here was going to be defaced, torn apart – that would be a greater pain than the physical torture his body gave him. What better time to take his own life?'

'*Goddamn you!*' roared Matlock. 'You're saying *I killed him!*'

'Perhaps I am,' Kressel said quietly. 'I hadn't thought of it in those terms. I'm sure Adrian didn't either.'

'But that's what you're *saying*! You're saying I went off half-cocked and killed him as much as if I'd slashed his wrists! . . . Well, you weren't there. *I was!*'

Kressel spoke gently. 'I didn't say you went off half-cocked. I said you were an amateur. A very well-intentioned amateur. I think Greenberg knows what I mean.'

Jason Greenberg looked at Matlock. 'There's an old Slovak proverb: "When the old men kill themselves, the cities are dying."'

The telephone bell suddenly pierced the air; its sound acted as a jolt to the three men. Matlock answered it, then turned to Greenberg. 'It's for you.'

'Thanks.' The federal agent took the phone from Matlock. 'Greenberg . . . O.K. I understand. When will you know? . . . I'll probably be on the road by then. I'll call you back. Talk later.' He replaced the telephone and stood by the desk, his back to Matlock and Kressel. The dean of colleges couldn't contain himself.

'What was it? What happened?'

Greenberg turned and faced them. Matlock thought his eyes seemed sadder than usual, which Matlock had learned was a sign of trouble in Greenberg.

'We're making a request of the police – the courts – for an autopsy.'

'*Why?!*' Kressel shouted as he approached the agent. 'For God's sake, *why*?! The man killed himself! He was in *pain*! . . . Jesus Christ, you can't *do* this! If news of it gets out . . .'

'We'll handle it quietly.'

'That can't be done and you *know* it! It'll leak out and all hell'll break loose around here! I won't *permit* it!'

'You can't stop it. Even I couldn't stop it. There's sufficient evidence to indicate that Herron didn't take his own life. That he was killed.' Greenberg smiled wryly at Matlock. 'And not by words.'

Kressel argued, threatened, made another call to Sealfont, and finally, when it was obvious that all were to no avail, he left Matlock's apartment in fury.

No sooner had Kressel slammed the door than the telephone rang again. Greenberg saw that the sound disturbed Matlock – not merely annoyed him, but disturbed him; perhaps frightened him.

'I'm sorry. . . . I'm afraid this place has to be a kind of patrol base for a while. Not long. . . . Maybe it's the girl.'

Matlock picked up the phone, listened, but did not say anything into it. Instead, he turned to Greenberg. He said only one word.

'You.'

Greenberg took the telephone, uttered his name softly, and then spent the next minute staring straight ahead. Matlock watched Greenberg for half the time and then wandered into his kitchen. He didn't wish to stand awkwardly to one side while the agent listened to a superior's instructions.

The voice at the other end of the line had initially identified itself by saying, 'Washington calling.'

On the counter lay the empty envelope in which the brutally hypocritical statement had come from the Department of Justice. It had been one more sign that his worst fantasies were gradually becoming real. From that infinitesimal portion of the mind which concerns itself with the unthinkable, Matlock had begun to perceive that the land he had grown up in was changing into something ugly and destructive. It was far more than a political manifestation, it was a slow, all-embracing sense of morality by strategy. A corruption of intentions. Strong feelings were being replaced with surface anger, convictions and compromise. The land was becoming something other than its promise, its commitment. The grails were empty vessels of flat wine, impressive solely because they were possessed.

'I'm off the phone now. Would you like to try reaching Miss Ballantyne?'

Matlock looked up at Greenberg, standing in the frame of the kitchen door. Greenberg, the walking contradiction, the proverb-quoting agent deeply suspicious of the system for which he worked.

'Yes. Yes, I'd like to.' He started into the living room as Greenberg stepped aside to let him pass. Matlock reached the center of the room and stopped. 'That's one hell of a quotation. What was it? "When the old men kill themselves, the cities are dying."' He turned and looked at the agent. 'I think that's the saddest proverb I've ever heard.'

'You're not Hassidic. Of course, neither am I, but the Hassidim wouldn't think it sad. . . . Come to think of it, no true philosopher would.'

'Why not? It *is* sad.'

'It's truth. Truth is neither joyful nor sad, neither good nor bad. It is simply truth.'

'Someday let's debate that, Jason.' Matlock picked up the telephone, dialed Pat's number, and let it ring a dozen times. There was no answer. Matlock thought of several of Pat's friends and wondered whether to call them or not. When angry or upset, Pat usually did one of two things. She either went off by herself for an hour or so, or, conversely, sought out one or two friends and drove off to a film in Hartford or an out-of-the-way bar. It was just over an hour. He'd give her another fifteen minutes before phoning around. It had, of course, occurred to him that she might have been taken involuntarily – that had been his first thought. But it wasn't logical. The Cheshire Cat had been filled with people, the tables close together. Greenberg was right. Wherever she went, she went because she wanted to go.

Greenberg stood by the kitchen door. He hadn't moved. He'd been watching Matlock.

'I'll try in a quarter of an hour. Then, if there's no answer, I'll call some friends of hers. As you said, she's one strong-willed young lady.'

'I hope you're not from the same cloth.'

'What does that mean?'

Greenberg took several steps into the living room. When he spoke, he looked directly into Matlock's eyes.

'You're out. Finished. Forget the letter, forget Loring, forget me. . . . That's the way it's got to be. We understand you have reservations for St. Thomas on Pan Am for Saturday. Enjoy it, because that's where you're going. Much better this way.'

Matlock returned the government man's look. 'Any decision like that will be made by me. I've got a gentle old man on my conscience; and you've got that stinkpot in your pocket. I signed it, remember?'

'The stinkpot doesn't count anymore. D.C. wants you out. You go.'

'Why?'

'Because of the gentle old man. If he *was* killed, you could be, too. If that happened, certain records might be subpoenaed, certain men who had reservations about recruiting you might voice those reservations to the press. You were maneuvered. I don't have to tell you that.'

'So?'

'The directors at Justice have no wish to be called executioners.'

'I see.' Matlock took his eyes off Greenberg and wandered toward the coffee table. 'Suppose I refuse?'

'Then I remove you from the scene.'

'How?'

'I have you arrested on suspicion of murder one.'

'*What?*'

'You were the last person on record to see Lucas Herron alive. By your own admission, you went out to his house to threaten him.'

'To *warn* him!'

'That's subject to interpretation, isn't it?'

When the thunderous crash came, it was so ear-shattering both men threw themselves to the floor. It was as if the whole side of the building had collapsed in rubble. Dust was everywhere, furniture toppled, glass shattered, splinters of wood and plaster flew through the air, and the terrible stench of burning sulfur settled over the room. Matlock knew the smell of that kind of bomb, and his reflexes knew how to operate. He clung to the base of his couch waiting, waiting for a second explosion – a delayed detonator which would kill any who rose in panic. Through the mist, he saw Greenberg start to get up, and he leaped forward, tackling the agent at his knees.

'Get down! Stay. . . .'

The second explosion came. Parts of the ceiling blackened. But Matlock knew it was not a killer explosive. It was something else, and he could not figure it out at the moment. It was an eye-grabber, a camouflage – not meant to kill, but to deflect all concentration. A huge firecracker.

Screams of panic could now be heard mounting from all parts of the building. The sounds of rushing feet pounded on the floor above his apartment.

And then a single screech of terror from outside Matlock's front door. It would not stop. The horror of it caused Matlock and Greenberg to struggle to their feet and race to the source. Matlock pulled the door open and looked down upon a sight no human being should ever see more than once in a lifetime, if his life must continue beyond that instant.

On his front step was Patricia Ballantyne wrapped in a blood-soaked sheet. Holes were cut in the areas of her naked breasts, blood flowing from gashes beneath the nipples. The front of her head was shaved; blood poured out of lacerations where once had been the soft brown hair. Blood, too, came from the half-open mouth, her lips bruised and split. The eyes were blackened into deep crevasses of sore flesh – but they moved! The eyes moved!

Saliva began forming at the corners of her lips. The half-dead corpse was trying to speak.

'Jamie . . .' was the only word she managed and then her head slipped to one side.

Greenberg threw his whole weight against Matlock, sending him sprawling into the gathering crowd. He roared orders of 'Police!' and 'Ambulance!' until he saw enough people running to execute his commands. He put his mouth to the girl's mouth, to force air into the collapsing lungs, but he knew it wasn't really necessary. Patricia Ballantyne wasn't dead; she'd been tortured by experts, and the experts knew their business well. Every slash, every crack, every bruise meant utmost pain but did not mean death.

He started to pick the girl up but Matlock stopped him. The English professor's eyes were swollen with tears of hate. He gently removed Greenberg's hands and lifted Pat into his arms. He carried her inside and stretched her out on the half-destroyed sofa. Greenberg went into the bedroom and returned with a blanket. Then he brought a bowl of warm water from the kitchen and several towels. He lifted the blanket and held a towel beneath the bleeding breasts. Matlock, staring in horror at the brutally beaten face, then took the edge of another towel and began wiping away the blood around the shaven head and the mouth.

'She'll be all right, Jim. I've seen this before. She'll be all right.'

And as Greenberg heard the sounds of the sirens in the near distance, he wondered, really, if this girl would ever be right again.

Matlock, helpless, continued to wipe the girl's face, his tears now streaming down his cheeks, his eyes unblinking. He spoke through his controlled sobs.

'You know what this means, don't you? No one pulls me out now. They try, I'll kill them.'

'I won't let them,' said Greenberg simply.

The screeching of brakes could be heard outside and the flashing lights of the police cars and the ambulances whipped in circles through the windows.

Matlock's face fell into the cushion beside the unconscious girl and he wept.

Fourteen

Matlock awoke in the antiseptic whiteness of a hospital room. The shade was up, and the sun reflected harshly on the three walls he could see. At his feet a nurse was writing efficiently, emphatically, on top of a clipboard attached to the base of the bed by a thin keychain. He stretched his arms, then quickly brought his left back, aware of a sharp pain in his forearm.

'You feel those the next morning, Mr. Matlock,' droned the nurse without looking up from the clipboard. 'Heavy intravenous sedations are murder, I can tell you. Not that I've ever had one, but Lord knows, I've seen enough who have.'

'Is Pat . . . Miss Ballantyne here?'

'Well, not in the same *room*! Lord, you campus types!'

'She's here?'

'Of course. Next room. Which I intend to keep *locked*! Lord, you people from the hill! . . . There! You're all accounted for.' The nurse let the clipboard crash down and vibrate back and forth. 'Now. *You've* got special privileges. *You're* allowed breakfast even though it's past breakfast time – *way* past! That's probably because they want you to pay your bill. . . . You can be discharged any time after twelve.'

'What time is it? Someone took my watch.'

'It's eight minutes to nine,' said the nurse, glancing at her wrist. 'And no one *took* your watch. It's with any other valuables you had when you were admitted.'

'How *is* Miss Ballantyne?'

'We don't discuss other patients, Mr. Matlock.'

'Where's her doctor?'

'He's the same as yours, I understand. Not one of *ours*.' The nurse made sure the statement was hardly complimentary. 'According to your chart, he'll be here at nine-thirty unless we phone for an emergency.'

'Call him. I want him here as soon as possible.'

'Now, really. There's no emergency. . . .'

'Goddamn it, get him here!'

As Matlock raised his voice the door of his room opened. Jason Greenberg came in quickly. 'I could hear you in the corridor. That's a good sign.'

'How's Pat?!'

'Just a minute, sir. We have regulations. . . .'

Greenberg took out his identification and showed it to the nurse. 'This man is in my custody, Miss. Check the front desk, if you like, but leave us alone.'

The nurse, ever professional, scrutinized the identification and walked rapidly out the door.

'How's Pat?'

'A mess, but with it. She had a bad night; she's going to have a worse morning when she asks for a mirror.'

'The hell with that! Is she *all right*?'

'Twenty-seven stitches – body, head, mouth, and, for variety, one on her left foot. But she's going to be fine. X-rays show only bone bruises. No fractures, no ruptures, no internal bleeding. The bastards did their usual professional job.'

'Was she able to talk?'

'Not really. And the doctor didn't advise it. She needs sleep more than anything else. . . . You need a little rest, too. That's why we put you here last night.'

'Anyone hurt at the apartment?'

'Nope. It was a crazy bombing. We don't think it was intended to kill anyone. The first was a short two-inch stick taped below the window exterior; the second – activated by the first – wasn't much more than a July Fourth rocket. You expected the second blast, didn't you?'

'Yes. I guess I did. . . . Terror tactics, wasn't it?'

'That's what we figure.'

'Can I see Pat?'

'Rather you waited. The doctor thinks she'll sleep into the afternoon. There's a nurse in there with ice packs and stuff if localized pain bothers her. Let her rest.'

Matlock cautiously sat on the edge of the bed. He began flexing his legs, arms, neck, and hands, and found that he wasn't much below par. 'I feel sort of like a hangover without the headache.'

'The doctor gave you a heavy dose. You were . . . understandably . . . very emotional.'

'I remember everything. I'm calmer, but I don't retract one goddamned word. . . . I have two classes today. One at ten and the other at two. I want to make them.'

'You don't have to. Sealfont wants to see you.'

'I'll talk to him after my last class. . . . Then I'll see Pat.' Matlock stood on his feet and walked slowly to the large hospital window. It was a bright, sunlit morning; Connecticut had had a string of beautiful days. As he stared outside, Matlock remembered he'd looked out another window five days ago when he'd first met Jason Greenberg. He'd made a decision then as he was making one now. 'Last night you said you wouldn't let them pull me out. I hope you haven't changed your mind. I'm *not* going to be on that Pan Am flight tomorrow.'

'You won't be arrested. I promised you that.'

'Can you prevent it? You also said you were going to be replaced.'

'I can prevent it. . . . I can morally object, an enigmatic phrase which is translated to mean I can embarrass people. However, I don't want to mislead you. If you create problems, you could be taken into protective custody.'

'They can if they can find me.'

'That's a condition I don't like.'

'Forget you heard it. Where are my clothes?' Matlock walked to the single closet door and opened it. His slacks, jacket, and shirt were hung on hangers; his loafers were on the floor with his socks carefully inserted. The lone bureau held his undershorts and a hospital-furnished toothbrush. 'Will you go down and see whoever you've got to see to get me out of here? Also, I'll need my wallet, cash, and watch. Will you do that, please?'

'What do you mean – if they could find you? What are you going to do?' Greenberg made no move to leave.

'Nothing earth-shattering. Merely continue making those inquiries . . . of a minor nature. That's the way the statement from your employers phrased it, wasn't it? Loring said it. Somewhere out there is the other half of that paper. I'm going to find it.'

'You listen to me first! I don't deny you have a right . . .'

'You don't *deny!*' Matlock turned on the federal agent. His voice was controlled but vicious. 'That's not good enough. That's *negative* approval! I've got several *big* rights! They include a kid brother in a sailboat, a black son of a bitch named Dunois or whatever you call him, a man by the name of Lucas Herron, and that girl in there! I suspect you and the doctor know the rest of what happened to her last night, and I can *guess!* Don't talk to me about *a right!*'

'In principle, we agree. I just don't want your "rights" to land you next to your brother. This is a job for professionals. Not an amateur! If you work at all, I want you to work with whoever takes my place. That's important. I want your word on it.'

Matlock took off the top of his pajamas and gave Greenberg a short, embarrassed smile. 'You have it. I don't really see myself as a one-man ranger team. Do you know who's taking your place?'

'Not yet. Probably someone from D.C. They won't take a chance on using a Hartford or a New Haven man. . . . The truth is . . . they don't know who's been bought. He'll be in touch. I'll have to brief him myself. No one else can. I'll instruct him to identify himself with . . . what would you like?'

'Tell him to use your proverb. "When the old men kill themselves, the cities are dying."'

'You like that, don't you?'

'I don't like it or dislike it. It's simply the truth. Isn't that the way it should be?'

'And very applicable. I see what you mean.'

'Very.'

'Jim, before I go this afternoon, I'm going to write out a telephone number for you. It's a Bronx number – my parents. They won't know where I am, but I'll check with them every day. Use it if you have to.'

'Thanks, I will.'

'I want your word on it.'

'You have it.' Matlock laughed a short laugh of gratitude.

'Of course, under the circumstances, I may just be on the other end of the line if you do call.'

'Back in private practice?'

'The possibility is less remote than you think.'

Fifteen

Between his two classes, Matlock drove to the small brokerage office in the town of Carlyle and emerged with a check for $7,312. It represented his total investment in the market, mostly from royalties. The broker had tried to dissuade him; it was no time to sell, especially at current prices. But Matlock had made up his mind. The cashier reluctantly issued the check.

From there Matlock went to his bank and transferred his entire savings into his checking account. He added the $7,312 to the slip and looked at the sum total of his immediate cash value.

It came to $11,501.72.

Matlock stared at the figure for several minutes. He had mixed feelings about it. On the one hand, it proved solvency; on the other, it was a little frightening to think that after thirty-three years of living he was able to pinpoint so accurately his net financial worth. There was no house, no land, no hidden investments anywhere. Only an automobile, a few possessions of minor value, and some published words of such a specialized nature that there would be no significant rewards.

Yet by many standards, it was a great deal of money.

Only nowhere *near* enough. He knew that. It was why Scarsdale, New York, was on the day's schedule.

The meeting with Sealfont had been unnerving, and Matlock wasn't sure how much more his shattered nerves could take. The cold fury of Carlyle's president was matched only by the depth of his anguish.

The bewildering shadow world of violence and corruption was a world he could never come to grips with because it was not within the realm of his comprehension. Matlock had been startled to hear Sealfont say, as he sat in his chair staring out the bay window overlooking the most beautiful lawn on the Carlyle campus, that he might well resign.

'If this whole sordid, unbelievable business is true – and who can doubt it – I have no right to sit in this chair.'

'That's not so,' Matlock had answered. 'If it's true, this place is going to need you more than ever before.'

'A blind man? No one needs a blind man. Not in this office.'

'Not blind. Unexposed.'

And then Sealfont had swung around in his chair and pounded on the top of his desk in an enormous display of strength.

'Why *here*?! *Why here?!*'

As he sat in front of Sealfont's desk, Matlock looked at the pained face of Carlyle's president. And for a second he thought the man might weep.

The trip down the Merritt Parkway was made at high speed. He had to race; it was necessary for him. It helped take his mind off the sight of Pat Ballantyne as he had seen her a few minutes before leaving. He had gone from Sealfont's to the hospital; still he hadn't been able to talk with her. No one had yet.

She had awakened at noon, he'd been told. She'd gone into severe hysterics. The doctor from Litchfield had administered further sedatives. The doctor was worried, and Matlock knew it was Pat's mind he was worried about. The nightmare of terror inflicted upon her body had to touch her brain.

The first minutes with his parents at the huge Scarsdale house were awkward. His father, Jonathan Munro Matlock, had spent decades in the highest spheres of his marketplace and knew instinctively when a man came to him without strength.

Without strength but with need.

Matlock told his father as simply and unemotionally as he could that he wanted to borrow a large sum of money; he could not guarantee its repayment. It would be used to help – ultimately help – young people like his dead brother.

The dead son.

'How?' asked Jonathan Matlock softly.

'I can't tell you that.' He looked into his father's eyes and the irrevocable truth of the son's statement was accepted by the father.

'Very well. Are you qualified for this undertaking?'

'Yes. I am.'

'Are there others involved?'

'By necessity, yes.'

'Do you trust them?'

'I do.'

'Have they asked for this money?'

'No. They don't know about it.'

'Will it be at their disposal?'

'No. Not that I can foresee. . . . I'll go further than that. It would be wrong for them to learn of it.'

'I'm not restricting you, I'm asking.'

'That's my answer.'

'And you believe that what you're doing will help, in some way, boys like David? Practical help, not theoretical, not dream stuff, not charity.'

'Yes. It has to.'

'How much do you want?'

Matlock took a deep breath silently. 'Fifteen thousand dollars.'

'Wait here.'

Several minutes later, the father came out of his study and gave his son an envelope.

The son knew better than to open it.

Ten minutes after the exchange – and Matlock knew it *was* an exchange – he left, feeling the eyes of his parents as they stood on the enormous porch and watched him drive out through the gates.

Matlock pulled into the apartment driveway, shut off the lights and the engine, and wearily climbed out. As he approached the old Tudor house, he saw that every light he owned was turned on. Jason Greenberg wasn't taking chances, and Matlock assumed that some part of Greenberg's silent, unseen army was watching his place from varying distances – none too far away.

He unlocked the door and pushed it open. There was no one there. At least, not in sight. Not even his cat. 'Hello? Jason? . . . Anybody here? It's Matlock.'

There was no answer and Matlock was relieved. He wanted only to crawl into bed and sleep. He'd stopped at the hospital to see Pat, and the request had been denied. At least he'd learned that '. . . she is resting and her condition is deemed satisfactory.' That was a step up. That afternoon she'd still been on the critical list. He would see her at nine in the morning.

Now was the time for him to sleep – peaceably if possible. Sleep at all costs. There was a great deal to do in the morning.

He went into his bedroom, passing the still unrepaired sections of wall and window as he did so. Carpenter's and plasterer's tools were neatly stacked in corners. He removed his jacket and his shirt and then thought, with a degree of self-ridicule, that he was becoming far too confident. He walked rapidly out of the bedroom and into his bathroom. Once the door was shut, he reached down to the litter box and lifted up the newspaper to the layer of canvas. The Corsican paper was there, the tarnished silver coating reflecting the light.

Back in the bedroom, Matlock removed his wallet, cash, and car keys, placing them on top of his bureau. As he did so, he remembered the envelope.

He hadn't been fooled. He knew his father, perhaps better than his father realized. He presumed there was a short note with the check stating clearly that the money was a gift, not a loan, and that no repayment was anticipated.

The note was there, folded inside the envelope, but the written words were not what Matlock expected.

> I believe in you. I always have.
> Love,
> Dad

On top of the note, clipped to the paper on the reverse side, was the check. Matlock slipped it off and read the figure.

It was for fifty thousand dollars.

Sixteen

Much of the swelling on her face and around her eyes had subsided. He took her hand and held it tightly, putting his face once more next to hers.

'You're going to be fine,' were the innocuous words he summoned. He had to hold himself in check to stop himself from screaming out his anger and his guilt. That this could be done to a human being by other human beings was beyond his endurance. And he was responsible.

When she spoke, her voice was hardly audible, like a small child's, the words only partially formed through the immobile lips.

'Jamie . . . Jamie?'

'Shh . . . Don't talk if it hurts.'

'*Why?*'

'I don't know. But we'll find out.'

'No! . . . No, don't! They're . . . they're . . .' The girl had to swallow; it was nearly impossible for her. She pointed to a glass of water on the bedside table. Matlock quickly reached for it and held it to her lips, supporting her by the shoulders.

'How did it happen? Can you tell me?'

'Told . . . Greenberg. Man and woman . . . came to the table. Said you were . . . waiting . . . outside.'

'Never mind, I'll talk to Jason.'

'I . . . feel better. I hurt but . . . feel better, I . . . really do. . . . Am I going to be all right?'

'Of course you are. I spoke with the doctor. You're bruised, but nothing broken, nothing serious. He says you'll be out of bed in a few days, that's all.'

Patricia Ballantyne's eyes brightened, and Matlock saw the terrible attempt of a smile on her sutured lips. 'I fought. . . . I fought and I fought . . . until I . . . couldn't remember any more.'

It took all of Matlock's strength not to burst into tears. 'I know you did. Now, no more talking. You rest, take it easy. I'll just sit here and we'll talk with our eyes. Remember? You said we always communicate around other people with our eyes. . . . I'll tell you a dirty joke.'

When the smile came, it *was* from her eyes.

He stayed until a nurse forbade him to stay longer. Then he kissed her softly on the lips and left the room. He was a relieved man; he was an angry man.

'Mr. Matlock?' The young doctor with the freshly scrubbed face of an intern approached him by the elevator.

'Yes?'

'There's a telephone call for you. You can take it at the second floor reception, if you'll follow me.'

The caller's voice was unknown. 'Mr. Matlock, my name's Houston. I'm a friend of Jason Greenberg's. I'm to get in touch with you.'

'Oh? How's Jason?'

'Fine. I'd like to get together with you as soon as possible.'

Matlock was about to name a place, any place, after his first class. And then he stopped. 'Did Jason leave any message . . . where he is now, or anything?'

'No sir. Just that I was to make contact pronto.'

'I see.' Why didn't the man say it? Why didn't Houston identify himself? 'Greenberg definitely told me he'd leave word . . . a message . . . where he'd be. I'm sure he said that.'

'Against department regulations, Mr. Matlock. He wouldn't be allowed to.'

'Oh? . . . Then he didn't leave any message at all?'

The voice on the other end of the line hesitated slightly, perceptively. 'He may have forgotten. . . . As a matter of fact, I didn't speak to him myself. I received my orders directly from Washington. Where shall we meet?'

Matlock heard the anxiety in the man's voice. When he referred to Washington, his tone had risen in a small burst of nervous energy. 'Let me call you later. What's your number?'

'Now listen, Matlock. I'm in a telephone booth and we have to meet. I've got my orders!'

'Yes, I'll bet you do. . . .'

'What?'

'Never mind. Are you downtown? In Carlyle?'

The man hesitated again. 'I'm in the area.'

'Tell me, Mr. Houston. . . . Is the city dying?'

'What? What are you talking about?'

'I'm going to be late for my class. Try me again. I'm sure you'll be able to reach me.' Matlock hung up the phone. His left hand shook and perspiration had formed on his brow.

Mr. Houston was the enemy.

The enemy was closing in.

His first Saturday class was at eleven, which gave him just about an hour to make what he felt were the most logical arrangements for the money. He didn't want to think that he had to physically be in the town of Carlyle – at the Carlyle Bank – on Monday morning. He wasn't sure it would be possible. He wasn't sure where he would be on Monday.

Since, on the surface, Carlyle was a typical New England college town, it had a particular way of life common to such places. One knew, generally on a first-name basis, all the people whose jobs made day-to-day living the effortless, unhurried existence that it was. The garage mechanic was 'Joe' or 'Mac,' the manager at J. Press was 'Al,' the dentist 'John' or 'Warren,' the girl at the dry cleaners 'Edith.' In Matlock's case, the banker was 'Alex.' Alex Anderson, a Carlyle graduate of forty, a local boy who'd made the jump from town to gown and then coordinated both. Matlock called him at home and explained his problem. He was carrying around a large check from his father. He was making some private family investments in his own name, and they were confidential. Since the robbery at his apartment, he wanted to divest himself of the check immediately. Could Alex suggest anything? Should he put it in the mail? How best to get it into his account, since he wasn't sure he would be in Carlyle on Monday, and he needed it cleared, the money available. Alex Anderson suggested the obvious. Matlock should endorse the check, put it in an envelope marked for Anderson's attention, and drop it in the night deposit box at the bank. Alex would take care of the rest first thing Monday morning.

And then Alex Anderson asked him the denomination and Matlock told him.

The account problem solved, Matlock concentrated on what he began to think of as his point of departure. There was no other phrase he could find, and he needed a phrase – he needed the discipline of a definition. He had to start precisely right, knowing that what might follow could be totally *undisciplined* – completely without plan or orthodoxy. For he had made up his mind.

He was going to enter the world of Nimrod. The builder of Babylon and Nineveh, the hunter of wild animals, the killer of children and old men, the beater of women.

He was going to find Nimrod.

As were most adults not wedded to the precept that all things enjoyable were immoral, Matlock was aware that the state of Connecticut, like its sister states to the north, the south, and the west, was inhabited by a network of men only too eager to supply those divertissements frowned upon by the pulpits and the courts. What Hartford insurance executive in the upper brackets never heard of that string of 'Antique Shoppes' on New Britain Avenue where a lithe young girl's body could be had for a reasonable amount of petty cash? What commuter from Old Greenwich was oblivious to the large estates north of Green Farms where the gambling often rivaled the Vegas stakes? How many tired businessmen's wives from New Haven or Westport were really ignorant of the various 'escort' services operating out of Hamden and Fairfield? And over in the 'old country,' the Norfolks? Where the rambling mansions were fading apotheoses to the *real* money, the blooded first families who migrated just a little west to avoid the new rich? The 'old country' had the strangest diversions, it was rumored. Houses in shadows, lighted by candles, where the bored could become aroused by observation. Voyeurs of the sickest scenes. Female, male, animal – all types, all combinations.

Matlock knew that in this world Nimrod could be found. It had to be. For although narcotics were but one aspect of the services rendered within this network, they were available – as was everything else.

And of all these games of indulgence, none had the fire and ice, none had the magnetism, of the gambling houses. For those thousands who couldn't find time for the junkets to San Juan, London, or Paradise Island, there were the temporary excursions into the manic moments where daily boredom could be forgotten – a stone's throw from home. Reputations were made quickly over the green felt tables – with the roll of the dice or a turn of a card. It was here that Matlock would find his point of departure. It was in these places where a young man of thirty-three years was prepared to lose thousands – until someone asked who he was.

At twelve-thirty Matlock walked across the quadrangle toward his apartment. The time had come to initiate his first move. The vague outline of a plan was coming into focus.

He should have heard the footsteps, but he didn't. He only heard the cough, a smoker's cough, the cough of a man who'd been running.

'Mr. Matlock?'

Matlock turned and saw a man in his middle thirties, like himself, perhaps a bit older and, indeed, out of breath.

'Yes?'

'Sorry, I keep missing you. I got to the hospital just as you'd left, then waited in the wrong damn building for you, after your class. There's a very confused biology teacher with a name similar to yours. Even looks a little like you. Same height, build, hair . . .'

'That's Murdock. Elliot Murdock. What's the matter?'

'He couldn't understand why I kept insisting that when "old men kill themselves, the cities are dying"!'

'You're from Greenberg!'

'That's it. Morbid code, if you don't mind my saying so. Keep walking. We'll separate at the end of the path. Meet me in twenty minutes at Bill's Bar & Grill by the freight depot. It's six blocks south of the railroad station. O.K.?'

'Never heard of it.'

'I was going to suggest you remove your necktie. I'll be in a leather jacket.'

'You pick classy spots.'

'Old habit. I cheat on the expense account.'

'Greenberg said I was to work with you.'

'You better believe it! He's up to his Kosher ass in boiling oil for you. I think they're shipping him out to a job in Cairo. . . . He's one hell of a guy. We field men like him. Don't louse him up.'

'All I wanted to ask was your name. I didn't expect a sermon.'

'It's Houston. Fred Houston. See you in twenty minutes. Get rid of the tie.'

Seventeen

Bill's Bar & Grill was a part of Carlyle Matlock had never seen before. Railroad laborers and freight-yard drifters were its predominant clientele. He scanned the filthy room; Houston sat in a back booth.

'It's cocktail hour, Matlock. A little early by campus standards, but the effects aren't much different. Not even the clothes these days.'

'It's quite a place.'

'It serves the purpose. Go up to the bar and get yourself a drink. The bunnies don't come on till sundown.'

Matlock did as Houston instructed and brought back the best bourbon he could find. It was a brand he had given up when he reached a living wage.

'I think I should tell you right away. Someone using your name telephoned me at the hospital.'

It was as if Houston had been hit in the stomach. 'My God,' he said quietly. 'What did he say? How did you handle it?'

'I waited for him to identify himself . . . with Greenberg's proverb. I gave him a couple of chances but he didn't. . . . So I told him to call me later and hung up.'

'He used *my* name?! *Houston*. You're sure?'

'Absolutely.'

'That doesn't make sense. He *couldn't*!'

'Believe me. He did.'

'No one knew I was the replacement. . . . *I* didn't know it until three this morning.'

'Someone found out.'

Houston took several swallows of his beer. 'If what you say is true, I'll be out of here within a couple of hours. Incidentally, that was good thinking. . . . Let me give you an extra hint, though. Never accept a contact made by telephone.'

'Why not?'

'If that *had* been me calling – how would *I* know it was *you* I was talking to?'

'I see what you mean. . . .'

'Common sense. Most everything we do is common sense. . . . We'll keep the same code. The "old men" and "the cities." Your next contact will be made tonight.'

'You're sure you'll be leaving?'

'I've been *spotted*. I'm not *about* to stick around. Maybe you forgot Ralph Loring. . . . We gave big at the office.'

'All right. Have you talked to Jason? Did he brief you?'

'For two hours. From four till six this morning. My wife said he drank thirteen cups of coffee.'

'What can you tell me about Pat? Patricia Ballantyne. What happened?'

'You know the medical facts. . . .'

'Not all of them.'

'I don't know *all* of them, either.'

'You're lying.'

Houston looked at Matlock without offense. When he replied, he did so compassionately. 'All right. There was evidence of rape. That's what you want to know, isn't it?'

Matlock gripped his glass. 'Yes,' he said softly.

'However, you should know this, too. The girl doesn't know it. Not at this stage of her recovery. I understand the mind plays tricks. It rejects things until it thinks – or something tells it – that the remembering can be handled.'

'Thanks for the lesson in psychology. . . . Animals. Filthy animals . . .' Matlock pushed his glass away. The liquor was intolerable to him now. The thought of dulling his senses even slightly was abhorrent.

'I'm supposed to play this by ear, so if I read you wrong, all I can do is apologize. . . . Be around when the puzzle gets put together for her. She's going to need you.'

Matlock looked up from the table, from the sight of his tensed hands. 'It was that bad?' he asked almost inaudibly.

'Preliminary lab tests – fingernails, hair, what have you – indicate that the assault was carried out by more than one person.'

Matlock's hatred could find only one expression. He closed his eyes and lashed out at the glass, sending it across the floor, where it smashed in front of the bar. The bartender dropped his soiled rag and started toward his latch, looking over at the man who threw the glass. Then he stopped. Houston held up a bill quickly, gesturing the man to stay away.

'Get hold of yourself!' Houston said. 'You're not going to do anyone any good like that. You're just calling attention to us. . . . Now, listen. You're cleared to make further inquiries, but there are two stipulations. The first is to check with our man – it was supposed to be me – before approaching anyone. The second – keep your subjects to students and only students. No faculty, no staff, no one outside – just students. . . . Make your reports every night between ten and eleven. Your contact will reach you daily as to where. Have you got that?'

Matlock stared at the agent in disbelief. He understood what the man was saying – even why he said it – but he couldn't believe that anyone who'd been briefed by Jason Greenberg would think he could deliver such instructions. 'Are you serious?'

'The orders are explicit. No deviations. That's holy writ.'

It was there again for Matlock. Another sign, another compromise. Another plastic order from the unseen plastic leaders.

'I'm there but I'm *not* there, is that the idea? I'm consigned to the outer limits and that fulfills the bargain?'

'Frig that.'

Matlock's eyes wandered upward, at nothing. He was trying to buy a few seconds of sweet reason. 'Frigga is the Norse goddess of the sky. She shares the heavens with Odin. Don't insult the lady, Houston.'

'You're a nut!' said the agent. 'I'm not sorry I'm getting out of here. . . . Look, it's for the best, take my word for it. And one last thing. I've got to take back the paper Loring gave you. That's a *must* do.'

'Is it, really?' Matlock slid across the filthy leatherette seat and started to get up. 'I don't see it that way. You go back to Washington and tell them I see it as a *must don't*. Take care of yourself, holy writ.'

'You're playing around with preventive custody!'

'We'll see who's playing,' said Matlock as he pushed himself away from the table, angling it to block the agent's exit, and started for the door. He could hear the screech of the table's legs as Houston moved it out of his way. He heard Houston call his name softly, intensely, as if he were confused, wanting to make Matlock come back, yet afraid of identifying him. Matlock reached the door, turned right on the sidewalk, and started running as fast as he could. He found a narrow alley and realized that it was, at least, in the right direction. He raced into it and stopped, pressing himself into a doorway. At the base of the alley, on the freight-yard thoroughfare, he saw Houston walking rapidly past the phlegmatic noonday laborers on their lunch breaks. Houston looked panicked; Matlock knew he couldn't return to his apartment.

It was a funny thing to do, he considered, as he sat in the booth of Bill's Bar & Grill. Returning to the place he couldn't wait to get out of twenty minutes ago. But it made vague sense to him – as much as anything made sense at the moment. He had to be by himself and think. He couldn't take the chance of wandering the streets where some part of the Greenberg-Houston unseen army might spot him. Ironically, the bar seemed safest.

He'd made his apologies to a wary bartender, offering to pay for the broken glass. He implied that the man he'd had words with before was a deadbeat – into him for a lot of money with no ability to pay. This explanation, given by the now-relaxed customer, was not only accepted by the bartender, it elevated him to a status not often seen in Bill's Bar & Grill.

He had to marshal his thoughts. There were checkpoints he'd mentally outlined which were to be passed before he began his journey to Nimrod. Now, there was another checkpoint. Houston had supplied it, although he'd never know. Pat had to be totally safe. He couldn't have that worry on his mind. All other items on his list were subservient to this. The clothes, the ready cash, the unfamiliar automobile, all would have to wait. He might have to alter his strategy now, Matlock thought. Nimrod's associates would be watched, his apartment would be watched, every name and location on the Justice list would be under surveillance.

But first, Pat. He'd have her guarded night and day, around the clock, every minute. Guarded openly, with no pretense of secrecy. Guarded in such a way as to be a signal to both the unseen armies, a warning that she was out of the game. Money was no problem now, none at all. And there were men in Hartford whose professions would fit his requirements. He knew that. The huge insurance companies used them incessantly. He remembered an ex-faculty member from the math department who'd left Carlyle for the lucrative field of insurance actuaries. He worked for Aetna. He looked for a telephone inside the dingy bar.

Eleven minutes later, Matlock returned to the booth. The business was concluded with Blackstone Security, Incorporated, Bond Street, Hartford. There would be three men daily on eight-hour shifts, three hundred dollars for each twenty-four-hour period the subject was covered by Blackstone, Inc. There would, of course, be the additional charges for any expenses incurred and a fee attached for the use of a 'Tel-electronic' if it was required. The Tel-electronic was a small device which signaled the bearer with short beeps if the telephone number designated was called. Blackstone, of course, suggested a different telephone number from a resident phone – which, of course, they would have activated within twelve hours and for which, of course, there was an additional charge.

Matlock agreed to everything, was grateful *for* everything, and said he'd be in Hartford to sign the papers later in the afternoon. He wanted to meet Mr. Blackstone – for another reason now. Blackstone, however, made it clear that since the head of Aetna's actuarial department had personally contacted him regarding Mr. Matlock, the formalities were not pressing. He'd dispatch his team to the Carlyle Hospital within the hour. And by any chance, was Mr. Matlock related to Jonathan Munro Matlock. . .? The head of Aetna's actuarial department had mentioned. . . .

Matlock was relieved. Blackstone *could* be useful. The exfaculty member at Aetna had assured him that there was none better than Blackstone. Expensive, but the best. Blackstone's personnel for the most part were former officers of the Special Forces and Marine Intelligence teams. It was more than a business gimmick. They were smart, resourceful, and tough. They were also licensed and respected by the state and local police.

The next item on his list was clothes. He had planned to go to his apartment and pack a suit, several pairs of slacks, and a jacket or two. Now that was out. At least for the time being. He would buy clothes – what he needed – as he went along. The ready cash could prove more of a problem, considering the amount he wanted. It was Saturday – he wasn't going to waste a Saturday night. The banks were closed, the large money sources unavailable.

Alex Anderson would have to solve the problem. He'd lie to Alex Anderson, tell him Jonathan Munro Matlock would look kindly – financially kindly – on Anderson if the banker would make available a large sum of cash on a Saturday afternoon. It would be confidential on both sides, of course. There would be a gratuity rendered for a coveted favor on a Saturday afternoon. Nothing which could be construed remotely indelicate. And, of course, again, confidential.

Matlock rose from the ripped, stained, dirty leatherette seat and returned to the telephone.

Anderson had only fleeting doubts about accommodating Jonathan Munro Matlock's son, and they concerned not the act but the confidence of the act. Once that concern was allayed, the fact that he was giving aid in the best traditions of banking became clear. It was important for any bank to accommodate the better client. If a particular client wished to show gratitude . . . well, that was up to the client.

Alex Anderson would secure James Matlock five thousand dollars in cash on a Saturday afternoon. He would deliver it to him at three outside the Plaza Movie Theatre, which was showing a revival of *A Knife in the Water* – with subtitles.

An automobile would be the least of his problems. There were two rent-a-car offices in the town, a Budget-National and a Luxor-Elite. The first for students, the second for affluent parents. He would rent a Luxor Cadillac or Lincoln and drive into Hartford to another Luxor lot and change cars. From Hartford he'd go to a Luxor branch in New Haven and do the same. With money, there would be the minimum of questions; with decent tips, there might even be cooperation.

He'd moved to his point of departure.

'Hey, mister. Your name Matlock?' The hairy bartender leaned over the table, the soiled bar rag squeezed in his right hand.

'Yes,' answered the startled Matlock with a short, violent intake of breath.

'Guy just came up t' me. Said for me to tell you you forgot something outside. On the curb, he said. You should hurry, he said.'

Matlock stared at the man. The pain in his stomach was the fear again, the panic. He reached into his pocket and pulled out several bills. Separating a five, he held it up to the bartender. 'Come to the door with me. Just to the window. Tell me if he's outside.'

'Sure. . . . To the window.' The hairy bartender switched the soiled rag to his left hand and took the bill. Matlock got out of the booth and walked beside the man to the half-curtained, filthy glass looking out on the street. 'No, he's not there. There's no one there. . . Just a dead. . .'

'I see,' said Matlock, cutting the man off. He didn't have to go outside, it wasn't necessary.

Lying on the edge of the curb, its body draping down into the gutter, was Matlock's cat.

Its head was severed, held to the rest of its body by a small piece of flesh. The blood poured out, staining the sidewalk.

Eighteen

The killing preyed on Matlock's mind as he approached the West Hartford town line. Was it another warning or had they found the paper? If they *had* found the paper, it didn't vitiate the warning, only reinforced it. He wondered whether to have a member of the Blackstone team check his apartment, check the litter box. He wasn't even sure why he hesitated. Why not have a Blackstone man find out? For three hundred dollars a day, plus charges, such an errand was hardly too much to ask. He was going to ask far more of Blackstone, Incorporated, but they didn't know it. Yet he kept balking. If the paper *was* secure, sending a man to check it might reveal its location.

He'd almost made up his mind to take the chance when he noticed the tan sedan in his rear-view mirror. It was there again. It had been there, off and on, since he'd entered Highway 72 a half hour ago. Whereas other cars turned off, passed him, or fell behind, this tan sedan was never really out of sight. Weaving in and around the traffic, it always managed to stay three or four cars behind him. There was one way to find out if it was coincidence. Off the next exit into West Hartford was a narrow street which wasn't a street at all but a cobblestone alley used almost exclusively for deliveries. He and Pat thought it was a shortcut one hectic afternoon and had been hemmed in for five minutes.

He swung off the exit and down the main street toward the alley. He made a sharp left and entered the narrow cobblestone lane. Since it was Saturday afternoon, there were no delivery trucks, and the alley was clear. He raced through, emerging in a crowded A & P parking lot, which in turn led to a parallel main road. Matlock drove to an empty parking space, shut off his motor, and lowered himself on the seat. He angled his side-view mirror so that it reflected the entrance of the alley. In roughly thirty seconds, the tan sedan came into view.

The driver was obviously confused. He slowed down, looking at the dozens of automobiles. Suddenly, behind the tan sedan, another car began blowing its horn. The driver was impatient; the tan sedan was blocking his progress. Reluctantly, the driver of the tan sedan started up; but before he did, he turned his face, craning his neck over his right shoulder in such a way that Matlock, now looking directly at the automobile, recognized him.

It was the patrolman. The police officer who'd been in his demolished apartment after the Beeson episode, the man who had covered his face with a towel and raced down the corridor of the squash alley two days ago.

Greenberg's 'coincidence.'

Matlock was perplexed. He was also frightened.

The patrolman in mufti drove the tan sedan haltingly toward a parking lot exit, still obviously searching. Matlock saw the car turn into the flow of traffic and drive away.

The offices of Blackstone Security, Incorporated, Bond Street, Hartford, looked more like a wealthy, sedate insurance company than an investigatory agency. The furniture was heavy colonial, the wallpaper a subdued, masculine stripe. Expensive hunting prints above the glow of brass table lamps. The effect was immediately one of strength, virility, and financial solidity. Why not? thought Matlock, as he sat in the Early American two-seater in the outer office. At three hundred dollars a day, Blackstone Security, Incorporated, probably rivaled Prudential in ratio of investment to profits.

When he was at last ushered into the office, Michael Blackstone rose from his chair and walked around the cherrywood desk to greet him. Blackstone was a short, compact man, neatly dressed. He was in his early fifties, obviously a physical person, very active, probably very tough.

'Good afternoon,' he said. 'I hope you didn't drive down here just for the papers. They could have waited. Just because *we* work seven days a week, doesn't mean we expect the rest of the world to do so.'

'I had to be in Hartford, anyway. No problem.'

'Sit down, sit down. Can I offer you anything? A drink? Coffee?'

'No thanks.' Matlock sat in a huge black leather chair, the kind of chair usually found in the oldest, most venerated men's clubs. Blackstone returned to his desk. 'Actually, I'm in somewhat of a hurry. I'd like to sign our agreement, pay you, and leave.'

'Certainly. The file's right here.' Blackstone picked up a folder on his desk and smiled. 'As I mentioned on the phone, there are questions we'd like answered, of course. Beyond what you've instructed us to do. It would help us carry out your orders. Take just a few minutes.'

Matlock expected the request. It was part of his plan, why he wanted to see Blackstone. His assumption – once Blackstone entered the picture – was that Blackstone might be able to offer him shortcuts. Perhaps not willingly, but if it was a question of 'an additional charge.' . . . It was for this reason that he had to meet Blackstone face to face. If Blackstone could be bought, a great deal of time could be saved.

'I'll answer what I can. As I'm sure you've checked out, the girl was beaten severely.'

'We know that. What puzzles us is the reluctance of anyone to say why. No one's given that sort of beating for kicks. Oh, it's possible, but that kind of case is generally handled quickly and efficiently by the police. There's no need for us. . . . Obviously you have information the police don't have.'

'That's true. I do.'

'May I ask why you haven't given it to them? Why you hired us? . . . The local police will gladly furnish protection if there's sufficient cause, and far less expensively.'

'You sound like you're turning away business.'

'We often do.' Blackstone smiled. 'It's never done happily, I can tell you that.'

'Then why . . .'

'You're a highly recommended client,' interrupted Blackstone, 'the son of a very prominent man. We want you to know your alternatives. That's our reasoning. What's yours?'

'You're plainspoken. I appreciate it. I assume what you're saying is that you don't want your reputation tarnished.'

'That's good enough.'

'Good. That's my reasoning, too. Only it's not *my* reputation. It's the girl's. Miss Ballantyne's. . . . The simplest way to put it is that she showed bad judgment in her choice of friends. She's a brilliant girl with an exciting future, but unfortunately that intelligence didn't carry over into other areas.' Matlock purposely stopped and took out a pack of cigarettes. Unhurriedly, he removed one and lit it. The pause had its effect. Blackstone spoke.

'Did she profit financially from these associations?'

'Not at all. As I see it, she was used. But I can understand why you asked. There's a lot of money to be made on campuses these days, isn't there?'

'I wouldn't know. Campuses aren't our field.' Blackstone smiled again, and Matlock knew he was lying. Professionally, of course.

'I guess not.'

'All right, Mr. Matlock. Why was she beaten? And what do you intend to do about it?'

'It's my opinion she was beaten to frighten her from revealing information *she doesn't have*. I intend to find the parties involved and tell tham that. Tell them to leave her alone.'

'And if you go to the police, her associations – past associations, I assume – become a matter of record and jeopardize this brilliant future of hers.'

'Exactly.'

'That's a tight story. . . . Who are these parties involved?'

'I don't know them by name. . . . However, I know their occupations. The main line of work seems to be gambling. I thought you might be able to help me here. Naturally, I would expect an additional charge for the service.'

'I see.' Blackstone got up and walked around his chair. For no particular reason, he fingered the dials on his inoperative air conditioner. 'I think you presume too much.'

'I wouldn't expect names. I'd like them, of course, and I'd pay well for them. . . . But I'd settle for locations. I can find them myself, and you know I can. You'd be saving me time, though.'

'I gather you're interested in . . . private clubs. *Private* social organizations where members may meet to pursue activities of their choice.'

'Outside the eye of the law. Where private citizens can follow their perfectly natural inclinations to place bets. That's where I'd like to start.'

'Could I dissuade you? Is it possible I could convince you to go to the police, instead?'

'No.'

Blackstone walked to a file cabinet on the left wall, took out a key, and opened it. 'As I said, a tight story. Very plausible. And I don't believe a word of it. . . . However, you seem determined; that concerns me.' He took a thin metal case from the file cabinet and carried it back to the desk. Selecting another key from his chain, he unlocked it withdrew a single sheet of paper. 'There's a Xerox machine over there,' he said pointing to a large gray copier in the corner. 'To use it one places a page face down under the metal flap and dials the required duplicates. Records are kept of the numbers automatically. There's rarely a reason for more than one. . . . If you'll excuse me for approximately two minutes, Mr. Matlock, I must make a phone call in another office.'

Blackstone held up the single sheet of paper, then placed it face down on top of Matlock's file folder. He stood erect, and, with the fingers of both hands, tugged at the base of his jacket in the manner of a man used to displaying expensive suits. He smiled and walked around his desk toward the office door. He opened it and turned back.

'It may be what you're looking for, and then again, it may not. I wouldn't know. I've simply left a confidential memorandum on my desk. The charge will be listed on your billing as . . . additional surveillance.'

He went out the door, closing it firmly behind him. Matlock rose from the black leather chair and crossed behind the desk. He turned the paper over and read the typed heading.

FOR SURVEILLANCE: HARTFORD-NEW HAVEN AXIS
PRIVATE CLUBS: LOCATIONS AND CONTACTS (MANAGERS)
AS OF 3–15. NOT TO BE REMOVED FROM OFFICE

Beneath the short, capitalized paragraph were twenty-odd addresses and names.

Nimrod was closer now.

Nineteen

The Luxor-Elite Rental Agency on Asylum Street, Hartford, had been cooperative. Matlock now drove a Cadillac convertible. The manager had accepted the explanation that the Lincoln was too funereal, and since the registration papers were in order, the switch was perfectly acceptable.

So was the twenty-dollar tip.

Matlock had analysed Blackstone's list carefully. He decided to concentrate on the clubs northwest of Hartford for the simple reason that they were nearer the Carlyle area. They weren't the nearest, however. Two locations were within five and seven miles of Carlyle respectively – in opposite directions – but Matlock decided to hold them off for a day or so. By the time he reached them – if he did so – he wanted the managements to know he was a heavy plunger. Not a mark, just heavy. The network gossip would take care of that – if he handled himself properly.

He checked off his first location. It was a private swimming club west of Avon. The contact was a man named Jacopo Bartolozzi.

At nine-thirty Matlock drove up the winding driveway to a canopy extending from the entrance of the Avon Swim Club. A uniformed doorman signaled a parking attendant, who appeared out of nowhere and slid into the driver's seat the moment Matlock stepped onto the pavement. Obviously no parking ticket was to be given.

As he walked toward the entrance, he looked at the exterior of the club. The main building was a sprawling, one-story white brick structure with a tall stockade fence extending from both ends into the darkness. On the right, quite far behind the fence, was the iridescent glow of greenish blue light and the sound of water splashing. On the left was a huge tentlike canopy under which could be seen the shimmering light of dozens of patio torches. The former was obviously an enormous pool, the latter some kind of dining area. Soft music could be heard.

The Avon Swim Club appeared to be a very luxurious complex.

The interior did nothing to dispel this observation. The foyer was thickly carpeted and the various chairs and odd tables against the damask walls seemed genuine antiques. On the left was a large checkroom, and further down on the right was a white marble counter not unlike a hotel information desk. At the end of the narrow lobby was the only incongruous structure. It was a black, ornate wrought-iron gate, and it was closed, obviously locked. Beyond the grilled enclosure could be seen an open-air corridor, subtly lit, with an extended covering supported by a series of thin Ionic pillars. A large man in a tuxedo was standing at attention behind the iron gate.

Matlock approached him.

'Your membership card, sir?'

'I'm afraid I don't have one.'

'Sorry, sir, this is a private swimming club. Members only.'

'I was told to ask for Mr. Bartolozzi.'

The man behind the grill stared at Matlock, frisking him with his eyes.

'You'd better check the front desk, sir. Right over there.'

Matlock walked back to the counter, to be greeted by a middle-aged, slightly paunchy desk clerk who had not been there when he first came in.

'May I help you?'

'You may. I'm fairly new in the area. I'd like to become a member.'

'We're sorry. Membership's full right now. However, if you'll fill out an application, we'll be glad to call you if there's an opening. . . . Would that be a family application or individual, sir?' The clerk, very professionally, reached below the counter and brought up two application forms.

'Individual. I'm not married. . . . I was told to ask for Mr. Bartolozzi. I was told specifically to ask for him. Jacopo Bartolozzi.'

The clerk gave the name only the slightest indication of recognition. 'Here, fill out an application and I'll put it on Mr. Bartolozzi's desk. He'll see it in the morning. Perhaps he'll call you, but I don't know what he can do. Membership's full and there's a waiting list.'

'Isn't he here now? On such a busy night.' Matlock said the words with a degree of incredulity.

'I doubt it, sir.'

'Why don't you find out? Tell him we have mutual friends in San Juan.' Matlock withdrew his money clip and removed a fifty-dollar bill. He placed it in front of the clerk, who looked at him sharply and slowly picked up the money.

'San Juan?'

'San Juan.'

Matlock leaned against the white marble counter and saw the man behind the wrought-iron gate watching him. If the San Juan story worked and he got through the gate, he realized that he would have to part with another large-sized bill. The San Juan story *should* work, thought Matlock. It was logical to the point of innocence. He had spent a winter vacation in Puerto Rico two years ago, and although no gambler, he'd traveled with a crowd – and a girl – who made the nightly rounds of the casinos. He'd met a number of people from the Hartford vicinity, although he couldn't for the life of him remember a single name.

A foursome emerged from inside the grilled entrance, the girls giggling, the men laughing resignedly. The women had probably won twenty or thirty dollars, thought Matlock, while the men had probably lost several hundred. Fair exchange for the evening. The gate closed behind them; Matlock could hear the electric click of the latch. It was a very well-locked iron gate.

'Excuse me, sir?' It was the paunchy desk clerk, and Matlock turned around.

'Yes?'

'If you'll step inside, Mr. Bartolozzi will see you.'

'Where? How?' There was no door except the wrought-iron gate and the clerk had gestured with his left hand, away from the gate.

'Over here, sir.'

Suddenly a knobless, frameless panel to the right of the counter swung open. The outline was barely discernible when the panel was flush against the damask wall; when shut, no border was in evidence. Matlock walked in and was taken by the clerk to the office of Jacopo Bartolozzi.

'We got mutual friends?' The obese Italian spoke hoarsely as he leaned back in his chair behind the desk. He made no attempt to rise, gave no gesture of welcome. Jacopo Bartolozzi was a short, squat caricature of himself. Matlock couldn't be sure, but he had the feeling that Bartolozzi's feet weren't touching the floor beneath his chair.

'It amounts to the same thing, Mr. Bartolozzi.'

'What amounts? Who's in San Juan?'

'Several people. One fellow's a dentist in West Hartford. Another's got an accounting firm in Constitution Plaza.'

'Yeah. . . . Yeah?' Bartolozzi was trying to associate people with the professions and locations Matlock described. 'What's the names? They members here?'

'I guess they are. They gave me *your* name.'

'This is a swim club. Private membership. . . . Who are they?'

'Look, Mr. Bartolozzi, it was a crazy night at the Condado casino. We all had a lot to drink and . . .'

'They don't drink in the Puerto Rican casinos. It's a law!' The Italian spoke sharply, proud of his incisive knowledge. He was pointing his fat finger at Matlock.

'More honored in the breach, believe me.'

'What?'

'We drank. Take my word for it. I'm just telling you I don't remember their names. . . . Look, I can go downtown on Monday and stand all day outside the Plaza and I'll find the CPA. I could also go out to West Hartford and ring every dentist's doorbell. What difference does it make? I like to play and I've got the money.'

Bartolozzi smiled. 'This is a swim club. I don't know what the hell you're talking about.'

'O.K.,' said Matlock with a disgruntled edge to his voice. 'This place happened to be convenient, but if you want to show three lemons, there are others. My San Juan friends also told me about Jimmy Lacata's down in Middletown, and Sammy Sharpe's in Windsor Shoals. . . . Keep your chips, fink.' He turned to the door.

'Hold it! Wait a minute!'

Matlock watched the fat Italian get out of the chair and stand up. He'd been right. Bartolozzi's feet couldn't have been touching the floor.

'What for? Maybe your limit's too small here.'

'You know Lacata? Sharpe?'

'Know *of* them, I told you. . . . Look, forget it. You've got to be careful. I'll find my CPA on Monday and we'll both come back some other time. . . . I just felt like playing tonight.'

'O.K. O.K. Like you said, we gotta be careful.' Bartolozzi opened his top drawer and pulled out some papers. 'C'mere. Sign 'em. You got an itch. Maybe I'll take your money. Maybe you'll take mine.'

Matlock approached the desk. 'What am I signing?'

'Just a couple of forms. Initiation's five hundred. Cash. You got it? No checks, no credit.'

'I've got it. What are the forms?'

'The first is a statement that you understand that this is a nonprofit corporation and that any games of chance are for charitable purposes. . . . What are you laughing at? I built the Church of the Blessed Virgin down in Hamden.'

'What's this other? It's a long one.'

'That's for our files. A certificate of general partnership. For the five hundred you get a classy title. You're a partner. Everybody's a partner. . . . Just in case.'

'In case?'

'In case anything good happens to us, it happens just as good to you. Especially in the newspapers.'

The Avon Swim Club was certainly a place for swimming, no doubt about it. The enormous pool curved back nearly two hundred feet, and scores of small, elegant cabanas bordered the far side. Beach chairs and tables were dotted about the grassy edges beyond the tiled deck of the pool, and the underwater floodlights made the setting inviting. All this was on the right of the open-air corridor. On the left, Matlock could see fully what was only hinted at from the outside. A huge green-and-white-striped tent rose above dozens of tables. Each table had a candled lantern in the center, and patio torches were safely placed about the whole enclosure. At the far end was a long table filled with roasts, salads, and buffet food. A bar was adjacent to the long table; scores of couples were milling about.

The Avon Swim Club was a lovely place to bring the family.

The corridor led to the rear of the complex, where there was another sprawling, white-bricked structure similar to the main building. Above the large, black-enameled double doors was a wooden sign, in old English scroll:

The Avon Spa

This part of the Avon Swim Club was not a lovely place to bring the family.

Matlock thought he was back in San Juan casino – his only experience in gambling rooms. The wall-to-wall carpet was sufficiently thick to muffle sound almost completely. Only the click of the chips and low-keyed but intense mutterings of the players and the board men were heard. The craps tables were lined along the walls, the blackjack counters in the center. In between, in staggered positions to allow for the flow of traffic, were the roulette wheels. In the middle of the large room, raised on a platform, was the cashier's nest. All of the Avon Spa's employees were in tuxedos, neatly groomed and subservient. The players were less formal.

The gate man, pleased with Matlock's crisp fifty-dollar bill, led him to the half-circle counter in front of the cashier's platform. He spoke to a man counting out slips of paper.

'This is Mr. Matlock. Treat him good, he's a personal friend.'

'No other way,' said the man with a smile.

'I'm sorry, Mr. Matlock,' muttered the gate man quietly. 'No markers the first time around.'

'Naturally. . . . Look, I'm going to wander about. . .'

'Sure. Get the feel of the action. . . . I tell you, it ain't Vegas. Between you and me, it's Mickey Mouse most of the time. I mean for a guy like you, you know what I mean?'

Matlock knew exactly what the gate man meant. A fifty-dollar bill was not the ordinary gratuity in Avon, Connecticut.

It took him three hours and twelve minutes to lose $4,175. The only time he felt panic was when he had a streak at the craps table and had built up his reserves to nearly $5,000. He had begun the evening properly – for his purposes. He went to the cashier often enough to realize that the average purchase of chips was $200 to $300. Hardly 'Mickey Mouse' in his book. So his first purchase was $1,500. The second was $1,000; the third, $2,000.

By one in the morning, he was laughing with Jacopo Bartolozzi at the bar underneath the green-and-white-striped tent.

'You're a game one. Lots'a creeps would be screaming "ice pick" if they went for a bundle like you did. Right now I'd be showing them a few papers in my office.'

'Don't you worry, I'll get it back. I always do. . . . You said it before. My itch was too much. Maybe I'll come back tomorrow.'

'Make it Monday. Tomorrow it's only swimming.'

'How come?'

'Sunday. Holy day.'

'Shit! I've got a friend coming in from London. He won't be here Monday. He's a big player.'

'Tell you what. I'll call Sharpe over in Windsor Shoals. He's a Jew. Holy days don't mean a fucking thing to him.'

'I'd appreciate that.'

'I may even drop over myself. The wife's got a Mothers of Madonna meeting, anyway.'

Matlock looked at his watch. The evening – his point of departure – had gone well. He wondered if he should press his luck. 'Only real problem coming into a territory is the time it takes to find the sources.'

'What's your problem?'

'I've got a girl over in the motel. She's sleeping, we traveled most of the day. She ran out of grass – no hard stuff – just grass. I told her I'd pick some up for her.'

'Can't help you, Matlock. I don't keep none here, what with the kids around during the day. It's not good for the image, see? A few pills, I got. No needle crap, though. You want some pills?'

'No, just grass. That's all I let her use.'

'Very smart of you. . . . Which way you headed?'

'Back into Hartford.'

Bartolozzi snapped his fingers. A large bartender sprang into position instantly. Matlock thought there was something grotesque about the squat little Italian commandeering in such fashion. Bartolozzi asked the man for paper and pencil.

'Here. Here's an address. I'll make a phone call. It's an afterhours place right off the main drag. Down the street from G. Fox. Second floor. Ask for Rocco. What you couldn't use, he's got.'

'You're a prince.' And as Matlock took the paper, he meant it.

'For four grand the first night, you got privileges. . . . Hey, y'know what? You never filled out an application! That's a gas, huh?'

'You don't need credit references. I play with cash.'

'Where the hell do you keep it?'

'In thirty-seven banks from here to Los Angeles.' Matlock put down his glass and held out his hand to Bartolozzi. 'It's been fun. See you tomorrow?'

'Sure, sure. I'll walk you to the door. Don't forget now. Don't give Sammy all the action. Come on back here.'

'My word on it.'

The two men walked back to the open-air corridor, the short Italian placing his fat hand in the middle of Matlock's back, the gesture of a new friend. What neither man realized as they stepped onto the narrow causeway was that one well-dressed gentleman at a nearby table who kept punching at a fluidless lighter was watching them. As the two men passed his table, he put his lighter back into his pocket while the woman across from him lit his cigarette with a match. The woman spoke quietly through a smile.

'Did you get them?'

The man laughed softly. 'Karsh couldn't have done better. Even got close-ups.'

Twenty

If the Avon Swim Club was an advantageous point of departure, the Hartford Hunt Club – under the careful management of Rocco Aiello – was an enviable first lap. For Matlock now thought of his journey to Nimrod as a race, one which had to end within two weeks and one day. It would end with the convocation of the Nimrod forces and the Mafiosi somewhere in the Carlyle vicinity. It would be finished for him when someone, somewhere produced another silver Corsican paper.

Bartolozzi's telephone call was effective. Matlock entered the old red stone building – at first he thought he had the wrong address, for no light shone through the windows, and there was no sign of activity within – and found a freight elevator at the end of the hallway with a lone Negro operator sitting in a chair in front of the door. No sooner had he come in than the black rose to his feet and indicated the elevator to Matlock.

In an upstairs hallway a man greeted him. 'Very nice to make your acquaintance. Name's Rocco. Rocco Aiello.' The man held out his hand and Matlock took it.

'Thanks. . . . I was puzzled. I didn't hear anything. I thought maybe I was in the wrong place.'

'If you had heard, the construction boys would have taken me. The walls are eighteen inches thick, sound-proofed both sides; the windows are blinds. Very secure.'

'That's really something.'

Rocco reached into his pocket and withdrew a small wooden cigarette case. 'I got a box of joints for you. No charge. I'd like to show you around, but Jock-O said you might be in a hurry.'

'Jock-O's wrong. I'd like to have a drink.'

'Good! Come on in. . . . Only one thing, Mr. Matlock. I got a nice clientele, you know what I mean? Very rich, very cube. Some of them know about Jock-O's operation, most of them don't. You know what I mean?'

'I understand. I was never much for swimming anyway.'

'Good, good. . . . Welcome to Hartford's finest.' He opened the thick steel door. 'I hear you went for a bundle tonight.'

Matlock laughed as he walked into the complex of dimly lit rooms crowded with tables and customers. 'Is that what it's called?'

'In Connecticut, that's what it's called. . . . See? I got two floors – a duplex, like. Each floor's got five big rooms, a bar in each room. Very private, no bad behavior. Nice place to bring the wife, or somebody else, you know what I mean?'

'I think I do. It's quite something.'

'The waiters are mostly college boys. I like to help them make a few dollars for their education. I got niggers, spics, kikes – I got no discrimination. Just the hair, I don't go for the long hair, you know what I mean?'

'College kids! Isn't that dangerous? Kids talk.'

'Hey, what d'you think?! This place was originally started by a Joe College. It's like a fraternity home. Everybody's a bona fide, dues-paying member of a private organization. They can't getcha for that.'

'I see. What about the other part?'

'What other part?'

'What I came for.'

'What? A little grass? Try the corner newsstand.'

Matlock laughed. He didn't want to overdo it. 'Two points, Rocco. . . . Still, if I knew you better, maybe I'd like to make a purchase. Bartolozzi said what I couldn't use, you've got. . . . Forget it, though. I'm bushed. I'll just get a drink and shove off. The girl's going to wonder where I've been.'

'Sometimes Bartolozzi talks too much.'

'I think you're right. By the way, he's joining me tomorrow night at Sharpe's over in Windsor Shoals. I've got a friend flying in from London. Care to join us?'

Aiello was obviously impressed. The players from London were beginning to take precedence over the Vegas and Caribbean boys. Sammy Sharpe's wasn't that well known, either.

'Maybe I'll do that. . . . Look, you need something, you feel free to ask, right?'

'I'll do that. Only I don't mind telling you, the kids make me nervous.'

Aiello took Matlock's elbow with his left hand and walked him toward the bar. 'You got it wrong. These kids – they're not kids, you know what I mean?'

'No, I don't. Kids are kids. I like my action a little more subdued. No sweat. I'm not curious.' Matlock looked up at the bartender and withdrew what was left of his bankroll. He removed a twenty-dollar bill and placed it on the bar. 'Old Fitz and water, please.'

'Put your money away,' Rocco said.

'Mr. Aiello?' A young man in a waiter's jacket approached them. He was perhaps twenty-two or twenty-three, Matlock thought.

'Yeah?'

'If you'll sign this tab. Table eleven. It's the Johnsons. From Canton. They're O.K.'

Aiello took the waiter's pad and scribbled his initials. The young man walked back toward the tables.

'See that kid? That's what I mean. He's a Yalie. He got back from Nam six months ago.'

'So?'

'He was a lieutenant. An officer. Now he's studying business administration. . . . He fills in here maybe twice a week. Mostly for contacts. By the time he gets out, he'll have a real nest egg. Start his own business.'

'What?'

'He's a supplier. . . . These kids, that's what I mean. You should hear their stories. Saigon, Da Nang. Hong Kong, even. Real peddling. Hey, these kids today, they're great! They know what's up. Smart, too. No worries, believe me!'

'I believe you.' Matlock took his drink and swallowed quickly. It wasn't that he was thirsty, he was trying to conceal his shock at Aiello's revelation. The graduates of Indochina were not the pink-cheeked, earnest, young-old veterans of Armentières, Anzio, or even Panmunjom. They were something else, something faster, sadder, infinitely more knowing. A hero in Indochina was the soldier who had contacts on the docks and in the warehouses. That man in Indochina was the giant among his peers. And such young-old men were almost all black.

Matlock drank the remainder of his bourbon and let Rocco show him the other rooms on the third floor. He displayed the controlled appreciation Aiello expected and promised he'd return. He said no more about Sammy Sharpe's in Windsor Shoals. He knew it wasn't necessary. Aiello's appetite had been whetted.

As he drove away, two thoughts occupied his mind. Two objectives had to be accomplished before Sunday afternoon was over. The first was that he had to produce an Englishman; the second was that he had to produce another large sum of money. It was imperative that he have both. He had to be at Sharpe's in Windsor Shoals the next evening.

The Englishman he had in mind lived in Webster, an associate professor of mathematics at a small parochial campus, Madison University. He had been in the country less than two years; Matlock had met him – quite unprofessionally – at a boat show in Saybrook. The Britisher had lived on the Cornwall coast most of his life and was a sailing enthusiast. Matlock and Pat had liked him immediately. Now Matlock hoped to God that John Holden knew something about gambling.

The money was a more serious problem. Alex Anderson would have to be tapped again, and it was quite possible that he'd find enough excuses to put him off. Anderson was a cautious man, easily frightened. On the other hand, he had a nose for rewards. That instinct would have to be played upon.

Holden had seemed startled but not at all annoyed by Matlock's telephone call. If he was anything other than kind, it was curious. He repeated the directions to his apartment twice and Matlock thanked him, assuring him that he remembered the way.

'I'll be perfectly frank, Jim,' said Holden, admitting Matlock into his neat three-room apartment. 'I'm simply bursting. Is anything the matter? Is Patricia all right?'

'The answers are yes and no. I'll tell you everything I can, which won't be a hell of a lot. . . . I want to ask you a favor, though. Two favors, actually. The first, can I stay here tonight?'

'Of course – you needn't ask. You look peaked. Come, sit down. Can I get you a drink?'

'No, no thanks.' Matlock sat on Holden's sofa. He remembered that it was one of those hide-a-beds and that it was comfortable. He and Pat had slept in it one happy, alcoholic night several months ago. It seemed ages ago.

'What's the second favor? The first is my pleasure. If it's cash, I've something over a thousand. You're entirely welcome to it.'

'No, not money, thanks just the same. . . . I'd like you to impersonate an Englishman for me.'

Holden laughed. He was a small-boned man of forty, but he laughed the way older, fatter men laughed.

'That shouldn't be too demanding, now should it? I suspect there's still a trace of Cornwall in my speech. Hardly noticeable, of course.'

'Hardly. With a little practice you may even lose the Yankee twang. . . . There's something else, though, and it may not be so easy. Have you ever gambled?'

'Gambled? You mean horses, football matches?'

'Cards, dice, roulette?'

'Not substantially, no. Of course, as any reasonably imaginative mathematician, I went through a phase when I thought that by applying arithmetical principles – logarithmic averages – one could beat the gambling odds.'

'Did they work?'

'I said I went through the phase, I didn't stay there. If there's a mathematical system, it eluded me. Still does.'

'But you've played? You know the games.'

'Rather well, when you come right down to it. Laboratory research, you might say. Why?'

Matlock repeated the story he had told Blackstone. However, he minimized Pat's injuries and lightened the motives of those who assaulted her. When he finished, the Englishman, who'd lit his pipe, knocked the ashes out of the bowl into a large glass ashtray.

'It's right out of the cinema, isn't it? . . . You say Patricia's not seriously hurt. Frightened but nothing much more than that?'

'Right. If I went to the police it might louse up her scholarship money.'

'I see. . . . Well, I don't really, but we'll let it go. And you'd rather I lost tomorrow night.'

'That doesn't matter. Just that you bet a great deal.'

'But you're *prepared* for heavy losses.'

'I am.'

Holden stood up. 'I'm perfectly willing to go through with this performance. It should prove rather a lark. However, there's a great deal you're not telling me and I wish you would. But I shan't insist upon it. I will tell you that your story is boggled with a large mathematical inconsistency.'

'What's that?'

'As I understand it, the money you are prepared to lose tomorrow evening is far in excess of any amount Patricia might realize in scholarship aid. The logical assumption, therefore, is that you do not wish to go to the police. Or perhaps, you can't.'

Matlock looked up at the Englishman and wondered at his own stupidity. He felt embarrassed and very inadequate. 'I'm sorry. . . . I haven't consciously lied to you. You don't have to go through with it; maybe I shouldn't have asked.'

'I never implied that you lied – not that it matters. Only that there was much you haven't told me. Of course, I'll do it. I just want you to know I'm a willing audience when and if you decide to tell me everything that's happened. . . . Now, it's late and you're tired. Why don't you take my room.'

'No, thanks. I'll sack out here. It has pleasant memories. A blanket's all I need. Also I have to make a phone call.'

'Anything you say. A blanket you'll get, and you know where the phone is.'

When Holden left, Matlock went to the phone. The Tel-electronic device he'd agreed to lease would not be ready until Monday morning.

'Blackstone.'

'This is James Matlock. I was told to call this number for any messages.'

'Yes, Mr. Matlock. There is a message, if you'll hold on while I get the card. . . . Here it is. From the Carlyle team. Everything is secure. The subject is responding nicely to medical treatment. The subject had three visitors. A Mr. Samuel Kressel, a Mr. Adrian Sealfont, and a Miss Lois Meyers. The subject received two telephone calls, neither of which the physician allowed to be taken. They were from the same individual, a Mr. Jason Greenberg. The calls were placed from Wheeling, West Virginia. At no time was the subject separated from the Carlyle team. . . . You can relax.'

'Thank you. I will. You're very thorough. Good night.' Matlock breathed deeply in relief and exhaustion. Lois Meyers lived across the hall from Pat in the graduate apartment house. The fact that Greenberg had called was comforting. He missed Greenberg.

He reached up and turned off the table lamp by the sofa. The bright April moon shone through the windows. The man from Blackstone's service was right – he could relax.

What he couldn't allow to relax were his thoughts about tomorrow – and after tomorrow. Everything had to remain accelerated; one productive day had to lead into another. There could be no letup, no sense of momentary satisfaction which might slow his thrust.

And after tomorrow. After Sammy Sharpe's in Windsor Shoals. If all went according to his calculations, it would be the time to head into the Carlyle area. Matlock closed his eyes and saw Blackstone's printed page in front of his mind.

CARMOUNT COUNTRY CLUB – CONTACT: HOWARD STOCKTON
WEST CARLYLE SAIL AND SKI RESORT – CONTACT: ALAN CANTOR

Carmount was east of Carlyle near the border of Mount Holly. The Sail and Ski was west, on Lake Derron – a summer and winter resort area.

He'd find some reason to have Bartolozzi or Aiello, or, perhaps, Sammy Sharpe, make the proper introductions. And once in the Carlyle area, he would drop the hints. Perhaps more than hints – commands, requirements, necessities. This was the boldness he needed to use, this was the way of Nimrod.

His eyes remained closed, the muscles in his body sagged, and the pitch darkness of exhausted sleep came over him. But before sleeping he remembered the paper. The Corsican paper. He had to get the paper now. He would need the silver paper. He would need the invitation to Nimrod.

His invitation now. His paper.

The Matlock paper.

Twenty-one

If the elders at the Windsor Shoals Congregational Church had ever realized that Samuel Sharpe, attorney at law, the very bright Jewish lawyer who handled the church's finances, was referred to as Sammy the Runner by most of North Hartford and South Springfield, Massachusetts, vespers would have been canceled for a month. Fortunately, such a revelation had never been made to them and the Congregational Church looked favorably on him. He had done remarkable things for the church's portfolio and gave handsomely himself during fund drives. The Congregational Church of Windsor Shoals, as indeed most of the town, was nicely disposed toward Samuel Sharpe.

Matlock learned all of this in Sharpe's office inside the Windsor Valley Inn. The framed citations on the wall told half the story, and Jacopo Bartolozzi good-naturedly supplied the rest. Jacopo was actually making sure that Matlock and his English friend were aware that Sharpe's operation, as well as Sharpe himself, lacked the fine traditions of the Avon Swim Club.

Holden surpassed Matlock's expectations. Several times he nearly laughed out loud as he watched Holden take hundred-dollar bills – rushed into

Webster by a harassed, nervous Alex Anderson – and flick them nonchalantly at a croupier, never bothering to count the chips but somehow letting everyone at whatever table he was at realize that he knew – to the dollar – the amount given him. Holden played intelligently, cautiously, and at one point was ahead of the house by nine thousand dollars. By the end of the evening, he had cut his winnings to several hundred and the operators of the Windsor Valley breathed grateful sighs of relief.

James Matlock cursed his second night of terrible luck and took his twelve-hundred-dollar loss for what it meant to him – nothing.

At four in the morning Matlock and Holden, flanked by Aiello, Bartolozzi, Sharpe, and two of their cronies, sat at a large oak table in the colonial dining room. They were alone. A waiter and two busboys were cleaning up; the gambling rooms on the third floor of the inn had closed.

The husky Aiello and the short, fat Bartolozzi kept up a running commentary about their respective clientele, each trying to upstage the other with regard to their customers' status; each allowing that 'it might be nice' for the other to become 'acquainted' with a Mr. and Mrs. Johnson of Canton or a certain Dr. Wadsworth. Sharpe, on the other hand, seemed more interested in Holden and the action in England. He told several funny, self-effacing stories about his visits to London clubs and his insurmountable difficulty with British currency in the heat of betting.

Matlock thought, as he watched Sammy Sharpe, that he was a very charming man. It wasn't hard to believe that Sharpe was considered a respectable asset to Windsor Shoals, Connecticut. He couldn't help comparing Sharpe to Jason Greenberg. And in the comparison, he found an essential difference. It was told in the eyes. Greenberg's were soft and compassionate, even in anger. Sharpe's were cold, hard, incessantly darting – strangely in conflict with the rest of his relaxed face.

He heard Bartolozzi ask Holden where he was off to next. Holden's offhand reply gave him the opportunity he was looking for. He waited for the right moment.

'I'm afraid I'm not at liberty to discuss my itinerary.'

'He means where he's going,' interjected Rocco Aiello.

Bartolozzi shot Aiello a withering glance. 'I just thought you should drop over to Avon. I got a real nice place I think you'd enjoy.'

'I'm sure I would. Perhaps another time.'

'Johnny'll be in touch with me next week,' Matlock said. 'We'll get together.' He reached for an ashtray and crushed out his cigarette. 'I have to be in . . . Carlyle, that's the name of the place.'

There was the slightest pause in the conversation. Sharpe, Aiello, and one of the other two men exchanged looks. Bartolozzi, however, seemed oblivious to any deep meaning.

'The college place?' asked the short Italian.

'That's right,' answered Matlock. 'I'll probably stay at Carmount or the Sail and Ski. I guess you fellows know where they are.'

'I guess we do.' Aiello laughed softly.

'What's your business in Carlyle?' The unidentified man – at least no one had bothered to introduce him by name – drew deeply on a cigar as he spoke.

'*My* business,' said Matlock pleasantly.

'Just asking. No offense.'

'No offense taken. . . . Hey, it's damned near four-thirty! You fellows are too hospitable.' Matlock pushed his chair back, prepared to stand.

The man with the cigar, however, had to ask another question.

'Is your friend going to Carlyle with you?'

Holden held up his hand playfully. 'Sorry, no itineraries. I'm simply a visitor to your pleasant shores and filled with a tourist's plans. . . . We really must go.'

Both men rose from the table. Sharpe stood, too. Before the others could move, Sharpe spoke.

'I'll see the boys to their car and show them the road out. You fellows wait here – we'll settle accounts. I owe you money, Rocco. Frank owes me. Maybe I'll come out even.'

The man with the cigar, whose name was obviously Frank, laughed. Aiello looked momentarily perplexed but within seconds grasped the meaning of Sharpe's statement. The men at the table were to remain.

Matlock wasn't sure he'd handled the situation advantageously.

He had wanted to pursue the Carlyle discussion just enough to have someone offer to make the necessary calls to Carmount and the Sail and Ski. Holden's refusal to speak about his itinerary precluded it, and Matlock was afraid that it also implied that he and Holden were so important that further introductions were unnecessary. In addition, Matlock realized that as his journey progressed, he banked more and more on the dead Loring's guarantee that none of those invited to the Carlyle conference would discuss delegates among themselves. The meaning of 'Omerta' was supposedly so powerful that silence was inviolate. Yet Sharpe had just commanded those at the table to remain.

He had the feeling that perhaps he had gone too far with too little experience. Perhaps it was time to reach Greenberg – although he'd wanted to wait until he had more concrete knowledge before doing so. If he made contact with Greenberg now, the agent might force him – what was the idiotic phrase? – out of strategy. He wasn't prepared to face that problem.

Sharpe escorted them to the near-deserted parking lot. The Windsor Valley Inn wasn't crowded with overnight guests.

'We don't encourage sleeping accommodations,' Sharpe explained. 'We're known primarily as a fine restaurant.'

'I can understand that,' said Matlock.

'Gentlemen,' began Sharpe haltingly. 'May I make a request that might be considered impolite?'

'Go right ahead.'

'May I have a word with you, Mr. Matlock? Privately.'

'Oh, don't concern yourself,' said Holden, moving off. 'I understand fully. I'll just walk around.'

'He's a very nice fellow, your English friend,' Sharpe said.

'The nicest. What is it, Sammy?'

'Several points of information, as we say in court.'

'What are they?'

'I'm a cautious man, but I'm also very curious. I run a fine organization, as you can see.'

'I can see.'

'I'm growing nicely – cautiously, but nicely.'

'I'll accept that.'

'I don't make mistakes. I've a trained legal mind and I'm proud that I don't make mistakes.'

'What are you driving at?'

'It strikes me – and I must be honest with you, it has also occurred to my partner Frank and to Rocco Aiello – that you may have been sent into the territory to make certain observations.'

'Why do you think that?'

'Why? . . . From nowhere comes a player like you. You got powerful friends in San Juan. You know our places like the back of your hand. Then you have a very rich, very nice associate from the London scene. That all adds up. . . . But most important – and I think you know it – you mention this business in Carlyle. Let's be honest. That speaks a whole big book, doesn't it?'

'Does it?'

'I'm not foolhardy. I told you, I'm a cautious man. I understand the rules and I don't ask questions I'm not supposed to ask or talk about things I'm not privileged to know about. . . . Still, I want the generals to realize they have a few intelligent, even ambitious, lieutenants in the organization. Anyone can tell you. I don't skim, I don't hold back.'

'Are you asking me to give you a good report?'

'That about sizes it up. I have value. I'm a respected attorney. My partner's a very successful insurance broker. We're naturals.'

'What about Aiello? It seems to me you're friendly with him.'

'Rocco's a good boy. Maybe not the quickest, but solid. He's a kind person, too. However, I don't believe he's in our league.'

'And Bartolozzi?'

'I have nothing to say about Bartolozzi. You'll have to make up your own mind about him.'

'By saying nothing, you're saying a lot, aren't you?'

'In my opinion, he talks too much. But that could be his personality. He rubs me the wrong way. Not Rocco, though.'

Matlock watched the methodical Sharpe in the predawn light of the parking lot and began to understand what had happened. It was logical; he, himself, had planned it, but now that it was taking place, he felt curiously objective. Observing himself; watching reacting puppets.

He had entered Nimrod's world a stranger; possibly suspect, certainly devious.

Yet suddenly, that suspicion, that deviousness, was not to be scorned but *honored*.

The suspect honored for his deviousness – because it *had* to come from a higher source. He was an emissary from the upper echelons now. He was feared.

What had Greenberg called it? The shadow world. Unseen armies positioning their troops in darkness, constantly on the alert for stray patrols, unfriendly scouts.

The thin line he had to tread was precarious. But it was his now.

'You're a good man, Sharpe. Goddamn smart, too. . . . What do you know about Carlyle?'

'Nothing! Absolutely nothing.'

'Now you're lying, and that's *not* smart.'

'It's true. I don't *know anything*. Rumors I've heard. Knowledge and hearsay are two different kinds of testimony.' Sharpe held up his right hand, his two forefingers separated.

'What rumors? Give it straight, for your own sake.'

'Just rumors. A gathering of the clan, maybe. A meeting of very highly placed individuals. An agreement which has to be reached between certain people.'

'Nimrod?'

Sammy Sharpe closed his eyes for precisely three seconds. During those moments he spoke.

'Now you talk language I don't want to hear.'

'Then you didn't hear it, did you?'

'It's stricken from the record, I assure you.'

'O.K. You're doing fine. And when you go back inside, I don't think it would be such a good idea to discuss the rumors you've heard. That would be acting like a stupid lieutenant, wouldn't it?'

'Not only stupid – insane.'

'Why did you tell them to stay, then? It's late.'

'For real. I wanted to know what everybody thought of you and your English friend. I'll tell you now, though – since you have mentioned a certain name, no such discussion will take place. As I said, I understand the rules.'

'Good. I believe you. You've got possibilities. You'd better go back in. . . . Oh, one last thing. I want you . . . *we* want you to call Stockton at Carmount and Cantor at the Sail and Ski. Just say I'm a personal friend and I'll be showing up. Nothing else. We don't want any guards up. That's important, Sammy. Nothing else.'

'It's my pleasure. And you won't forget to convey my regards to the others?'

'I won't forget. You're a good man.'

'I do my best. It's all a person can do. . .'

Just then, the quiet of the predawn was shattered by five loud reports. Glass smashed. The sounds of people running and screaming and furniture crashing came from within the inn. Matlock threw himself to the ground.

'John! John!'

'Over here! By the car! Are you all right?!'

'Yes. Stay there!'

Sharpe had run into the darkness by the base of the building. He crouched into a corner, pressing himself against the brick. Matlock could barely see the outline of his form, but he could see enough to watch Sharpe withdraw a revolver from inside his jacket.

Again there was a volley of shots from the rear of the building, followed once more by screams of terror. A busboy crashed through the side door and crawled on his hands and knees toward the edge of the parking lot. He shouted hysterically in a language Matlock could not understand.

Several seconds later, another of the inn's employees in a white jacket ran through the door pulling a second man behind him, this one obviously wounded, blood pouring from his shoulder, his right arm dangling, immobile.

Another shot rang out of nowhere and the waiter who had been screaming fell over. The wounded man behind him went pummeling forward, crashing face down into the gravel. Within the building, men were shouting.

'Let's go! Get *out!* Get to the *car!*'

He fully expected to see men come scrambling out of the side door into the parking lot, but no one came. Instead, from another section of the property, he heard the gunning of an engine and, moments later, the screeching of tires as an automobile made a sharp turn. And then, to his left, about fifty yards away, a black sedan came racing out of the north driveway toward the main road. The car had to pass under a street light, and Matlock saw it clearly.

It was the same automobile that had plunged out of the darkness moments after Ralph Loring's murder.

Everything was still again. The grayish light of dawn was getting brighter.

'Jim! Jim, come here! I think they've gone!'

It was Holden. He had left the sanctuary of the automobile and was crouching over the man in the white jacket.

'Coming!' said Matlock, getting off the ground.

'This fellow's dead. He was shot between the shoulders. . . . This one's still breathing. Better get an ambulance.' Holden had walked over to the unconscious busboy with the bloodied, immobile right arm.

'I don't hear anything. Where's Sharpe?'

'He just went inside. That door. He had a gun.'

The two men walked carefully to the side entrance of the inn. Matlock slowly opened the door and preceded Holden into the foyer. Furniture was overturned, chairs and tables on their sides; blood was glistening on the wooden floor.

'Sharpe? Where are you?' Matlock raised his voice cautiously. It was several seconds before the reply came. When it did, Sharpe could hardly be heard.

'In here. In the dining room.'

Matlock and Holden walked through the oak-framed arch. Nothing in either man's life had prepared him for what he saw.

The overpowering horror was the sight of the bodies literally covered with blood. What was left of Rocco Aiello was sprawled across the red-soaked tablecloth, most of his face blown off. Sharpe's partner, the unintroduced man named Frank, was on his knees, his torso twisted back over the seat of a chair, blood flowing out of his neck, his eyes wide open in death. Jacopo Bartolozzi was on the floor, his obese body arched around the leg of a table, the front of his shirt ripped up to the collar, revealing his bulging stomach, the flesh pierced with a score of bullet holes, blood still trickling out over the coarse black hair. Bartolozzi had tried to tear his shirt away from his battered chest, and a portion of cloth was clutched in his dead hand. The fourth man lay behind Bartolozzi, his head resting on Bartolozzi's right foot, his arms and legs extended in a spread-eagle pattern, his entire back covered with a thick layer of blood, portions of his intestines pushed through the skin.

'Oh, my God!' muttered Matlock, not fully believing what he saw. John

Holden looked as though he might become sick. Sharpe spoke softly, rapidly, wearily.

'You'd better go. You and your English friend better leave quickly.'

'You'll have to call the police,' said Matlock, bewildered.

'There's a man outside, a boy. He's still alive.' Holden stuttered as he spoke.

Sharpe looked over at the two men, the revolver at his side, his eyes betraying only the slightest degree of suspicion. 'I have no doubt the lines have been cut. The nearest houses are farms at least half a mile from here. . . . I'll take care of everything. You'd better get out of here.'

'Do you think we should?' asked Holden, looking at Matlock.

Sharpe replied. 'Listen, Englishman, personally I couldn't care less what either of you do. I've got enough to think about, enough to figure out. . . . For your own good, get out of here. Less complications, less risk. Isn't that right?'

'Yes, you're right,' Matlock said.

'In case you're picked up, you left here a half hour ago. You were friends of Bartolozzi, that's all I know.'

'All right.'

Sharpe had to turn away from the sight of the murdered men. Matlock thought for a moment that the Windsor Shoals attorney was going to weep. Instead, he took a deep breath and spoke again.

'A trained legal mind, Mr. Matlock. I'm valuable. You tell them that.'

'I will.'

'You also tell them I need protection, *deserve* protection. You tell them that, too.'

'Of course.'

'Now, get out.' Suddenly Sharpe threw his revolver on the floor in disgust. And then he screamed, as the tears came to his eyes, 'Get out for Christ's sake! *Get out!*'

Twenty-two

Matlock and Holden agreed to separate immediately. The English professor dropped off the mathematician at his apartment and then headed south to Fairfield. He wanted to register at a highway motel far enough away from Windsor Shoals to feel less panicked, yet near enough to Hartford so he could get to Blackstone's by two in the afternoon.

He was too exhausted, too frightened to think. He found a third-rate motel just west of Stratford and surprised the early morning clerk by being alone.

During the registration, he mumbled unpleasant criticisms about a suspicious wife in Westport, and with a ten-dollar bill convinced the clerk to enter his arrival at 2:00 A.M., single. He fell into bed by seven and left a call for twelve-thirty. If he slept for five hours, he thought, things had to become clearer.

Matlock slept for five hours and twenty minutes and nothing much had changed. Very little had cleared up for him. If anything, the massacre at Windsor Shoals now appeared more extraordinary than ever. Was it possible that he was meant to be a victim? Or were the killers waiting outside, waiting silently for him to leave before committing their executions?

Mistake or warning?

By one-fifteen he was on the Merritt Parkway. By one-thirty he entered the Berlin Turnpike, taking the back roads into Hartford. By five minutes past two he walked into Blackstone's office.

'Look,' said Michael Blackstone, leaning over his desk, staring at Matlock, 'we ask a minimum of questions, but don't for one minute think that means we give our clients blank checks!'

'It seems to me you like that process reversed.'

'Then take your money and go somewhere else. We'll survive!'

'Just hold it! You were hired to protect a girl, that's all! That's what I'm paying three hundred dollars a day for! Anything else is marginal, and I'm paying for that, too, I expect.'

'There'll be no extra charges. I don't know what you're talking about.' Suddenly Blackstone bent his elbows, crouching forward. He whispered hoarsely. 'Christ, Matlock? *Two men!* Two men on that goddamn list were murdered last night! If you're a hopped-up maniac, I don't want anything to do with you! That's no part of any deal here! I don't care *who* your old man is or *how* much money you've got!'

'Now I don't know what *you're* talking about. Except what I read in the papers. I was at a motel in Fairfield last night. I was registered there at two this morning. According to the papers, those killings took place around five.'

Blackstone pushed himself off the desk and stood up. He looked at Matlock suspiciously. 'You can verify that?'

'Do you want the name and number of the motel? Give me a phone book, I'll get it for you.'

'No! . . . No. I don't want to know a thing. You were in Fairfield?'

'Get the phone book.'

'All right. All right, . forget it. I think you're lying, but you've covered yourself. As you say, we're only hired to protect the girl.'

'Any change from Sunday afternoon? Is everything all right?'

'Yes. . . . Yes.' Blackstone seemed preoccupied. 'I've got your Tel-electronic. It's operative. It's an additional twenty dollars a day.'

'I see. Wholesale price.'

'We never implied we were cheap.'

'You couldn't.'

'We don't.' Blackstone remained standing, pushed a button on his office intercom, and spoke into it. 'Bring in Mr. Matlock's Tel-electronic, please.'

Seconds later an attractive girl came into the office carrying a metal device no larger than a pack of cigarettes. She put it on Blackstone's desk and placed an index card beside it. She left as rapidly as she had entered.

'Here you are,' Blackstone said. 'Your code is Charger Three-zero. Meaning – Carlyle area, three-man team. The telephone number you call is five, five, five, six, eight, six, eight. We keep a list of numbers on reserve which we feel are easy to commit. The Tel-electronic will signal you by short beeps. You can shut it off by pushing this button here. When the signal is emitted, you are to call the number. A recording machine on that telephone will give you the message from the team. Often it will be to phone another number to make direct contact. Do you understand everything? It's really very simple.'

'I understand,' said Matlock, taking the small metal box. 'What confuses me is why you don't just have the men call this office and then you contact me. Outside of whatever profit there is, wouldn't it be easier?'

'No. Too much room for error. We handle a great many clients. We want our clients to be in direct contact with the men they're paying for.'

'I see.'

'Also, we respect the privacy of our clients. We don't think it's such a good idea for information to be transmitted through third and fourth parties. Incidentally, you can reach the team by the same procedures. Each one has a machine. Just phone the number and record the message for them.'

'Commendable.'

'Professional.' And then Blackstone, for the first time since Matlock had entered the office, sat in his chair and leaned back. 'Now I'm going to tell you something, and if you want to take it as a threat, you'd be justified. Also, if you want to cancel our services on the strength of what I say, that's O.K., too. . . . We know that you're being actively sought by agents of the Justice Department. However, there are no charges leveled against you, no warrants for your arrest. You have certain rights which the federal men often overlook in their zealousness – it's one of the reasons we're in business. However, *again*, we want you to know that should your status change, should there *be* charges or a warrant for your arrest, our services are terminated immediately, and we won't hesitate to cooperate with the

authorities regarding your whereabouts. Whatever information we possess
will be held for your attorneys – it's privileged – but not your whereabouts.
Capiche?'

'I do. That's fair.'

'We're more than fair. That's why I'm going to demand ten days' advance
payment from you – unused portion returnable. . . . In the event the
situation changes and the federal men get a court order for you, you will
receive – *only once* – the following message on the telephone recorder. Just
these words.'

Blackstone paused for emphasis.

'What are they?'

'*"Charger Three-zero is canceled."'*

Out on Bond Street Matlock felt a sensation he knew wouldn't leave him
until his journey, his race was over. He thought people were staring at him.
He began to think strangers were watching him. He found himself involuntarily turning around, trying to find the unseen, observing eyes. Yet there
were none.

None that he could distinguish.

The Corsican paper now had to be gotten out of his apartment. And
considering Blackstone's statements, there was no point in his attempting to
get it himself. His apartment would be under surveillance – from both
camps, the seekers and the quarry.

He would use the Blackstone team, one of them, putting to the test the
sartorial Blackstone's guarantee of privileged information. He would reach
them – him – as soon as he placed one prior telephone call. A call that would
make it clear whether the silver Corsican invitation was really necessary or
not. A call to Samuel Sharpe, attorney at law, Windsor Shoals, Connecticut.

Matlock decided to show Sharpe a temporary, more compassionate side of
his acquired personality. Sharpe himself had displayed a momentary lapse of
control. Matlock thought it was the moment to indicate that even such men
as himself – men who had influential friends in San Juan and London – had
feelings beyond personal survival.

He walked into the lobby of the Americana Hotel and called him. Sharpe's
secretary answered.

'Are you in an office where Mr. Sharpe can return your call momentarily?'

'No, I'm in a telephone booth. I'm also in a hurry.'

There was silence, preceded by the click of a hold button. The wait was
less than ten seconds.

'May I have the number you're calling from, Mr. Matlock? Mr. Sharpe
will get back to you within five minutes.'

Matlock gave the girl the number and hung up.

As he sat in the plastic seat, his memory wandered back to another telephone booth and another plastic seat. And a black sedan which raced past the dead man slouched in that booth, on that seat, with a bullet hole in his forehead.

The bell sounded; Matlock lifted the receiver.

'Matlock?'

'Sharpe?'

'You shouldn't call me at the office. You should know better. I had to go down to the lobby here, to a pay phone.'

'I didn't think a respected attorney's telephone would be any risk. I'm sorry.'

There was a pause at the other end of the line. Sharpe obviously never expected an apology. 'I'm a cautious man, I told you. What is it?'

'I just wanted to know how you were. How everything went. It was a terrible thing, last night.'

'I haven't had time for a reaction. There's so much to do. Police, funeral arrangements, reporters.'

'What are you saying? How are you handling it?'

'There won't be any major mistakes. In a nutshell – if it comes to that – I'm an innocent victim. Frank's a victim, too, only he's dead. . . . I'm going to miss Frank. He was a very good fellow. I'll close down the upstairs, of course. The state police have been paid. By you people, I assume. It'll be what the papers say it was. A bunch of Italian hoodlums shot up in a nice country restaurant.'

'You're a cool operator.'

'I told you,' replied Sharpe sadly, 'I'm a cautious man. I'm prepared for contingencies.'

'Who did it?'

Sharpe did not answer the question. He did not speak at all.

'I asked you, who do you think did it?'

'I expect you people will find out before I do. . . . Bartolozzi had enemies; he was an unpleasant person. Rocco, too, I suppose. . . . But why Frank? You tell me.'

'I don't know. I haven't been in touch with anyone.'

'Find out for me. Please. It wasn't right.'

'I'll try. That's a promise. . . . And, Sammy, make those calls to Stockton and Cantor, don't forget.'

'I won't. I've got them listed on my afternoon calendar. I told you, I'm a methodical man.'

'Thanks. My sympathies about Frank. He seemed like a nice guy.'

'He was a prince.'

'I'm sure he was. . . . I'll be in touch, Sammy. I haven't forgotten what I said I'd do for you. You've really impressed me. I'll . . .'

The sound of coins dropping into the telephone receptacle at Windsor Shoals interrupted Matlock. The time limit was up, and there was no point in prolonging the conversation. He had found out what he needed to know. He had to have the Corsican paper now. The horror of the dawn massacre had not caused the methodical Sharpe to forget the telephone calls he'd promised to make. Why it hadn't was a miracle to Matlock, but there it was. The cautious man had not panicked. He was ice.

The telephone booth was stuffy, close, uncomfortable, filled with smoke. He opened the door and walked rapidly across the hotel lobby to the front exit.

He rounded the corner of Asylum Street looking for an appropriate restaurant. One in which he could have lunch while awaiting the return call from Charger Three-zero. Blackstone had said that he should leave a number; what better than a restaurant?

He saw the sign: The Lobster House. The kind of place frequented by business executives.

He was given a booth to himself, not a table. It was nearly three; the luncheon crowd had thinned. He sat down and ordered a bourbon on the rocks, asking the waitress the whereabouts of the nearest telephone. He was about to get out of the booth to make his call to 555–6868 when he heard the muted, sharp, terrifying sound of the Tel-electronic from within his jacket. At first it paralysed him. It was as if some part of his person, an hysterical organ perhaps, had gone mad and was trying to signal its distress. His hand shook as he reached inside his coat and withdrew the small metal device. He found the shut-off button and pressed it as hard as he could. He looked around, wondering if the sound had attracted attention.

It had not. No one returned his looks. No one had heard a thing.

He got out of his seat and walked quickly toward the telephone. His only thought was Pat – something had happened, something serious enough for Charger Three-zero to activate the terrible, insidious machine which had panicked him.

Matlock pulled the door shut and dialed 555–6868.

'Charger Three-zero reporting.' The voice had the once-removed quality of a taped recording. 'Please telephone five, five, five; one, nine, five, one. There is no need for alarm, sir. There's no emergency. We'll be at this number for the next hour. The number again is five, five, five; one, nine, five, one. Out.'

Matlock realized that Charger Three-zero took pains to allay his fears immediately, perhaps because it was his first experience with the Tel-electronic. He had the feeling that even if the town of Carlyle had gone up in thermonuclear smoke, Charger Three-zero's words would have a palliative quality about them. The other reasoning, perhaps, was that a man thought more clearly when unafraid. Whatever, Matlock knew that the method worked. He was calmer now. He reached into his pocket and took out some change, making a mental note as he did so to convert some dollar bills into coins for future use. The pay telephone had become an important part of his life.

'Is this five, five, five; nineteen fifty-one?'

'Yes,' said the same voice he had heard on the recording. 'Mr. Matlock?'

'Yes. Is Miss Ballantyne all right?'

'Doing very well, sir. That's a good doctor you've got. She sat up this morning. A lot of the swelling's gone down. The doctor's quite pleased. . . . She's asked for you a number of times.'

'What are you telling her?'

'The truth. That we've been hired by you to make sure she's not bothered.'

'I mean about where I am.'

'We've simply said you had to be away for several days. It might be a good idea to telephone her. She can take calls starting this afternoon. We'll screen them, of course.'

'Of course. Is that why you contacted me?'

'In part. The other reason is Greenberg. Jason Greenberg. He keeps calling for you. He insists that you get in touch with him.'

'What did he say? Who talked to him?'

'I did. Incidentally, my name's Cliff.'

'O.K., Cliff, what did he say?'

'That I should tell you to call him the minute I reached you. It was imperative, critical. I've got a number. It's in Wheeling, West Virginia.'

'Give it to me.' Matlock withdrew his ballpoint pen and wrote the number on the wooden shelf under the telephone.

'Mr. Matlock?'

'What?'

'Greenberg also said to tell you . . . that "the cities weren't dying, they were dead." Those were his words. "The cities were dead."'

Twenty-three

Cliff agreed without comment to retrieve the Corsican paper from Matlock's apartment. A rendezvous would be arranged later by telephone. In the event the paper was missing, Charger Three-zero would alert him immediately.

Matlock restricted himself to one drink. He picked at his lunch and left the Lobster House by three-thirty. It was time to regroup his forces, resupply his ammunition. He had parked the Cadillac in a lot several blocks south of Blackstone's office on Bond Street. It was one of those municipal parking areas, each slot with its own meter. It occurred to Matlock as he approached it that he hadn't returned to insert additional coins since going to Blackstone's. The meters were only good for an hour; he'd been there for nearly two. He wondered what rental-car businesses did with the slew of traffic violations which had to mount up with transients. He entered the lot and momentarily wondered if he was in the right aisle. Then he realized he was not. The Cadillac was two lanes over, in the fourth aisle. He started to sidle past the closely parked vehicles toward his own and then he stopped.

In between the automobiles, he saw the blue and white stripes of a Hartford patrol car. It was parked directly behind his Cadillac. One police officer was trying the Cadillac's door handle, a second patrolman was leaning against the police vehicle talking into a radio phone.

They'd found the car. It frightened him, but somehow it didn't surprise him.

He backed away cautiously, prepared to run if he was spotted. His thoughts raced ahead to the problems to which this newest complication gave rise. First and most immediate was an automobile. Second was the fact that they knew he was in the Hartford vicinity. That ruled out other means of transportation. The rail-road stations, the bus terminals, even the hack bureaus would be alerted. It came back to finding another car.

And yet he wondered. Blackstone made it clear there were no charges against him, no warrants. If there were, he would have received the message from 555–6868. He would have heard the words: 'Charger Three-zero is canceled.'

He hadn't. There'd been no hint of it. For a moment he considered going back to the patrol car, accepting a ticket for overtime.

He dismissed the thought. These police were not meter maids. There had been a previous parking lot beyond an alley, at the rear of an A&P. And another policeman – in civilian clothes – following him. A pattern was there, though it eluded definition. Matlock walked swiftly up Bond Street away from the municipal lot. He turned into the first side street and found himself beginning to break into a run. Instantly he slowed down. There is nothing in a crowded street more noticeable than a man running – unless it is a woman. He resumed a pace equal to the afternoon shoppers, doing his best to melt into the flow of human traffic. He even paused now and then to stare blankly into store-front windows, not really seeing the displays of merchandise. And then he began to reflect on what was happening to him. The primitive instincts of the hunted were suddenly working inside his brain. The protective antennae of the would-be trapped animal were thrusting, parrying with their surroundings and, chameleonlike, the body did its best to conform to the environment.

Yet he wasn't the hunted! He was the hunter! Goddamn it, he was the *hunter*!

'Hello, Jim! How the hell are you? What are you doing in the big city?'

The shock of the greeting caused Matlock to lose his balance. To actually *lose his balance* and trip. He fell to the sidewalk and the man who had spoken to him reached down and helped him up.

'Oh! Oh, hello, Jeff! Christ, you startled me. Thanks.' Matlock got up and brushed himself off. He looked around wondering who else beside Jeff Kramer was watching him.

'A long lunch, buddy?' Kramer laughed. He was a Carlyle alumnus with a graduate degree in psychology that had been impressive enough for an expensive public relations firm.

'Lord, no! Just have something on my mind. My bumbling old professor bag.' And then Matlock looked at Jeff Kramer. Jeff Kramer was not only with an expensive firm, but he also had an expensive wife and two very expensive kids in extremely expensive prep schools. Matlock felt he should reemphasize his previous point. 'For a fact, I had one unfinished bourbon.'

'Why don't we rectify that,' said Kramer, pointing at the Hogshead Tavern across the street. 'I haven't seen you in months. I read in *The Courant* you got yourself robbed.'

'Goddamn, *did* I! The robbery I could take, but what they did to the apartment! And the *car*!' Matlock headed toward the Hogshead Tavern with Jeff Kramer. 'That's why I'm in town. Got the Triumph in a garage here. That's my problem, as a matter of fact.'

The hunted not only had antennae which served to warn the host of its enemies, but also the uncanny – if temporary – ability to turn disadvantage into advantage. Conceivable liabilities into positive assets.

Matlock sipped his bourbon and water while Kramer went through half his Scotch in several swallows. 'The idea of a bus down to Scarsdale, with changes at New Haven and Bridgeport, defeats me.'

'*Rent* a car, for Christ's sake.'

'Just tried two places. The first can't let me have one until tonight, the second not until tomorrow. Some kind of convention, I guess.'

'So wait until tonight.'

'Can't do it. Family business. My father called his council of economic advisers. For dinner – and if you think I'm going to Scarsdale without my own wheels, you're out of it!' Matlock laughed and ordered another round of drinks. He reached into his pocket and put a fifty-dollar bill on the bar. The bill had to attract the attention of Jeff Kramer, who had such an expensive wife.

'Never thought you could balance a checkbook, say nothing of being an economic adviser.'

'Ah, but I'm the prince royal. Can't forget that, can we?'

'Lucky bastard, that's what I can't forget. Lucky bastard.'

'Hey! I've got one hell of an idea. Your car in town?'

'Hey, wait a minute, good buddy. . . .'

'No, listen.' Matlock took out his bills. 'The old man'll pay for it. . . . Rent me *your* car. Four or five days. . . . Here. I'll give you two, three hundred.'

'You're nuts!'

'No, I'm not. He wants me down. He'll pay!'

Matlock could sense Kramer's mind working. He was estimating the cost of a low-priced rent-a-car for a week. Seventy-nine-fifty and ten cents a mile with an average daily mileage of, perhaps, fifteen or twenty. Tops, $105, and maybe $110, for the week.

Kramer had that expensive wife and those two very expensive kids in extremely expensive prep schools.

'I wouldn't want to take you like that.'

'Not *me*! Christ, no. *Him!*'

'Well . . .'

'Here, let me write out a bill. I'll give it to him the minute I get there.' Matlock grabbed a cocktail napkin and turned it over to the unprinted side. He took out his ballpoint pen and began writing. 'Simple contract. . . . "I, James B. Matlock, agree to pay Jeffrey Kramer three hundred" . . . what the hell, it's his money . . ."four hundred dollars for the rental of his . . ." – what's the make?'

'Ford wagon. A white Squire. Last year's.' Kramer's eyes alternately looked at the napkin and the roll of bills Matlock carelessly left next to Kramer's elbow on the bar.

'"Ford Wagon, for a period of" . . . let's say one week, O.K.?'

'Fine.' Kramer drank the remainder of his second Scotch.

'"One week. . . . Signed, James B. Matlock!" There you are, friend. Countersign. And here's four hundred. Courtesy of Jonathan Munro. Where's the car?'

The hunted's instincts were infallible, thought Matlock, as Kramer pocketed the bills and wiped his chin, which had begun to perspire. Kramer removed the two car keys and the parking lot ticket from his pocket. True to Matlock's anticipation, Jeff Kramer wanted to part company. With his four hundred dollars.

Matlock said he would phone Kramer in less than a week and return the automobile. Kramer insisted on paying for the drinks and rapidly left the Hogshead Tavern. Matlock, alone, finished his drink and thought out his next move.

The hunted and the hunter were now one.

Twenty-four

He sped out Route 72 toward Mount Holly in Kramer's white station wagon. He knew that within the hour he would find another pay telephone and insert another coin and make another call. This time to one Howard Stockton, owner of the Carmount Country Club. He looked at his watch; it was nearly eight-thirty. Samuel Sharpe, attorney at law, should have reached Stockton several hours ago.

He wondered how Stockton had reacted. He wondered about Howard Stockton.

The station wagon's headlights caught the reflection of the road sign.

MOUNT HOLLY. INCORPORATED 1896

And just beyond it, a second reflection.

MOUNT HOLLY ROTARY
HARPER'S REST
TUESDAY NOON
ONE MILE

Why not? thought Matlock. There was nothing to lose. And possibly something to gain, even learn.

The hunter.

The white stucco front and the red Narragansett neons in the windows said all there was to say about Harper's cuisine. Matlock parked next to a pickup truck, got out, and locked the car. His newly acquired suitcase with the newly acquired clothes lay on the back seat. He had spent several hundred dollars in Hartford; he wasn't about to take a chance.

He walked across the cheap, large gravel and entered the bar area of Harper's Restaurant.

'I'm on my way to Carmount,' said Matlock, paying for his drink with a twenty-dollar bill. 'Would you mind telling me where the hell it is?'

'About two and a half miles west. Take the right fork down the road. You got anything smaller than a twenty? I only got two fives and singles. I need my singles.'

'Give me the fives and we'll flip for the rest. Heads you keep it, tails I have one more and you still keep it.' Matlock took a coin from his pocket and threw it on the formica bar, covering it with his hand. He lifted his palm and picked up the coin without showing it to the bartender. 'It's your unlucky night. You owe me a drink – the ten's yours.'

His conversation did not go unheeded by the other customers – three men drinking draft beer. That was fine, thought Matlock, as he looked around for a telephone.

'Men's room's in the rear around the corner,' said a rustic-looking drinker in a chino jacket, wearing a baseball cap.

'Thanks. Telephone around?'

'Next to the men's room.'

'Thanks again.' Matlock took out a piece of paper on which he had written: Howard Stockton, Carmount C.C., # 203-421-1100. He gestured for the bartender, who came toward him like a shot. 'I'm supposed to phone this guy,' said Matlock quietly. 'I think I got the name wrong. I'm not sure whether it's Stackton or Stockton. Do you know him?'

The bartender looked at the paper and Matlock saw the instant reflex of recognition. 'Sure. You got it right. It's Stockton. Mr. Stockton. He's vice-president of the Rotary. Last term he was president. Right boys?' The bartender addressed this last to his other customers.

'Sure.'

'That's it. Stockton.'

'Nice fella.'

The man in the chino jacket and baseball cap felt the necessity of elaborating. 'He runs the country club. That's a real nice place. Real nice.'

'Country club?' Matlock implied the question with a trace of humor.

'That's right. Swimming pool, golf course, dancing on the weekends. Very nice.' It was the bartender who elaborated now.

'I'll say this, he's highly recommended. This Stockton, I mean.' Matlock drained his glass and looked toward the rear of the bar. 'Telephone back there, you say?'

'That's right, Mister. Around the corner.'

Matlock reached into his pocket for some change and walked to the narrow corridor where the rest rooms and telephone were located. The instant he rounded the corner, he stopped and pressed himself against the wall. He listened for the conversation he knew would be forthcoming.

'Big spender, huh?' The bartender spoke.

'They all are. Did I tell you? My kid caddied there a couple of weeks ago – some guy got a birdie and give the kid a fifty-dollar bill. Che-ryst! Fifty dollars!'

'My old woman says all them fancy dames there are *whoores*. Real whoores. She works a few parties there, my old woman does. Real whoores. . . .'

'I'd like to get my hands on some of them. Jee-*sus!* I swear to Christ most of 'em got no brazzieres!'

'Real whoores. . . .'

'Who gives a shit? That Stockton's O.K. He's O.K. in my book. Know what he did? The Kings. You know, Artie King who had a heart attack – dropped dead doin' the lawns up there. Old Stockton not only give the family a lotta dough – he set up a regular charge account for 'em at the A&P. No shit. He's O.K.'

'Real whoores. They lay for money. . . .'

'Stockton put most of the cash up for the grammar school extension, don't forget that. You're fuckin' right, he's O.K. I got two kids in that school!'

'Not only – y'know what? He give a pocketful to the Memorial Day picnic.'

'Real, honest-to-Christ whoores. . . .'

Matlock silently sidestepped his way against the wall to the telephone booth. He closed the door slowly with a minimum of noise. The men at the bar were getting louder in their appreciation of Howard Stockton, proprietor of the Carmount Country Club. He was not concerned that they might hear his delayed entrance into the booth.

What concerned him in an odd way was himself. If the *hunted* had instincts – protective in nature – the *hunter* had them also – aggressive by involvement. He understood now the necessity of tracking the scent, following the spoor, building a fabric of comprehensive habit. It meant that the hunter had abstract tools to complement his weapons. Tools which could build a base of entrapment, a pit in which the hunted might fall.

He ticked them off in his mind.

Howard Stockton: former president, current vice-president of the Mount Holly Rotary; a charitable man, a compassionate man. A man who took care of the family of a deceased employee named Artie King; who financed the extension of a grammar school. The proprietor of a luxurious country club in which men gave fifty-dollar tips to caddies and girls were available for members in good standing. Also a good American who made it possible for the town of Mount Holly to have a fine Memorial Day picnic.

It was enough to start with. Enough to shake up Howard Stockton if – as Sammy Sharpe had put it – 'it came to that.' Howard Stockton was not the formless man he was fifteen minutes ago. Matlock still didn't know the man's features, but other aspects, other factors were defined for him. Howard Stockton had become a *thing* in Mount Holly, Connecticut.

Matlock inserted the dime and dailed the number of the Carmount Country Club.

'It *suh*tainly is a pleasure, Mr. Matlock!' exclaimed Howard Stockton, greeting Matlock on the marble steps of the Carmount Country Club. 'The boy'll take your car. Heah! Boy! Don't wrap it up, now!'

A Negro parking attendant laughed at his southern gentleman's command. Stockton flipped a half-dollar in the air and the black caught it with a grin.

'Thank you, suh!'

'Treat 'em good, they'll treat you good. That right, boy? Do I treat you good?'

'*Real* good, Mister Howard!'

Matlock thought for a moment that he was part of an odious television commercial until he saw that Howard Stockton was the real item. Right up to his grayish blond hair, which topped a sun-tanned face, which, in turn, set off his white moustache and deep blue eyes surrounded by crow's nests of wrinkles belonging to a man who lived well.

'Welcome to Carmount, Mr. Matlock. It's not Richmond, but on the other hand, it ain't the Okefenokee.'

'Thank you. And the name is Jim.'

'Jim? Like that name. It's got a good, honest ring to it! My friends call me Howard. You call me Howard.'

The Carmount Country Club, what he could see of it, reminded Matlock of all those pictures of antebellum architecture. And why not, considering the owner? It was rife with potted palms and delicate chandeliers and light blue toile wallpaper depicting rococo scenes in which cavorted prettified figures in powdered wigs. Howard Stockton was a proselytizer of a way of life which had collapsed in 1865, but he wasn't going to admit it. Even the servants, mostly black, were in liveries – honest-to-god liveries, knickers and all. Soft, live music came from a large dining room, at the end of which was a string orchestra of perhaps eight instruments gracefully playing in a fashion long since abandoned. There was a slowly winding staircase in the center of the main hall which would have done honor to Jefferson Davis – or David O. Selznick. Attractive women were wandering around, linked with not-so-attractive men.

The effect was incredible, thought Matlock, as he walked by his host's side toward what his host modestly claimed was his private library.

The southerner closed the thick paneled door and strode to a well-stocked mahogany bar. He poured without asking a preference.

'Sam Sharpe says you drink sour mash. You're a man of taste, I tell you that. That's *my* drink.' He carried two glasses to Matlock. 'Take your pick. A Virginian has to disarm a northerner with his complete lack of bias these days.'

'Thank you,' said Matlock, taking a glass and sitting in the armchair indicated by Stockton.

'This Virginian,' continued Howard Stockton, sitting opposite Matlock, 'also has an unsouthern habit of getting to the point. . . . I don't even know if it's wise for you to be in my place. I'll be honest. That's why I ushered you right in here.'

'I don't understand. You could have told me on the phone not to come. Why the game?'

'Maybe you can answer that better than I can. Sammy says you're a real big man. You're what they call . . . *international*. That's just dandy by me. I like a bright young fella who goes up the ladder of success. Very commendable, that's a fact. . . . But I pay my bills. I pay every month on the line. I got the best combined operation north of Atlanta. I don't want trouble.'

'You won't get it from *me*. I'm a tired businessman making the rounds, that's all I am.'

'What happened at Sharpe's? The papers are full of it! I don't want *nothin'* like that!'

Matlock watched the southerner. The capillaries in the suntanned face were bloodred, which was probably why the man courted a year-round sunburn. It covered a multitude of blemishes.

'I don't think you understand.' Matlock measured his words as he lifted the glass to his lips. 'I've come a long way because I *have* to be here. I don't *want* to be here. Personal reasons got me into the area early, so I'm doing some sightseeing. But it's only that. I'm just looking around. . . . Until my appointment.'

'What appointment?'

'An appointment in Carlyle, Connecticut.'

Stockton squinted his eyes and pulled at his perfectly groomed white moustache. 'You've got to be in Carlyle?'

'Yes. It's confidential, but I don't have to tell you that, do I?'

'You haven't told me anything.' Stockton kept watching Matlock's face, and Matlock knew the southerner was looking for a false note, a wrong word, a hesitant glance which might contradict his information.

'Good. . . . By any chance, do you have an appointment in Carlyle, too? In about a week and a half?'

Stockton sipped his drink, smacking his lips and putting the glass on a side table as though it were some precious *objet d'art*. 'I'm just a southern cracker tryin' to make a dollar. Livin' the good life and makin' a dollar. That's all. I don't know about any appointments in Carlyle.'

'Sorry I brought it up. It's a . . . major mistake on my part. For both our sakes. I hope you won't mention it. Or *me*.'

'That's the *last* thing I'd do. Far as I'm concerned, you're a friend of Sammy's lookin' for a little action . . . and a little hospitality.' Suddenly Stockton leaned forward in his chair, his elbows on his knees, his hands folded. He looked like an earnest minister questioning a parishioner's sins. 'What in tarnation happened at Windsor Shoals? What in hell was it?'

'As far as I can see, it was a local vendetta. Bartolozzi had enemies. Some said he talked too goddamn much. Aiello, too, I suppose. They were show-offs. . . . Frank was just there, I think.'

'Goddamn *Eye*talians! Mess up everything! *That* level, of course, you know what I mean?'

There it was again. The dangling interrogative – but in this southerner's version, it wasn't really a question. It was a statement.

'I know what you mean,' said Matlock wearily.

'I'm afraid I got a little bad news for you, Jim. I closed the tables for a few days. Just plum scared as a jackrabbit after what happened at the Shoals.'

'That's not bad news for me. Not the way my streak's been going.'

'I heard. Sammy told me. But we got a couple of other diversions. You won't find Carmount lacking in hospitality, I promise you that.'

The two men finished their drinks, and Stockton, relieved, escorted his guest into the crowded, elegant Carmount dining room. The food was extraordinary, served in a manner befitting the finest and wealthiest plantation of the antebellum South.

Although pleasant – even relaxing, in a way – the dinner was pointless to Matlock. Howard Stockton would not discuss his 'operation' except in the vaguest terms and with the constant reminder that he catered to the 'best class of Yankee.' His speech was peppered with descriptive anachronisms, he was a walking contradiction in time. Halfway through the meal, Stockton excused himself to say good-bye to an important member.

It was the first opportunity Matlock had to look at Stockton's 'best class of Yankee' clientele.

The term applied, thought Matlock, if the word *class* was interchangeable with *money*, which he wasn't willing to concede. Money screamed from every table. The first sign was the proliferation of sun tans in the beginning of a Connecticut May. These were people who jetted to the sun-drenched islands at will. Another was the easy, deep-throated laughter echoing throughout the room; also the glittering reflection of jewelry. And the clothes – softly elegant suits, raw silk jackets, Dior ties. And the bottles of sparkling vintage wines, standing majestically in sterling silver stands upheld by cherrywood tripods.

But something was wrong, thought Matlock. Something was missing or out of place, and for several minutes he couldn't put his finger on what it was. And then he did.

The suntans, the laughter, the wrist jewelry, the jackets, the Dior ties – the money, the elegance, the aura was predominantly *male*.

The contradiction was the women – the girls. Not that there weren't some who matched their partners, but in the main, they didn't. They were younger. Much, much younger. And different.

He wasn't sure what the difference was at first. Then, abstractly, it came to him. For the most part, the girls – and they *were* girls – had a look about them he knew very well. He'd referred to it often in the past. It was the campus look – as differentiated from the office look, the secretary look. A slightly more intense expression around the eyes, a considerably more careless attitude in conversation. The look of girls not settling into routines, not welded to file cabinets or typewriters. It was definable because it was real. Matlock had been exposed to that look for over a decade – it was unmistakable.

Then he realized that within this contradiction there was another – minor – discrepancy. The clothes the girls wore. They weren't the clothes he expected to find on girls with the campus look. They were too precisely cut, too designed, if that was the word. In this day of unisex, simply too feminine.

They wore costumes!

Suddenly, in a single, hysterically spoken sentence from several tables away, he knew he was right.

'Honest, I mean it – it's too groovy!'

That voice! *Christ, he knew that voice!*

He wondered if he was meant to hear it.

He had his hand up to his face and slowly turned toward the direction of the giggling speaker. The girl was laughing and drinking champagne, while her escort – a much older man – stared with satisfaction at her enormous breasts.

The girl was Virginia Beeson. The 'pinky groovy' perennial undergraduate wife of Archer Beeson, Carlyle University's history instructor.

The man in an academic hurry.

Matlock tipped the black who carried his suitcase up the winding staircase to the large, ornate room Stockton had offered him. The floor was covered with a thick wine-colored carpet, the bed canopied, the walls white with fluted moldings. He saw that on the bureau was an ice bucket, two bottles of Jack Daniels, and several glasses. He opened the suitcase, picked out his toilet articles, and put them on the bedside table. He then removed a suit, a light-weight jacket and two pairs of slacks, and carried them to the closet. He returned to the suitcase, lifted it from the bed, and laid it across the two wooden arms of a chair.

There was a soft tapping on his door. His first thought was that the caller was Howard Stockton, but he was wrong.

A girl, dressed in a provocative deep-red sheath, stood in the frame and smiled. She was in her late teens or very early twenties and terribly attractive.

And her smile was false.

'Yes?'

'Compliments of Mr. Stockton.' She spoke the words and walked into the room past Matlock.

Matlock closed the door and stared at the girl, not so much bewildered as surprised.

'That's very thoughtful of Mr. Stockton, isn't it?'

'I'm glad you approve. There's whisky, ice, and glasses on your bureau. I'd like a short drink. Unless you're in a hurry.'

Matlock walked slowly to the bureau. 'I'm in no hurry. What would you like?'

'It doesn't matter. Whatever's there. Just ice, please.'

'I see.' Matlock poured the girl a drink and carried it over to her. 'Won't you sit down?'

'On the bed?'

The only other chair, besides the one on which the suitcase was placed, was across the room by a French window.

'I'm sorry.' He removed the suitcase and the girl sat down. Howard Stockton, he thought, had good taste. The girl was adorable. 'What's your name?'

'Jeannie.' She drank a great deal of her drink in several swallows. The girl may not have perfected a selection in liquor, but she knew how to drink. And then, as the girl took the glass from her mouth, Matlock noticed the ring on her third right finger.

He knew that ring very well. It was sold in a campus bookstore several blocks from John Holden's apartment in Webster, Connecticut. It was the ring of Madison University.

'What would you say if I told you I wasn't interested?' asked Matlock, leaning against the thick pole of the bed's anachronistic canopy.

'I'd be surprised. You don't look like a fairy.'

'I'm not.'

The girl looked up at Matlock. Her pale blue eyes were warm – but professionally warm – meaning, yet not meaning at all. Her lips were young. And full; and taut.

'Maybe you just need a little encouragement.'

'You can provide that?'

'I'm good.' She made the statement with quiet arrogance.

She was so young, thought Matlock, yet there was age in her. And hate. The hate was camouflaged, but the cosmetic was inadequate. She was performing – the costume, the eyes, the lips. She may have detested the role, but she accepted it.

Professionally.

'Suppose I just want to talk?'

'Conversation's something else. There are no rules about that. I've equal rights in that department. Quid pro, Mister No-name.'

'You're facile with words. Should that tell me something?'

'I don't know why.'

'"Quid pro quo" isn't the language of your eight to three hooker.'

'This place – in case you missed it – isn't the Avenida de las Putas, either.'

'Tennessee Williams?'

'Who knows?'

'I think you do.'

'Fine. All right. We can discuss Proust in bed. I mean, that *is* where you want me, isn't it?'

'Perhaps I'd settle for the conversation.'

The girl suddenly, in alarm, whispered hoarsely, 'Are you a cop?'

'I'm the furthest thing from a cop,' laughed Matlock. 'You might say that some of the most important policemen in the area would like to find me. Although I'm no criminal. . . . Or a nut, by the way.'

'Now *I'm* not interested. May I have another drink?'

'Surely.' Matlock got it for her. Neither spoke until he returned with her glass.

'Do you mind if I stay here awhile? Just long enough for you to have balled me.'

'You mean you don't want to lose the fee?'

'It's fifty dollars.'

'You'll probably have to use part of it to bribe the dormitory head.

Madison University's a little old-fashioned. Some coed houses still have weekday check-ins. You'll be late.'

The shock on the girl's face was complete. 'You *are* a cop! You're a lousy *cop!*' She started to get out of the chair, but Matlock quickly stood in front of her, holding her shoulders. He eased her back into the chair.

'I'm not a cop, I told you that. And you're not interested, remember? But *I'm* interested. I'm *very* interested, and you're going to tell me what I want to know.'

The girl started to get up and Matlock grabbed her arms. She struggled; he pushed her back violently. 'Do you always get "balled" with your ring on? Is that to show whoever gets laid there's a little class to it?!'

'Oh, my God! Oh, Jesus!' She grabbed her ring and twisted her finger as if the pressure might make it disappear.

'Now, listen to me! You answer my questions or I'll be down in Webster tomorrow morning and I'll start asking them down there! Would you like that better?'

'Please! *Please!*' Tears came to the girl's eyes. Her hands shook and she gasped for breath.

'How did you get here?!'

'No! No. . .'

'*How?*'

'I was recruited. . . .'

'By whom?'

'Others . . . Others. We recruit each other.'

'How many are there?'

'Not many. Not very many. . . . It's quiet. We have to keep it quiet. . . . Let me go, *please*. I want to *go*.'

'Oh, no. Not yet. I want to know how many and *why!*'

'I told you! Only a few, maybe seven or eight girls.'

'There must be thirty downstairs!'

'I don't *know* them. They're from other places. We don't ask each other's *names!*'

'But you know where they're from, don't you!'

'Some. . . . Yes.'

'Other schools?'

'Yes . . .'

'*Why*, Jeannie? For Christ's sake, *why?*'

'Why do you *think*? *Money!*'

The girl's dress had long sleeves. He grabbed her right arm and ripped the fabric up past the elbow. She fought him back but he overpowered her.

There were no marks. No signs.

She kicked at him and he slapped her face, hard enough to shock her into momentary immobility. He took her left arm and tore the sleeve.

There they were. Faded. Not recent. But there.

The small purple dots of a needle.

'I'm not on it now! I haven't been in *months!*'

'But you need the money! You need fifty or a hundred dollars every time you come over here!. . . What is it *now?* Yellows? Reds? *Acid? Speed?* What the hell is it *now?* Grass isn't that expensive!'

The girl sobbed. Tears fell down her cheeks. She covered her face and spoke – moaned – through her sobs.

'There's so much trouble! So much . . . *trouble!* Let me *go, please!'*

Matlock knelt down and cradled the girl's head in his arms, against his chest.

'What trouble? Tell me, please. What trouble?'

'They *make* you do it. . . . You *have* to. . . . So many need help. They won't help *anyone* if you don't do it. Please, whatever your name is, let me alone. Let me go. Don't say anything. Let me *go!. . . Please!'*

'I will, but you've got to clear something up for me. Then you can go and I won't say anything. . . . Are you down here because they threatened you? Threatened the other kids?'

The girl nodded her head, gasping quietly, breathing heavily. Matlock continued. 'Threatened you with what? Turning you in? . . . Exposing a habit? That's not worth it. Not today. . . .'

'Oh, you're outta sight!' The girl spoke through her tears. 'They can ruin you. For life. Ruin your family, your school, maybe later. Maybe. . . . Some rotten prison. Somewhere! Habit, pushing, supplying . . . a boy you know's in trouble and *they* can get him off. . . . Some girl's in her third month, she needs a doctor . . . *they* can get one. No noise.'

'You don't need *them!* Where've you *been?!* There are agencies, counseling!'

'Oh, Jesus Christ, mister! Where have *you* been?!. . . The drug courts, the doctors, the judges! They run them *all!. . .* There's nothing *you* can do about it. Nothing *I* can do about it. So leave me alone, leave *us* alone. Too many people'll get hurt!'

'And you're just going to keep doing what they say! Frightened, spoiled little bastards who keep on whining! Afraid to wash your hands, or your *mouths,* or your *arms!'* He pulled at her left elbow and yanked it viciously.

The girl looked up at him, half in fear, half in contempt.

'That's right,' she said in a strangely calm voice. 'I don't think you'd understand. You don't know what it's all about. . . . We're different from you. My friends are all I've got. All any of us have got. We help each other. . . . I'm not interested in being a hero. I'm only interested in my friends. I don't have a flag decal in my car window and I don't like John Wayne. I think he's a shit. I think you all are. All shits.'

Matlock released the girl's arm. 'Just how long do you think you can keep it up?'

'Oh, I'm one of the lucky ones. In a month I'll have that scroll my parents paid for and I'm out of it. They hardly ever try to make contact with you later. They say they will, but they rarely do. . . . You're just supposed to live with the possibility.'

He understood the implications of her muted testimony and turned away. 'I'm sorry. I'm very, very sorry.'

'Don't be. I'm one of the lucky ones. Two weeks after I pick up that piece of engraved crap my parents want so badly, I'll be on a plane. I'm leaving this goddamn country. And I'll never come back!'

Twenty-five

He had not been able to sleep, nor had he expected to. He had sent the girl away with money, for he had nothing else he could give her, neither hope nor courage. What he advocated was rejected, for it involved the risk of danger and pain to untold children committed to the well-being of each other. He could not demand; there was no trust, no threat equal to the burdens they carried. Ultimately, it was the children's own struggle. They wanted no help.

He remembered the Bagdhivi admonition: *Look ye to the children; look and behold. They grow tall and strong and hunt the tiger with greater cunning and stronger sinews than you. They shall save the flocks better than you. Ye are old and infirm. Look to the children. Beware of the children.*

Were the children hunting the tiger better? And even if they were, whose flocks would they save? And who was the tiger?

Was it the 'goddamn country'?

Had it come to that?

The questions burned into his mind. How many Jeannies were there? How extensive was Nimrod's recruiting?

He had to find out.

The girl admitted that Carmount was only one port of call; there were others, but she didn't know where. Friends of hers had been sent to New Haven, others to Boston, some north to the outskirts of Hanover.

Yale. Harvard. Dartmouth.

The most frightening aspect was Nimrod's threat of a thousand futures. What had she said?

'They hardly ever make contact. . . . They say they will. . . . You live with the possibility.'

If such was the case, Bagdhivi was wrong. The children had far less cunning, possessed weaker sinews; there was no reason to beware. Only to pity.

Unless the children were subdivided, led by other, stronger children.

Matlock made up his mind to go down to New Haven. Maybe there were answers there. He had scores of friends at Yale University. It would be a side trip, an unconsidered excursion, but intrinsic to the journey itself. Part of the Nimrod odyssey.

Short, high-pitched sounds interrupted Matlock's concentration. He froze, his eyes swollen in shock, his body tense on top of the bed. It took him several seconds to focus his attention on the source of the frightening sound. It was the Tel-electronic, still in his jacket pocket. But where had he put his jacket? It wasn't near his bed.

He turned on the bedside lamp and looked around, the unrelenting, unceasing sounds causing his pulse to hammer, his forehead to perspire. Then he saw his coat. He had put it on top of the chair in front of the French window, halfway across the room. He looked at his watch: 4:35 A.M. He ran to the jacket, pulled out the terrible instrument, and shut it off.

The panic of the hunted returned. He picked up the telephone on the bedside table. It was a direct line, no switchboard.

The dial tone was like any other dial tone outside the major utility areas. A little fuzzy, but steady. And if there was a tap, he wouldn't be able to recognize it anyway. He dialed 555–6868 and waited for the call to be completed.

'Charger Three-zero reporting,' said the mechanized voice. 'Sorry to disturb you. There is no change with the subject, everything is satisfactory. However, your friend from Wheeling, West Virginia, is very insistent. He telephoned at four-fifteen and said it was imperative you call him at once. We're concerned. Out.'

Matlock hung up the telephone and forced his mind to go blank until he found a cigarette and lit it. He needed the precious moments to stop the hammering pulse.

He hated that goddamn machine! He hated what its terrifying little beeps did to him.

He drew heavily on the smoke and knew there was no alternative. He had to get out of the Carmount Country Club and reach a telephone booth. Greenberg wouldn't have phoned at four in the morning unless it was an emergency. He couldn't take the chance of calling Greenberg on the Carmount line.

He threw his clothes into the suitcase and dressed quickly.

He assumed there'd be a night watchman, or a parking attendant asleep in a booth, and he'd retrieve his, Kramer's, automobile. If not, he'd wake up someone, even if it was Stockton himself. Stockton was still frightened of trouble, Windsor Shoals trouble – he wouldn't try to detain him. Any story would do for the purveyor of young, adorable flesh. The sunburned southern flower of the Connecticut Valley. The stench of Nimrod.

Matlock closed the door quietly and walked down the silent corridor to the enormous staircase. Wall sconces were lighted, dimmed by rheostats to give a candlelight effect. Even in the dead of night, Howard Stockton couldn't forget his heritage. The interior of the Carmount Country Club looked more than ever like a sleeping great hall of a plantation house.

He started for the front entrance, and by the time he reached the storm carpet, he knew it was as far as he would go. At least for the moment.

Howard Stockton, clad in a flowing velour, nineteenth-century dressing gown, emerged from a glass door next to the entrance. He was accompanied by a large, Italian-looking man whose jet black eyes silently spoke generations of the Black Hand. Stockton's companion was a killer.

'Why, Mr. Matlock! Are you leavin' us?'

He decided to be aggressive.

'Since you tapped my goddamn phone, I assume you gather I've got problems! They're *my business, not yours*! If you want to know, I resent your intrusion!'

The ploy worked. Stockton was startled by Matlock's hostility.

'There's no reason to be angry. . . . I'm a businessman, like you. Any invasion of your privacy is for your protection. Goddamn! That's *true*, boy!'

'I'll accept the lousy explanation. Are my keys in the car?'

'Well, not in your *car*. My friend Mario here's got 'em. He's a real high-class Eyetalian, let me tell you.'

'I can see the family crest on his pocket. May I have my keys?'

Mario looked at Stockton, obviously confused.

'Now, just a minute,' Stockton said. 'Wait a bit, Mario. Let's not be impulsive. . . . I'm a reasonable man. A very reasonable, rational person. I'm merely a Virginia . . .'

'*Cracker*, trying to make a dollar!' interrupted Matlock. 'I'll buy that! Now get the hell out of my way and give me the keys!'

'Good Lord, *you all* are downright *mean*! I mean, *mean*! Put yourself in my place! . . . Some crazy code like "Chargin' Three-zero" and an urgent call from Wheelin', West *Virginia*! And instead of usin' my perfectly good telephone, you gotta make space and get *outta* here! C'mon, Jim. What would *you* do?!'

Matlock kept his voice chillingly precise. 'I'd try to understand *who* I was dealing with. . . . We've made a number of inquiries, Howard. My superiors are concerned about you.'

'What-do-you-mean?' Stockton's question was asked so swiftly the words had no separation.

'They think . . . we think you've called too much attention to yourself. President and vice-president of a *Rotary Club*! Jesus! A one-man fund-raiser for new school buildings; the big provider for widows and orphans – charge accounts included; Memorial Day picnics! Then hiring locals to spread rumors about the girls! Half the time the kids walk around half naked. You think the local citizens don't talk? *Christ*, Howard!'

'Who the hell are you?'

'Just a tired businessman who gets annoyed when he sees another businessman make an ass of himself. What the hell do you think you're running for? Santa Claus? Have you any idea how prominent that costume is?'

'Goddamn it, you got it in for me! I've got the finest combined operation north of Atlanta! I don't know who you people been talkin' to, but I tell you – this l'il old Mount Holly'd go to hell in a basket for me! Those things you people dug up – they're *good* things! *Real* good! . . . You twist 'em, make 'em sound bad! That ain't *right*!'

Stockton took out a handkerchief and patted his flushed, perspiring face. The southerner was so upset his sentences spilled over into one another, his voice strident. Matlock tried to think swiftly, cautiously. Perhaps the time was now – with Stockton. It had to be some time. He had to send out his own particular invitation. He had to start the last lap of his journey to Nimrod.

'Calm down, Stockton. Relax. You may be right. . . . I haven't time to think about it now. We've got a crisis. All of us. That phone call was serious.' Matlock paused, looking hard at the nervous Stockton, and then put his suitcase on the marble floor. 'Howard,' he said slowly, choosing his words carefully, 'I'm going to trust you with something and I hope to hell you're up to it. If you pull it off, no one'll bother your operation – ever.'

'What's that?'

'Tell *him* to take a walk. Just down the hall, if you like.'

'You heard the man. Go smoke a cigar.'

Mario looked both hostile and confused as he trudged slowly toward the staircase. Stockton spoke.

'What do you want me to do? I told you, I don't want trouble.'

'We're *all* going to have trouble unless I reach a few delegates. That's what Wheeling was telling me.'

'What do you mean . . . delegates?'

'The meeting over at Carlyle. The conference with our people and the Nimrod organization.'

'That's not my affair!' Stockton spat out the words. 'I don't know a thing about that!'

'I'm sure you don't; you weren't meant to. But now it concerns all of us. . . . Sometimes rules have to be broken; this is one of those times. Nimrod's gone too far, that's all I can tell you.'

'You tell *me*? I live with those *preachers*! I *parlay* with them, and when I complain, you know what our own people say? They say, "That's the way it is, old Howie, we all do business"! What kind of talk is that? Why do *I* have to do business with them?'

'Perhaps you won't much longer. That's why I have to reach some of the others. The delegates.'

'They don't include me in those meetings. I don't know anyone.'

'Of course you don't. Again, you weren't meant to. The conference is heavy; very heavy and very quiet. So quiet we may have screwed ourselves: we don't know who's in the area. From what organization; from what family? But I have my orders. We've got to get through to one or two.'

'I can't help you.'

Matlock looked harshly at the southerner. 'I think you can. Listen to me. In the morning, get on the phone and pass the word. *Carefully!* We don't want panic. Don't talk to anyone you don't know and don't use my name! Just say you've met someone who has the Corsican paper, the silver Corsican paper. He's *got* to meet quietly with someone else who has it, too. We'll start with one person if we have to. Have you got that?'

'I got it but I don't like it! It's none of *my business*!'

'Would you rather close down? Would you rather lose this magnificent relic of yours and stare out of a cell window for ten or twenty years? I understand prison funerals are very touching.'

'All right! . . . All right. I'll call my bag boy. I'll say I don't know nothin'! I'm just passin' along a message.'

'Good enough. If you make a contact, tell whoever it is that I'll be at the Sail and Ski tonight or tomorrow. Tell him to bring the paper. I won't talk to anyone without the paper!'

'Without the paper. . . .'

'Now let me have my keys.'

Stockton called Mario back. Matlock got his keys.

★ ★ ★

He swung south on Route 72 out of Mount Holly. He didn't remember precisely where, but he knew he'd passed several highway telephone booths on his way up from Hartford. It was funny how he was beginning to notice public telephones, his only connecting link with solidity. Everything else was transient, hit or miss, unfamiliar and frightening. He'd phone Greenberg as Charger Three-zero requested, but before he did, he was going to reach one of Blackstone's men.

A rendezvous would have to be arranged immediately. He now had to have the Corsican paper. He'd put out the word; he'd have to keep his end of the bargain or he would learn nothing. *If* Stockton's message got through and *if* someone *did* make contact, that someone would kill or be killed before breaking the oath of 'Omerta' unless Matlock produced the paper.

Or was it all for nothing? Was he the amateur Kressel and Greenberg said he was? He didn't know. He tried so hard to think things through, look at all sides of every action, use the tools of his trained, academic imagination. But was it enough? Or was it possible that his sense of commitment, his violent feelings of vengeance and disgust were only turning him into a Quixote?

If that were so, he'd live with it. He'd do his goddamnedest and live with it. He had good reasons – a brother named David; a girl named Pat; a gentle old man named Lucas; a nice fellow named Loring; a confused, terrified student from Madison named Jeannie. The sickening whole *scene!*

Matlock found a booth on a deserted stretch of Route 72 and called the inanimate receiver at the other end of 555–6868. He gave the number of the telephone booth and waited for Charger Three-zero to answer his call.

A milk truck lumbered by. The driver was singing and waved to Matlock. Several minutes later a huge Allied Van Lines sped past, and shortly after a produce truck. It was nearing five-thirty, and the day was brightening. Brightening to a dull gray, for there were rain clouds in the sky.

The telephone rang.

'Hello!'

'What's the problem, sir? Did you reach your friend in West Virginia? He said he's not kidding anymore.'

'I'll call him in a few minutes. Are you the fellow named Cliff?' Matlock knew it was not; the voice was different.

'No, sir. I'm Jim. Same name as yours.'

'All right, Jim. Tell me, did the other fellow do what I asked him to? Did he get the paper for me?'

'Yes, sir. If it's the one on silver paper, written in Italian. I think it's Italian.'

'That's the one. . . .'

Matlock arranged for the pickup in two hours. It was agreed that the

Blackstone man named Cliff would meet him at an all-night diner on Scofield Avenue near the West Hartford town line. Charger Three-zero insisted that the delivery be made rapidly, in the parking lot. Matlock described the car he was driving and hung up the phone.

The next call would have to be Jason Greenberg in Wheeling. And Greenberg was furious.

'Schmuck! It isn't bad enough you break your word, you've got to hire your own army! What the hell do you think those clowns can do that the United States Government can't?'

'Those clowns are costing me three hundred dollars a day, Jason. They'd better be good.'

'You ran out! Why did you do that? You gave me your word you wouldn't. You said you'd work with our man!'

'Your man gave me an ultimatum I couldn't live with! And if it was your idea, I'll tell you the same thing I told Houston.'

'What does that mean? What ultimatum?'

'You know goddamn well! Don't play that game. And you listen to me. . . .' Matlock took a break before plunging into the lie, giving it all the authority he could summon. 'There's a lawyer in Hartford who has a very precise letter signed by me. Along the same lines as the letter I signed for you. Only the information's a bit different: it's straight. It describes in detail the story of my recruitment; how you bastards sucked me in and then how you let me hang. How you forced me to sign a lie. . . . You try anything, he'll release it and there'll be a lot of embarrassed manipulators at the Justice Department. . . . You gave me the idea, Jason. It was a damn good idea. It might even make a few militants decide to tear up the Carlyle campus. Maybe launch a string of riots, with luck, right across the country. The academic scene's ready to be primed out of its dormancy; isn't that what Sealfont said? Only this time it won't be the war or the draft or drugs. They'll find a better label: government infiltration, police state . . . *Gestapo* tactics. Are you prepared for that?'

'For Christ's sake, cut it out! It won't do you any good. You're not that important. . . . Now, what the hell are you talking about? *I briefed him!* There weren't any conditions except that you keep him informed of what you were doing.'

'Bullshit! I wasn't to leave the campus; I wasn't to talk to anyone on the faculty or the staff. I was restricted to student inquiries, and I gathered those were to be cleared *first*! Outside of those minor restrictions, I was free as a bird! Come on! You *saw* Pat! You saw what they did to her. You know what else they did – the word is *rape*, Greenberg! Did you people expect me to *thank* Houston for being so *understanding*?'

'Believe me,' said Greenberg softly, in anger. 'Those conditions were added after the briefing. They should have told me, that's true. But they were added for your own protection. You can see that, can't you?'

'They weren't part of our bargain!'

'No, they weren't. And they should have told me. . . .'

'Also, I wonder whose protection they were concerned with. Mine or theirs.'

'A good question. They should have told me. They can't delegate responsibility and always take away the authority. It's not logical.'

'It's not *moral*. Let me tell you something. This little odyssey of mine is bringing me closer and closer to the sublime question of morality.'

'I'm glad for you, but I'm afraid your odyssey's coming to an end.'

'Try it!'

'They're going to. Statements in lawyers' offices won't mean a damn. I told them I'd try first. . . . If you don't turn yourself over to protective custody within forty-eight hours, they'll issue a warrant.'

'On what grounds?!'

'You're a menace. You're mentally unbalanced. You're a nut. They'll cite your army record – two courts-martial, brig time, continuous instability under combat conditions. Your use of drugs. And alcohol – they've got witnesses. You're also a racist – they've got that Lumumba affidavit from Kressel. And now I understand, although I haven't the facts, you're consorting with known criminals. They have photographs – from a place in Avon. . . . Turn yourself in, Jim. They'll ruin your life.'

Twenty-six

Forty-eight hours! Why forty-eight hours? Why not twenty-four or twelve or immediately? It didn't make sense! Then he understood and, alone in the booth, he started to laugh. He laughed out loud in a telephone booth at five-thirty in the morning on a deserted stretch of highway in Mount Holly, Connecticut.

The practical men were giving him just enough time to accomplish something – if he *could* accomplish something. If he couldn't, and anything happened, they were clean. It was on record that they considered him a mentally unbalanced addict with racist tendencies who consorted with known criminals, and they had given him warning. In deference to the delicate balance of dealing with such madmen, they allocated *time* in the hopes of reducing the danger. Oh, Christ! The manipulators!

★ ★ ★

He reached the West Hartford diner at six-forty-five and ate a large breakfast, somehow believing that the food would take the place of sleep and give him the energy he needed. He kept glancing at his watch, knowing that he'd have to be in the parking lot by seven-thirty.

He wondered what his contact at Charger Three-zero would look like.

The man was enormous, and Matlock had never considered himself small. Cliff of Charger Three-zero reminded Matlock of those old pictures of Primo Carnera. Except the face. The face was lean and intelligent and smiled broadly.

'Don't get out, Mr. Matlock.' He reached in and shook Matlock's hand. 'Here's the paper; I put it in an envelope. By the way, we had Miss Ballantyne laughing last night. She's feeling better. Encephalograph's steady, metabolism's coming back up to par, pupil dilation's receding. Thought you'd like to know.'

'I imagine that's good.'

'It is. We've made friends with the doctor. He levels.'

'How's the hospital taking your guard duty?'

'Mr. Blackstone solves those problems in advance. We have rooms on either side of the subject.'

'For which, I'm sure, I'll be charged.'

'You know Mr. Blackstone.'

'I'm getting to. He goes first class.'

'So do his clients. I'd better get back. Nice to meet you.' The Blackstone man walked rapidly away and got into a nondescript automobile several years old.

It was time for Matlock to drive to New Haven.

He had no set plan, no specific individuals in mind; he wasn't leading, he was being led. His information was, at best, nebulous, sketchy, far too incomplete to deal in absolutes. Yet perhaps there was enough for someone to make a connection. But whoever made it, or was capable of making it, had to be someone with an overall view of the university. Someone who dealt, as did Sam Kressel, with the general tensions of the campus.

However, Yale was five times the size of Carlyle; it was infinitely more diffuse, a section of the New Haven city, not really isolated from its surroundings as was Carlyle. There *was* a focal point, the Office of Student Affairs; but he didn't know anyone there. And to arrive off the street with an improbable story of college girls forming – or being formed into – a prostitution ring reaching, as so far determined, the states of Connecticut, Massachusetts, and New Hampshire, would create havoc if he was taken seriously. And he wasn't sure he *would* be taken seriously, in which case he'd learn nothing.

There was one possibility; a poor substitute for Student Affairs, but with its own general view of the campus: the Department of Admissions. He knew a man, Peter Daniels, who worked in Yale's admissions office. He and Daniels had shared a number of lecterns during prep school recruitment programs. He knew Daniels well enough to spell out the facts as he understood them; Daniels wasn't the sort to doubt him or to panic. He'd restrict his story to the girl, however.

He parked on Chappel Street near the intersection of York. On one side of the thoroughfare was an arch leading to the quadrangle of Silliman College, on the other a large expanse of lawn threaded with cement paths to the Administration Building. Daniels's office was on the second floor. Matlock got out of the car, locked it, and walked toward the old brick structure with the American flag masted next to the Yale banner.

'That's preposterous! This is the age of Aquarius and then some. You don't pay for sex; it's exchanged freely.'

'I know what I saw. I know what the girl told me; she wasn't lying.'

'I repeat. You can't be sure.'

'It's tied in with too many other things. I've seen them, too.'

'May I ask the obvious question? Why don't you go to the police?'

'Obvious answer. Colleges have been in enough trouble. What facts I have are isolated. I need more information. I don't want to be responsible for indiscriminate name-calling, any widespread panic. There's been enough of that.'

'All right, I'll buy it. But I can't help you.'

'Give me several names. Students *or* faculty. People you know . . . you're certain are messed up, seriously messed up. Near the center. You've got those kinds of names, I know you do; we do. . . . I swear, they'll never know who gave them to me.'

Daniels got out of his chair, lighting his pipe. 'You're being awfully general. Messed up how? Academically, politically . . . narcotics, alcohol? You're covering a wide territory.'

'Wait a minute.' Daniels's words evoked a memory. Matlock recalled a dimly lit, smoke-filled room inside a seemingly deserted building in Hartford. Rocco Aiello's Hunt Club. And a tall young man in a waiter's jacket who had brought over a tab for Aiello to sign. The veteran of Nam and Da Nang. The Yalie who was *making contacts, building up his nest egg . . . the business administration* major. 'I know who I want to see.'

'What's his name?'

'I don't know. . . . But he's a veteran – Indochina, about twenty-two or three; he's pretty tall, light brown hair . . . majoring in business administration.'

'A description which might fit five hundred students. Except for premed, law, and engineering, it's all lumped under liberal arts. We'd have to go through every file.'

'Application photographs?'

'Not allowed anymore, you know that.'

Matlock stared out the window, his eyebrows wrinkled in thought. He looked back at Daniels. 'Pete, it's May. . . .'

'So? It could be November; that wouldn't change the Fair Practices law.'

'Graduation's in a month. . . . Senior class photographs. Year-book portraits.'

Daniels understood instantly. He took his pipe from his mouth and started for the door.

'Come with me.'

His name was Alan Pace. He was a senior and his curriculum was not centered on business administration; he was a government major. He lived off campus on Church Street near the Hamden town line. According to his records, Alan Pace was an excellent student, consistent honors in all subjects, a fellowship in the offing at the Maxwell School of Political Science at Syracuse. He had spent twenty-eight months in the army, four more than was required of him. As with most veterans, his university extracurricular activities were minimal.

While Pace was in service, he was an officer attached to inventory and supply. He had volunteered for a four-month extended tour of duty in the Saigon Corps – a fact noted with emphasis on his reapplication form. Alan Pace had given four months of his life more than necessary to his country. Alan Pace was obviously an honorable man in these days of cynicism.

He was a winner, thought Matlock.

The drive out Church Street toward Hamden gave Matlock the chance to clear his mind. He had to take one thing at a time; one item crossed off – on to the next. He couldn't allow his imagination to interpret isolated facts beyond their meaning. He couldn't lump everything together and total a sum larger than the parts.

It was entirely possible that this Alan Pace played a solo game. Unattached, unencumbered.

But it wasn't logical.

Pace's apartment house was an undistinguished brown brick building, so common on the outskirts of cities. Once – forty or fifty years ago – it had been the proud symbol of a rising middle class extending themselves out beyond the cement confines toward the country, but not so courageous as to leave the city completely. It wasn't so much run down as it was . . . not spruced up. The most glaring aspect of the apartment house to Matlock, however, was that it seemed to be a most unlikely place for a student to reside.

But he was there now; Peter Daniels had ascertained that.

Pace had not wanted to unlatch the door. It was only Matlock's strong emphasis on two points that made the student relent. The first point was that he wasn't from the police; the second, the name Rocco Aiello.

'What do you want? I've got a lot of work to do; I don't have time to talk. I've got comprehensives tomorrow.'

'May I sit down?'

'What for? I told you, I'm busy.' The tall, brown-haired student crossed back to his desk, piled with books and papers. The apartment was neat – except for the desk – and quite large. There were doors and short corridors leading to other doors. It was the sort of apartment that usually was shared by four or five students. But Alan Pace had no roommates.

'I'll sit down anyway. You owe that much to Rocco.'

'What does that mean?'

'Just that Rocco was my friend. I was the one with him the other night when you brought him a tab to sign. Remember? And he was good to you. . . . He's dead.'

'I know. I read about it. I'm sorry. But I didn't owe him anything.'

'But you bought from him.'

'I don't know what you're talking about.'

'Come on, Pace. You don't have the time and neither do I. You're not connected to Aiello's death, I know that. But I've got to have information, and you're going to supply it.'

'You're talking to the wrong person. I don't know you. I don't know *anything*.'

'I know *you*. I've got a complete rundown on you. Aiello and I were considering going into business together. Now, that's none of your concern, I realize that, but we exchanged . . . personnel information. I'm coming to you because, frankly, Rocco's gone and there are areas that need filling. I'm really asking a favor, and I'll pay for it.'

'I told you, I'm not your man. I hardly knew Aiello. I picked up a few dollars waiting tables. Sure, I heard rumors, but that's *all*. I don't know what you want, but you'd better go to someone else.'

Pace was sharp, thought Matlock. He was disengaging himself but not foolishly claiming complete innocence. On the other hand, perhaps he was telling the truth. There was only one way to find out.

'I'll try again. . . . Fifteen months in Vietnam. Saigon, Da Nang; excursions to Hong Kong, Japan. I&S officer; the dullest, most exasperating kind of work for a young man with the potential that earns him honors at a very tough university.'

'I&S was good duty; no combat, no sweat. Everybody made the tourist hops. Check the R&R route sheets.'

'Then,' continued Matlock without acknowledging Pace's interruption, 'the dedicated officer returns to civilian life. After a four-month voluntary extension in Saigon – I'm surprised you weren't caught up on *that* one – he comes back with enough money to make the proper investments, and certainly not from his army pay. He's one of the biggest suppliers in New Haven. Do you want me to go on?'

Pace stood by the desk and seemed to stop breathing. He stared at Matlock, his face white. When he spoke, it was the voice of a frightened young man.

'You can't prove anything. I haven't done anything. My army record, my record here – they're both good. They're very good.'

'The best. Unblemished. They're records to be proud of; I mean that sincerely. And I wouldn't want to do anything to spoil them; I mean that, too.'

'You couldn't. I'm clean!'

'No, you're not. You're up to your fellowship neck. Aiello made that *clear*. On *paper*.'

'You're lying!'

'You're stupid. You think Aiello would do business with *anyone* he didn't run a check on? Do you think he'd be *allowed* to? He kept very extensive books, Pace, and I've *got* them. I told you; we were going into business together. You don't form a partnership without audit disclosures, you should know that.'

Pace spoke barely above a whisper. 'There are no books like that. There never are. Cities, towns, codes. No names. Never any names.'

'Then why am I here?'

'You saw me in Hartford; you're reaching for a connection.'

'You know better than that. Don't be foolish.'

Matlock's quickly put implications were too much for the tall, shocked young man. 'Why did you come to me? I'm not that important. You say you know about me; then you know I'm not important.'

'I told you. I need information. I'm reluctant to go to the high priests, anyone with real authority. I don't want to be at a disadvantage. That's why I'm willing to pay; why I'm prepared to tear up everything I've got on you.'

The prospect of being cut free of the stranger's grip was obviously all that was on Pace's mind. He replied quickly.

'Suppose I can't answer your questions? You'll think I'm lying.'

'You can't be worse off. All you can do is try me.'

'Go ahead.'

'I met a girl . . . from a nearby college. I met her under circumstances that can only be described as professional prostitution. Professional in every sense of the word. Appointments, set fees, no prior knowledge of clients, the works. . . . What do you know about it?'

Pace took several steps toward Matlock. 'What do you mean, what do I know? I know it's there. What else is there to know?'

'How extensive?'

'All over. It's not news.'

'It is to me.'

'You don't know the scene. Take a walk around a few college towns.'

Matlock swallowed. Was he really that far out of touch? 'Suppose I were to tell you I'm familiar with a lot of . . . college towns?'

'I'd say your circles were cubed. Also, I'm no part of that action. What else?'

'Let's stick to this for a minute. . . . Why?'

'Why what?'

'Why do the girls do it?'

'Bread, man. Why does anyone do anything?'

'You're too intelligent to believe that. . . . Is it organized?'

'I guess so. I told you, I'm no part of it.'

'Watch it! I've got a lot of paper on you. . . .'

'All right. Yes, it's organized. Everything's organized. If it's going to work.'

'Where *specifically* are the operations?'

'I *told* you! All *over*.'

'Inside the colleges?'

'No, not inside. On the outskirts. A couple of miles usually, if the campuses are rural. Old houses, away from the suburbs. If they're in cities – downtown hotels, private clubs, apartment houses. But not *here*.'

'Are we talking about . . . Columbia, Harvard, Radcliffe, Smith, Holyoke? And points south?'

'Everyone always forgets Princeton,' replied Pace with a wry smile. 'A lot of nice old estates in those back roads. . . . Yes, we're talking about those places.'

'I never would have believed it. . . .' Matlock spoke as much to himself as to Pace. 'But, *why?* Don't give me the "bread" routine. . . .'

'Bread is *freedom*, man! For these kids it's freedom. They're not psyched-up freaks; they're not running around in black berets and field jackets. Very few of us are. We've *learned*. Get the money, fella, and the nice people will like you. . . . Also, whether you've noticed it or not, the straight money's not as easy to come by as it once was. Most of these kids need it.'

'The girl I mentioned before; I gathered she was forced into it.'

'Oh, Jesus, nobody's *forced!* That's crap.'

'She was. She mentioned a few things. . . . Controls is as good a word as any. Courts, doctors, even jobs. . . .'

'I wouldn't know anything about that.'

'And afterward. Making contact later – perhaps a few years later. Plain old-fashioned blackmail. Just as I'm blackmailing you now.'

'Then she was in trouble before; this girl, I mean. If it's a bummer, she doesn't have to make the trip. Unless she's into somebody and owes what she can't pay for.'

'Who is Nimrod?' Matlock asked the question softly, without emphasis. But the question caused the young man to turn and walk away.

'I don't know that. I don't have that information.'

Matlock got out of the chair and stood motionless. 'I'll ask you just once more, and if I don't get an answer, I'll walk out the door and you'll be finished. A very promising life will be altered drastically – if you have a life. . . . Who is Nimrod?'

The boy whipped around and Matlock saw the fear again. The fear he had seen on Lucas Herron's face, in Lucas Herron's eyes.

'So help me Christ, I can't answer that!'

'Can't or won't?'

'Can't. I *don't know!*'

'I think you do. But I said I'd only ask you once. That's it.' Matlock started for the apartment door without looking at the student.

'No! . . . Goddamn it, I *don't know!* . . . How *could* I know? You can't!' Pace ran to Matlock's side.

'Can't what?'

'Whatever you said you'd do. . . . Listen to me! I don't know who they are! I don't have . . .'

'They?'

Pace looked puzzled. 'Yeah. . . . I guess "they." I don't know. I don't have any contact. Others do; I don't. They haven't bothered me.'

'But you're aware of them.' A statement.

'Aware. . . . Yes, I'm aware. But *who*, honest to God, *no!*'

Matlock turned and faced the student. 'We'll compromise. For now. Tell me what you *do* know.'

And the frightened young man did. And as the words came forth, the fear infected James Matlock.

Nimrod was an unseen master puppeteer. Faceless, formless, but with frightening, viable authority. It wasn't a *he* or a *they* – it was a *force*, according to Alan Pace. A complex abstraction that had its elusive tentacles in every major university in the Northeast, every municipality that served

the academic landscape, all the financial pyramids that funded the complicated structures of New England's higher education. 'And points south,' if
the rumors had foundation.

Narcotics was only one aspect, the craw in the throats of the criminal
legions – the immediate reason for the May conference, the Corsican letter.

Beyond drugs and their profits, the Nimrod imprimatur was stamped on
scores of college administrations. Pace was convinced that curriculums were
being shaped, university personnel hired and fired, degree and scholarship
policies, all were expedited on the Nimrod organization's instructions.
Matlock's memory flashed back to Carlyle. To Carlyle's assistant dean of
admissions – a Nimrod appointee, according to the dead Loring. To Archer
Beeson, rapidly rising in the history department; to a coach of varsity soccer;
to a dozen other faculty and staff names on Loring's list.

How many more were there? How deep was the infiltration?

Why?

The prostitution rings were subsidiary accommodations. Recruitments
were made by the child-whores among themselves; addresses were provided,
fees established. Young flesh with ability and attractiveness could find its
way to Nimrod and make the pact. And there was 'freedom,' there was
'bread' in the pact with Nimrod.

And 'no one was hurt'; it was a victimless crime.

'No crime at all, just freedom, man. No pressures over the head. No
screaming zonkers over scholarship points.'

Alan Pace saw a great deal of good in the elusive, practical Nimrod. More
than good.

'You think it's all so different from the outside – straight? You're wrong,
mister. It's mini-America: organized, computerized, and very heavy with
the corporate structure. Hell, it's patterned on the American syndrome; it's
company *policy*, man! It's GM, ITT, and Ma Bell – only someone was smart
enough to organize the groovy groves of academe. And it's growing fast.
Don't fight it. Join it.'

'Is that what you're going to do?' asked Matlock.

'It's the way, man. It's the faith. For all I know *you're* with it now. Could
be, you're a recruiter. You guys are everywhere; I've been expecting you.'

'Suppose I'm not?'

'Then you're out of your head. And over it, too.'

Twenty-seven

If one watched the white station wagon and its driver heading back toward the center of New Haven, one would have thought – if he thought at all – that it was a rich car, suitable to a wealthy suburb, the man at the wheel appropriately featured for the vehicle.

Such an observer would not know that the driver was barely cognizant of the traffic, numbed by the revelations he'd learned within the hour; an exhausted man who hadn't slept in forty-eight hours, who had the feeling that he was holding onto a thin rope above an infinite chasm, expecting any instant that his lifeline would be severed, plunging him into the infinite mist.

Matlock tried his best to suspend whatever thought processes he was capable of. The years, the specific months during which he'd run his academic race against self-imposed schedules had taught him that the mind – at least his mind – could not function properly when the forces of exhaustion and overexposure converged.

Above all, he had to function.

He was in uncharted waters. Seas where tiny islands were peopled by grotesque inhabitants. Julian Dunoises, Lucas Herrons; the Bartolozzis, the Aiellos, the Sharpes, the Stocktons, and the Paces. The poisoned and the poisoners.

Nimrod.

Uncharted waters?

No, they weren't uncharted, thought Matlock.

They were well traveled. And the travelers were the cynics of the planet.

He drove to the Sheraton Hotel and took a room.

He sat on the edge of the bed and placed a telephone call to Howard Stockton at Carmount. Stockton was out.

In brusque, officious tones, he told the Carmount switchboard that Stockton was to return his call – he looked at his watch; it was ten to two – in four hours. At six o'clock. He gave the Sheraton number and hung up.

He needed at least four hours' sleep. He wasn't sure when he would sleep again.

He picked up the telephone once more and requested a wake-up call at five-forty-five.

As his head sank to the pillow, he brought his arm up to his eyes. Through the cloth of his shirt he felt the stubble of his beard. He'd have to go to a barbershop; he'd left his suitcase in the white station wagon. He'd been too tired, too involved to remember to bring it to his room.

The short, sharp three rings of the telephone signified the Sheraton's adherence to his instructions. It was exactly quarter to six. Fifteen minutes later there was another ring, this one longer, more normal. It was precisely six, and the caller was Howard Stockton.

'I'll make this short, Matlock. You got a contact. Only he doesn't want to meet *inside* the Sail and Ski. You go to the East Gorge slope – they use it in spring and summer for tourists to look at the scenery – and take the lift up to the top. You be there at eight-thirty this evenin'. He'll have a man at the top. That's all I've got to say. It's none of *mah business!*'

Stockton slammed down the telephone and the echo rang in Matlock's ear.

But he'd made it! *He'd made it!* He had made the contact with Nimrod! With the conference.

He walked up the dark trail toward the ski lift. Ten dollars made the attendant at the Sail and Ski parking lot understand his problem: the nice-looking fellow in the station wagon had an assignation. The husband wasn't expected till later – and, what the hell, that's life. The parking lot attendant was very cooperative.

When he reached the East Gorge slope, the rain, which had threatened all day, began to come down. In Connecticut, April showers were somehow always May thunderstorms, and Matlock was annoyed that he hadn't thought to buy a raincoat.

He looked around at the deserted lift, its high double lines silhouetted against the increasing rain, shining like thick strands of ship hemp in a fogged harbor. There was a tiny, almost invisible light in the shack which housed the complicated, hulking machines that made the lines ascend. Matlock approached the door and knocked. A small, wiry-looking man opened the door and peered at him.

'You the fella goin' up?'

'I guess I am.'

'What's your name?'

'Matlock.'

'Guess you are. Know how to catch a crossbar?'

'I've skied. Arm looped, tail on the slat, feet on the pipe.'

'Don't need no help from me. I'll start it, you get it.'

'Fine.'

'You're gonna get wet.'

'I know.'

Matlock positioned himself to the right of the entrance pit as the lumbering machinery started up. The lines creaked slowly and then began their halting countermoves, and a crossbar approached. He slid himself onto the lift, pressed his feet against the footrail, and locked the bar in front of his waist. He felt the swinging motion of the lines lifting him off the ground.

He was on his way to the top of the East Gorge, on his way to his contact with Nimrod. As he swung upward, ten feet above the ground, the rain became, instead of annoying, exhilarating. He was coming to the end of his journey, his race. Whoever met him at the top would be utterly confused. He counted on that, he'd planned it that way. If everything the murdered Loring and the very-much-alive Greenberg had told him was true, it couldn't be any other way. The total secrecy of the conference; the delegates, unknown to each other; the oath of 'Omerta,' the subculture's violent insistence on codes and countercodes to protect its inhabitants – it *was* all true. He'd seen it all in operation. And such complicated logistics – when sharply interrupted – inevitably led to suspicion and fear and ultimately confusion. It was the confusion Matlock counted on.

Lucas Herron had accused him of being influenced by plots and counter-plots. Well, he wasn't *influenced* by them – he merely *understood* them. That was different. It was this understanding which had led him one step away from Nimrod.

The rain came harder now, whipped by the wind which was stronger off the ground than on it. Matlock's crossbar swayed and dipped, more so each time he reached a rung up the slope. The tiny light in the machine shack was now barely visible in the darkness and the rain. He judged that he was nearly halfway to the top.

There was a jolt; the machinery stopped. Matlock gripped the waist guard and peered above him through the rain trying to see what obstruction had hit the wheel or the rung. There was none.

He turned awkwardly in the narrow perch and squinted his eyes down the slope toward the shack. There was no light now, not even the slightest illumination. He held his hand up in front of his forehead, keeping the rain away as best he could. He had to be mistaken, the downpour was blurring his vision, perhaps the pole was in his line of sight. He leaned first to the right, then to the left. But still there was no light from the bottom of the hill.

Perhaps the fuses had blown. If so, they would have taken the bulb in the shack with them. Or a short. It was raining, and ski lifts did not ordinarily operate in the rain.

He looked beneath him. The ground was perhaps fifteen feet away. If he suspended himself from the footrail, the drop would only be eight or nine feet. He could handle that. He would walk the rest of the way up the slope.

He had to do it quickly, however. It might take as long as twenty minutes to climb to the top, there was no way of telling. He couldn't take the chance of his contact's panicking, deciding to leave before he got to him.

'Stay right where you are! Don't unlatch that harness!'

The voice shot out of the darkness, cutting through the rain and wind. Its harsh command paralysed Matlock as much from the shock of surprise as from fear. The man stood beneath him, to the right of the lines. He was dressed in a raincoat and some kind of cap. It was impossible to see his face or even determine his size.

'Who are you?! What do you want?'

'I'm the man you came to meet. I want to see that paper in your pocket. Throw it down.'

'I'll show you the paper when I see *your* copy. That's the deal! That's the deal I made.'

'You don't understand, Matlock. Just throw the paper down. That's all.'

'What the hell are you talking about?!'

The glare of a powerful flashlight blinded him. He reached for the guard rail latch.

'Don't touch that! Keep your hands straight out or you're dead!'

The core of the high-intensity light shifted from his face to his chest, and for several seconds all Matlock saw were a thousand flashing spots inside his eyes. As his sight returned, he could see that the man below him was moving closer to the lines, swinging the flashlight toward the ground for a path. In the glow of the beam, he also saw that the man held a large, ugly automatic in his right hand. The blinding light returned to his face, now shining directly beneath him.

'Don't threaten me, punk!' yelled Matlock, remembering the effect his anger had on Stockton at four that morning. 'Put that goddamn gun away and help me down! We haven't much time and I don't like games!'

The effect now was not the same. Instead, the man beneath him began to laugh, and the laugh was sickening. It was, more than anything else, utterly genuine. The man on the ground was enjoying himself.

'You're very funny. You look funny sitting there on your ass in midair. You know what you look like? You look like one of those bobbing monkey targets in a shooting gallery! *You know what I mean?* Now, cut the bullshit and throw down the paper!'

He laughed again, and at the sound everything was suddenly clear to Matlock.

He hadn't made a contact. He hadn't cornered anyone. All his careful planning, all his thought-out actions. All for nothing. He was no nearer Nimrod now than he was before he knew Nimrod existed.

He'd been trapped.

Still, he had to try. It was all that was left him now.

'You're making the mistake of your life!'

'Oh, for Christ's sake, knock it off! Give me the paper! We've been looking for that fucking thing for a week! My orders are to get it *now*!'

'I can't give it to you.'

'I'll blow your head off!'

'I said I *can't*! I didn't say I *wouldn't*!'

'Don't shit me. You've got it on you! You wouldn't have come here without it!'

'It's in a packet strapped to the small of my back.'

'Get it out!'

'I told you, I can't! I'm sitting on a four-inch slat of wood with a footrail and I'm damn near twenty feet in the air!'

His words were half lost in the whipping rain. The man below was frustrated, impatient.

'*I said get it out!*'

'I'll have to drop down. I can't reach the straps!' Matlock yelled to be heard. 'I can't *do* anything! I haven't got a gun!'

The man with the large, ugly automatic moved back several feet from the lines. He pointed both the powerful beam and his weapon at Matlock.

'O.K., come on down! You cough wrong and your head's blown off!'

Matlock undid the latch, feeling like a small boy on top of a ferris wheel wondering what could happen if the wheel stopped permanently and the safety bar fell off.

He held onto the footrail and let the rest of him swing beneath it. He dangled in the air, the rain soaking him, the beam of light blinding him. He had to think now, he had to create an instant strategy. His life was worth far less than the lives at Windsor Shoals to such men as the man on the ground.

'Shine the light down! I can't see!'

'Fuck that! Just drop!'

He dropped.

And the second he hit the earth, he let out a loud, painful scream and reached for his leg.

'Aaaahhh! My ankle, my foot! I broke my goddamn ankle!' He twisted and turned on the wet overgrowth, writhing in pain.

'Shut up! Get me that paper! *Now!*'

'*Jesus Christ!* What do you *want* from me? My ankle's turned *around*! It's *broken*!'

'Tough! Give me the paper!'

Matlock lay prostrate on the ground, his head moving back and forth, his neck straining to stand the pain. He spoke between short gasps.

'Strap's here. Undo the strap.' He tore at his shirt displaying part of the canvas belt.

'Undo it yourself. Hurry up!'

But the man came closer. He wasn't sure. And closer. The beam of light was just above Matlock now. Then it moved to his midsection and Matlock could see the large barrel of the ugly black automatic.

It was the second, the instant he'd waited for.

He whipped his right hand up towards the weapon, simultaneously springing his whole body against the legs of the man in the raincoat. He held the automatic's barrel, forcing it with all his strength toward the ground. The gun fired twice, the impact of the explosions nearly shattering Matlock's hand, the sounds partially muted by wet earth and the slashing rain.

The man was beneath him now, twisting on his side, thrashing with his legs and free arm against the heavier Matlock. Matlock flung himself on the pinned arm and sank his teeth into the wrist above the hand holding the weapon. He bit into the flesh until he could feel the blood spurting out, mingled with the cold rain.

The man released the automatic, screaming in anguish. Matlock grabbed for the gun, wrested it free, and smashed it repeatedly into the man's face. The powerful flashlight was in the tall grass, its beam directed at nothing but drenched foliage.

Matlock crouched over the half-conscious, bloody face of his former captor. He was out of breath, and the sickening taste of the man's blood was still in his mouth. He spat a half dozen times trying to cleanse his teeth, his throat.

'O.K.!' He grabbed the man's collar and yanked his head up. 'Now you tell me what happened! This was a trap, wasn't it?'

'The paper! I gotta get the paper.' The man was hardly audible.

'I was *trapped, wasn't I*! The whole last week was a trap!'

'Yeah. . . . Yeah. The paper.'

'That paper's pretty important, isn't it?'

'They'll kill you . . . they'll kill you to get it! You stand no chance, mister. . . . No chance . . .'

'Who's *they*?!'

'I don't know . . . don't know!'

'*Who's Nimrod?*'

'I don't know . . . "Omerta"! . . . "Omerta"!'

The man opened his eyes wide, and in the dim spill of the fallen flashlight, Matlock saw that something had happened to his victim. Some thought, some concept overpowered his tortured imagination. It was painful to watch. It was too close to the sight of the panicked Lucas Herron, the terrified Alan Pace.

'Come on, I'll get you down the slope. . . .'

It was as far as he got. From the depths of his lost control, the man with the blood-soaked face lunged forward, making a last desperate attempt to reach the gun in Matlock's right hand. Matlock yanked back; instinctively he fired the weapon. Blood and pieces of flesh flew everywhere. Half the man's neck was blown off.

Matlock stood up slowly. The smoke of the automatic lingered above the dead man, the rain forcing it downward toward the earth.

He reached into the grass for the flashlight, and as he bent over he began to vomit.

Twenty-eight

Ten minutes later he watched the parking lot below him from the trunk of a huge maple tree fifty yards up the trail. The new leaves partially protected him from the pouring rain, but his clothes were filthy, covered with wet dirt and blood. He saw the white station wagon near the front of the area, next to the stone gate entrance of the Sail and Ski. There wasn't much activity now; no automobiles entered, and those drivers inside would wait until the deluge stopped before venturing out on the roads. The parking lot attendant he'd given the ten dollars to was talking with a uniformed doorman under the carport roof of the restaurant entrance. Matlock wanted to race to the station wagon and drive away as fast as he could, but he knew the sight of his clothes would alarm the two men, make them wonder what had happened on the East Gorge slope. There was nothing to do but wait, wait until someone came out and distracted them, or both went inside.

He hated the waiting. More than hating it, he was frightened by it. There'd been no one he could see or hear near the wheel shack, but that didn't mean no one was there. Nimrod's dead contact probably had a partner somewhere, waiting as Matlock was waiting now. If the dead man was found, they'd stop him, kill him – if not for revenge, for the Corsican paper.

He had no choice now. He'd gone beyond his depth, his abilities. He'd been manipulated by Nimrod as he'd been maneuvered by the men of the Justice Department. He would telephone Jason Greenberg and do whatever Greenberg told him to do.

In a way, he was glad his part of it was over, or soon would be. He still felt the impulse of commitment, but there was nothing more he could do. He had failed.

Down below, the restaurant entrance opened and a waitress signaled the uniformed doorman. He and the attendant walked up the steps to speak with the girl.

Matlock ran down to the gravel and darted in front of the grills of the cars parked on the edge of the lot. Between automobiles he kept looking toward the restaurant door. The waitress had given the doorman a container of coffee. All three were smoking cigarettes, all three were laughing.

He rounded the circle and crouched in front of the station wagon. He crept to the door window and saw to his relief that the keys were in the ignition. He took a deep breath, opened the door as quietly as possible, and leaped inside. Instead of slamming it, he pulled the door shut quickly, silently, so as to extinguish the interior light without calling attention to the sound. The two men and the waitress were still talking, still laughing, oblivious.

He settled himself in the seat, switched on the ignition, threw the gears into reverse, and roared backward in front of the gate. He raced out between the stone posts and started down the long road to the highway.

Back under the roof, on the steps by the front door, the three employees were momentarily startled. Then, from being startled they became quickly bewildered – and even a little curious. For, from the rear of the parking lot, they could hear the deep-throated roar of a second, more powerful engine. Bright headlights flicked on, distorted by the downpour of rain, and a long black limousine rushed forward.

The wheels screeched as the ominous-looking automobile swerved toward the stone posts. The huge car went to full throttle and raced after the station wagon.

There wasn't much traffic on the highway, but he still felt he'd make better time taking the back roads into Carlyle. He decided to go straight to Kressel's house, despite Sam's proclivity toward hysteria. Together they could both call Greenberg. He had just brutally, horribly killed another human being, and whether it was justified or not, the shock was still with him. He suspected it would be with him for the remainder of his life. He wasn't sure Kressel was the man to see.

But there was no one else. Unless he returned to his apartment and stayed there until a federal agent picked him up. And then again, instead of an agent, there might well be an emissary from Nimrod.

There was a winding S-curve in the road. He remembered that it came before a long stretch through farmland where he could make up time. The highway was straighter, but the back roads were shorter as long as there was no traffic to speak of. As he rounded the final half-circle, he realized that he was gripping the wheel so hard his forearms ached. It was the muscular defenses of his body taking over, controlling his shaking limbs, steadying the car with sheer unfeeling strength.

The flat stretch appeared; the rain had let up. He pushed the accelerator to the floor and felt the station wagon surge forward in overdrive.

He looked twice, then three times, up at his rear-view mirror, wary of patrol cars. He saw headlights behind him coming closer. He looked down at his speedometer. It read eighty-seven miles per hour and still the lights in the mirror gained on him.

The instincts of the hunted came swiftly to the surface; he knew the automobile behind him was no police car. There was no siren penetrating the wet stillness, no flashing light heralding authority.

He pushed his right leg forward, pressing the accelerator beyond the point of achieving anything further from the engine. His speedometer reached ninety-four miles per hour – the wagon was not capable of greater speed.

The headlights were directly behind him now. The unknown pursuer was feet, inches from his rear bumper. Suddenly the headlights veered to the left, and the car came alongside the white station wagon.

It was the same black limousine he had seen after Loring's murder! The same huge automobile that had raced out of the darkened driveway minutes after the massacre at Windsor Shoals! Matlock tried to keep part of his mind on the road ahead, part on the single driver of the car, which was crowding him to the far right of the road. The station wagon vibrated under the impact of the enormous speed; he found it more and more difficult to hold the wheel.

And then he saw the barrel of the pistol pointed at him through the window of the adjacent automobile. He saw the look of desperation in the darting eyes behind the outstretched arm, trying to steady itself for a clean line of fire.

He heard the shots and felt the glass shattering into his face and over the front seat. He slammed his foot into the brake and spun the steering wheel to the right, jumping the shoulder of the road, careening violently into and through a barbed-wire fence and onto a rock-strewn field. The wagon lunged into the grass, perhaps fifty or sixty feet, and then slammed into a cluster of rocks, a property demarcation. The headlights smashed and went out, the grill buckled. He was thrown into the dashboard, only his upheld arms keeping his head from crashing into the windshield.

But he was conscious, and the instincts of the hunted would not leave him.

He heard a car door open and close, and he knew the killer was coming into the field after his quarry. After the Corsican paper. He felt a trickle of blood rolling down his forehead – whether it was the graze of a bullet or a laceration from the flying glass, he couldn't be sure – but he was grateful it was there. He'd need it now, he needed the sight of blood on his forehead. He remained slumped over the wheel, immobile, silent.

And under his jacket he held the ugly automatic he had taken from the dead man in the raincoat on the slope of East Gorge. It was pointed under his left arm at the door.

He could hear the mushed crunch of footsteps on the soft earth outside the station wagon. He could literally feel – as a blind man feels – the face peering through the shattered glass looking at him. He heard the click of the door button as it was pushed in and the creaking of the hinges as the heavy panel was pulled open.

A hand grabbed his shoulder. Matlock fired his weapon.

The roar was deafening; the scream of the wounded man pierced the drenched darkness. Matlock leaped out of the seat and slammed the full weight of his body against the killer, who had grabbed his left arm in pain. Wildly, inaccurately, Matlock pistol-whipped the man about his face and neck until he fell to the ground. The man's gun was nowhere to be seen, his hands were empty. Matlock put his foot on the man's throat and pressed.

'I'll stop when you signal you're going to talk to me, you son of a bitch! Otherwise I *don't* stop!'

The man sputtered, his eyes bulged. He raised his right hand in supplication.

Matlock took his foot away and knelt on the ground over the man. He was heavy set, black-haired, with the blunt features of a brute killer.

'Who sent you after me? How did you know this car?'

The man raised his head slightly as though to answer. Instead, the killer whipped his right hand into his waist, pulled out a knife, and rolled sharply to his left, yanking his gorilla-like knee up into Matlock's groin. The knife slashed into Matlock's shirt, and he knew as he felt the steel point crease his flesh that he'd come as close as he would ever come to being killed.

He crashed the barrel of the heavy automatic into the man's temple. It was enough. The killer's head snapped back; blood matted itself around the hairline. Matlock stood up and placed his foot on the hand with the knife.

Soon the killer's eyes opened.

And during the next five minutes, Matlock did what he never thought he would be capable of doing – he tortured another man. He tortured the killer with the killer's own knife, penetrating the skin around and below the eyes, puncturing the lips with the same steel point that had scraped his own flesh. And when the man screamed, Matlock smashed his mouth with the barrel of the automatic and broke pieces of ivory off the killer's teeth.

It was not long.

'The paper!'

'What else?'

The writhing killer moaned and spat blood, but would not speak. Matlock did; quietly, in total conviction, in complete sincerity.

'You'll answer me or I'll push this blade down through your eyes. I don't care anymore. Believe me.'

'The old man!' The guttural words came from deep inside the man's throat. 'He said he wrote it down. . . . No one knows. . . . You talked to him. . . .'

'What old . . .' Matlock stopped as a terrifying thought came into his mind. '*Lucas Herron?! Is that who you mean?!*'

'He said he wrote it down. They think you know. Maybe he lied. . . . For Christ's sake, he could have lied. . . .'

The killer fell into unconsciousness.

Matlock stood up slowly, his hands shaking, his whole body shivering. He looked up at the road, at the huge black limousine standing silently in the diminishing rain. It would be his last gamble, his ultimate effort.

But something was stirring in his brain, something elusive but palpable. He had to trust that feeling, as he had come to trust the instincts of the hunter and the hunted.

The old man!

The answer lay somewhere in Lucas Herron's house.

Twenty-nine

He parked the limousine a quarter of a mile from Herron's Nest and walked toward the house on the side of the road, prepared to jump into the bordering woods should any cars approach.

None did.

He came upon one house, then another, and in each case he raced past, watching the lighted windows to see if anyone was looking out.

No one was.

He reached the edge of Herron's property and crouched to the ground. Slowly, cautiously, silently he made his way to the driveway. The house was dark; there were no cars, no people, no signs of life. Only death.

He walked up the flagstone path and his eye caught sight of an official-looking document, barely visible in the darkness, tacked onto the front door. He approached it and lit a match. It was a sheriff's seal of closure.

One more crime, thought Matlock.

He went around to the back of the house, and as he stood in front of the patio door, he remembered vividly the sight of Herron racing across his manicured lawn into the forbidding green wall which he parted so deftly and into which he disappeared so completely.

There was another sheriff's seal on the back door. This one was glued to a pane of glass.

Matlock removed the automatic from his belt and as quietly as possible broke the small-paned window to the left of the seal. He opened the door and walked in.

The first thing that struck him was the darkness. Light and dark were relative, as he'd come to understand during the past week. The night had light which the eyes could adjust to; the daylight was often deceptive, filled with shadows and misty blind spots. But inside Herron's house the darkness was complete. He lit a match and understood why.

The windows in the small kitchen was covered with shades. Only they weren't ordinary window shades, they were custom built. The cloth was heavy and attached to the frames with vertical runners, latched at the sills by large aluminum hasps. He approached the window over the sink and lit another match. Not only was the shade thicker than ordinary, but the runners and the stretch lock at the bottom insured that the shade would remain absolutely flat against the whole frame. It was doubtful that any light could go out or come in through the window.

Herron's desire – or need – for privacy had been extraordinary. And if all the windows in all the rooms were sealed, it would make his task easier.

Striking a third match, he walked into Herron's living room. What he saw in the flickering light caused him to stop in his tracks, his breath cut short.

The entire room was a shambles. Books were strewn on the floor, furniture overturned and ripped apart, rugs upended, even sections of the wall smashed. He could have been walking into his own apartment the night of the Beeson dinner. Herron's living room had been thoroughly, desperately searched.

He went back to the kitchen to see if his preoccupation with the window shades and the darkness had played tricks on his eyes. They had. Every drawer was pulled open, every cabinet ransacked. And then he saw on the floor of a broom closet two flashlights. One was a casement, the other a long-stemmed Sportsman. The first wouldn't light, the second did.

He walked rapidly back into the living room and tried to orient himself, checking the windows with the beam of the flashlight. Every window was covered, every shade latched at the sill.

Across the narrow hallway in front of the narrower stairs was an open door. It led to Herron's study, which was, if possible, more of a mess than his living room. Two file cabinets were lying on their sides, the backs torn off; the large leather-topped desk was pulled from the wall, splintered, smashed on every flat surface. Parts of the wall, as the living room, were broken into. Matlock assumed these were sections which had sounded hollow when tapped.

Upstairs, the two small bedrooms and the bath were equally dismantled, equally dissected.

He walked back down the stairs, even the steps had been pried loose from their treads.

Lucas Herron's home had been searched by professionals. What could he find that they hadn't? He wandered back into the living room and sat down on what was left of an armchair. He had the sinking feeling that his last effort would end in failure also. He lit a cigarette and tried to organize his thoughts.

Whoever had searched the house had not found what they were looking for. Or had they? There was no way to tell, really. Except that the brute killer in the field had screamed that the old man 'had written it down.' As if the fact was almost as important as the desperately coveted Corsican document. Yet he had added: '. . . maybe he lied, he could have lied.' *Lied?* Why would a man in the last extremity of terror add that qualification to something so vital?

The assumption had to be that in the intricate delicacy of a mind foundering on the brink of madness, the worst evil was rejected. Had to be rejected so as to hold onto what was left of sanity.

No. . . . No, they had not found whatever it was they *had to find*. And since they hadn't found it after such exhaustive, extraordinary labors – it didn't *exist*.

But he knew it did.

Herron may have been involved with Nimrod's world, but he was not born of it. His was not a comfortable relationship – it was a tortured one. Somewhere, someplace he had left an indictment. He was too good a man not to. There had been a great decency in Lucas Herron. Somewhere . . . someplace.

But where?

He got out of the chair and paced in the darkness of the room, flicking the flashlight on and off, more as a nervous gesture than for illumination.

He re-examined minutely every word, every expression used by Lucas that early evening four days ago. He was the hunter again, tracking the spoor, testing the wind for the scent. And he was close; goddamn it, he was close! . . . Herron had *known* from the second he'd opened his front door what Matlock was after. That instantaneous, fleeting moment of recognition had been in his eyes. It had been unmistakable to Matlock. He'd even said as much to the old man, and the old man had laughed and accused him of being influenced by plots and counterplots.

But there'd been something else. Before the plots and counterplots. . . .
Something *inside*. In this room. Before Herron suggested sitting *outside*. . . .
Only he hadn't *suggested*, he'd made a statement, given a command.

And just before he'd given the command to rear-march toward the
backyard patio, he'd walked in silently, *walked in silently*, and startled
Matlock. He had opened the swinging door, *carrying* two filled glasses, and
Matlock *hadn't heard* him. Matlock pushed the button on the flashlight and
shot the beam to the base of the kitchen door. There was no rug, nothing to
muffle footsteps – it was a hardwood floor. He crossed to the open swing-
hinged door, walked through the frame, and shut it. Then he pushed it
swiftly open in the same direction Lucas Herron had pushed it carrying the
two drinks. The hinges clicked as such hinges do if they are old and the door
is pushed quickly – *normally*. He let the door swing shut and then he pressed
against it slowly, inch by inch.

It was silent.

Lucas Herron had made the drinks and then *silently* had eased himself
back into the living room so he wouldn't be heard. So he could observe
Matlock without Matlock's knowing it. And then he'd given his firm
command for the two of them to go outside.

Matlock forced his memory to recall *precisely* what Lucas Herron said and
did at that *precise* moment.

'. . . we'll go out on the patio. It's too nice a day to stay inside. Let's go.'

Then, *without waiting for an answer*, even a mildly enthusiastic agreement,
Herron had walked *rapidly* back through the kitchen door. No surface
politeness, none of the courtly manners one expected from Lucas.

He had given an order, the firm command of an officer and a gentleman.

By Act of Congress.

That was *it!* Matlock swung the beam of light over the writing desk.

The photograph! The photograph of the marine officer holding the map
and the Thompson automatic in some tiny section of jungle on an insignificant island in the South Pacific.

'*I keep that old photograph to remind myself that time wasn't always so
devastating.*'

At the precise moment Herron walked through the door, Matlock had
been looking closely at the photograph! The fact that he was doing so
disturbed the old man, disturbed him enough for him to insist that they go
outside instantly. In a curt, abrupt manner so unlike him.

Matlock walked rapidly to the desk. The small cellophane-topped photo-
graph was still where it had been – on the lower right wall above the desk.
Several larger glass-framed pictures had been smashed; this one was intact.
It was small, not at all imposing.

He grabbed the cardboard frame and pulled the photo off the single thumbtack which held it to the wall. He looked at it carefully, turning it over, inspecting the thin edges.

The close, harsh glare of the flashlight revealed scratches at the upper corner of the cardboard. Fingernail scratches? Perhaps. He pointed the light down on the desk top. There were unsharpened pencils, scraps of note paper, and a pair of scissors. He took the scissors and inserted the point of one blade between the thin layers of cardboard until he could rip the photograph out of the frame.

And in that way he found it.

On the back of the small photograph was a diagram drawn with a broad-tipped fountain pen. It was in the shape of a rectangle, the bottom and top lines filled in with dots. On the top were two small lines with arrows, one straight, the other pointing to the right. Above each arrowhead was the numeral 30. Two 30s.

Thirty.

On the sides, bordering the lines, were childishly drawn trees.

On the top, above the numbers, was another simplified sketch. Billowy half-circles connected to one another with a wavy line beneath. A cloud. Underneath, more trees.

It was a map, and what it represented was all too apparent. It was Herron's back yard; the lines on three sides represented Herron's forbidding green wall.

The numerals, the 30s, were measurements – but they were also something else. They were contemporary symbols.

For Lucas Herron, chairman for decades of Romance Languages, had an insatiable love for words and their odd usages. What was more appropriate than the symbol '30' to indicate finality?

As any first year journalism student would confirm, the number 30 at the bottom of any news copy meant the story was finished. It was over.

There was no more to be said.

Matlock held the photograph upside down in his left hand, his right gripping the flashlight. He entered the woods at mid-section – slightly to the left – as indicated on the diagram. The figure 30 could be feet, yards, meters, paces – certainly not inches.

He marked off thirty twelve-inch spaces. Thirty feet straight, thirty feet to the right.

Nothing.

Nothing but the drenched, full overgrowth and underbrush which clawed at his feet.

He returned to the green wall's entrance and decided to combine yards and paces, realizing that paces in such a dense, junglelike environment might vary considerably.

He marked off the spot thirty paces directly ahead and continued until he estimated the point of yardage. Then he returned to the bent branches where he had figured thirty paces to be and began the lateral trek.

Again nothing. An old rotted maple stood near one spot Matlock estimated was thirty steps. There was nothing else unusual. He went back to the bent branches and proceeded to his second mark.

Thirty yards straight out. Ninety feet, give or take a foot or two. Then the slow process of thirty yards through the soaking wet foliage to his next mark. Another ninety feet. Altogether, one hundred and eighty feet. Nearly two-thirds of a football field.

The going was slower now, the foliage thicker, or so it seemed. Matlock wished he had a machete or at least some kind of implement to force the wet branches out of his way. Once he lost count and had to keep in mind the variation as he proceeded – was it twenty-one or twenty-three large steps? Did it matter? Would the difference of three to six feet really matter?

He reached the spot. It was either twenty-eight or thirty. Close enough if there was anything to be seen. He pointed the flashlight to the ground and began slowly moving it back and forth laterally.

Nothing. Only the sight of a thousand glistening weeds and the deep-brown color of soaked earth. He kept swinging the beam of light, inching forward as he did so, straining his eyes, wondering every other second if he had just covered that particular section or not – everything looked so alike.

The chances of failure grew. He could go back and begin again, he thought. Perhaps the 30s connoted some other form of measurement. Meters, perhaps, or multiples of another number buried somewhere in the diagram. The dots? Should he count the dots on the bottom and top of the rectangle? Why were the dots there?

He had covered the six-foot variation and several feet beyond.

Nothing.

His mind returned to the dots, and he withdrew the photograph from his inside pocket. As he positioned himself to stand up straight, to stretch the muscles at the base of his spine – pained by crouching – his foot touched a hard, unyielding surface. At first he thought it was a fallen limb, or perhaps a rock.

And then he knew it was neither.

He couldn't see it – whatever it was, was underneath a clump of overgrown weeds. But he could feel the outline of the object with his foot. It was straight, precisely tooled. It was no part of a forest.

He held the light over the cluster of weeds and saw that they weren't weeds. They were some kind of small-budded flower in partial bloom. A flower which did not need sunlight or space.

A jungle flower. Out of place, purchased, replanted.

He pushed them out of the way and bent down. Underneath was a thick, heavily varnished slab of wood about two feet wide and perhaps a foot and a half long. It had sunk an inch or two into the ground; the surface had been sanded and varnished so often that the layers of protective coating reached a high gloss, reflecting the beam of the flashlight as though it were glass.

Matlock dug his fingers into the earth and lifted up the slab. Beneath it was a weathered metal plaque, bronze perhaps.

For Major Lucas N. Herron, USMCR
In Gratitude from the Officers and Men of Bravo Company,
Fourteenth Raider Battalion, First Marine Division
Solomon Islands – South Pacific
May 1943

Seeing it set in the ground under the glare of light, Matlock had the feeling he was looking at a grave.

He pushed away the surrounding mud and dug a tiny trench around the metal. On his hands and knees, he slowly, awkwardly lifted the plaque up and carefully placed it to one side.

He had found it.

Buried in earth was a metal container – the type used in library archives for valuable manuscripts. Airtight, weatherproofed, vacuumed, a receptacle for the ages.

A coffin, Matlock thought.

He picked it up and inserted his cold, wet fingers under the lever of the coiled hasp. It took considerable strength to pull it up, but finally it was released. There was the rush of air one hears upon opening a tin of coffee. The rubber edges parted. Inside Matlock could see an oilcloth packet in the shape of a notebook.

He knew he'd found the indictment.

Thirty

The notebook was thick, over three hundred pages, and every word was handwritten in ink. It was in the form of a diary, but the lengthy entries varied enormously. There was no consistency regarding dates. Often days followed one another; at other times entries were separated by weeks, even months. The writing also varied. There were stretches of lucid narrative followed by incoherent, disjointed rambling. In the latter sections the hand had shaken, the words were often illegible.

Lucas Herron's diary was a cry of anguish, an outpouring of pain. A confessional of a man beyond hope.

As he sat on the cold wet ground, mesmerized by Herron's words, Matlock understood the motives behind Herron's Nest, the forbidding green wall, the window shades, the total isolation.

Lucas Herron had been a drug addict for a quarter of a century. Without the drugs, his pain was unendurable. And there was absolutely nothing anyone could do for him except confine him to a ward in a Veterans' Hospital for the remainder of his unnatural life.

It was the rejection of this living death that had plunged Lucas Herron into another.

Major Lucas Nathaniel Herron, USMCR, attached to Amphibious Assault Troops, Raider Battalions, Fleet Marine Force, Pacific, had led numerous companies of the Fourteenth Battalion, First Marine Division, in ranger assaults on various islands throughout the Japanese-held Solomons and Carolinas.

And Major Lucas Herron had been carried off the tiny island of Peleliu in the Carolinas on a stretcher, having brought two companies back to the beach through jungle fire. None thought he could survive.

Major Lucas Herron had a Japanese bullet imbedded at the base of his neck, lodged in a section of his nervous system. He was not expected to live. The doctors, first in Brisbane, then San Diego, and finally at Bethesda, considered further operations unfeasible. The patient could not survive them; he would be reduced to a vegetable should even the slightest complication set in. No one wished to be responsible for that.

They put the patient under heavy medication to relieve the discomfort of his wounds. And he lay there in the Maryland hospital for over two years.

The stages of healing – partial recovery – were slow and painful. First, there were the neck braces and the pills; then the braces and the metal frames for walking, and still the pills. At last the crutches, along with the braces and always the pills. Lucas Herron came back to the land of the living – but not without the pills. And in moments of torment – the needle of morphine at night.

There were hundreds, perhaps thousands, like Lucas Herron, but few had his extraordinary qualifications – for those who sought him out. An authentic hero of the Pacific war, a brilliant scholar, a man above reproach.

He was perfect. He could be used perfectly.

On the one hand, he could not live, could not endure, without the relief afforded him by the narcotics – the pills and the increasingly frequent needles. On the other hand, if the degree of his dependence was known medically, he would be returned to a hospital ward.

These alternatives were gradually, subtly made clear to him. Gradually in the sense that his sources of supply needed favors now and then – a contact to be made in Boston, men to be paid in New York. Subtly in that when Herron questioned the involvement, he was told it was really quite harmless. Harmless but *necessary*.

As the years went by, he became enormously valuable to the men he needed so badly. The contact in Boston, the men to be paid in New York, became more and more frequent, more and more *necessary*. Then Lucas was sent farther and farther afield. Winter vacations, spring midterms, summers: Canada, Mexico, France . . . the Mediterranean.

He became a courier.

And always the thought of the hospital ward on his tortured body and brain.

They had manipulated him brilliantly. He was never exposed to the results of his work, never specifically aware of the growing network of destruction he was helping to build. And when finally he learned of it all, it was too late. The network had been built.

Nimrod had his power.

'*April 22, 1951*. At midterm they're sending me back to Mexico. I'll stop at the U. of M. – as usual – and on the way back at Baylor. A touch of irony: the bursar here called me in, saying Carlyle would be pleased to help defray my "research" expenses. I declined, and told him the *disability allowance* was sufficient. Perhaps I should have accepted. . . .

'*June 13, 1956*. To Lisbon for three weeks. A routing map, I'm told, for a small ship. Touching the Azores, through Cuba (a mess!), finally into Panama. Stops – for me – at the Sorbonne, U. of Toledo, U. of Madrid. I'm becoming an academic gadfly! I'm not happy about methods – who could be? – but neither am I responsible for the archaic laws. So many, many can be helped. They need help! I've been in touch with scores on the telephone

– they put me in touch – men like myself who couldn't face another day without help. . . . Still, I worry. . . . Still, what can I do? Others would do it, if not me. . . .

'*February 24, 1957*. I'm alarmed but calm and responsible (I hope!) about my concerns. I'm told now that when they send me to make contacts I am the *messenger* from "*Nimrod*"! The name is a code – a meaningless artifice, they say – and will be honored. It's all so foolish – like the intelligence information we'd receive from MacArthur's HQ in So-Pac. *They* had *all* the codes and *none* of the *facts*. . . . The pain is worse, the medics said it would get worse. But . . . "Nimrod's" considerate. . . . As I am. . . .

'*March 10, 1957*. They were angry with me! They withheld my dosage for two days – I thought I would kill myself! I started out in my car for the VA hospital in Hartford, but they stopped me on the highway. They were in a Carlyle *patrol car* – I should have known they had the police here! . . . It was either *compromise* or the *ward*! . . . They were right! . . . I'm off to Canada and the job is to bring in a man from North Africa . . . I *must* do it! The calls to me are constant. This evening a man – Army, 27th – Naha casualty – from East Orange, N.J., said that he and six others *depended* on me! There are so many like ourselves! Why? Why, for God's sake, are we *despised*? We need *help* and all that's offered to us are the *wards*!. . .

'*August 19, 1960*. I've made my position clear! They go too far! . . . "Nimrod" is not just a code name for a location, it's also a *man*! The geography doesn't change but the man does. They're not helping men like me any longer – well, maybe they are – but it's more than *us*! They're reaching out – they're *attracting* people – for a great deal of money! . . .

'*August 20, 1960*. Now they're threatening me. They say I'll have no more once my cabinet's empty. . . . I don't care! I've enough for a week – with luck – a week and a half. . . . I wish I liked alcohol more, or that it didn't make me sick. . . .

'*August 28, 1960*. I shook to my ankles but I went to the Carlyle Police Station. I wasn't thinking. I asked to speak with the highest man in authority and they said it was after five o'clock – he had gone home. So I said I had information about narcotics and within ten minutes the chief of police showed up. . . . By now I was obvious – I couldn't control myself – I urinated through my trousers. The chief of police took me into a small room and opened his kit and administered a needle. He was from Nimrod! . . .

'*October 7, 1965*. This Nimrod is displeased with me. I've always gotten along with the Nimrods – the two I've met, but this one is sterner, more concerned with my accomplishments. I refuse to touch *students*, he accepts that, but he says I am getting silly in my classroom lectures, I'm not bearing down. He doesn't care that I don't *solicit* – he doesn't want me to – but he tells me that I should be – well, be more conservative in my outlook. . . .

It's strange. His name is Matthew Orton and he's an insignificant aide to the lieutenant governor in Hartford. But he's Nimrod. And I'll obey. . . .

'*November 14, 1967.* The back is intolerable now – the doctors said it would *disintegrate* – that was *their* word – but not like *this*! I can get through forty minutes of a lecture and then I *must* excuse myself! . . . I ask always – is it worth it? . . . It must be or I wouldn't go on. . . . Or am I simply too great an egoist – or too much a coward – to take my life? . . . Nimrod sees me tonight. In a week it's *Thanksgiving* – I wonder where I will go. . . .

'*January 27, 1970.* It *has* to be the end now. In C. Fry's beautiful words, the "seraphic strawberry, beaming in its bed" must turn and show its nettles. There's nothing more for me and Nimrod has infected too many, too completely. I will take my life – as painlessly as possible – there's been so much pain. . . .

'*January 28, 1970.* I've tried to kill myself! I can't *do* it! I bring the gun, then the knife to the point, but it *will not happen*! Am I *really* so infused, so infected that I cannot accomplish that which is most to be desired? . . . Nimrod will kill me. I know that and he knows it better.

'*January 29, 1970. Nimrod –* he's now *Arthur Latona!* Unbelievable! The same *Arthur Latona* who built the middle-income housing projects in Mount Holly! – At any rate, he's given me an unacceptable order. I've *told* him it's *unacceptable.* I'm far too valuable to be discarded and I've told him that, *too.* . . . He wants me to carry a great deal of money to Toros Daglari in Turkey! . . . Why, oh why, can't my life be *ended*? . . .

'*April 18, 1971.* It's a wondrously strange world. To survive, to exist and breathe the air, one does so much one comes to loathe. The total is frightening . . . the excuses and the rationalizations are worse. . . . Then something happens which suspends – or at least postpones – all necessity of judgment. . . . The pains shifted from the neck and spine to the lower sides. I knew it had to be something else. Something *more.* . . . I went to Nimrod's doctor – as I must – always. My weight has dropped, my reflexes are pathetic. He's worried and tomorrow I enter the private hospital in Southbury. He says for an exploratory. . . . I know they'll do their best for me. They have other trips – very important trips, Nimrod says. I'll be traveling throughout most of the summer, he tells me. . . . If it wasn't me, it would be someone else. The pains are terrible.

'*May 22, 1971.* The old, tired soldier is home. Herron's Nest is my salvation! I'm minus a kidney. No telling yet about the other, the doctor says. But I know better. I'm dying. . . . Oh, God, I welcome it! There'll be no more trips, no more threats. Nimrod can do no more. . . . They'll keep me alive, too. As long as they can. *They have to now!* . . . I hinted to the doctor that I've kept a record over the years. He just stared at me speechless. I've never seen a man so frightened. . . .

'*May 23, 1971.* Latona – Nimrod – dropped by this morning. Before he could discuss anything, I told him I knew I was dying. That nothing mattered to me now – the decision to end my life was made, not by me. I even told him that I was prepared – relieved; that I had tried to end it myself but couldn't. He asked about "*what you told the doctor.*" He wasn't able to say the *words*! His *fear* blanketed the living room like a heavy mist. . . . . I answered calmly, with great authority, I think. I told him that whatever records there were would be given to him – *if my last days or months were made easier for me.* He was furious but he knew there wasn't anything he could do. What can a person do with an old man in pain who knows he's going to die? What arguments are left?

'*August 14, 1971.* Nimrod is dead! Latona died of a coronary! Before *me*, and there's irony in that! . . . Still the business continues without change. Still I'm brought my supplies every week and every week the frightened messengers ask the questions – where are they? Where are the records? – they come close to threatening me but I remind them that Nimrod had the word of a dying old man. Why would I change that? . . . They retreat into their fear. . . . A new Nimrod will be chosen soon. . . . I've said I didn't want to know – and I don't!

'*September 20, 1971.* A new year begins for Carlyle. My last year, I know that – what responsibilities I can assume, that is. . . . Nimrod's death has given me courage. Or is it the knowledge of my own? God knows I can't undo much but I can try! . . . I'm reaching out, I'm finding a few who've been hurt badly, and if nothing else I offer help. It may only be words, or advice, but just the knowledge that *I've been there* seems to be comforting. It's always such a shock to those I speak with! Imagine! The "grand old bird"! The pains and the numbness are nearly intolerable. I may not be able to wait. . . .

'*December 23, 1971.* Two days before my last Christmas. I've said to so many who've asked me to their homes that I was going into New York. Of course, it's not so. I'll spend the days here at the Nest. . . . A disturbing note. The messengers tell me that the new Nimrod is the sternest, strongest one of all. They say he's ruthless. He orders executions as easily as his predecessors issued simple requests. Or are they telling me these things to frighten me? That can't frighten me!

'*February 18, 1972.* The doctor told me that he'd prescribe heavier "medication" but warned me not to overdose. He, too, spoke of the new Nimrod. Even he's worried – he implied that the man was mad. I told him I didn't want to know anything. I was out of it.

'*February 26, 1972.* I can't believe it! Nimrod *is* a *monster*! He's *got* to be *insane*! He's demanded that all those who've been working here over three years be cut off – sent out of the country – and if they refuse – be killed!

The doctor's leaving next week. Wife, family, practice. . . . Latona's widow was murdered in an "automobile accident"! One of the messengers – Pollizzi – was shot to death in New Haven. Another – Capalbo – OD'd and the rumor is that the dose was administered!

'*April 5, 1972.* From Nimrod to me – deliver to the messenger any and all records or he'll shut off my supplies. My house will be watched around the clock. I'll be followed wherever I go. I'll not be allowed to get any medical attention whatsoever. The combined effects of the cancer and the withdrawal will be beyond anything I can imagine. What Nimrod doesn't know is that before he left the doctor gave me enough for several months. He frankly didn't believe I'd last that long. . . . For the first time in this terrible, horrible life, I'm dealing from a position of strength. My life is firmer than ever because of death.

'*April 10, 1972.* Nimrod is near the point of hysterics with me. He's threatened to expose me – which is meaningless. I've let him know that through the messengers. He's said that he'll destroy the whole Carlyle campus, but if he does that he'll destroy himself as well. The rumor is that he's calling together a conference. An important meeting of powerful men. . . . My house is now watched – as Nimrod said it would be – around the clock. By the Carlyle police, of course. Nimrod's private army!

'*April 22, 1972.* Nimrod has won! It's horrifying, but he's won! He sent me two newspaper clippings. In each a student was killed by an overdose. The first a girl in Cambridge, the second a boy from Trinity. He says that he'll keep adding to the list for every week I withhold the records. . . . Hostages are executed! – He's got to be *stopped*! But how? What can I *do*? . . . I've got a plan but I don't know if I can do it – I'm going to try to *manufacture* records. Leave them intact. It will be difficult – my hands shake so sometimes! Can I possibly get through it? – I have to. I said I'd deliver a *few* at a time. For my *own* protection. I wonder if he'll agree to that?

'*April 24, 1972.* Nimrod's unbelievably evil, but he's a realist. He knows he can do nothing else! We both are racing against the time of my death. Stalemate! I'm alternating between a typewriter and different fountain pens and various types of paper. The killings are suspended but I'm told they will resume if I miss *one* delivery! Nimrod's hostages are in my hands! Their executions can be prevented only by me!

'*April 27, 1972.* Something strange is happening! The Beeson boy phoned our contact at Admissions. Jim Matlock was there and Beeson suspects him. He asked questions, made an ass of himself with Beeson's wife. . . . Matlock isn't on any list! He's no part of Nimrod – on either side. He's never purchased a thing, never sold. . . . The Carlyle patrol cars are always outside now. Nimrod's army is alerted. What is it?

'*April 27, 1972 – P.M.* The messengers came – two of them – and what they led me to believe is so incredible I cannot write it here. . . . I've never asked the identity of Nimrod, I never wanted to know. But panic's rampant now, something is happening beyond even Nimrod's control. And the messengers told me who Nimrod is. . . . They *lie! I cannot, will not believe it!* If it is true we are all in hell!'

Matlock stared at the last entry helplessly. The handwriting was hardly readable; most of the words were connected with one another as if the writer could not stop the pencil from racing ahead.

'*April 28.* Matlock was here. He knows! Others know! He says the government men are involved now. . . . It's over! But what they can't understand is what will happen – a bloodbath, killings – executions! Nimrod can do *no less!* There will be so much *pain.* There will be mass killing and it will be provoked by an insignificant teacher of the Elizabethans. . . . A messenger called. Nimrod *himself* is coming out. It is a confrontation. Now I'll know the truth – who he really is. . . . If he's who I've been led to believe – somehow I'll get this record out – somehow. It's all that's left. It's my turn to threaten. . . . It's over now. The pain will soon be over, too. . . . There's been so much pain . . . I'll make one final entry when I'm sure. . . .'

Matlock closed the notebook. What had the girl named Jeannie said? *They* have the *courts,* the *police,* the *doctors.* And Alan Pace. He'd added the major university administrations – all over the Northeast. Whole academic policies; employments, deployments, curriculums – sources of enormous financing. *They* have it *all.*

But Matlock had the indictment.

It was enough. Enough to stop Nimrod – whoever he was. Enough to stop the bloodbath, the executions.

Now he *had* to reach Jason Greenberg.

Alone.

Thirty-one

Carrying the oilcloth packet, he began walking toward the town of Carlyle, traveling the back roads on which there was rarely any night traffic. He knew it would be too dangerous to drive. The man in the field had probably recovered sufficiently to reach someone – reach Nimrod. An alarm would be sent out for him. The unseen armies would be after him now. His only chance was to reach Greenberg. Jason Greenberg would tell him what to do.

There was blood on his shirt, mud caked on his trousers and jacket. His appearance brought to mind the outcasts of Bill's Bar & Grill by the railroad freight yards. It was nearly two-thirty in the morning, but such places stayed open most of the night. The blue laws were only conveniences for them, not edicts. He reached College Parkway and descended the hill to the yards.

He brushed his damp clothes as best he could and covered the bloodstained shirt with his jacket. He walked into the filthy bar; the layers of cheap smoke were suspended above the disheveled customers. A jukebox was playing some Slovak music, men were yelling, a stand-up shuffleboard was being abused. Matlock knew he melted into the atmosphere. He would find a few precious moments of relief.

He sat down at a back booth.

'What the hell happened to *you?*'

It was the bartender, the same suspicious bartender whom he'd finally befriended several days ago. Years . . . ages ago.

'Caught in the rainstorm. Fell a couple of times. Lousy whisky. . . . Have you got anything to eat?'

'Cheese sandwiches. The meat I wouldn't give you. Bread's not too fresh either.'

'I don't care. Bring me a couple of sandwiches. And a glass of beer. Would you do that?'

'Sure. Sure, mister. . . . You sure you want to eat here? I mean, I can tell, this ain't your kind of place, you know what I mean?'

There it was again. The incessant, irrelevant question; the dangling interrogative. *You know what I mean . . .?* Not a question at all. Even in his few moments of relief he had to hear it once more.

'I know what you mean . . . but I'm sure.'

'It's your stomach.' The bartender trudged back to his station.

Matlock found Greenberg's number and went to the foul-smelling pay phone on the wall. He inserted a coin and dialed.

'I'm sorry, sir,' the operator said, 'the telephone is disconnected. Do you have another number where the party can be reached?'

'Try it again! I'm sure you're wrong.'

She did and she wasn't. The supervisor in Wheeling, West Virginia, finally informed the operator in Carlyle, Connecticut, that any calls to a Mr. Greenberg were to be routed to Washington, D.C. It was assumed that whoever was calling would know where in Washington.

'But Mr. Greenberg isn't expected at the Washington number until early A.M.,' she said. 'Please inform the party on the line.'

He tried to think. Could he trust calling Washington, the Department of Justice, Narcotics Division? Under the circumstances, might not Washington – for the sake of speed – alert someone in the Hartford vicinity to get to him? And Greenberg had made it clear – he didn't trust the Hartford office, the Hartford agents.

He understood Greenberg's concern far better now. He had only to think of the Carlyle police – Nimrod's private army.

No, he wouldn't call Washington. He'd call Sealfont. His last hope was the university president. He dialed Sealfont's number.

'James! Good Lord, James! Are you all right?! Where in heaven's name have you *been*?!'

'To places I never knew were there. Never knew existed.'

'But you're all right? That's all that matters! Are you all right?!'

'Yes, sir. And I've got everything. I've got it all. Herron wrote everything down. It's a record of twenty-three years.'

'Then he *was* part of it?'

'Very much so.'

'Poor, *sick* man. . . . I don't understand. However, that's not important now. That's for the authorities. Where are you? I'll send a car. . . . No, I'll come myself. We've all been so worried. I've been in constant touch with the men at the Justice Department.'

'Stay where you are,' Matlock said quickly. 'I'll get to you myself – everyone knows your car. It'll be less dangerous this way. I know they're looking for me. I'll have a man here call me a taxi. I just wanted to make sure you were home.'

'Whatever you say. I must tell you I'm relieved. I'll call Kressel. Whatever you have to say, he should know about it. That's the way it's to be.'

'I agree, sir. See you shortly.'

He went back to the booth and began to eat the unappetizing sandwiches. He had swallowed half the beer when from inside his damp jacket, the short, hysterical beeps of Blackstone's Tel-electronic seared into his ears. He pulled out the machine and pressed the button. Without thinking of anything but the number 555-6868 he jumped up from the seat and walked rapidly back to the telephone. His hand trembling, he awkwardly manipulated the coin and dialed.

The recorded words were like the lash of a whip across his face.

'Charger Three-zero is canceled.'

Then there was silence. As Blackstone had promised, there was nothing else but the single sentence – stated but once. There was no one to speak to, no appeal. Nothing.

But there had to be! He would not, *could not*, be cut off like this! If Blackstone was canceling him, he had a right to know *why*! He had a right to know that Pat was *safe*!

It took several minutes and a number of threats before he reached Blackstone himself.

'I don't have to talk to you!' The sleepy voice was belligerent. 'I made that clear! . . . But I don't mind because if I can put a trace on this call I'll tell them where to find you the second you hang up!'

'Don't threaten me! You've got too much of my money to threaten me. . . . Why am I canceled? I've got a right to know that.'

'Because you stink! You stink like garbage!'

'That's not good enough! That doesn't *mean* anything!'

'I'll give you the rundown then. A warrant is out for you. Signed by the court and . . .'

'For *what*, goddamn it?! Protective custody?! *Preventive detention?!*'

'For *murder*, Matlock! For conspiracy to distribute *narcotics*! For aiding and abetting known narcotics *distributors*! . . . You sold *out*! Like I said, you *smell*! And I hate the business you're in!'

Matlock was stunned. Murder? Conspiracy! What was Blackstone talking about?

'I don't know what you've been told, but it's not true. None of it's *true*! I risked my life, my *life*, do you *hear* me! To bring what I've got . . .'

'You're a good talker,' interrupted Blackstone, 'but you're careless! You're also a ghoulish bastard! There's a guy in a field outside of Carlyle with his throat slit. It didn't take the government boys ten minutes to trace that Ford wagon to its owner!'

'I didn't *kill* that man! I swear to Christ I *didn't kill him*!'

'No, of course not! And you didn't even *see* the fellow whose head you shot off at East Gorge, did you? Except that there's a parking lot attendant and a couple of others who've got you on the scene! . . . I forgot. You're also stupid. You left the parking ticket under your windshield wiper!'

'No, wait a minute! *Wait a minute!* This is all *crazy*! The man at East Gorge asked to meet me there! He tried to *murder me*!'

'Tell that to your lawyer. We got the whole thing – straight – from the Justice boys! I demanded that. I've got a damned good reputation. . . . I'll say this. When you sell out, you sell *high*! Over sixty thousand dollars in a *checking* account. Like I said, you *smell*, Matlock!'

He was so shocked he could not raise his voice. When he spoke, he was out of breath, hardly audible. 'Listen to me. You've *got* to listen to me. Everything you say . . . there are explanations. Except the man in the field. I don't understand that. But I don't care if you believe me or not. It doesn't matter. I'm holding in my hand all the vindication I'll ever need. . . . What *does* matter is that you watch *that girl*! Don't cancel me out! *Watch her!*'

'Apparently you don't understand English very well. You *are* canceled! Charger Three-zero is *canceled*!'

'What about the girl?'

'We're not irresponsible,' said Blackstone bitterly. 'She's perfectly safe. She's under the protection of the Carlyle police.'

There was a general commotion at the bar. The bartender was closing up and his customers resented it. Obscenities were shouted back and forth over the beer-soaked, filthy mahogany, while cooler or more drunken heads slowly weaved their way toward the front door.

Paralysed, Matlock stood by the foul-smelling telephone. The roaring at the bar reached a crescendo but he heard nothing; the figures in front of his eyes were only blurs. He felt sick to his stomach, and so he held the front of his trousers, the oilcloth packet with Lucas Herron's notebook between his hands and his belt. He thought he was going to be sick as he had been sick beside the corpse on the East Gorge slope.

But – there was no time. Pat was held by Nimrod's private army. He had to act *now*. And when he acted, the spring would be sprung. There would be no rewinding.

The horrible truth was that he didn't know where to begin.

'What's the matter, mister? The sandwiches?'

'What?'

'Ya look like you're gonna throw up.'

'Oh? . . . No.' Matlock saw for the first time that almost everyone had left the place.

The notebook! The notebook would be the ransom! There would be no tortured decision – not for the plastic men! Not for the *manipulators*! Nimrod could have the notebook! The indictment!

But then what? Would Nimrod let her live? Let him live?! . . . What had Lucas Herron written: 'The new Nimrod is a monster . . . ruthless. He orders executions. . . .'

Nimrod had murdered with far less motive than someone's knowledge of Lucas Herron's diaries.

'Look, mister. I'm sorry, but I gotta close up.'

'Will you call a taxi for me, please?'

'A taxi? It's after three o'clock. Even if there was one, he wouldn't come down *here* at three o'clock in the morning.'

'Have you got a car?'

'Now wait a minute, mister. I gotta clean up and ring out. I had some action tonight. The register'll take me twenty minutes.'

Matlock withdrew his bills. The smallest denomination was a hundred. 'I've got to have a car – right away. How much do you want? I'll bring it back in an hour – maybe less.'

The bartender looked at Matlock's money. It wasn't a normal sight. 'It's a pretty old heap. You might have trouble driving it.'

'I can drive *anything*! Here! Here's a hundred! If I wreck it you can have the whole roll. Here! Take it, for Christ's sake!'

'Sure. Sure, mister.' The bartender reached under his apron and took out his car keys. 'The square one's the ignition. It's parked in the rear. Sixty-two Chevy. Go out the back door.'

'Thanks.' Matlock started for the door indicated by the bartender.

'Hey, mister!'

'What?'

'What's your name again? . . . Something "rock"? I forgot. I mean, for Christ's sake, I give you the car, I don't even know your name!'

Matlock thought for a second. 'Rod. Nimrod. The name's Nimrod.'

'That's no name, mister.' The burly man started toward Matlock. 'That's a spin fly for catchin' trout. Now, what's your name? You got my car, I gotta know your name.'

Matlock still held the money in his hand. He peeled off three additional hundreds and threw them on the floor. It seemed right. He had given Kramer four hundred dollars for his station wagon. There should be symmetry somewhere. Or, at least, meaningless logic.

'That's four hundred dollars. You couldn't get four hundred dollars for a '62 Chevy. I'll bring it back!' He ran for the door. The last words he heard were those of the grateful but confused manager of Bill's Bar & Grill.

'Nimrod. Fuckin' joker!'

The car was a heap, as its owner had said. But it moved, and that was all that mattered. Sealfont would help him analyse the facts, the alternatives. Two opinions were better than one; he was afraid of assuming the total responsibility – he wasn't capable of it. And Sealfont would have people in high places he could contact. Sam Kressel, the liaison, would listen and object and be terrified for his domain. No matter; he'd be dismissed. Pat's safety was uppermost. Sealfont would see that.

Perhaps it was time to threaten – as Herron ultimately had threatened. Nimrod had Pat; he had Herron's indictment. The life of one human being for the protection of hundreds, perhaps thousands. Even Nimrod had to see their bargaining position. It was irrefutable, the odds were on their side.

He realized as he neared the railroad depot that this kind of thinking, by itself, made him a manipulator, too. Pat had been reduced to *quantity X*, Herron's diaries, *quantity Y*. The equation would then be postulated and the mathematical observers would make their decisions based on the data presented. It was the ice-cold logic of survival; emotional factors were disregarded, consciously despised.

Frightening!

He turned right at the station and started to drive up College Parkway.

Sealfont's mansion stood at the end. He went as fast as the '62 Chevy would go, which wasn't much above thirty miles an hour on the hill. The streets were deserted, washed clean by the storm. The store fronts, the houses, and finally the campus were dark and silent.

He remembered that Kressel's house was just a half block off College Parkway on High Street. The detour would take him no more than thirty seconds. It was worth it, he thought. If Kressel hadn't left for Sealfont's, he would pick him up and they could talk on the way over. Matlock *had* to talk, *had* to begin. He couldn't stand the isolation any longer.

He swung the car to the left at the corner of High Street. Kressel's house was a large gray colonial set back from the street by a wide front lawn bordered by rhododendrons. There were lights on downstairs. With luck, Kressel was still home. There were two cars, one in the driveway; Matlock slowed down.

His eyes were drawn to a dull reflection at the rear of the driveway. Kressel's kitchen light was on; the spill from the window illuminated the hood of a third car, and the Kressels were a two-car family.

He looked again at the car in front of the house. It was a Carlyle patrol car. The Carlyle police were in Kressel's house!

Nimrod's private army was with *Kressel*!

Or was Nimrod's private army with *Nimrod*?

He swerved to the left, narrowly missing the patrol car, and sped down the street to the next corner. He turned right and pressed the accelerator to the floor. He was confused, frightened, bewildered. If Sealfont had called Kressel – which he had obviously done – and Kressel worked with Nimrod, or *was* Nimrod, there'd be other patrol cars, other soldiers of the private army waiting for him.

His mind went back to the Carlyle Police Station – a century ago, capsuled in little over a week – the night of Loring's murder. Kressel had disturbed him then. And even before that – with Loring and Greenberg – Kressel's hostility to the federal agents had been outside the bounds of reason.

Oh, Christ! It was so clear now! His instincts had been right. The instincts which had served him as the *hunted* as well as the *hunter* had been true! He'd been watched *too* thoroughly, his every action anticipated. Kressel, the *liaison*, was, in fact, Kressel the tracker, the seeker, the supreme killer.

Nothing was ever as it appeared to be – only what one sensed behind the appearance. Trust the senses.

Somehow he had to get to Sealfont. Warn Sealfont that the Judas was Kressel. Now they *both* had to protect themselves, establish some base from which they could strike back.

Otherwise the girl he loved was lost.

There couldn't be a second wasted. Sealfont had certainly told Kressel that he, Matlock, had Lucas Herron's diaries, and that was all Kressel would need to know. All Nimrod needed to know.

Nimrod had to get possession of both the Corsican paper *and* the diaries; now he knew where they were. His private army would be told that this was its moment of triumph or disaster. They would be waiting for him at Sealfont's; Sealfont's mansion was the trap they expected him to enter.

Matlock swung west at the next corner. In his trouser pocket were his keys, and among them was the key to Pat's apartment. To the best of his knowledge, no one knew he had such a key, certainly no one would expect him to go there. He had to chance it; he couldn't risk going to a public telephone, risk being seen under a street lamp. The patrol cars would be searching everywhere.

He heard the roar of an engine behind him and felt the sharp pain in his stomach. A car was following him – closing in on him. And the '62 Chevrolet was no match for it.

His right leg throbbed from the pressure he exerted on the pedal. His hands gripped the steering wheel as he turned wildly into a side street, the muscles in his arms tensed and aching. Another turn. He spun the wheel to the left, careening off the edge of the curb back into the middle of the road. The car behind him maintained a steady pace, never more than ten feet away, the headlights blinding in the rear-view mirror.

His pursuer was *not* going to close the gap between them! Not then. Not at that moment. He could have done so a hundred, two hundred yards ago. He was waiting. Waiting for something. But what?

There was so *much* he couldn't understand! So much he'd miscalculated, misread. He'd been outmaneuvered at every important juncture. He was what they said – an amateur! He'd been beyond his depth from the beginning. And now, at the last, his final assault was ending in ambush. They would kill him, take the Corsican paper, the diaries of indictment. They would kill the girl he loved, the innocent child whose life he'd thrown away so brutally. Sealfont would be finished – he knew too much now! God knew how many others would be destroyed.

So be it.

If it had to be this way, if hope really had been taken from him, he'd end it all with a gesture, at least. He reached into his belt for the automatic.

The streets they now traveled – the pursuer and the pursued – ran through the outskirts of the campus, consisting mainly of the science buildings and a number of large parking lots. There were no houses to speak of.

He swerved the Chevrolet as far to the right as possible, thrusting his right arm across his chest, the barrel of the pistol outside the car window, pointed at the pursuing automobile.

He fired twice, the car behind him accelerated; he felt the repeated jarring of contact, the metal against metal as the car behind hammered into the Chevrolet's left rear chassis. He pulled again at the trigger of the automatic. Instead of a loud report, he heard and felt only the single click of the firing pin against an unloaded chamber.

Even his last gesture was futile.

His pursuer crashed into him once more. He lost control; the wheel spun, tearing his arm, and the Chevrolet reeled off the road. Frantic, he reached for the door handle, desperately trying to steady the car, prepared to jump if need be.

He stopped all thought; all instincts of survival were arrested. Within those split seconds, time ceased. For the car behind him had drawn parallel and he saw the face of his pursuer.

There were bandages and gauze around the eyes, beneath the glasses, but they could not hide the face of the black revolutionary, Julian Dunois.

It was the last thing he remembered before the Chevrolet swerved to the right and skidded violently off the road's incline.

Blackness.

Thirty-two

Pain roused him. It seemed to be all through his left side. He rolled his head, feeling the pillow beneath him.

The room was dimly lit; what light there was came from a table lamp on the other side. He shifted his head and tried to raise himself on his right shoulder. He pushed his elbow into the mattress, his immobile left arm following the turn of his body like a dead weight.

He stopped abruptly.

Across the room, directly in line with the foot of the bed, sat a man in a chair. At first Matlock couldn't distinguish the features. The light was poor and his eyes were blurred with pain and exhaustion.

Then the man came into focus. He was black and his dark eyes stared at Matlock beneath the perfectly cut semicircle of an Afro haircut. It was Adam Williams, Carlyle University's firebrand of the Black Left.

When Williams spoke, he spoke softly and, unless Matlock misunderstood – once again – there was compassion in the black's voice.

'I'll tell Brother Julian you're awake. He'll come in to see you.' Williams got out of the chair and went to the door. 'You've banged up your left shoulder. Don't try to get out of bed. There are no windows in here. The hallway is guarded. Relax. You need rest.'

'I don't have *time* to rest, you *goddamn fool!*' Matlock tried to raise himself further but the pain was too great. He hadn't adjusted to it.

'You don't have a choice.' Williams opened the door and walked rapidly out, closing it firmly behind him.

Matlock fell back on the pillow . . . Brother Julian. . . . He remembered now. The sight of Julian Dunois's bandaged face watching him through the speeding car window, seemingly inches away from him. And his ears had picked up Dunois's words, his commands to his driver. They had been shouted in his Caribbean dialect.

'Hit him, mon! Hit him again! Drive him *off*, mon!'

And then everything had become dark and the darkness had been filled with violent noise, crashing metal, and he had felt his body twisting, turning, spiraling into the black void.

Oh, God! How long ago was it? He tried to lift up his left hand to look at his watch, but the arm barely moved; the pain was sharp and lingering. He reached over with his right hand to pull the stretch band off his wrist, but it wasn't there. His watch was gone.

He struggled to get up and finally managed to perch on the edge of the bed, his legs touching the floor. He pressed his feet against the wood, thankful that he could sit up. . . . He had to put the pieces together, to reconstruct what had happened, where he was going.

He'd been on his way to Pat's. To find a secluded telephone on which to reach Adrian Sealfont. To warn him that Kressel was the enemy, Kressel was Nimrod. And he'd made up his mind that Herron's diaries would be Pat's ransom. Then the chase had begun, only it wasn't a chase. The car behind him, commanded by Julian Dunois, had played a furious game of terror. It had toyed with him as a lethal mountain cat might play with a wounded goat. Finally it had attacked – steel against steel – and driven him to darkness.

Matlock knew he had to escape. But *from where* and *to whom?*

The door of the windowless room opened. Dunois entered, followed by Williams.

'Good morning,' said the attorney. 'I see you've managed to sit up. That's good. It augurs well for your very abused body.'

'What time is it? Where am I?'

'It's nearly four-thirty. You are in a room at Lumumba Hall. You see? I withhold nothing from you . . . Now, you must reciprocate. You must withhold nothing from me.'

'Listen to me!' Matlock kept his voice steady. 'I have no fight with you, with *any* of you! I've got . . .'

'Oh, I disagree,' Dunois smiled. 'Look at my *face*. It's only through enormous good fortune that I wasn't blinded by you. You tried to crush the lenses of my glasses into my eyes. Can you imagine how my work would suffer if I were blind?'

'Goddamn it! You filled me with acid!'

'And you provoked it! You were actively engaged in pursuits inimicable to our brothers! Pursuits you had no *right* to engage in! . . . But this is concentric debate. It will get us nowhere. . . . We *do* appreciate what you've brought us. Beyond our most optimistic ambitions.'

'You've got the notebook. . . .'

'*And* the Corsican document. The Italian invitation we knew existed. The notebook was only a rumor. A rumor which was fast being ascribed to fiction until tonight – this morning. You should feel proud. You've accomplished what scores of your more experienced betters failed to accomplish. You found the treasure. The *real* treasure.'

'I've got to have it back!'

'Fat chance!' said Williams, leaning against the wall, watching.

'If I don't get it back, a girl will *die*! Do whatever you goddamn well please with me, but let me *use* it to get her back. Christ! Please, *please*!'

'You feel deeply, don't you? I see tears in your eyes. . . .'

'Oh, *Jesus*! You're an *educated man*! You can't *do* this! . . . *Listen!* Take whatever information you want out of it! Then give it to me and let me go! . . . I swear to you I'll come back. Give her a chance. Just give her a *chance*!'

Dunois walked slowly to the chair by the wall, the chair in which Adam Williams sat when Matlock awoke. He pulled it forward, closer to the bed, and sat down, crossing his knees gracefully. 'You feel helpless, don't you? Perhaps . . . even without hope.'

'I've been through a great deal!'

'I'm sure you have. And you appeal to my reason . . . as an *educated man*. You realize that it is within my scope to help you and therefore I am superior to you. You would not make such an appeal if it were not so.'

'Oh, Christ! Cut that out!'

'Now you know what it's like. You are helpless. Without hope. You wonder if your appeal will be lost on a deaf ear. . . . Do you really, for one second, think that I care for the life of Miss Ballantyne? Do you honestly believe she has any priority for me? Any more than the lives of *our* children, *our* loved ones mean anything to you!'

Matlock knew he had to answer Dunois. The black would offer nothing if he evaded him. It was another game – and he had to play, if only briefly.

'I don't deserve this and you know it. I loathe the people who won't do anything for them. You know me – you've made that clear. So you must know that.'

'Ahh, but I *don't* know it! You're the one who made the choice, the decision to work for the superior mon! The *Washington* mon! For decades, two *centuries*, *my* people have appealed to the *superior Washington mon*! "Help us," they cry. "Don't leave us without hope!" they scream. But nobody listens. Now, you expect me to listen to you?'

'Yes, I *do*! Because I'm not your enemy. I may not be everything you want me to be, but I'm not your enemy. If you turn me – and men like me – into objects of hatred, you're *finished*. You're out-numbered, don't forget that, Dunois. We won't storm the barricades every time you yell "foul," but we hear you. We're willing to help; we want to help.'

Dunois looked coldly at Matlock. 'Prove it.'

Matlock returned the black's stare. 'Use me as your bait, your hostage. Kill me if you have to. But get the girl out.'

'We can do that – the hostaging, the killing – without your consent. Brave but hardly proof.'

Matlock refused to allow Dunois to disengage the stare between them. He spoke softly. 'I'll give you a statement. Written, verbal – on tape; freely, without force or coercion. I'll spell it all out. How I was used, what I did. Everything. You'll have your Washington men as well as Nimrod.'

Dunois folded his arms and matched Matlock's quiet voice. 'You realize you would put an end to your professional life; this life you love so much. No university administration worthy of its name would consider you for a position. You'd never be trusted again. By any factions. You'd become a pariah.'

'You asked for proof. It's all I can offer you.'

Dunois sat immobile in the chair. Williams had straightened up from his slouching position against the wall. No one spoke for several moments. Finally Dunois smiled gently. His eyes, surrounded by the gauze, were compassionate.

'You're a good man. Inept, perhaps, but persevering. You shall have the help you need. We won't leave you without hope. Do you agree, Adam?'

'Agreed.'

Dunois got out of the chair and approached Matlock.

'You've heard the old cliché, that politics has strange bedfellows. Conversely, practical objectives often make for strange political alliances. History bears this out. . . . We want this Nimrod as much as you do. As well as the Mafiosi he tries to make peace with. It is they and their kind who prey upon the children. An example must be made. An example which will instill terror in other Nimrods, other Mafiosi. . . . You shall have help, but this is the condition we demand.'

'What do you mean?'

'The disposition of Nimrod and the others will be left to us. We don't trust your judges and your juries. Your courts are corrupt, your legalistics no more than financial manipulations. . . . The barrio addict is thrown into jail. The rich gangsters appeal. . . . No, the disposition must be left to us.'

'I don't care about that. You can do whatever you like.'

'Your not caring is insufficient. We demand more than that. We must have our guarantee.'

'How can I give a guarantee?'

'By your silence. By not acknowledging our presence. We will take the Corsican paper and somehow we will find the conference and be admitted. We will extract what we want from the diaries – that's being done now, incidentally. . . . But your *silence* is the paramount issue. We will help you now – on a best-efforts basis, of course – but you must never mention our involvement. Irrespective of what may happen, you must not, directly or indirectly, allude to our participation. Should you do so, we will take your life and the life of the girl. Is this understood?'

'It is.'

'Then we are in agreement?'

'We are.'

'Thank you,' said Dunois, smiling.

Thirty-three

As Julian Dunois outlined their alternatives and began to formulate strategy, it became clearer to Matlock why the blacks had sought him out with such concentration – and why Dunois was willing to offer help. He, Matlock, had the basic information they needed. Who were his contacts? Both inside and without the university? Who and where were the government men? How were communications expedited?

In other words – whom should Julian Dunois *avoid* in his march to Nimrod?

'I must say, you were extraordinarily unprepared for contingencies,' Dunois said. 'Very slipshod.'

'That occurred to me, too. But I think I was only partially to blame.'

'I dare say you were!' Dunois laughed, joined by Williams. The three men remained in the windowless room. A card table had been brought in along with several yellow pads. Dunois had begun writing down every bit of information Matlock supplied. He double-checked the spelling of names, the accuracy of addresses – a professional at work; Matlock once again experienced the feeling of inadequacy he had felt when talking with Greenberg.

Dunois stapled a number of pages together and started on a fresh pad. 'What are you doing?' asked Matlock.

'These will be duplicated by a copier downstairs. The information will be sent to my office in New York. . . . As will a photostat of every page in Professor Herron's notebook.'

'You don't fool around, do you?'

'In a word – no.'

'It's all I've got to give you. Now, what do we do? What do *I* do? I'm frightened, I don't have to tell you that. I can't even let myself think what might happen to her.'

'*Nothing* will happen. Believe me when I tell you that. At the moment, your Miss Ballantyne is as safe as if she were in her mother's arms. Or yours. She's the bait, not you. The bait will be kept fresh and unspoiled. For you have what they want. They can't survive without it.'

'Then let's make the offer. The sooner the better.'

'Don't worry. It will be made. But we must decide carefully – aware of the nuances – how we do it. So far, we have two alternatives, we agreed upon that. The first is Kressel, himself. The direct confrontation. The second, to use the police department, to let your message to Nimrod be delivered through it.'

'Why do that? Use the police?'

'I'm only listing alternatives . . . Why the police? I'm not sure. Except that the Herron diaries state clearly that Nimrod was replaced in the past. This current Nimrod is the third since the position's inception, is that not correct?'

'Yes. The first was a man named Orton in the lieutenant governor's office. The second, Angelo Latona, a builder. The third, obviously, Kressel. What's your point?'

'I'm speculating. Whoever assumes the position of Nimrod has authoritarian powers. Therefore, it is the position, not the man. The man can make whatever he can of the office.'

'But the office,' interrupted Williams, 'is given and taken away. Nimrod isn't the last voice.'

'Exactly. Therefore, it might be to Matlock's advantage to let the word leak out very specifically that it is *he* who possesses the weapon. That Kressel – Nimrod – must exercise great caution. For everyone's sake.'

'Wouldn't that mean that more people would be after me?'

'Possibly. Conversely, it could mean that there'd be a legion of anxious criminals protecting you. Until the threat you impose is eliminated. No one will act rashly until that threat is taken away. No one will want Nimrod to act rashly.'

Matlock lit a cigarette, listening intently. 'What you're trying to do then is to partially separate Nimrod from his own organization.'

Dunois snapped the fingers of both hands, the sound of castanets, applause. He smiled as he spoke.

'You're a quick student. It's the first lesson of insurgency. One of the prime objectives of infiltration. Divide. Divide!'

The door opened; an excited black entered. Without saying a word, he handed Dunois a note. Dunois read it and closed his eyes for several moments. It was his way of showing dismay. He thanked the black messenger calmly and dismissed him politely. He looked at Matlock but handed the note to Williams.

'Our stratagems may have historic precedence, but I'm afraid for us they're empty words. Kressel and his wife are dead. Dr. Sealfont has been taken forcibly from his house under guard. He was driven away in a Carlyle patrol car.'

'What? Kressel! I don't believe it! It's not true!'

'I'm afraid it is. Our men report that the two bodies were carried out not more than fifteen minutes ago. The word is murder and suicide. Naturally. It would fit perfectly.'

'Oh, Christ! Oh, Jesus Christ! It's my fault! I made them do it! I *forced* them! Sealfont! Where did they take him?'

'We don't know. The brothers on watch didn't dare follow the patrol car.'

He had no words. The paralysis, the fear, was there again. He reeled blindly into the bed and sank down on it, sitting, staring at nothing. The sense of futility, of inadequacy, of defeat was now overwhelming. He had caused so much pain, so much death.

'It's a severe complication,' said Dunois, his elbows on the card table. 'Nimrod has removed your only contacts. In so doing, he's answered a vital question, prevented us from making an enormous error – I refer to Kressel, of course. Nevertheless, to look at it from another direction, Nimrod has reduced our alternatives. You have no choice now. You must deal through his private army, the Carlyle police.'

Matlock looked numbly across at Julian Dunois. 'Is that all you can *do*? Sit there and coolly decide a next move? . . . Kressel's *dead*. His *wife* is *dead*. Adrian Sealfont's probably killed by now. These were my friends!'

'And you have my sympathies, but let me be honest; I don't regret the loss of the three individuals. Frankly. Adrian Sealfont is the only *real* casualty – we might have worked with him, he was brilliant – but this loss does not break my heart. We lose thousands in the barrios every month. I weep for them more readily. . . . However, to the issue at hand. You really don't have a choice. You must make your contact through the police.'

'But that's where you're wrong.' Matlock felt suddenly stronger. 'I *do* have a choice. . . . Greenberg left West Virginia early this morning. He'll be in Washington by now. I have a number in New York that can put me in touch with him. I'm getting hold of Greenberg.' He'd done enough, caused enough anguish. He couldn't take the chance with Pat's life. Not any longer. He wasn't capable.

Dunois leaned back in his chair, removing his arms from the card table. He stared at Matlock. 'I said a little while ago that you were an apt student. I amend that observation. You are quick but obviously superficial. . . . You will *not* reach Greenberg. He was not part of our agreement and you *will not* violate that agreement. You will carry through on the basis we agree upon or you will be subject to the penalties I outlined.'

'Goddamn it, don't threaten me! I'm sick of threats!' Matlock stood up. Dunois reached under his jacket and took out a gun. Matlock saw that it was the black automatic he had taken from the dead man on the East Gorge slope. Dunois, too, rose to his feet.

'The medical report will no doubt estimate your death to be at dawn.'

'For God's sake! The girl is being held by killers!'

'So are you,' Dunois said quietly. 'Can't you *see* that? Our motives are different, but make no mistake about it. We are *killers*. We *have* to be.'

'You wouldn't go that far!'

'Oh, but we would. We have. And much, much further. We would drop your insignificant corpse in front of the police station with a note pinned to your bloodstained shirt. We would *demand* the death of the girl prior to any negotiations. They would readily agree, for neither of us can take the chance of her living. Once she, too, is dead, the giants are left to do battle by themselves.'

'You're a monster.'

'I am what I have to be.'

No one spoke for several moments. Matlock shut his eyes, his voice a whisper. 'What do I do?'

'That's much better.' Dunois sat down, looking up at the nervous Adam Williams. Briefly, Matlock felt a kinship with the campus radical. He, too, was frightened, unsure. As Matlock, he was ill-equipped to deal with the world of Julian Dunois or Nimrod. The Haitian seemed to read Matlock's thoughts.

'You must have confidence in yourself. Remember, you've accomplished far more than anyone else. With far less resources. And you have extraordinary courage.'

'I don't feel very courageous.'

'A brave man rarely does. Isn't that remarkable? Come, sit down.' Matlock obeyed. 'You know, you and I are not so different. In another time, we might even be allies. Except, as many of my brothers have noted, I look for saints.'

'There aren't any,' Matlock said.

'Perhaps not. And then again, perhaps . . . we'll debate it some other time. Right now, we must plan. Nimrod will be expecting you. We can't disappoint him. Yet we must be sure to guard ourselves on all flanks.' He pulled closer to the table, a half-smile on his lips, his eyes shining.

The black revolutionary's strategy, if nothing else, was a complex series of moves designed to protect Matlock and the girl. Matlock grudgingly had to acknowledge it.

'I have a double motive,' Dunois explained. 'The second is, frankly, more important to me. Nimrod will not appear himself unless he has no other choice, and I want Nimrod. I will not settle for a substitute, a camouflage.'

The essence of the plan was Herron's notebook itself, the last entries in the diary.

The identity of Nimrod.

'Herron states explicitly that he *would* not write the name intimated by the messengers. Not that he couldn't. His feeling obviously was that he could not implicate that man if the information was incorrect. Guilt by innuendo would be abhorrent to him. Like yourself, Matlock; you refused to offer up Herron on the basis of an hysterical phone call. He knew that he might die at any given moment; his body had taken about as much abuse as it could endure. . . . He had to be positive.' Dunois, by now, was drawing meaningless geometric shapes on a blank page of yellow paper.

'And then he was murdered,' said Matlock. 'Made to look like suicide.'

'Yes. If nothing else, the diaries confirm that. Once Herron had proved to himself who Nimrod was, he would have moved heaven and earth to include it in the notebook. Our enemy cannot know that he did not. That is our Damocletian sword.'

Matlock's first line of protection was to let the chief of the Carlyle police understand that he, Matlock, knew the identity of Nimrod. He would reach an accommodation solely with Nimrod. This accommodation was the lesser of two evils. He was a hunted man. There was a warrant out for his arrest of which the Carlyle police surely were aware. He might conceivably be exonerated from the lesser indictments, but he would not escape the charge of murder. Possibly, two murders. For he had killed, the evidence was overwhelming, and he had no tangible alibis. He did not know the men he had killed. There were no witnesses to corroborate self-defense; the manner of each killing was grotesque to the point of removing the killer from society. The best he could hope for was a number of years in prison.

And then he would spell out his terms for an accommodation with Nimrod. Lucas Herron's diaries for his life – and the life of the girl. Certainly the diaries were worth a sum of money sufficient for both of them to start again somewhere.

Nimrod could do this. Nimrod *had* to do it.

'The key to this . . . let's call it phase one . . . is the amount of conviction you display.' Dunois spoke carefully. 'Remember, you are in panic. You have taken lives, killed other human beings. You are not a violent man but you've been forced, coerced into frightening crimes.'

'It's the truth. More than you know.'

'Good. Convey that feeling. All a panicked man wants is to get away from the scene of his panic. Nimrod must believe this. It guarantees your immediate safety.'

A second telephone call would then be made by Matlock – to confirm Nimrod's acceptance of a meeting. The location, at this point, could be chosen by Nimrod. Matlock would call again to learn where. But the meeting must take place before ten o'clock in the morning.

'By now, you, the fugitive, seeing freedom in sight, suddenly possess doubts,' said Dunois. 'In your gathering hysteria, you need a guarantee factor.'

'Which is?'

'A third party; a mythical third party. . . .'

Matlock was to inform the contact at the Carlyle Police Headquarters that he had written up a complete statement about the Nimrod operation; Herron's diaries, identities, everything. This statement had been sealed in an envelope and given to a friend. It would be mailed to the Justice Department at ten in the morning unless Matlock instructed otherwise.

'Here, phase two depends again on conviction, but of another sort. Watch a caged animal whose captors suddenly open the gate. He's wary, suspicious; he approaches his escape with caution. So, too, must our fugitive. It will be expected. You have been most resourceful during the past week. By logic you should have been dead by now, but you survived. You must continue that cunning.'

'I understand.'

The last phase was created by Julian Dunois to guarantee – as much as was possible in a 'best-efforts situation' – the reclaiming of the girl and the safety of Matlock. It would be engineered by a third and final telephone call to Nimrod's contact. The object of the call was to ascertain the specific location of the meeting and the precise time.

When informed of both, Matlock was to accept without hesitation.

At first.

Then moments later – seemingly with no other reason than the last extremity of panic and suspicion – he was to reject Nimrod's choice.

Not the time – the location.

He was to hesitate, to stutter, to behave as close to irrationality as he could muster. And then, suddenly, he was to blurt out a second location of his *own* choice. As if it had just come to mind with no thoughts of it before that moment. He was then to restate the existence of the nonexistent statement which a mythical friend would mail to Washington at ten in the morning. He was then to hang up without listening further.

'The most important factor in phase three is the recognizable consistency of your panic. Nimrod must see that your reactions are now primitive. The act itself is about to happen. You lash out, recoil, set up barriers to avoid his net, should that net exist. In your hysteria, you are as dangerous to him as a wounded cobra is deadly to the tiger. For rationality doesn't exist, only survival. He now must meet you himself, he now must bring the girl. He will, of course, arrive with his palace guard. His intentions won't change. He'll take the diaries, perhaps discuss elaborate plans for your accommodation, and when he learns that there is no written statement, no friend about to mail it, he'll expect to kill you both. . . . However, none of his intentions will be carried out. For we'll be waiting for him.'

'How? How will you be waiting for him?'

'With my own palace guard. . . . We shall now, you and I, decide on that hysterically arrived at second location. It should be in an area you know well, perhaps frequent often. Not too far away, for it is presumed you have no automobile. Secluded, because you are hunted by the law. Yet accessible, for you must travel fast, most likely on back roads.'

'You're describing Herron's Nest. Herron's house.'

'I may be, but we can't use it. It's psychologically inconsistent. It would be a break in our fugitive's pattern of behavior. Herron's Nest is the root of his fear. He wouldn't go back there. . . . Someplace else.'

Williams started to speak. He was still unsure, still wary of joining Dunois's world. 'I think, perhaps . . .'

'What, Brother Williams? What do you think?'

'Professor Matlock often dines at a restaurant called the Cheshire Cat.'

Matlock snapped his head up at the black radical. 'You too? You've had me followed.'

'Quite often. We don't enter such places. We'd be conspicuous.'

'Go on, brother,' broke in Dunois.

'The Cheshire Cat is about four miles outside Carlyle. It's set back from the highway, which is the normal way to get there, about half a mile, but it also can be reached by taking several back roads. Behind and to the sides of the restaurant are patios and gardens used in the summer for dining. Beyond these are woods.'

'Anyone on the premises?'

'A single night watchman, I believe. It doesn't open until one. I don't imagine cleanup crews or kitchen help get there before nine-thirty or ten.'

'Excellent.' Dunois looked at his wristwatch. 'It's now ten past five. Say we allow fifteen minutes between phases one, two, and three and an additional twenty minutes for traveling between stations, that would make it approximately six-fifteen. Say six-thirty for contingencies. We'll set the rendezvous for seven. Behind the Cheshire Cat. Get the notebook, brother. I'll alert the men.'

Williams rose from his chair and walked to the door. He turned and addressed Dunois. 'You won't change your mind? You won't let me come with the rest of you?'

Dunois didn't bother to look up. He answered curtly. 'Don't annoy me. I've a great deal to think about.'

Williams left the room quickly.

Matlock watched Dunois. He was still sketching his meaningless figures on the yellow pad, only now he bore down on the pencil, causing deep ridges on the paper. Matlock saw the diagram emerging. It was a series of jagged lines, all converging.

They were bolts of lightning.

'Listen to me,' he said. 'It's not too late. Call in the authorities. Please, for Christ's sake, you can't risk the lives of these kids.'

From behind his glasses, surrounded by the gauze bandages, Dunois's eyes bore into Matlock. He spoke with contempt. 'Do you for one minute think I would allow these children to tread in waters I don't even know *I* can survive? We're not your Joint Chiefs of Staff, Matlock. We have greater respect, greater love for our young.'

Matlock recalled Adam Williams' protestations at the door. 'That's what Williams meant then? About coming with you.'

'Come with me.'

Dunois led Matlock out of the small, windowless room and down the corridor to a staircase. There were a few students milling about, but only a few. The rest of Lumumba Hall was asleep. They proceeded down two flights to a door Matlock remembered as leading to the cellars, to the old, high-ceilinged chapter room in which he'd witnessed the frightening performance of the African tribal rite. They descended the stairs and, as Matlock suspected, went to the rear of the cellars, to the thick oak door of the chapter room. Dunois had not spoken a word since he'd bade Matlock follow him.

Inside the chapter room were eight blacks, each well over six feet tall.

They were dressed alike: dark, tight-fitting khakis with open shirts and black, soft leather ankle boots with thick rubber soles. Several were sitting, playing cards; others were reading, some talking quietly among themselves. Matlock noticed that a few had their shirt sleeves rolled up. The arms displayed were tautly muscular, veins close to the skin. They all nodded informally to Dunois and his guest. Two or three smiled intelligently at Matlock, as if to put him at ease. Dunois spoke softly.

'The palace guard.'

'My God!'

'The elite corps. Each man is trained over a period of three years. There is not a weapon he cannot fire or fix, a vehicle he cannot repair . . . or a philosophy he cannot debate. Each is familiar with the most brutal forms of combat, traditional as well as guerrilla. Each is committed until death.'

'The terror brigade, is that it? It's not new, you know.'

'Not with that description, no, it wouldn't be. Don't forget, I grew up with such dogs at my heels. Duvalier's Ton Ton Macoute were a pack of hyenas; I witnessed their work. These men are no such animals.'

'I wasn't thinking of Duvalier.'

'On the other hand, I acknowledge the debt to Papa Doc. The Ton Ton's concept was exciting to me. Only I realized it had to be restructured. Such units are springing up all over the country.'

'They sprung up once before,' Matlock said. 'They were called "elite" then, too. They were also called "units" – SS units.'

Dunois looked at Matlock and Matlock saw the hurt in his eyes. 'To reach for such parallels is painful. Nor is it justified. We do what we have to do. What is right for us to do.'

'*Ein Volk, Ein Reich, Ein Fuehrer*,' said Matlock softly.

Thirty-four

Everything happened so fast. Two of Dunois's elite guard were assigned to him, the rest left for the rendezvous with Nimrod, to prepare themselves to meet another elite guard – the selected few of Nimrod's private army who undoubtedly would accompany him. Matlock was ushered across the campus by the two huge blacks after the word came back from scouts that the path was clear. He was taken to a telephone booth in the basement of a freshman dormitory, where he made his first call.

He found that his fear, his profound fear, aided the impression Dunois wanted to convey. It wasn't difficult for him to pour out his panicked emotions, pleading for sanctuary, for, in truth, he *felt* panicked. As he spoke hysterically into the phone, he wasn't sure which was the reality and which the fantasy. He wanted to be free. He wanted Pat to live and be free with him. If Nimrod could bring it all about, why not deal with Nimrod in good faith?

It was a nightmare for him. He was afraid for a moment that he might yell out the truth and throw himself on the mercy of Nimrod.

The sight of Dunois's own Ton Ton Macoute kept bringing him back to his failing senses, and he ended the first telephone call without breaking. The Carlyle police 'superintendent' would forward the information, receive an answer, and await Matlock's next call.

The blacks received word from their scouts that the second public telephone wasn't clear. It was on a street corner, and a patrol car had been spotted in the area. Dunois knew that even public phones could be traced, although it took longer, and so he had alternate sites for each of the calls, the last one to be made on the highway. Matlock was rushed to the first alternate telephone booth. It was on the back steps of the Student Union.

The second call went more easily, although whether that was an advantage was not clear. Matlock was emphatic in his reference to the mythical statement that was to be mailed at ten in the morning. His strength had its effect, and he was grateful for it. The 'superintendent' was frightened now, and he didn't bother to conceal it. Was Nimrod's private army beginning to have its doubts? The troops were, perhaps, picturing their own stomachs blown out by the enemy's shells. Therefore, the generals had to be more alert, more aware of the danger.

He was raced to a waiting automobile. It was an old Buick, tarnished, dented, inconspicuous. The exterior, however, belied the inside. The interior was as precisely tooled as a tank. Under the dashboard was a powerful radio; the windows were at least a half-inch thick, paned, Matlock realized, with bulletproof glass. Clipped to the sides were high-powered, short-barreled rifles, and dotted about the body were rubber-flapped holes into which these barrels were to be inserted. The sound of the engine impressed Matlock instantly. It was as powerful a motor as he'd ever heard.

They followed an automobile in front of them at moderate speed; Matlock realized that another car had taken up the rear position. Dunois had meant it when he said they were to cover themselves on all flanks. Dunois was, indeed, a professional.

And it disturbed James Matlock when he thought about the profession.

It was black. It was also *Ein Volk, Ein Reich, Ein Fuehrer.*

As was Nimrod and all he stood for.

The words came back to him.

'. . . *I'm getting out of this goddamn country, mister.* . .'

Had it come to that?

And: '. . . *You think it's all so different?*. . . *It's mini-America!* . . . *It's company policy, man!*'

The land was sick. Where was the cure?

'Here we are. Phase three.' The black revolutionary in command tapped him lightly on the arm, smiling reassuringly as he did so. Matlock got out of the car. They were on the highway south of Carlyle. The car in front had pulled up perhaps a hundred yards ahead of them and parked off the road, its lights extinguished. The automobile behind had done the same.

In front of him stood two aluminum-framed telephone booths, placed on a concrete platform. The second black walked to the right booth, pushed the door open – which turned on the dull overhead light – and quickly slid back the pane of glass under the light, exposing the bulb. This he rapidly unscrewed so that the booth returned to darkness. It struck Matlock – impressed him, really – that the Negro giant had eliminated the light this way. It would have been easier, quicker, simply to have smashed the glass.

The objective of the third and final call, as Dunois had instructed, was to reject Nimrod's meeting place. Reject it in a manner that left Nimrod no alternative but to accept Matlock's panicked substitute: the Cheshire Cat.

The voice over the telephone from the Carlyle police was wary, precise.

'Our mutual friend understands your concerns, Matlock. He'd feel the same way you do. He'll meet you with the girl at the south entrance of the athletic field, to the left of the rear bleachers. It's a small stadium, not far from the gym and the dormitories. Night watchmen are on; no harm could come to you. . . .'

'All right. All right, that's O.K.' Matlock did his best to sound quietly frantic, laying the groundwork for his ultimate refusal. 'There are people around; if any of you tried anything, I could scream my head off. And I *will*!'

'Of course. But you won't have to. Nobody wants anyone hurt. It's a simple transaction; that's what our friend told me to tell you. He admires you. . . .'

'How can I be sure he'll bring Pat? I have to be sure!'

'The *transaction*, Matlock.' The voice was oily, there was a hint of desperation. Dunois's 'cobra' was unpredictable. 'That's what it's all about. Our friend wants what you found, remember?'

'I remember. . . .' Matlock's mind raced. He realized he had to maintain his hysteria, his unpredictability. But he had to switch the location. Change it without being suspect. If Nimrod became suspicious, Dunois had sentenced Pat to death. 'And you tell our *friend* to remember that there's a statement in an envelope addressed to men in Washington!'

'He knows that, for Christ's sake. I mean . . . he's concerned, you know what I mean? Now, we'll see you at the field, O.K.? In an hour, O.K.?'

This was the moment. There might not come another.

'No! Wait a minute. . . . I'm not going on that campus! The Washington people, they've got the whole place watched! They're all around! They'll put me away!'

'No, they won't. . . .'

'How the hell do you know?'

'There's nobody. So help me, it's *O.K.* Calm down, please.'

'That's easy for you, not me! No, I'll tell you where. . . .'

He spoke rapidly, disjointedly, as if thinking desperately while talking. First he mentioned Herron's house, and before the voice could either agree or disagree, he rejected it himself. He then pinpointed the freight yards, and immediately found irrational reasons why he could not go there.

'Now, don't get so excited,' said the voice. 'It's a simple transaction . . .'

'That restaurant! Outside of town. The Cheshire Cat! Behind the restaurant, there's a garden. . . .'

The voice was confused trying to keep up with him, and Matlock knew he was carrying off the ploy. He made last references to the diaries and the incriminating affidavit and slammed the telephone receiver into its cradle.

He stood in the booth, exhausted. Perspiration was dripping down his face, yet the early morning air was cool.

'That was handled very nicely,' said the black man in command. 'Your adversary chose a place within the college, I gather. An intelligent move on his part. Very nicely done, sir.'

Matlock looked at the uniformed Negro, grateful for his praise and not a little astonished at his own resourcefulness. 'I don't know if I could do it again.'

'Of course you could,' answered the black, leading Matlock toward the car. 'Extreme stress activates a memory bank, not unlike a computer. Probing, rejecting, accepting – all instantaneously. Until panic, of course. There are interesting studies being made regarding the varying thresholds.'

'Really?' said Matlock as they reached the car door. The Negro motioned him inside. The car lurched forward and they sped off down the highway flanked by the two other automobiles.

'We'll take a diagonal route to the restaurant using the roads set back in the farm country,' said the black behind the wheel. 'We'll approach it from the southwest and let you off about a hundred yards from a path used by employees to reach the rear of the building. We'll point it out to you. Walk directly to the section of the gardens where there's a large white arbor and a circle of flagstones surrounding a goldfish pond. Do you know it?'

'Yes, I do. I'm wondering how *you* do, though.'

The driver smiled. 'I'm not clairvoyant. While you were in the telephone booth, I was in touch with our men by radio. Everything's ready now. We're prepared. Remember, the white arbor and the goldfish pond. . . . And here. Here's the notebook and the envelope.' The driver reached down to a flap pocket on the side of his door and pulled out the oilcloth package. The envelope was attached to it by a thick elastic band.

'We'll be there in less than ten minutes,' said the man in command, shifting his weight to get comfortable. Matlock looked at him. Strapped to his leg – sewn into the tight-fitting khaki, actually – was a leather scabbard. He hadn't noticed it before and knew why. The bone-handled knife it contained had only recently been inserted. The scabbard housed a blade at least ten inches long.

Dunois's elite corps was now, indeed, prepared.

Thirty-five

He stood at the side of the tall white arbor. The sun had risen over the eastern curve, the woods behind him still heavy with mist, dully reflecting the light of the early morning. In front of him the newly filled trees formed corridors for the old brick paths that converged into this restful flagstone haven. There were a number of marble benches placed around the circle, all glistening with morning moisture. From the center of the large patio, the bubbling sounds of the man-made goldfish pond continued incessantly with no break in the sound pattern. Birds could be heard activating their myriad signals, greeting the sun, starting the day's foraging.

Matlock's memory wandered back to Herron's Nest, to the forbidding green wall which isolated the old man from the outside world. There were similarities, he thought. Perhaps it was fitting that it should all end in such a place.

He lit a cigarette, extinguishing it after two intakes of smoke. He clutched the notebook, holding it in front of his chest as though it were some impenetrable shield, his head snapping in the direction of every sound, a portion of his life suspended with each movement.

He wondered where Dunois's men were. Where had the elite guard hidden itself? Were they watching him, laughing quietly among themselves at his nervous gestures – his so obvious fear? Or were they spread out, guerrilla fashion? Crouched next to the earth or in the low limbs of the trees, ready to spring, prepared to kill?

And who would they kill? In what numbers and how armed would be Nimrod's forces? Would Nimrod come? Would Nimrod bring the girl he loved safely back to him? And if Nimrod did, if he finally saw Pat again, would the two of them be caught in the massacre which surely had to follow?

Who *was* Nimrod?

His breathing stopped. The muscles in his arms and legs contorted spastically, stiffened with fear. He closed his eyes tightly – to listen or to pray, he'd never really know, except that his beliefs excluded the existence of God. And so he listened with his eyes shut tight until he was sure.

First one, then two automobiles had turned off the highway and had entered the side road leading to the entrance of the Cheshire Cat. Both vehicles were traveling at enormous speeds, their tires screeching as they rounded the front circle leading into the restaurant parking area.

And then everything was still again. Even the birds were silent; no sound came from anywhere.

Matlock stepped back under the arbor, pressing himself against its lattice frame. He strained to hear – anything.

Silence. Yet not silence! Yet, again, a sound so blended with stillness as to be dismissed as a rustling leaf is dismissed.

It was a scraping. A hesitant, halting scraping from one of the paths in front of him, one of the paths hidden amongst the trees, one of the old brick lanes leading to the flagstone retreat.

At first it was barely audible. Dismissible. Then it became slightly clearer, less hesitant, less unsure.

Then he heard the quiet, tortured moan. It pierced into his brain.

'Jamie . . . Jamie? Please, Jamie. . . .'

The single plea, his name, broke off into a sob. He felt a rage he had never felt before in his life. He threw down the oilcloth packet, his eyes blinded by tears and fury. He lunged out of the protective frame of the white arbor and yelled, roared so that his voice startled the birds, who screeched out of the trees, out of their silent sanctuary.

'Pat! Pat! Where are you? Pat, my God, where? *Where!*'

The sobbing – half relief, half pain – became louder.

'Here. . . . Here, Jamie! Can't see.'

He traced the sound and raced up the middle brick path. Halfway to the building, against the trunk of a tree, sunk to the ground, he saw her. She was on her knees, her bandaged head against the earth. She had fallen. Rivulets of blood were on the back of her neck; the sutures in her head had broken.

He rushed to her and gently lifted up her head.

Under the bandages on her forehead were layers of three-inch adhesive tape, pushed brutally against the lids of her eyes, stretched tight to her temples – as secure and unmovable as a steel plate covering her face. To try and remove them would be a torture devised in hell.

He held her close and kept repeating her name over and over again.

'Everything will be all right now. . . . Everything will be all right. . . .'

He lifted her gently off the ground, pressing her face against his own. He kept repeating those words of comfort which came to him in the midst of his rage.

Suddenly, without warning, without any warning at all, the blinded girl screamed, stretching her bruised body, her lacerated head.

'Let them have it, for God's sake! Whatever it is, *give it to them!*'

He stumbled down the brick path back to the flagstone circle.

'I will, I will, my darling. . . .'

'Please, Jamie! Don't let them touch me again! *Ever again!*'

'No, my darling. Not ever, not ever. . . .'

He slowly lowered the girl onto the ground, onto the soft earth beyond the flagstones.

'Take the tape off! Please take the tape off.'

'I can't now, darling. It would hurt too much. In a little . . .'

'I don't *care!* I can't stand it any longer!'

What could he do? What was he supposed to *do?* Oh, God! Oh, God, you son-of-a-bitching God! *Tell me! Tell me!*

He looked over at the arbor. The oilcloth packet lay on the ground where he had thrown it.

He had no choice now. He did not care now.

'*Nimrod! . . . Nimrod! Come to me now, Nimrod! Bring your goddamn army! Come on and get it, Nimrod! I've got it here!*'

Through the following silence, he heard the footsteps.

Precise, surefooted, emphatic.

On the middle path, Nimrod came into view.

Adrian Sealfont stood on the edge of the flagstone circle.

'I'm sorry, James.'

Matlock lowered the girl's head to the ground. His mind was incapable of functioning. His shock was so total that no words came, he couldn't assimilate the terrible, unbelievable fact in front of him. He rose slowly to his feet.

'Give it to me, James. You have your agreement. We'll take care of you.'

'No. . . . No. No, I don't, I *won't believe* you! This isn't so. This isn't the way it can be. . . .'

'I'm afraid it is.' Sealfont snapped the fingers of his right hand. It was a signal.

'No. . . . No! No! No!' Matlock found that he was screaming. The girl, too, cried out. He turned to Sealfont. 'They said you were taken away! I thought you were dead! I blamed myself for your death!'

'I wasn't taken, I was escorted. Give me the diaries.' Sealfont, annoyed, snapped his fingers again. 'And the Corsican paper. I trust you have both with you.'

There was the slightest sound of a muffled cough, a rasp, an interrupted exclamation. Sealfont looked quickly behind him and spoke sharply to his unseen forces.

'Get out here!'

'Why?'

'Because we *had* to. *I* had to. There was no alternative.'

'No alternative?' Matlock couldn't believe he had heard the words. 'No alternative to *what?*'

'Collapse! We were financially exhausted! Our last reserves were committed; there was no one left to appeal to. The moral corruption was complete: the pleas of higher education became an unprofitable, national bore. There was no other answer but to assert our own leadership . . . over the corruptors. We did so, and we survived!'

In the agonizing bewilderment of the moment, the pieces of the puzzle fell into place for Matlock. The unknown tumblers of the unfamiliar vault locked into gear and the heavy steel door was opened. . . . Carlyle's extraordinary endowment. . . . But it was more than Carlyle; Sealfont had just said it. The *pleas* had become a *bore!* It was subtle, but it was there! Everywhere!

The raising of funds throughout all the campuses continued but there were no cries of panic these days; no threats of financial collapse that had been the themes of a hundred past campaigns in scores of colleges and universities.

The general assumption to be made – if one bothered to make it – was that the crises had been averted. Normality had returned.

But it *hadn't*. The norm had become a monster.

'Oh, my God,' said Matlock softly, in terrified consternation.

'He was no help, I can assure you,' replied Sealfont. 'Our accomplishments are extremely human. Look at us now. *Independent!* Our strength growing systematically. Within five years every major university in the Northeast will be part of a self-sustaining federation!'

'You're diseased. . . . You're a *cancer!*'

'We *survive!* The choice was never really that difficult. No one was going to stop the way things were. Least of all ourselves. . . . We simply made the decision ten years ago to alter the principal players.'

'But *you* of all people . . .'

'Yes. I was a good choice, wasn't I? Sealfont turned once again in the direction of the restaurant, toward the sleeping hill with the old brick paths. He shouted. 'I told you to come out here! There's nothing to worry about.

Our friend doesn't care who you are. He'll soon be on his way. . . . Won't you, James?'

'You're *insane*. You're . . .'

'Not for a *minute*! There's no one saner. Or more practical. . . . History repeats, you should know that. The fabric is torn, society divided into viciously opposing camps. Don't be fooled by the dormancy; scratch the surface – it bleeds profusely.'

'You're *making* it bleed!' Matlock screamed. There was nothing left; the spring had sprung.

'On the contrary! You pompous, self-righteous *ass*!' Sealfont's eyes stared at him in cold fury, his voice scathing. 'Who gave you the right to make pronouncements? Where were you when men like myself – in *every institution* – faced the very real prospects of closing our doors! You were safe; we *sheltered* you . . . And our appeals went unanswered. There wasn't room for our needs. . . .'

'You didn't try! Not hard enough . . .'

'Liar! *Fool!*' Sealfont roared now. He was a man possessed, thought Matlock. Or a man tormented. 'What was *left*? Endowments? Dwindling. There are other, more *viable tax incentives*! . . . Foundations? Small-minded tyrants – smaller allocations! . . . The Government? *Blind! Obscene!* Its priorities are bought! Or returned in kind at the ballot box! We had no funds; we bought no votes! For us, the system had collapsed! It was finished! . . . And no one knew it better than I did. For years . . . begging, pleading; palms outstretched to the ignorant men and their pompous *committees*. . . . It was hopeless; we were killing ourselves. Still no one listened. And always . . . *always* – behind the excuses and the delays – there was the snickering, the veiled reference to our common God-given frailty. After all . . . we were *teachers*. Not *doers*. . . .'

Sealfont's voice was suddenly low. And hard. And utterly convincing as he finished. 'Well, young man, we're *doers now*. The system's damned and rightly so. The leaders never learn. Look to the children. They saw. They understood. . . . And we've enrolled them. Our alliance is no coincidence.'

Matlock could do no more than stare at Sealfont. Sealfont had said it: *Look to the children. . . . Look, and behold. Look and beware.* The leaders never learn. . . . Oh, God! Was it so? Was it really the way things were? The Nimrods and the Dunoises. The 'federations,' the 'elite guards.' Was it happening all over again?

'Now James. Where is the letter you spoke of? Who has it?'

'Letter? What?'

'The letter that is to be mailed this morning. We'll stop it now, won't we?'

'I don't understand.' Matlock was trying, trying *desperately* to make contact with his senses.

'Who has the letter!'

'The letter?' Matlock knew as he spoke that he was saying the wrong words, but he couldn't help himself. He couldn't stop to think, for he was incapable of thought.

'The letter! . . . There *is* no *letter, is there*?! There's . . . no "incriminating statement" typed and ready to be mailed at ten o'clock in the morning! You were lying!'

'I was lying. . . . Lying.' His reserves had been used up. There was nothing now but what was so.

Sealfont laughed softly. It wasn't the laugh Matlock was used to hearing from him. There was a cruelty he'd not heard before.

'Weren't you clever? But you're ultimately weak. I knew that from the beginning. You were the government's perfect choice, for you have no really firm commitments. They called it mobility. I knew it to be unconcerned flexibility. You talk but that's all you do. It's meaningless. . . . You're very representative, you know.' Sealfont spoke over his shoulder toward the paths. 'All right, *all* of you! Dr. Matlock won't be in a position to reveal any names, any identities. Come out of your hutches, you rabbits!'

'Augh . . .'

The guttural cry was short, punctuating the stillness. Sealfont whipped around.

Then there was another gasp, this the unmistakable sound of a human windpipe expunging its last draft of air.

And another, this coupled with the beginnings of a scream.

'Who is it? Who's up there?' Sealfont rushed to the path from which the last cry came.

He was stopped by the sound of a terrifying shout – cut short – from another part of the sanctuary. He raced back; the beginnings of panic were jarring his control.

'Who's up there?! Where are all of you? *Come down here!*'

The silence returned. Sealfont stared at Matlock.

'What have you done? What have you done, you unimportant little man? Whom have you brought with you? *Who is up there? Answer me!*'

Even if he'd been capable, there was no need for Matlock to reply. From a path at the far end of the garden, Julian Dunois walked into view.

'Good morning, Nimrod.'

Sealfont's eyes bulged. 'Who *are* you? Where are my men?!'

'The name is Jacques Devereaux, Heysoú Daumier, Julian Dunois – take your choice. You were no match for us. You had a complement of ten, I had eight. No match. Your men are dead and how their bodies are disposed of is no concern of yours.'

'Who *are you*?'

'Your enemy.'

Sealfont ripped open his coat with his left hand, plunging his right inside. Dunois shouted a warning. Matlock found himself lurching forward toward the man he'd revered for a decade. Lunging at him with only one thought, one final objective, if it had to be the end of his own life.

To kill.

The face was next to his. The Lincoln-like face now contorted with fear and panic. He brought his right hand down on it like the claw of a terrified animal. He ripped into the flesh and felt the blood spew out of the distorted mouth.

He heard the shattering explosion and felt a sharp, electric pain in his left shoulder. But still he couldn't stop.

'Get off, Matlock! For God's sake, get off!'

He was being pulled away. Pulled away by huge black muscular arms. He was thrown to the ground, the heavy arms holding him down. And through it all he heard the cries, the terrible cries of pain and his name being repeated over and over again.

'Jamie . . . Jamie . . . Jamie . . .'

He lurched upward, using every ounce of strength his violence could summon. The muscular black arms were taken by surprise; he brought his legs up in crushing blows against the ribs and spines above him.

For a few brief seconds, he was free.

He threw himself forward on the hard surface, pounding his arms and knees against the stone. Whatever had happened to him, whatever was meant by the stinging pain, now spreading throughout the whole left side of his body, he had to reach the girl on the ground. The girl who had been through such terror for him.

'Pat!'

The pain was more than he could bear. He fell once more, but he had reached her hand. They held each other's hands, each trying desperately to give comfort to the other, fully aware that both might die at that moment.

Suddenly Matlock's hand went limp.

All was darkness for him.

He opened his eyes and saw the large black kneeling in front of him. He had been propped up into a sitting position at the side of a marble bench. His shirt had been removed, his left shoulder throbbed.

'The pain, I'm sure, is far more serious than the wound,' said the black. 'The upper left section of your body was badly bruised in the automobile, and the bullet penetrated below your left shoulder cartilage. Compounded that way, the pain would be severe.'

'We gave you a local anesthetic. It should help.' The speaker was Julian

Dunois, standing to his right. 'Miss Ballantyne has been taken to a doctor. He'll remove the tapes. He's black and sympathetic, but not so much so to treat a man with a bullet wound. We've radioed our own doctor in Torrington. He should be here in twenty minutes.'

'Why didn't you wait for him to help Pat?'

'Frankly, we have to talk. Briefly, but in confidence. Secondly, for her own sake, those tapes had to be removed as quickly as possible.'

'Where's Sealfont?'

'He's disappeared. That's all you know, all you'll ever know. It's important that you understand that. Because, you see, if we must, we will carry out our threat against you and Miss Ballantyne. We don't wish to do that. . . . You and I, we are not enemies.'

'You're wrong. We are.'

'Ultimately, perhaps. That would seem inevitable. Right now, however, we've served each other in a moment of great need. We acknowledge it. We trust you do also.'

'I do.'

'Perhaps we've even learned from each other.'

Matlock looked into the eyes of the black revolutionary. 'I understand things better. I don't know what you could have learned from me.'

The revolutionary laughed gently. 'That an individual, by his actions – his courage, if you like – rises above the stigma of labels.'

'I don't understand you.'

'Ponder it. It'll come to you.'

'What happens now? To Pat? To me? I'll be arrested the minute I'm seen.'

'I doubt that sincerely. Within the hour, Greenberg will be reading a document prepared by my organization. By me, to be precise. I suspect the contents will become part of a file buried in the archives. It's most embarrassing. Morally, legally, and certainly politically. Too many profound errors were made. . . . We'll act this morning as your intermediary. Perhaps it would be a good time for you to use some of your well-advertised money and go with Miss Ballantyne on a long, recuperative journey. . . . I believe that will be agreed upon with alacrity. I'm sure it will.'

'And Sealfont? What happens to him. Are you going to kill him?'

'Does Nimrod deserve to die? Don't bother to answer; we'll not discuss the subject. Suffice it to say he'll remain alive until certain questions are answered.'

'Have you any idea what's going to happen when he's found to be missing?'

'There will be explosions, ugly rumors. About a great many things. When icons are shattered, the believers panic. So be it. Carlyle will have to live with it. . . . Rest, now. The doctor will be here soon.' Dunois turned his attention to a uniformed Negro who had come up to him and spoken softly. The kneeling black who had bandaged his wound stood up. Matlock watched the tall, slender figure of Julian Dunois, quietly, confidently issuing his instructions, and felt the pain of gratitude. It was made worse because Dunois suddenly took on another image.

It was the figure of death.

'Dunois?'

'Yes?'

'Be careful.'

Epilogue

The blue green waters of the Caribbean mirrored the hot afternoon sun in countless thousands of swelling, blinding reflections. The sand was warm to the touch, soft under the feet. This isolated stretch of the island was at peace with itself and with a world beyond that it did not really acknowledge.

Matlock walked down to the edge of the water and let the miniature waves wash over his ankles. Like the sand on the beach, the water was warm.

He carried a newspaper sent to him by Greenberg. Part of a newspaper, actually.

KILLINGS IN CARLYLE, CONN.

23 SLAIN, BLACKS AND WHITES, TOWN STUNNED, FOLLOWS DISAPPEARANCE OF UNIVERSITY PRESIDENT

CARLYLE, MAY 10 – On the outskirts of this small university town, in a section housing large, old estates, a bizarre mass killing took place yesterday. Twenty-three men were slain; the federal authorities have speculated the killings were the result of an ambush that claimed many lives of both the attackers and the attacked. . . .

There followed a cold recitation of identities, short summaries of police file associations.

Julian Dunois was among them.

The specter of death had not been false; Dunois hadn't escaped. The violence he engendered had to be the violence that would take his life.

The remainder of the article contained complicated speculations on the meaning and the motives of the massacre's strange cast of characters. And the possible connection to the disappearance of Adrian Sealfont.

Speculations only. No mention of Nimrod, nothing of himself; no word of any long-standing federal investigations. Not the truth; nothing of the truth.

Matlock heard his cottage door open, and he turned around. Pat was standing on the small veranda fifty yards away over the dune. She waved and started down the steps toward him.

She was dressed in shorts and a light silk blouse; she was barefoot and smiling. The bandages had been removed from her legs and arms, and the Caribbean sun had tanned her skin to a lovely bronze. She had devised a wide orange headband to cover the wounds above her forehead.

She would not marry him. She said there would be no marriage out of pity, out of debt – real or imagined. But Matlock knew there would be a marriage. Or there would be no marriages for either of them. Julian Dunois had made it so.

'Did you bring cigarettes?' he asked.

'No. No cigarettes,' she replied. 'I brought matches.'

'That's cryptic.'

'I used that word – cryptic – with Jason. Do you remember?'

'I do. You were mad as hell.'

'You were spaced out . . . In hell. Let's walk down to the jetty.'

'Why did you bring matches?' He took her hand, putting the newspaper under his arm.

'A funeral pyre. Archeologists place great significance in funeral pyres.'

'What?'

'You've been carrying around that damned paper all day. I want to burn it.' She smiled at him, gently.

'Burning it won't change what's in it.'

Pat ignored his observation. 'Why do you think Jason sent it to you? I thought the whole idea was several weeks of nothing. No newspapers, no radios, no contact with anything but warm water and white sand. He made the rules and he broke them.'

'He *recommended* the rules and knew they were difficult to live by.'

'He should have let someone else break them. He's not as good a friend as I thought he was.'

'Maybe he's a better one.'

'That's sophistry.' She squeezed his hand. A single, over-extended wave lapped across their bare feet. A silent gull swooped down from the sky into the water offshore; its wings flapped against the surface, its neck shook violently. The bird ascended screeching, no quarry in its beak.

'Greenberg knows I've got a very unpleasant decision to make.'

'You've made it. He knows that, too.'

Matlock looked at her. Of course Greenberg knew; she knew, too, he thought. 'There'll be a lot more pain; perhaps more than justified.'

'That's what they'll tell you. They'll tell you to let them do it their way. Quietly, efficiently, with as little embarrassment as possible. For everyone.'

'Maybe it's best; maybe they're right.'

'You don't believe that for a second.'

'No, I don't.'

They walked in silence for a while. The jetty was in front of them, its rocks placed decades, perhaps centuries ago, to restrain a long-forgotten current. It was a natural fixture now.

As Nimrod had become a natural fixture, a logical extension of the anticipated; undesirable but nevertheless expected. To be fought in deep cover.

Mini-America . . . just below the surface.

Company policy, man.

Everywhere.

The hunters, builders. The killers and their quarry were making alliances. *Look to the children. They understand. . . . We've enrolled them.*

The leaders never learn.

A microcosm of the inevitable? Made unavoidable because the needs were real? Had been real for years?

And still the leaders would not learn.

'Jason said once that truth is neither good nor bad. Simply truth. That's why he sent me this.' Matlock sat down on a large flat rock; Pat stood beside him. The tide was coming in and the sprays of the small waves splashed upward. Pat reached over and took the two pages of the newspaper.

'This is the truth then.' A statement.

'Their truth. Their judgment. Assign obvious labels and continue the game. The good guys and the bad guys and the posse will reach the pass on time. Just in time. This time.'

'What's your truth?'

'Go back and tell the story. All of it.'

'They'll disagree. They'll give you reasons why you shouldn't. Hundreds of them.'

'They won't convince me.'

'Then they'll be against you. They've threatened; they won't accept interference. That's what Jason wants you to know.'

'That's what he wants me to think about.'

Pat held the pages of the newspaper in front of her and struck a wooden island match on the dry surface of a rock.

The paper burned haltingly, retarded by the Caribbean spray.
But it burned.
'That's not a very impressive funeral pyre,' said Matlock.
'It'll do until we get back.'